I0628869

THE VANISHING
GOLD TRUCK

ALSO BY HARRY STEPHEN KEELER

The "Screwball Circus" series:

The Vanishing Gold Truck
The Ace of Spades Murder
The Case of the Jeweled Ragpicker
Stand By—London Calling!
The Case of the Crazy Corpse
The Circus Stealers
A Copy of Beowulf
Report on Vanessa Hewstone
The Six from Nowhere

The "Way Out" Series

The Peacock Fan
The Sharkskin Book
The Book with Orange Leaves
Two Strange Ladies
The Case of 16 Beans

Others Novels

The Amazing Web
The Box from Japan
The Case of the Ivory Arrow
The Case of the Mysterious Moll
The Case of the Transparent Nude
The Case of the Transposed Legs
The Face of the Man from Saturn
Find the Clock
The Five Silver Buddhas
The Fourth King
The Green Jade Hand
Hangman's Nights
The Iron Ring
The Man Who Changed His Skin
The Monocled Monster
The Murder of London Lew
The Mystery of the Fiddling Cracksman
Riddle of the Travelling Skull
The Search for X-Y-Z
Sing Sing Nights

THE VANISHING GOLD TRUCK

HARRY STEPHEN KEELER

The Screwball Circus Mysteries, Book 1

WILDSIDE PRESS

To
Hazel Goodwin Keeler
around whose beautiful little circus story
"SPANGLES"
first published in the Dell Publishing Company's
Best Love Stories Magazine
and appearing herein
I have woven
this mystery novel
of The Big Top.

Copyright © 1941, renewed 1969 by Harry Stephen Keeler.
Published by Wildside Press LLC.
wildsidepress.com | bcmystery.com

BOOK I

CHAPTER I

THIS SIDE OF NOWHERE!

Jim Craney, driver for the MacWhorter's Mammoth Motorized Shows, brought to a stop the huge lion cage on wheels in which, back of the gaudy gilt and crimson circus-wagon panels which covered it tightly, lay the show's big lioness and her five newly born cubs. With one sunburned hand he peered, against the hot 2 o'clock afternoon sun, down the deserted hard dirt road along which his gas-driven cylinders had been impelling him, thence toward the lone dilapidated clapboard constructed and tar-paper thatched store that hovered by the godforsaken wayside.

Desperately, Jim Craney, in his striking costume as a MacWhorter's Shows driver, wondered whether this lonely store, standing defiantly in this region of vast distances, no habitations and virtually no people, had a tap-in on the local countryside telephone line which, but a short while ago today, he had learned was installed in a conduit, far under the surface of the road—a bit of constructive elaboration out of old W.P.A. days; and also did he wonder whether—if the store did have such a tap-in—did, in short, have a telephone!—he could possibly get connection on it with the one man in this entire desolate area who could make it possible for him to get this big cat and her 5 kittens to Foleysburg before the show closed tonight. And last but not least, Jim wondered helplessly whether this man—hard-boiled sheriff as the latter was—devout hater of all cats as he was also, as Jim had learned, less than 30 minutes ago—a man who, as Jim had likewise been informed at the same time, had even once been cruelly despoiled and injured by a member of the cat family—would go one single 64th of an inch out of his way to expedite the movement of one large cat and her 5 kittens.

And unfortunately, as Jim realized with a heavy heart, unless he somehow, and some way, and in some miraculous manner, got to Foleysburg tonight before the show closed and went on to Spottsville, he had irrevocably and forever lost the one woman in the world he really loved—had ever loved—the woman who—

And once more, before trying his luck on there even being a telephone inside such a ramshackle store, he took out the folded letter he had found under the seat cushion of his lion-cage wagon, atop his roadmaps, about the time he'd started this morning from Pricetown, and opened it out again. Written only in pencil, on several sheets of coarse paper, it spelled—for Jim Craney—the veritable end of his life. Unless this hard-boiled sheriff—this hater of all cats—this victim of cats—this—

And gloomily and morosely Jim reread the letter.

CHAPTER II

"GYPSY'S" LETTER

Jim:

I'm frightfully sick of doing a palm-reading act as Gypsy Queen Rozequia in a small circus, and being engaged to a wagon-driver who's so darned stubborn that even when he's insulted a girl he refuses to apologize. You say your troubles and loneliness had gotten you down—and that you had "drunk a pint"—and that then, being jealous of a "certain man with waxed mustaches"—you had to get some certain bitter things off your chest. But even at that, Jim, a drunken man—or a drunken jealous man, so far as that goes—*can be* a cavalier.

I was always loyal to you, Jim—I stuck to you, faithfully—even though chances of your ever getting a thousand dollars together, so that we could marry, and buy a chicken farm—and get out of this life—were just about zero. Indeed, you have today, Jim—as against your 35 romantic colorful years, including a few in Australia, and a few in South Africa—just $10 toward the farm, haven't you?

Well, Jim, that "man with the waxed mustaches"—as you call him!—or Mondaine, the Illusionist, as we bill him—loves me too; he *has* $1000 saved up—I've seen the bankbook—and it all means, Jim, a chance for me to escape this life—which I hate with all my heart and soul. Especially so with MacWhorter's outfit—and Mr. MacWhorter's almost insane superstition that to go from one state to another means a lucky performance—and his insistence (which is also based on another one of his wild superstitions) on always breaking show immediately at close of performance and starting out at midnight sharp—and his insistence also that, after—often—the most horrible of long journeys, every person in the show play next night as though he—or she—had rested on soft mattresses all day and night, instead of on hard, spring-less, trailer bunks, and trailer-bunk pads. Of course my speaking thus will be, to Mr. Jim Craney lese majesty!—which is a phrase, Jim, that means Disloyalty to the King. In this case, Jim's King—whom he admires so much! And so let me say that I, too, admire Mr. MacWhorter—I admire, that is, his amazing genius for precision of show movement—the way he has trained his big-top crew to pull down, even while the platform show is holding one last showing to the lingering crowds—the ingenious mechanical devices and stunts Mr. MacWhorter has incorporated for swift pull-down and swift getaway—the manner in which good hot food is served to us, promptly and on the dot, at close of performance—all of those things. But those things, unfortunately, contribute only to MacWhorter's superstitions—and we, God help us, who work for him and with him, and ride his hard bunks, and make our sleeping and waking hours comport to his weird schedules, are the ones who have to pay the price for his Scotch—and eccentric—and really false ideas. Not you, perhaps—for being a driver exclusively, those horrible jumps, and long travelings, insure *you* work—and plenty of it. But for us women in the show—

But back to you and me again!

I might have fought on, and waited, and waited, and waited, Jim, for the impossible—the hopelessly impossible—to happen for us: a bit of money to start a different kind of life on—but there just is no use waiting, Jim, for a man who is stubborn—a man who is simply unable to apologize when he is in the wrong. Our life would only be a fizzle. And so, Jim, if you haven't apologized in person to me for your most terrible words by the night that the show pulls out from that godawful town west of the hills, Foleysburg—which we've now learned is, for some reason not given us, completely minus both telegraph and telephone service!—I'm leaving with Mondaine—to try our luck in getting into a big-city vaudeville or night-club act together. For if he and I are to jump the show, Jim—we have to do it *at* Foleysburg—or never. For 6 miles west of there, with a good hard dirt road to walk there on, there's a jerkwater single-track railroad with a train on it at 2 A.M., bound northward, that will stop for passengers if and when flagged with a red lantern; along that road, moreover, there's no less than 3 preachers, who will marry people, at any hour of the day or night, for whatever the people care to give, be it $1 or be it 25 cents, for, you see, in the state where Foleysburg is, neither licenses nor residence are needed to get married. And marriage Mondaine insists on, Jim—even as do I—if he and I are to travel together. Thus you can see, I guess, that if he and I postpone our show-jumping beyond Foleysburg, we're just hamstrung in every way. For the show goes on, as *you* of course know, to Spottsville, 100 miles further south—through the worst kind of railroadless territory—into a region that exceeds even this in the matter of downright—though, merciful heavens, *what* kind of a weird region is even this one we're coming through now?—America's West!—but without any herds of cows to justify a single cowboy—a mild edition of—of—of Yellowstone Park, no less, but without a single volcano, hot spring, glacier, geyser, or anything like that to break its—its blighted deadness—yet, at the same time, because of its geography, America's South!—but without a single magnolia tree or a cotton plant—a Mississippi-bottoms district in more ways than one, except that through it runs neither Mississippi River nor practically any other kind of a river—hillbilly region, no less, but without either a Kentucky or a Tennessee mountain looking down on it—a region where people speak a weird Western-Southern-riverbottom-hillbilly dialect so outlandish that *I,* at least, have never heard it before on land nor sea—not that, of course, Jim, I've seen all of either as you have!—but!—Spottsville!—100 more miles straight into region that is *this* region, only worse!—oh, merciful heavens and earth, how MacWhorter's eternal stepping out of states makes it hard for us who work for him, since—but anyway, once in the Spottsville region, the show will be further than ever, for Mondaine and me, from the big-city booking offices at—well, in this case—Southwest City to the north. So, Jim, it's Foleysburg or nothing, for my getaway; and show-closing hour—11 P.M. sharp—or never—for that getaway. For that's *the* hour when Mondaine and I would have to start on foot—just, however, as Mondaine and Florette Smith—to reach—but now as Mr. and Mrs. Cecil Mondaine!—that jerkwater railroad—*the* last road back to civilization—in safe, ample time.

And so, Jim, it's just up to you, you see. To make things right—before that hour I speak of. For once it has passed—and you haven't yet done so—I'm as much out of your life, Jim, as though I had never been in it. For even my own mother warned me once, when she was alive, never to—but skip it!

So now you have it all clear, I hope, Jim? Or shall I restate it—and underline it, even? All right! *I'm still with the show, as I write this—and will remain with it—waiting on you, of course—till 11 o'clock of the night it leaves Foleysburg—but not one minute later than that: that hour marks the absolute and ultimate extent of my stay with it. Unless, of course, you've apologized to me before that time.*

And so, Jim, to repeat—once more and again—what I said a dozen lines or so back, it's up to you, you see. To make things right—before that moment I speak of above.

But I know—I practically already know in advance, Jim, I'm sorry to say—*exactly* what *you'll* do! You'll just "solve" your duty and obligation of apologizing by purposely not catching up with the show by either the hour of break-up at Foleysburg, or, so far as that goes, by even the hour of pull-out—and then overtaking it afterward between Foleysburg and Spottsville. Or even only at Spottsville. And I'm just not going, Jim, to let you take care of your moral obligations by a subterfuge like that. You'll have to come in and face your duty—disagreeable as it may seem to you—*or else.*

Oh, I'm so sorry—to seem to have to give out an ultimatum like this, Jim. But aren't *you* being awfully unchivalrous and unkind—to *make* me? But whether or no, Jim, I'm giving it out. Even more than that: preparing—if needs must be—to put my life and destiny in the hands of a man who loves me, regardless of what *my full* feelings, right now, may be for him. For stubbornness such as you've displayed would wreck your and my love, and your and my life, if we married—hence my desire to get out from under everything—this hateful, detestable life included—before it's *all* too late.

Florette

CHAPTER III

OLD TWISTIBUS

Unhappily Jim Craney put the letter away in the breast-pocket of his rainproof jacket which lay on the seat beside him. Ironically, he gazed at himself—gay, yet penniless, bird of plumage as he was—with his striking driver's costume of short-sleeved green flannel shirt, belted into black trousers with red stripes on edges, the legs of the latter buckled into shin-high thong-laced yellow cowhide boots, his short bullwhip—mere symbol, no more, of old circus-wagon days—swinging, by a snap-catch, from his side; then tilting back on his head the flat broad-brimmed Australian-like grey hat, with brim rolled up one side, that was part and parcel of the costume, he swung his troubled gaze in a great arc across the desolate countryside region where the wagon stood—a region of uncultivable knolls, becoming apparently bigger and bigger toward the south, or left of him, with here and there, in all directions, patches of malignant-looking weeds, and here and there, too, clusters of scrub oak—and more patches, like actual woods of the same, in the distance, left, right, and forward—and no fences anywhere, because of apparently nothing that had to be kept in *or* out; after which troubled surveyal, he dourly regarded the lonely store that stood off from his wagon.

Such an isolated godforsaken thing it was, he reflected, its existence unjustified by even the usual crossroads; a thing of clapboards, covered with tarpaper, and its very godfor-sakenness further emphasized by the many indications that its keepers had to live right in it; for the store was unduly long from the roadway back, a rickety tin chimney, well toward the rear, was right now giving off a faint wisp of smoke that smelled pungently of wood; a pig rooted about in a small pen to one side of the rear corner, and a woman's bicycle, of most ancient type, leaned against one of the front corners. Over the narrow doorway that faced on the roadside, on a long white-painted wood panel, were the red-painted words

ELUM'S STORE

with, underneath them, on a white pine plank nailed below the panel—as though to answer *all* questions!—a further sign, more crudely lettered in black paint, which ran:

NO!—the 8-9-10-jak-kweenaway AIN'T opened yit an WONT be open fur nuther week.

Now Princess, back inside the cage—back, indeed, of the short open black cab in which Jim rode, virtually over the engine, disturbed evidently by the deep silence of the countryside—or else the long-persisting stopping of that gentle swaying motion which had been proceeding all morning—or else because one of her new precious kitten-lionesses And gotten a few inches out of paw reach, let out a low, gentle, throaty grumble—a sort of combination 1/3 purr and 2/3's rumble, that, despite the proportion of purr in it, yet held in it much of both captious query and deep irritation. And then, perhaps having scooped her blind, straying kitten back closer to her, promptly subsided again. While Jim, gently grumbled and rumbled, as it were, back to life and action, by the characteristic sounds coming around into the open cab, stood up, preparing to climb down and make certain exceedingly vital inquiries. Except that, now standing, but with his head well above the window that was customarily just back of it, he took occasion to peer through a small 1-inch hole drilled in the back of the cab, straight through another like hole drilled, a few inches lower down, in the red-and-gilt panel comprising the cage's entire front end, to the occupant of that cage. And thanks to plentiful light trickling in over the tops of the closely fitting side panels, was able to assure himself that all was well. The big cat was now, indeed, at peace with the world again, no matter what had been wrong a few seconds ago. Luxuriously, she lay on her side, her great tawny body arched backward, her eyes closed in delight, her kittens all lustily attached to her, her great front paws alternately making convulsive, spasmodic-like motions in which the digits, first stretching wide apart, with claws sticking far out, compressed into round fur balls, then relaxed again—first one—then the other—an exact reproduction, that action of sheer delight, of her motions when she too had been a kitten, and with alternate kitten-fists had pressed fiercely against the source and font of what then had been the most precious thing on earth: warm milk. And Jim, satisfied now by her low purr—her closed eyes—and her steady production of "ecstasy mitts"—that she was drinking deep of pure cat contentment, climbed hastily down from his cab, allowing the entire combination vehicle to stand right where it was, and entered the store.

He realized that he would have been a picturesque figure indeed, entering the store—except that the whole MacWhorter Shows had passed this point early, very early this morning—not that there was such a thing as "early" in these districts, for people all got up at dawn, and the day commenced then and there!—had even, as Jim was able to read from certain indisputable signs, those signs being discarded paper 2-pint cups and oily spots in the dried mud of the roadway, stopped along this very stretch of road for axle and gas inspection, and the ladling out of hot coffee to the drivers. And those same drivers—including several pairs of clowns riding in pairs, and spelling each other off every hour at the wheel—plus a few handymen and roustabouts doing the same thing—had been, to the extent of every single driver—and one out of every pair of impromptu ones—dressed, for publicity purposes, exactly like Jim Craney himself was now dressed; and thus he was enabled to realize that neither himself nor his gilt-and-panel-covered conveyance outside would probably prove to be much of a novelty.

A thin bony high-cheeked woman, in a drab colorless calico dress, and with hair done up in a tight topknot on her head, chewing a twig of sweet-wood, was dusting about apathetically in a store which was hung at the rear end with cheap calicos, both drab and flamboyant; to the side of the calico display stood an open doorway, hung with thick bead portieres through which a rocker edge could be seen, and revealing the existence of those living quarters Jim's deductions had foretold. Up front of the store, both sides, were shelves on which tinned goods sat, and, in front of the counters standing out from those shelves, were bulging barrels with flyspecked crackers in them. The papered walls of the store were adorned by many and various signs advertising chewing tobaccos, and, piled along the base of the store's front wall—but visible to Jim only after he got inside, and threw a glance back at the flash of color emanating therefrom—were several dozens of bright red 5-gallon cans—gasoline cans, full, empty, or both!—showing that this place was the only kind of gas station of which this sort of primitive region could boast. The woman in the back of the store glanced at Jim with, at best, only the mild disinterest of one who had seen circus stuff—such as he was now bringing to her very door!—to utter repletion, early today.

"Good aft'noon, Madam," he greeted her. "Have you, by any chance, a phone?"

"Phone?" she cackled in a high voice, taking out her sweet-wood, and dipping it into an open canister on the counter that Jim immediately knew must contain snuff. "'Cose we-uns got a phone. 'Cause ye don't see no tely-phone line up in th' air 'longside *this* 'ticlar road, mister, don't mean a thing. Phone line's burrit—an' burrit deep!—in a condyit!"

"So I heard. Well, c'n I get c'nnection on your instrument with th' next county—next one west, I mean—Willis Creek County, I guess it's called?"

"Kin git c'nnection on it," she told him imperturbably, "anywhar's—day *or* night—sence th' switchbo'd's right in the house whar the opyrator lives!—anywhar's in U-nited States whar they is a phone. In fack, yo're boss—at leas' I 'spose he was yo're boss, 'caze he rid in a gorjis checkered green trailer all by hisse'f, an'—but an'way, he even called a couple o' calls on our phone this mo'nin' when the procission stopped hyar raound dawn. Which 'uz raound 5 'clock. I don't know 'zackly whar he called to, becaze my old man 'uz inside at the time, an' I 'uz outside lookin' at ever'thing. But one of his calls, I know, 'uz to Hootens Falls—3 states over."

"Hootens Falls? Jupiter! That's one o' our advance points—beyond even Spottsville. He—he was talkin' to our advance man before, I 'spose, the show might maybe get cut off completely from wire connection with the outside world." But Jim's face had fallen. For he realized, from the fact of that other call that MacWhorter had made—and the fact that, as Jim also knew, the show had wound into the hills after leaving here—that it was barely possible that MacWhorter, on the way down this road in the night, had learned of the identical thing of which Jim had learned—had even, perhaps, tried the very thing which Jim himself was about to try—but had failed utterly and ignobly. In which case—However, that call, on the other hand, so Jim realized, could have been to any one of many other points. Most likely was, he assured himself. In which case—

The woman's blank face, in the meanwhile, showed that she did not know the difference between an advance man and a calcium light. But her subsequent words showed that she was exceedingly puzzled by the completely fallen look on Jim's face.

"Whut on earth's th' matter of you?" she demanded. "Air yo' calcilatin' to make some other call—an' air afeard our instryment cain't take it? Well, to put yo're mind to rest, you kin git Yurrup on our phone. You kin even git points fu'ther—like-say, London."

"London?" echoed Jim abstractedly, trying to think of his own problems.

"'At's whut I said," she announced triumphantly. "London! Fur a Englishman, who once vis'ted this hyar parts, spent twenty-five dollars an' twenty-five cents, fur jest 3 minutes, on our instryment—a-callin' of his pappy—who was a earl or duke or so'thin'—jest to no mo'n wish him a happy bu'thday. Now air you satisfied?"

Jim, however, was still lost in troubled reflection. The woman spoke, impatiently now.

"Wa-all" she said, with a vehement gesture of her thin wrists, "yo're boss talkin' cl'ar to Hootens Falls, 3 states over—ef not that Englishman a-talkin' oncet cl'ar 'crost the ocean—should ought to answer yo're question, I reckon, 'bout yo're bein' able to git whatever c'nnection yo' mought want on our instryment. In sho't—and to b'ile it down—yo' kin git c'nnection on it anywhar's in the whole world."

"Anywheres in the whole world," Jim grunted to himself only, under his breath, "'cept'n a dratted spit of a town called Foleysburg—that ain't got phone service." But, because Jim Coney was a careful man—and one who checked everything against everything—he asked, immediately: "Well, could I get c'nnection on it, maybe, with a town called Foleysburg—miles and miles southwest o' here—in the next state, in fact?"

"Foleysburg?" the woman exclaimed contemptuously. "Lorda'mighty no! I got a sister livin' in Foleysburg—know all 'bout it. You cain't git c'nnection neither with Foleysburg—nor nothin' nowhar 'round it—'r in its caounty—or even in th' teeny mite of a spit of a caounty what hugs it jest this side. Fur Ol' Man Foley, whut give the land f'r both them caounties—big Foleysburg Caounty—an' leetle Foley Caounty a-huggin' it—an' most o' the 'provements whar both has got—he thunk 'lectricity 'uz the devil—and made all his land grants 'pend on no phone nor telygrapht lines ever bein' brung in either."

"So *that's* the explanation?" said Jim darkly.

He thought a minute. Then, it occurring to him that maybe—by, in this case, the grace of God!—the circus had "piled up" somewhere along that long winding hill road which it had necessarily to traverse after leaving this fairish road—Old Twistibus, as one man Jim had met had called that winding road—Crazy Snake Trail, as the man with him had averred it was called in the long ago—and the thought of whose fierce convolutions right now was twisting Jim's very soul about—the "piling up" of the show on the road would mean that the show never would get to Foleysburg—would mean that Florette couldn't jump it at all!—that he could easily overtake it before she did—could—

He spoke. Hope crawling in him.

"Is they any way—by—by cross lines—or comb'nations o' lines—inside conduits—or atop poles!—or anything—that a feller could get in touch with a few of the people livin' 'long old Twistibus? I'd like f'r to check up the progress of my show."

"Check it—by them savages?" the woman ejaculated as contemptuously as when she had talked of Foleysburg. And she actually cackled. "Why, them savages livin' in them thar hills 'long Ol' Twistibus not on'y don't have hide nor hair o' no phone lines—but they wouldn't know w'ich end of a telyphone to talk into, ef'n they did. Them's the most turr'ble ig'nant peoples they is in this whole U.S.A. Don't know nothin'. Now ef'n yo're figga'hin' to check on an'thin'—vehicle or man!—passin' anywhar's 'long Ol' Twistibus—they ain't ary chanct whatsoever o' learnin' nuthin' atter whatever 'tis—mewl-drove, hoss-drug, or gas'line driv—passes on into th' hills at Perkins Junction, whut's nothin' but a lonely junction o' three roads layin' up ah'id yo' now on'y a sho't ways—'twell whatever 'tis comes out, hours an' hours later, onto th' Foleysburg Road at Simpson's Junction, 'nuther lonely 3-road junction layin' raound an' south onder Sout'west City Crossin'—cep'n as mebbe some o' them savages comes on out from th' hills raound hyar an' tells so'thin'."

"Well," pressed on Jim desperately, "have you, by any chance, heerd an'thing this morning—out of Old Twistibus—'bout a light bridge goin' down over a creek called Bear Creek—'count our elephant?—an' addin' a big bit o' mileage to the journey through?"

"Sho' did," said the woman imperturbably. "Why'nt yu ask befur? Ba'rfoot 'oman whut come out this mo'nin'—or ruther, jest befo' noon—to git some chawterbaccer hyar, said th' circus got pas' B'ar Creek okay this mo'nin'—B'ar Creek's 'bout a hour an' a half travel out o' Perkins Junction—circus got past, she said—ev'y danged wagon!—but that yo're whopper of an elyphant, who 'uz tailin' th' whole procession, ahid his—his go-truck, got skeered in middle o' the bridge—mebbe 'count the water bein' so danged deep as 'tis jest now in B'ar Creek—an' he started tremblin' an' swayin'—an' the hull bridge, she says, went down into an' onder th' water. Not, how'ver, befo' yo're elyphant got wise to himse'f—an' run fo' it. 'Ooman said that elyphant actually waltzed out'n that teeterin' bridge like he was a mouse. Though they hadda use a block an' tackle—hitched raound a off-side stump, to pull his 'hind half up over the bank."

The woman was contemplatively silent for a moment, as though trying to conjure up a picture of this bizarre occurrence. And then as one who was simply unable to conjure up pictures, she resumed.

"But answerin' yo're question e'zackly," she went on, "the B'ar Creek bridge *is* down, now. 'Ith deep water flowin' in the creek, too. And that do mean that *yo'll* hatter go cl'ar raound by th' B'ar Creek Bridge by-pass road now—all through Little B'ar Valley, in fack—to whar's 'nother bridge at its fu'thest end—jest to git through—jest t' git back onto Old Twistibus 'tother side o' that last bridge—an' w'ile all this don't add so much mileage as the crow flies—no!—it sho' do add hours travel—3 of 'em, to be e'zact."

"Damn!" groaned Jim to himself. "I—I—I hoped that feller might have been just a damned spoofer. Whooie! Well, that settles it, then. *Unless*—" And now he was thinking darkly of that cat-hating sheriff! But then, at some further possibilities inherent in the picture, hope again rose in him faintly. *"Or* unless the show *did* pile up somewhere else farther on on Old Twistibus." He was grimly silent. "But if it didn't, I hain't no chance. *Except*—" And aloud he said: "Well, c'n I use your phone?"

"Kin ef'n you'll prop open the door yo' jes' came in by—'ith the brick thar—so's the store'll air out a mite."

"Oh-oh!" commented Jim to himself. *"I* must smell 'cat.' And smell cat—bad! Good thing people can't smell over telephone wires."

"Easy done," Jim was assenting aloud, propping the door wide open, and putting the brick against it. The woman was gazing through the open door at the circus wagon with lackluster, no-longer-interested eyes.

"Got animiles in that wagon?" she asked, though markedly uninterestedly.

"Yeah. Now where is the ph—"

"Air they so' mo' little monkeys—like 'uz in that tur-r'ble big jeewhol-loper of a circus wagon whut went by 'ith th' others this mo'nin'—gibberin' an' chatterin'—an' smellin' too?"

"*Little*—monkeys?" echoed Jim, flabbergasted. "Little monk—" But immediately he realized that someone, this morning, had put off some point-ed question of hers with the usual subterfuges. "Darned big monkeys, you mean, Madam," he said quite frankly. "A g'rilla—a lady g'rilla, but a g'rilla no less!—at least a dwarf lady g'rilla—was in the special end section o' that huge cage that was covered with them panels—an' orangoutangs was in the section where the g'rilla wasn't. *Little* monkeys?—my gosh! That g'rilla lady—dwarf though she is—is got such arms and legs on her, and muscles atop them, that—that she could tote you on her shoulder from here to Jericho—and then toss you straight up into the limb of an oak tr— *little* monkeys—my gosh!"

"I see," said the woman with some asperity. "You folks shore don't show nothin' free, do you? Cep'n th' one orang'tang what driv th' wagon."

Jim snickered aloud. That would be a good one to tell whenever he reached the show again. A good one on Screw-Face, who piloted that huge cage on wheels. But brought back now to the very problem anent regaining that show, he got promptly back to business. "But now 'bout your pho—"

"What kind o' animiles air in *yo're* cage?" the woman persisted.

"I've only one," parried Jim. "And now—"

"What kind of a animile is it?"

Now indeed he knew that she was *no* interpreter of animal smells!

"A *felinus giganticus,*" said Jim cryptically. "But where is the phone?"

"Right thar on th' wall nixt the door—onder my old man's rain slicker what's a-hangin' on it."

Jim gently removed a rain slicker he did see clinging mysteriously to the wall—and there indeed, by the side of the open doorway, was an old-fashioned wall phone of the most ancient vintage with, of all things, a hand-operating handle to summon Central!

He lifted the heavy receiver, and twirled the handle. A girl answered.

"Will you put me, please," he asked her, "onto the Sher'ff O' Willis Creek County—next county up road, I think it is? I don't know 'zackly what town to ask for, though—for I'm a stranger here'bouts an' my roadmaps are old as all get-out. But I leave that to you, sence—"

"Town?" she interrupted him, suddenly getting the drift of his words. "Why, they ain't but one town in that caounty—an' that's the town o' Willis Creek itse'f."

"Oh—I see. Well, Willis Creek 'tis, then, that I'll be wantin'—an' the Sheriff."

"Okay. On'y, stranger, we charge 2 bits flat in this kentry to th'ow a c'nnection what's mo'n 50 miles as a crow flies, though they ain't no 'ticler time limit on talkin' on it—and this yere town o' Willis Creek itse'f is at least'bout—oh, 'bout 60 miles—as a crow flies, that is—from you."

"Jumping Jehoshaphat!" grunted Jim to himself. "Talk about a country o' great distances—this beats 'em all." Aloud, however, he said, "Okay, Sister—whatever th' charges is, I'll be payin' 'em to the folks where I'm phonin' from. Only—how you know how far Willis Creek is from *me*—when I ain't said yet where I am?"

"Oh, yo're talkin' from Elum's, ain't ye?"

"Well, yeah—but how—"

"'Cause yo're magneto's a-skippin' all its right-handed rings," the girl giggled. "An' ain' none in Yocum Caounty but Elum's what does *that*. Hold the wire."

There was a silence, exceedingly short for such archaic service, and after a clicking, a man's voice spoke. It was a voice dripping with the peculiar accents and phraseology of this rural hillbilly region—but full of the authority of one who was somebody in his own community.

"Sher'ff Bucyrus Duckhouse talkin'," it said sternly.

Jim winced. Not at the words—no!—but at a certain something in the tone of voice in which they were uttered. For that tone was, Jim perceived immediately, the tone of a really and truly hard-boiled man. A man who—

But Jim nevertheless stiffened resolutely up, there in front of the ancient telephone. And from the man he now had connection with—and all about whose cat-hating qualities Jim had heard completely and plentifully this morning!—proceeded to try and gently wangle one huge favor: a favor which, while it was one undoubtedly *to* and *for* a certain great cat and her 5 small cats, was one which—*if* Jim succeeded in getting it!—would stop Florette Smith from flying tonight, with Mondaine the Illusionist, straight out of Jim Craney's life forever!

CHAPTER IV

FAVOR WANTED!

My name," Jim explained at once, "is Jim Craney—"

"Craney?" It was the query of a careful man. "Jim Craney, eh? O-kay. Go ahid?"

"And I'm somew'ere on Carthage Road—though if th' telephone girl hasn't told you from where I'm callin', I better say as it's the Carthage Road that's on the other side o' Smoky Ridge Mountain from where you are—East Carthage Road, I think they call it, since they's one each side of the mountain—anyways, I'm on the Carthage Road that's in Yocum County—and not the Carthage Road that lays in your county—Willis Creek County. And I'm headin' straight west on *my* Carthage Road—and not east. Accordin' to my roadmaps, I'm—however, I'm at Elum's Store, if you know where that—"

"Elum's? Why, shore I know whar Elum's is. Think I never b'en out my own caounty? But what mought ye be wantin'—Craney?"

"Well, I'm a wagon-driver, Sheriff, f'r the MacWhorter's Shows—that went through here early this mornin', bound for Foleysburg in the tip of the next state down—in fact, our wagon train, as I happen to know, stopped off here 'round 5 o'clock this mornin' so's my boss could make a couple o' phone calls—" Jim paused significantly, and his spirits rose a bit, for the man on the other end was not interpolating any remark such as "'Twas me he called." But so that the other still could, Jim proceeded to gently stall a bit. "Shows you, heh, Sheriff, how easy and slow they took it, in that jet-black dark we had last night, usin' up 5 hours to cover from Pricetown to here, what *I've* covered in 3 hours flat!" Still the man on the other end was failing quite to say that he had been called. And now Jim felt more chipper than ever. "Anyway," he went on, "I'm with that show, and I'm fetchin' along, in a reg'lation circus-wagon cage—one o' them traveling cages, you know, built onto a truck chassis, and all covered with carved gilt an' red panels'—yes—well, I'm fetchin' along a—a—uh—a—a animal—I can't pertend it's jest a bunch o' paraphernalia, because it—it—hrmph—it smells animal!—but anyway, it's a animal that started to have young last night 'bout 2 hours before the show left Pricetown—which, as I implied, was midnight—'t always is!—and so they left me ahind. Y'see, they was a vet in that town what had once been with Frank Buck's Show—knew all about bringin' in a critter like this, when she was havin'—that is, o' course, helpin' from outside the cage on'y, to bring her through—when she was having ki—hrmph—that is, young—and—however, Sheriff, the young arrove all right—took, all in all, all o' 8 hours!—and now, thanks to that—and a 'ditional fool crazy delay I caught, on account of it—I'm tailin' on 'zackly 9 hours back o' the show, tryin' t' regain it."

"The last wagon, I take it?" the Sheriff inquired.

"I should say *so!*" averred Jim. "Too much so the last! F'r I got away from Pricetown far, far too late. The Boss, he figgered 2 more hours 'd suffice—and at th' very most—to get them young borned. But they didn't actually arrive—all of 'em, that is—till 6 A.M.! Then I caught this curious acc'dent I r'ferred to, which kep' m' from pull in' out until the sun was way, way, way high in the sky; and so, instead of startin' at 2 A.M.—or, let's say, dawn, which 'd been maybe *the* log'cal time for a lone follow-up driver to start out—*I* started hours and hours and hours late. 11—to be exact—of which I've made up 2, 'count of travelin' a stretch of road in full daylight instead of black darkness. Leavin' me 9 in the hole! But from here on—from now on—I'd hardly gain anything, since both the show, ahead of me, and myself, 'd both be movin' in daylight. And—" Jim realized he wasn't getting to the point—was almost floundering. And decided to at least introduce the subject. "I—I don't know whether my road-map is crazy, or I am—for this here Smoky Ridge Mountain is 'sposed to lay up ahead o' me—yet I can't see hide nor hair of it in the dist—"

"Hell f'ar, man!" interrupted the Sheriff. "It's a right-smart heap o' distance from you—a mite sho't o' 40 miles. And 'sides, 'tain't nothin' but a big hill o' impenytrable rock."

"Oh—I see? Well an'way, as things now stand, as at least I do know from my roadmap here—and what I hear too 'bout this so-called hills road what girdles Smoky Ridge t' the south of itself—Ol' Twistibus, as one feller I talked with called this hills road—Crazy Snake Trail, as 'nother claimed it used to be oncet—well, from what I hear 'bout that road, plus a certain sad somethin' that happened on it today, it's—it's jest 'bout impossible for me to make Foleysburg afore the show busts up t'night and takes a big lope west. I might maybe—yes—*jest* make it by time she pulls out—but it's plumb doubtful if I c'n make her by time she closes, and Florette—but you get the idee, I'm sure. An' so I—"

"Ezackly what," catechized the man on the other end, with the undoubted suspicion of one who believed that the true explanation of this delay might have been one circus-wagon driver lying drunk all night, "was this so-called 'fool, crazy accydent' what 'uz able to delay you at Pricetown?"

With a stifled groan, Jim threw up his two hands, the one holding the receiver, the other empty. "Of all the suspicious guys," he said to himself, "this guy is the wor—whoa, Tilley!—say!—I wonder?—I wonder?—if that 'accident'—was on the level?—in view o' the fact that—say, that Mondaine *is* a fox, all right; and he might have had a finger in—hm?—by God!—hm?"

He came to himself suddenly, and answered the question asked of him—truthfully—the more to examine its now odd facts himself as he did so.

"Well, the accident," he said musingly, "was that just as soon's these young I told you 'bout got borned—an' the vet an' me was throwin' a bit of breakfast together in his house—he was a bach'lor, you see?—he got some tel-phone call—hm?—and had to grab his bag an' rush out into the country on a 'mergency call to help a blooded Jersey cow d'liver a calf. That is," qualified Jim, downright suspicious now, "he said that's what the call was. Anyway, we said goo'-by—an' he told me how to lock up. But when I got out to the big double-brick garage in which we had the cage-wagon, he'd acc'dentally went an' shut the door on it—the spring-lock had caught!—he had the key—and there—I couldn't get my cage-wagon out! And the only window was barred on th' inside—an' so I couldn't get in. And on top o' that, he never did get back. So that, in brief, was the accident, and that's how 'twas that I never got away till—"

"But hyar, hyar," said the man on the other end with all the fascinated delight of one who evidently loved puzzles, "what in hell *did* you do?"

"Good God!" said Jim to himself. "I better give the story of my life and be done with it!" Resolutely he drove on, his own face dark as he wondered how much that blond-mustached illusionist had had to do with this.

"Why," he said simply, "after hangin' round like a fool for two hours, I examined the lock—found 'twas a Milledge lock—remembered that Milledgeville, where those locks are man'factured, was a suburb o' Price-town—chartered me a Ford, and went out there—the sup'ntendent had seen our show the night before, and liked it!—and he sent a man back with me with a bunch o' special skeleton keys. This feller, after taking a pike inside the window to see that I was tellin' the truth, read the code figures stamped on the lock—opened her up—and let me in. And out I drove with my cage-wagon—at 11 A.M. And so now I'm stymied—yes, stymied!—from catching up with my sh—"

"Ever hafta trail yo're show afore?" asked the Sheriff.

"Why, yeh—yeh—"

"Ever fail to catch up afore?"

"Why, yeh—sure—but not never under these same circ'mstances."

"Well, whatever *these* sarc'mstances may be, what didja do in them cases whar yo' didn't catch up—at th' next show-p'int?"

"Why, I kep' followin'—till I—I sapped up on the show—an' got it at some later show-point."

"W'ich involved travelin' 'spenses, o' course. You got money? Now, I mean?"

"'Course I got money," returned Jim indignantly. "I got $50 of Mr. Mac-Whorter's money for meals—gas, if I need it—red meat—"

"Red meat? What—"

"Hamburgers," said Jim hastily. "I love 'em."

"Oh, hamburgers? We don't have hamburger stands 'round this part o' the kentry. No mor'n we have ile an' gas stations—not, how'ver, that no-body cain't git hisse'f a can o' ile or a 5- or 10-gallon can o' gas at 'most any store outside th' dead an' onciv'lized hills region. But see hyar, I'm right glad to git a chanct t' talk to you—afore you do dive into them hills, on yo're labo'ius pu'suit o' yo're show—"—pointed forecast *that,* all right, which made Jim bite his lips fiercely!—"—that is, to swap a few words with you on th' phone hyar, becaze—wa-all, becaze my cooriosity's aroused 'bout showbusiness—yo're show, an'way—why, a feller down thisaway who now knows somep'n 'bout yo' people, tolt me t'day 'at yo'-all ca'y a big travelin' tank car right with you—so's to be indypendent o' all gas so'ces?"

"That's right," admitted Jim. In which admission, at least, there was nothing dangerous. "But gas is gas—and distance is dist—"

"And this feller," persisted the Sheriff, "said 'at all yo're cars—cep'n mebbe the special machines draggin' the trailer trains, which 'uz fitted up even mo' so—he said he was tolt 'at ev'y one o' yo're cars was spec'ally fitted 'ith a special gas-tank holdin' 50 gallons. Fifty gal—whooie! Is that right?"

"That's right," admitted Jim, but exceedingly troubledly now. "But gal-lons don't pay 'tention to clocks, since—"

"And how much," the Sheriff drove on, "d' you fellers git, out'n yo're cars—well, now take that circus cage yo're drivin' right now, how much d'ya get from—"

"Well, this veh'cle" explained Jim, with a sigh, "like most of our veh'cles, is a sort of—of synthetic affair! First, the cage's been built atop an over-wheel truck-chassis—you know what I mean?—type o' chassis what lets it ride over and clear o' the wheels?—so's to serve for exh'bition purposes as well as travelin' purposes?—in fact, the cage's been built atop the chassis of a standard ev'ryday, dyed-in-the-wool, black-nosed National Auto Company's truck. And—"

"Pshaw!" said the Sheriff, disappointedly. Obviously some boyhood castle had tumbled flat. "When I was a boy—but ain't that kind o' drab—f'r a circus? I mean—black cabs an' hoods—an' all?"

"Not," returned Jim, with supreme patience, "if you saw the busts o' color and fire draggin' in back of 'em—in my p'ticler case, the woodcarved framework o' the cage, plus the woodcarved shut-off panels what are set up around the chassis when the cage is exhibiting—woodcarved stuff did in Japan by Jap'nese woodcarvers earnin' all of 5 cents a day!—but tinted and gilded in a good old American carny-goods house!—no. But as for those black cabs, those cabs, don't forget, are—at least when the glass windows 'n all are up—are the rainproofedness, hailproofedness, sunproofe—"

"True," agreed the Sheriff. "Though I don't like the way a man, in one o' them type o' cabs, has t' ride a'most right over the engyne."

"I see," Jim almost groaned aloud. "Well, now I'll ask one! If you, Sheriff, were a-buying trucks and chassis—in big quantities—for anything at all—from, say, a trans-contynental truckin' line to—to a circus—what kind would *you* buy—to keep your costs down? And to—now wait!—to make it pos'ble to get parts anywheres?"

"You win!" laughed the Sheriff. "The standard National Auto Comp'ny truck, o' co'se. Same's 'bout 95-p'cent of the rest of Amer'ca now does, in this standa'dized day o' nineteen fo't—but yo' say most o' yo're veh'cles is synthetic? So how much d' y' get from yo're gas—but say, again, that very circus-wagon cage yo're drivin' right now, how much d'ya get from—"

"Our special engines," said Jim frowningly, "let us av'age 10 miles to the gallon. Fact is, the special engines in my machine, coupled with the compar'tive lightness o' the cage, gets *me* 12 to the gallon."

"Jehoshaphat! Why, you fellers could—ef you had to, that is—you could jump from—from Chycago to Omaha—500 miles—'thout pickin' up a single drap o' gas, couldn't you?"

"Right," said Jim, gritting his teeth. Gritting them, that is, at the manner in which he was failing completely to get to the point at issue. But was nevertheless careful to cater to this information-hungry man, to the last degree. "Not only is the license plate what's tacked to one o' the back panels hangin' against my cage one o' the new special gold an' black Fed'ral Inter-State licenses what Uncle Sam gives to showfolks like us—just as 'tis, so far as that goes, on ev'ry veh'cle we got—but we're fixed, all of us, to be able to cover twict as long a jump as ever we could poss'bly have—as a matter of fact, our boss rigged our outfit up the way it is because he figgers someday to take the whole shebang, aboard some old freighter, to Australia—which is a place o' huge distances—I know, because I've been there!—anyway, he figgers to take it there—a fact!—but anyway, we aim to be able to cover any fool jump our fool advance man lays out for us right here in the U.S.A.!—and b'lieve me, we sometimes cover some big ones. Though this present one, Sheriff, is perhaps the worst we ever had—or will have. Why, this country around here sure is—"

"'Leetle Australy,' this kentry has b'en called," declared the Sheriff imperturbably. "By some famous English trav'ler who once ventured into it. Though it seems a nat'ral 'nough kentry to me. Who's lived in it a plumb long time. So danged nat'ral, in fact, that—i'God!—*I* live full 7½ mile outside th' town I do most of m' sheriffin' in—an' neither me nor nobody else thinks nothin' of it, fur what's a leetle matter o' 10—20—30—minutes' commutin' time in a car, I'd like to know?—nothin' at all!—I do it 4—6—

sometimes 8 times a day, an' think noth—but gittin' back to yo're problem, it seems to me that fitted out like you air, with a ova'sized gas tank, plenty gas at yo're elbow thar at Elum's—*ef* you need it, and $50 in yo're pockets, yo're settin' pretty jest now fer not bein' a wanderin' tramp driver f'r the rest of yo're days. Oh, maybe a wanderin' one—yeah!—but not a hongry, starvin' one. Fact is, I don't think that yo're boss, about to catch his-se'f a piece o' sleep right now at Foleysburg, is worryin' none."

"Yeah? Well, I know plumb well that if the show ever *gets* there, they'll all be fixin' to grab themselves a piece o' sleep a'right!—all but him, that is, who'll be Johnny-on-the-Job—and the Big Top crew who'll have to step on it!—but seems *I* won't never know that they did get there till I get there myself; why—I can't even know, right now, so far's that goes, whether they even got out, by this here Simpson's Junction, wherever 'tis, into the better Foleysburg Road, because I understand they's a malary swamp 'longside that junction—and that nobody—not even a crossroads store—can risk livin' 'longside; so ya see—"

"Wa-all," broke in the Sheriff grimly, "I kin tell yo' 'bout *that*. W'ile it's true nobody lives—or even tries to live—'round Simpson's Junction, becaze o' th' p'izen swamp—I kin, as I said, tell yo' 'bout w'ether yo're show come out thar or not. F'r 'bout half the town o' Willis Creek hyar—w'ere I have the honor o' hangin' out as Sheriff!—walked or driv' this mornin' round and down to Simpson's Junction—fus' goin' west, yo' know, 'long our county's section o' Carthage Road?—then down, by th' end stretch o' Southwest City Road to the junction?—and see the whole circus come out o' th' hills this mornin'—'bout 10:30 o'clock. I didn't git to see it—no!—fur var'ous but good reasons—but I hear 'twas quite a sight 'ith all the red an' gilt wagons an' all."

"Pshaw!" Jim said. "They—they made it, okay. Well, I still say 's I won't ever know abs'lutely if they made Foleysburg, even on that better road, till I get there myself!"

"Oh, they got thar a'right," said the Sheriff. "Just fifteen minutes ago—to the dot. With ever'thing—'cludin' the ely-phant—in his go-truck!"

"They—did?" Jim's last hopes fell. But now complete bewilderment filled him. "But—but how d'*you* know, Sheriff—with Foleysburg not havin' no phone service nor telegr—"

"Oh, that's easy. When you know th' answer! A friend o' mine who's in Beeville today, a town 50 miles or so northeast o' Foleysburg—and out o' its caounty entirely—was phonin' me, at my request, no mo'n 3 minutes afore you called up—consarnin' a nigger whut 'scaped jail hyar las' week, and who I figgered had loped to thar. An' who was thar, a'right, disguised as— but the p'int what I'm tryin' to git at is that this friend, when he phoned me, on a circuit goin' clean plumb 'round the Unyverse, so it a'most seemed, was at the home of a kid nephew o' his'n whut's got a wi'less talkin' set 'ith a kid in Foleysburg, an'—"

"You—you don't mean?" put in Jim excitedly, "that they's a way to get commun'cation with that town? Say, by way o' this very phone, and that—"

"Now holt yo're hosses! These two kids got on'y one complete unit atween 'em!—and this happens t' be the week th' Beeville kid's got the receivin' end of it—an' the Foleysburg kid the talkin' end! And inc'dentally the end whut, mo' likely as not, could invalydate his old man's ve'y title to his house an' land. Since—but anyway, my friend, jest befo' he called me hyar, had jest listened in to the Foleysburg kid tellin' his Beeville boy friend that the circus had jest drawed in complete, 'cludin' the elyphant on the hind end. Atter w'ich—ef'n it intrusts you any—the set went 'pop' at the sendin' end!"

"Tubes blew up?" proffered Jim.

"Yeah?" drawled the Sheriff sardonically. "Wall, th' last wu'ds what come through wuz 'Jeehunkus, my ol' man's a-comin' with th' sledge ham—'—w'ich means that the old man smashed that transmittin' app'ratus to hell 'n gone. So they won't be no mo' commun'cation out'n Foleysburg now, let alone in! But yo're show's definitely in—so that's thar."

"Well, well, well," was all Jim could say, considerably dumfounded, but also amazed at the curious way in which circumstances had, momentarily at least, counteracted the complete lack of communications in this region. Now he asked a question.

"Sher'ff," he said, "'zackly how long—in your honest estymate—'ll it take me to cover Old Twistibus? I'm askin', because I can't go by what I hear 'round here from every Tom, Dick and Harry—nor by the show movements you just give me—since the show may have stood here or there in Old Twistibus—or laid up there or here—or even put on spurts on good stretches—I can't go by *its* movements. But you undoubt'ly know the low-down. And—but here—I'll put the question even more acc'rately: How long'll it take me to cover Old Twistibus, with this—this critter, which def'nitely and abs'lutely has to be drove not too rough?"

"Well, critter 'r no critter," said the Sheriff, "from Perkins Junction, whut's now ahead of you a bit—an' whar, o' co'se, Ol' Twistibus comes in—till yo' come out on this here Simpson's Junction, whar Ol' Twistibus hits—an' ends—in Foleysburg Road—y' got befo' yo' a bit o' tough drivin'. W'ich—but how much, yo'll ast, in sheer miles. Well, hain't nobody ever act'ally measured Old Twistibus 'ith a tapeline, an' so estymates differ like ever'thing—but one good so'ce—a suttin' gov'ment engyneer—says it's all of 140 mile o' twists an' dips, kivverin' on'y 70 miles or so o' distance as a crow flies. All we know for shore round hyar is the *exact* travelin' time through it. Sence the road's an out-'n-out na-t'ral, when it comes to bein' a speed damp'ner—a—a—a speed reg'lator, so fur's that goes—a—a so'te o' aut'matic d'terminer to'ds holtin' motor veh'cles goin' over it to a fixed minymum passage-time. And so I'm able to tell you def'nitely that it'll take you—an' quite rega'dless, please onderstand, o' whethah yo're travelin' 'ith a racin' car or a jallopy—or even the N.A.C. truck what you got!—it'll take you eveh bit of—and not a danged mite less'n—full 5 hours. Fack is, *I* never heerd o' nobody makin' it in less'n that. Yo're show—as it 'pears—well o'ganized as 'tis—and knowin' no doubt how to space out its veh'cles to prevent blockin', took 30 minutes mo'n the standa'd 5 hours."

"And—and if th' Bear Creek Bridge is down? And I hear that she—"

"Is she down? Well, th' Lord be praised! She'd oughta b'en condemned 2 y'ars ago. Best news I've heered t'day—fer hoomanity. Now them lazy savages in th' hills'll hatter build a new one—or l'arn to swim! However, yo've asked a question. Ef she's down, then yo' better fill up that ova'-sized gas tank o' yo'rn there at Elum's—in case 'tain't filled—for 'ith that bridge down, yo'll hatter circle it by goin' clear into Dead Man's Valley—that's a set o' dismal hills lyin' behint an' beyant these Old Twistibus Hills—hills what nothin' kin be growed atween'em, and so nobody lives in 'em 'tall—anyway, yo'll hatter go clear into this valley, by way of a road—the on'y road, in fack—an' one leadin' off o' Old Twistibus just about thutty feet ahead o' whar the bridge is—or was!—a road whut's danged near as crazy an' ornery as Old Twistibus itse'f—anyway, that road—an' they ain't ary other—circles the whole valley and takes you fin'lly t' th' 'tother bridge what exists over that creek, at the futh'most end o' Dead Man's Valley, and then fetches you 'ventually right plumb back to Old Twistibus jest 'tother side the downed bridge. Kinda in'ficient, heh, to hatter pass through a whole great valley an' range o' hills jest to circle a fool downed bridge?—but that's the way 'tis. But the travelin' time 'volved, you ast, didn't yo'? Wa-all, it takes easy a full 3 hours to pass through Dead Man's Valley. At least, I never heerd o' nobody kivverin' that beyant-hills region in less'n 3 hours."

"Ow!" said Jim silently. "Well, assumin' then, that by the grace o' God I'm out onto—and in—the Foleysburg Road—at Simpson's Junction—and still, thanks to that oversized gas tank of mine, splashin' plenty o' fuel—how much time then, to Foleysburg, 'long that road?"

"Oh—3 hours—that's a fairish good road. Three hours—so long's yo' kin read signs—an' see to it 'at when you take th' detour round at Mill Creek you take the *right* one o' the two!—caze 'tother's got a treach'rous bog in it—Old Devil Quicksand!—this region's got ever'thing in it, you know, that Mother Nature gives—quicksands—cyclones—ever'thin'. Anyway, ef'n yo' kin read c'rrect—and take the *right* bypass road—it'll be 3 hours. But all o' 3 hours. Ef'n you don't—and it's dark—dark, say, like las' night—and you take the wrong detour road—it'll mebbe be weeks—months—y'ars befo' yo' git to Foleysburg!"

"Well, that settles it then," Jim groaned to himself. And aloud he said: "5 hours—that bein' a figger *you* call a minimum, and *I* hafta—transportin' a—a critter with newly borned young—plus 3 hours—same conditions again—plus 3 hours—same again—11 hours. Con-drat that Bear Creek bridge and that fool elepha—hrmph—uh—er—elephant tender, who said he'd been over this same comb'nation route 20 years ago, and that it wasn't but a few hours. It's 11 hours a'right, as you give it, Sheriff. And 11 hours added to 2 o'clock, which is more'n went now—no!—11 hours added to certain time I need, as sure as heck, to change a tire here what's slowly splittin' open on me—and t' buy some canned goods and put on my nosebag, for I'm so starved I'm plumb weak—oh, call it 12 hours f'r safety's sake—an' addin' that to 2 o'clock that's a'ready gone and went—*why!*—I'll not only lose out—not only will Florette be gone by two—three hours—but skip that, Sherif!—the show'll be long gone too. Yeah, I'm sunk a'right—unless—" And Jim stopped. Hoping against hope that the Sheriff might perhaps interpolate the proper answer at this point.

But the Sheriff's answer was markedly belligerent.

"Yeah?" he said gelidly. "Onless—*what?*"

CHAPTER V

THE STRAIGHTAWAY

Well," retorted Jim uneasily, "I've heard 'bout—well, I been wonderin' if they's any chance 'tall to—but this is the setup as has been give me by one of the fellers I met up road—a man who says he jest came from this-away—and one, with him, from our the hills to boot. Of course he told me 'bout my bein' in f'r a heller of a drive, and all that—a'most th' very minute I leave Perkins Junction up ahead of me—windin' in and out of those mud-hills of Old Twistibus—even zigzagging straight backward and forward in places, he claimed—fordin' shallow streams in some places because of last week's floods—and makin' some detours, too, 'count the same reason, by local bypasses that has ruts in 'em, goin' clear down, he says, to China, but he also said—"

"Listen hyar," put in the Sheriff, in his voice a pronounced contempt. "Air yo' some lacy pants who, in spite o' th' hell-bender of a big gas tank on his machine, and the fack that, ef'n he didn't fill it at Pricetown, he kin dump 'nough tins o' gas in it right thar at Elum's to fill it to the gills, still cain't take a bit o' hard drivin'?"

"I'm no lacy pants—no," retorted Jim indignantly, "and I never see the stretch o' drivin' I cain't take or make. But there's reasons—pers'nal reasons—why I *got* to connect with the show tonight—and not later. I—but here's the point I'm tryin' to make. This feller told me that if I'd been comin' through here only a week later, the new Straightaway—as *he* called it—or, as Elum's sign outside here puts it—"

"Yeah," put in the Sheriff dryly, "Moss Elum he cain't spell—and I've heerd he had to spell that part of his sign with playin' kyard symbols. Go ahead?"

"Well," pressed on Jim flounderingly, "this feller said that the Straight-away—joinin' together the 2 Carthage Roads—East Carthage an' West Carthage—into one, an' goin' right through the—the Smoky Ridge tunnel—not only cuts the whole durn Old Twistibus right out of the pikter, and gives a straight east and west contin'us road between here and Southwest City Crossing, west o' you—not only, he says, cuts the distance 'way 'way 'way down, but, because of the beautiful new macadam on the Straightaway, cuts the travelin' time over ev'ry unit of th' distance—so far—so he says—that they simply ain't any comparison what-so-ever even."

"All that's keerect," admitted the Sheriff coolly. "I mought even say 'at it's b'en calkilated out by that suttin gov'ment road engyneer I r'ferred to'while back, that ef'n Old Twistibus—Old Twistibus, that is, 'thout the extry length now in it f'r *you*—'uz straightened out so's she was like a big hairpin, 'stid of a snake what had froze stiff while he was in a ep'lyptic fit, then all the straight good roadway—'cluding this new Straightaway stretch what j'ins it all up—connectin' that thar hairpin's two p'ints, 'd be like a jumper acrost them p'ints which, ef it an' th' hairpin 'uz both adjusted in len'ths 'codin' to th' rel'tive speeds possible on the two routes, 'd make the hairpin but $^{20}/_{,}$ths 's long as the jumper 'crost its ends."

"Then that would mean," said Jim, eagerly, and calculating mentally, "that one could go from beginning to end of Old Twistibus—*but via the Straightaway branch*—in no more'n 1 hour and 45 minutes, more or le—"

"Keerect," again admitted the Sheriff. "'Bout one hour, all in all, f'r th' strict Straightaway segment alone, w'ere one kin let a machine out for all she's wu'th—'bout one hour, roughishly, yes, f'r th' Straightaway segment alone—or, ef you like exactytude, 45 minutes f'r th' long part o' that segment what lays in the county where you now air—th' part kivverin' the extensive dried-out lowlands ahead o' you, an' still called Frog Gullies, then piercin' Smoky Ridge and bein' part o' my county—15 minutes f'r the shorter part o' th' Straightaway layin' in my county, an' kivverin' the much briefer dried-out lowlands this side th' Ridge called Catfish Gullies; then—'ith respect to yo'rese'f, o' course—'bout 'nother qua'ter hour from this end o' the Straightaway, on a danged fair dirt road, West Carthage, to my town o' Willis Creek; then 'nother qua'ter hour—say—an' on the same road, o' course—from Willis Creek to Southwest City Crossin' of Southwest City Road; an' mebbe 'nother 15 minutes down what's left o' Southwest City Road to Simpson's Junction, whar Southwest City Road, Ol' Twistibus, an' Foleysburg Road all end in an' at each other. But I mought also add that the 'ficial openin' of that Straightaway is to be 'ficially helt on the centynarial annyversary o' the town of Willis Creek, my town, what did all th' wire-pullin' t' ger Uncle Sam to spend all that forchune."

"Yes," assented Jim diplomatically. "This feller I talked with said 'twas one of the most 'spensive pieces o' highway construction in all U.S.A.—bein' on concrete pillars nearly all its len'th 'count them lowlands, which sometimes gets swampy—but that Uncle Sam was willin' to put it through 'cause it could be made later a part—"

"—a part—yes," put in the Sheriff, "a' th' Great National East-West Way 'crost th' kentry. So—what?"

"Well, this feller that talked to me," went on Jim fiercely, realizing more and more that he was up against a very uncompromising and forbidding representative of the law, "says that th' shorter end o' the Straightaway what lays in your county, your side the Ridge, has got only a chain acrost it—a chain unhookable by anybody, but carryin' a sign hangin' from it tellin' people that they's no road through; but at the end what lays in this county, he says, they's a barrier crost it—a powerful barrier—at the point, in fact, he says, where the Straightaway commences to lift up on its—its concrete stilts—above the lowlands around it—but he said it's a swing-around barrier for later toll purposes—and that the key ain't in the possession of the Sheriff of this county because it ain't a county road yet—he says it's in your pass—that is, he said that you're 'ficially road-caretaker for Uncle Sam till the road's opened, and that you know where a key to that barrier can be got—or found—and he says, Sheriff, that in a few 'mergencies you've let a few cars—or trucks, or whatnot—go onto the new highway—to cut off distance—and time—to cut off both, that is. Now I've more than half a hunch, Sheriff, that my boss, Mr. MacWhorter, musta tried to fix it for himself early this mornin'—by phone, same's I'm doing, and with you—for the circus to go thataway—for you're a silent sort of man, and don't tell ever'thing you know—but my hunch now is that he did—and prob'ly offered you a good piece of change to boot—and you must have told him no, plenty loud, otherwise he wouldn't have went by way of Old Twistibus. But jest the same, I'm—I'm asking you too, Sheriff, whether you wouldn't let me through—just the one circus wagon—the last wagon!—so's I can make Foleysburg—which'll be dog-plumb in the bag for me then!—before the show closes. For the other way, Sheriff, I'm sunk—sunk not only for show-closin' hour, but even prob'ly for show-pullin'-out hour."

And Jim waited, with heart in his mouth—for he knew not only all the sad details of the fearfully circuitous drive to get to Foleysburg via Old Twistibus—but he knew Florette; knew, as well as he ever knew anything in his life that when that big tent came down tonight, she would be pulling out from the show; and that when the show itself pulled out from Foleysburg, she would be trudging along a dark road with Mondaine—exactly as she said she would—would be being named wife to Mondaine by some country preacher—would be—

But the Sheriff was answering him.

"Wa-all now," the Sheriff was drawling remonstratively, "that thar's a p'utty bald so'te o' request, ain't it? 'Caze rules is—even as declar'd by Uncle Sam hisse'f, so fur's that goes—that nary a veh'cle—'tother than one 'volved in a 'mergency—kin go through that highway till *all* kin go through it. Chief 'mergency this feller must a-be'n talkin' 'bout to you was when I left th' fire comp'ny come through from Cedarville—a town off'n a road what comes into the road yo're now on, at Perkins Junction—to he'p put out a lot of coal a-smolderin' in our Mansion House cellar—and a su'geon from Pricetown—same town's yo' jest come from—git through 'caze a man hyar had busted his 'pendix, an' had to be opyrated at once—if not sooner. So far's MacWhorter tryin' to cross our palms, he did—yes!—though not mine d'reckly, no! Fur I've b'en in the town o' Janestown far, far west o' hyar—sence yest'day noon—testifyin' in a 2-day tryal—an' I never got back hyar 'twell noon today. That bein' th' complete reason why I didn't git to see yo're show file out this mo'nin' at Simpson's Junction. And why—but as I'm tryin' to say, I had a dep'ty of so'tes—a friend—kivverin' my office in my absence, an' yo're boss MacWhorter tolt this feller, early this mo'nin', on th' phone, that he'd pay him $50 when the circus, by way o' th' Straight-away, hove past whar our 'ficial office—such as 'tis! is, on Ca'thage Road west, some sev'ral miles—an' then some!—east o' town. Even lied like hell, sayin' yo'-all 'uz transportin' a sick gal—kid or so'thin'—which 'uz a fool lie on the very face of itse'f, 'caze anybody sick 'd b'en lef' ahind in a hos-pital whar doctors is—not clowns an' stake-drivers. However, cain't blame him fur tryin' to build up a case o' so'tes! My dep'ty, however, shore burned hell out o' him on the phone; he warned him 'bout either blowin' or shootin' that barr'er lock—not that, as he frankly tolt MacWhorter, *that* could be leg'lly proved ef 'twas did 'ith nary witnesses nigh—but, said he to Mac-Whorter, th' minute MacWhorter's procession o' cars hove up hyar—thanks to gittin' through 'count o' some skulduggery 'ith that lock, the whole passel of 'em 'd be arrested onder State Law 4889 prohibitin' processions of mo'n 12 cars 'thout county permission. So yo're boss *did* take Ol' Twistibus." The Sheriff paused a second or so. "'Cose," he admitted, "yo're on'y one cir-cus wagon—not a hull circus. Couldn't arrest *you* as no procession—that's shore! Fur law is law. But I don't even calkilate to wisht I could—sence I'm jest not fixin' it nohow f'r you to git a-holt of a suttin' key some'eres! F'r hell fa'r, driver, I jest cain't see as how yo're facin' no 'mergency 'cept makin'—or not makin'—a show what you kin keep follerin'up. And gittin' drivin' wages—f'r so doin'. Seems like I'd be doin' you a favor ef'n I was to keep you from makin' yo're c'nnection t'night. For—but I guess I'm sorry, but I jest cain't see how I kin waive rules an' reg'lations—but hyar—what kind of a animile mought it be that yo've got inside that thar circus-wagon yo're pilotin'?"

"He—would!" said Jim to himself. But was equal to the emergency, as he had been several times this morning.

"It's a *felinus giganticus,*" he said gracefully.

"Oh?" said the Sheriff, dimly. "Gi—gi—*giganticus* means big, o' course. But feeliness? I cain't say as I know that wu'd. But wait now—don't tell me! Le' me figger it out. *Giganticus* don't jest mean big; it means—now wait—don't tell me. It must be—but I got it! It's a hippo, heh? Fur I 'mem-ber now I have heerd 'em called gigantic cows. Well—well—well—'twould be a hippo that *yo're* askin' *me* favors for! The sad 'spressions on them critters' faces allus makes me damn near to a weaklin'—I want to turn to whoever I'm with, an' bawl m' fool eyes out—hm?—an' with little hippos all 'round her, with equally sad 'spressions? My God. I—" And Jim could hear the Sheriff floundering mentally about.

In fact, Jim was just about to admit that tlus animal he had just called a *felinus giganticus* was, indeed, much to be pitied—far from its native haunts, as it was—with little young ones like itself nursing on it—and—

But just as he opened his mouth to admit all this, something happened.

Princess let out a roar such as she might have given only in her native jungles—a roar thar reverberated over hill and plain and knoll—that whistled through near-by scrub oak and cactus—shook the clapboards of the little store till they actually vibrated—paralyzed even the drums of Jim's ears.

"A—cat!" said the Sheriff. "By the good God A'mighty—a great—big—cat!"

CHAPTER VI

MOB!

Al "Three-Gun" Mulhearn, bankrobber, faced his three companions in the thicket 2 miles north of the town of Cedarville, and prepared to rehearse, for the last and final time, the instructions that all already knew.

Not far from the four close-lying low stumps on which the four men sat, off the crude tree-cleared trail which led, by a sharp curve, out onto the regular roadway—in short, Cedarville Road, which itself, eventually, led down into Perkins Junction, stood a comparatively small overland-type truck, battleship grey in color. At least with respect to the oblong truck body itself, lying back of the exceedingly short squat black cab and engine hood which marked the chassis as that of a standard National Auto Company truck. For there was about the entire truck, on really close inspection, a curious suggestion of high speed—a suggestion, no less, that the battleship-grey truck body itself had been removed from some quite innocent industrial transportational vehicle, and mounted on a special fast-engined chassis, for the machine was heavy-tired as to wheels, and the grey truck body appeared to be actually braced, by steel angle irons, at its four vertical corners, and along all its horizontal edges, top and bottom, against possible vibration from the fiercest kind of roadpounding. Though such buttressing—if such it was—would have been a thing observable, at best, only by a close observer who could analyze what he saw. For the very flushness between the sides and ends of the truck body and the faces of the rigid, unwarped corners and horizontal edges, cried aloud, to such an observer, that wood had been cunningly mortised so that angle iron faces could sit snugly within; the gentle fusion—such as it was—in color, between corners, edges and truck body sides and ends, revealed that paint had been dexterously applied to make them do just that: but nothing, quite nothing, had been able to camouflage the line of demarcation in every case where one material ended—and another began! Nailed firmly and tightly to the end of the truck body—a simple form of affixion permitted in this easygoing section of the United States!—was its license plate; in this case, a bright green; and painted on the side of the truck body facing the four men—as it was, likewise, on the side now away from them!—in yellow letters outlined by snappy black, were the words:

TRANSCONTINENTAL TRUCKING COMPANY
FAST FREIGHT

Lashed to the side of the cab, as though a too heavy loading of the truck's interior had prevented further packing of goods inside—and lashed, moreover, by rope passing several times clear around the base of the cab, but containing in its turns various concatenations of curious and trickish-looking knots and loops, all of which suggested that the rope could be cleared away entirely by a jerk here, and a jerk chere, was a small but stout wooden case, with a hinged and padlocked lid, and with, apparently tied to *it* by twine only, a "dolly"—or 4-roller-skate-wheel platform—carrying a heavy draw rope and the whole indicating that the case was heavy and best transportable, when off the truck, by rolling it or drawing it.

"Now I hope," said Al Mulhearn, a big hulk of a man about 40 years of age, cold blue of eye, and black of hair, and dressed just now in the striped overalls and jumper, as well as cap of the same material, of a trucker, "that you birds have got ever'thing down pat in your beans. F'r t'day ain't no more, an' no longer, the day it's been for 3 long weeks 'r so—it's now—" As a concession to the necessities of clear expression, he spat from his mouth the cud of gum which, being a nonsmoker, he was seldom without. "F'r t'day," he repeated, more clearly now, "ain't, as I jest said, no more, an' no longer, the day it's been for 3 long weeks 'r so—th' day, I mean, when that box of gold was maybe *gonna* be in the Cedarville Bank vault; it's the day now that the box *is* there—we've cased the joint like no joint's ever been cased before, an' seen it brought there and what' hell not else—and so now is the hour when you birds have got to do some perfec' co-ordinatin' in the way of gat-slingin', box-liftin', car-drivin', an' what have you.

"So let's rehearse the heist all over again, durin' the last free minutes open to us. So that they'll be no excuse of anyon—"

"'Scuse me, Boss," came from a little wizened light-weight fellow facing the leader—a veritable youth, in fact, about 19 years of age, with yellow hair and a pockmarked face, and dressed in a dark brown suit and a black shirt, and wearing a green cap, "but I'd like to ask one question—off th' record—if you don't mind." And the speaker expectantly pursed a pair of cupid's-bow lips which broke his pock-marked face, and which, like that of his chief, held neither cigarette nor cigar.

"Dish it," ordered Al Mulhearn. "Though I don't think it'll have no sig-nifycance. F'r while you sure are the deadliest shot, Snipes, with a rod—freehand, hip, or pocket!—in all U.S.A.—the sperrit of old Robber Hood himself, by Christ, come back to earth!—you also got a cur'ous blindness to plain ever'day, hard facts." The big man regarded his youthful henchman troubledly, as something which could never be fully understood. "However," he went on, "I don't aim to drive you lugs—none o' you—into doin' your act so long's there's th' littlest, slightest, goddam'est small thing in any bean that ain't 101 p'cent clear. So what's your question, Snipes?"

"Well, Boss," said the little pock-marked fellow troubledly—or presumably so, "it's been occurrin' to me, durin' the last couple o' hours, what a fine bunch o' saps we'd be if this Cedarville jug—an' that Brocktown jug—had both pulled a beautiful shill yest'rday, so that what we seen bein' transferred was just—say—a box o' lead washers; and that th' real box o' gold—with the hundred grand in it!—was bein' held elsewhere in case of a heist. A heist, no less, than the one we're all set to pull!"

Al Mulhearn gazed sadly, but tolerantly, at Snipes Spurlock.

"Snipes, don't it mean nothin' to you that the feud that lays atween this Cedarville Bank and that Brocktown Bank—that is, th' presidents thereof!—is bitter as hell—and that they couldn't ever have got together to cook up a shill? That—but now lissen here. Suppose I rehearse the facts as *we know 'em;* it's—" He glanced at an exceedingly accurate-looking watch ticking away on his wrist. "—it's on'y 2:31½ right now—they's minutes a-plenty ahead of us before we even dare pull outa this thicket on the heist—so suppose, as I said, I rehearse the facts as we know 'em—and let these other boys, here, Slim and Scarface, figger out if there *is* a hole in that setup."

"But don't you know yet, Boss—" The speaker was a man who sat at Mulhearn's right in the circle, atop a stump whose base was littered with cigarette butts—a long, lanky, thin-faced and hard-faced man, about 33 years of age, dressed like Mulhearn, in striped trucker's clothing, complete even to the striped cap, and trailing a cigarette from the corner of his mouth so expeditely that he held it and talked clearly at the same time. "—that Snipes is a screwball that rides higher than a junky on a pack of muggles—just by starting arguments—worse, by having things 'proved' for him alone?"

"Aw nuts," protested Snipes. "I—"

"Nuts hell," retorted the other. "You don't smoke good tobacco. You don't—"

"Tobacco—icky!" said Snipes, thrusting his nose straight up in the air. "I—"

"I ain't so sure," put in Al Mulhearn darkly, "but that Slim is right. But Snipes has his good points. One of 'em bein' his shootin' eye! An' the other bein' his goddamnfool disregard of slugs whinin' around his bean. An' besides, this is one o' them moments in life when it don't hurt none to lean clear over backward so far's an'body's doubts and quallums goes—to discuss the whole situation as though they was, amongst us, one new man—and thus see if an'body finds a hole anywhere?"

"Why not?" returned the man referred to as Slim. "We've got to fill in our time some way till the zero moment. I'd just as soon spend it geeing up this mental defective so's his rodwork'll be super."

"Nuts," said Snipes.

"All right then," agreed the leader.

And paused, ruminating.

"Three weeks ago," he began, "it was, wasn't it, that we read, in our hideout there, sout' o' the Big Town, about this box o' gold coins—$100,000 worth at present gold rates—bein' unearthed in the home of this old miser—this old miser deceased, I better say!—Jason Whitforth, livin' about halfway between Cedarville and Brocktown. This crazy addleheaded old miser—so *I* call him!—seein' 'at he lined his wooden box wit' lead to protect his god-dam' gold, makin' the whole thing heft about 250 pounds!—and this makin' it, long later, into a 4-man heist—and—and a 3-man payoff." Al Mulhearn's lower lip came out as could only the lip of a man who *had* had to pay off many assistants in his day. But it drew immediately back in. And he went on. "And we read, up there in the hideout, about the two wills of old Miser Whitforth that were found, both dated the same calendar day, one namin' the Brocktown Bank as adminystrator of his estate—and the other namin' the Cedarville Bank. And about the presidents of both banks hatin' each other's very guts—but with the Brocktown pres holdin' on to the gold because the will namin' his bank was found first, and also because—"

"Possassion she eez 10 points of the law," pointed out a man at the speaker's left, who had been thoughtfully chewing, off and on, with firm white teeth, on a cold cigar butt. He was a dark Italian-like man, about 38 years of age, with a long scar running down his face, and dressed in grey flannel shirt and high boots, and wearing a black felt hat.

"As Scarface Scalisi here says, yes," confirmed Mulhearn. "And—" He looked sourly at the infinitely short cigar butt protruding from the other's lips. Then, opening his striped trucker's blouse slightly, and fumbling at a vest pocket within, withdrew a fat plump long cigar there, and extended it to Scarface.

"F'r God's sake, Scarface," he said disgustedly. "Have a decent smoke on me, will ya?"

Scarface reached eagerly out for the cigar. Which, however, was gone! Vanished completely! Al Mulhearn's open hand stood there, however. On his face a malevolent grin.

"Aw—C'rist!" grunted Scarface disgustedly. "An' I go fall ag'in, like ton of breecks, for boss w'at can do sleigh'-av-han'. Beega dam' fool, me. How you do dat, boss?"

"How?" echoed Al Mulhearn, quite delighted. "Didn'tcha see me hookin' somethin' on the cigar—what's a phoney anyway, made o' rub-ber—while I was fumblin' for it? You're so goddam' naeevy, Scarface, 'at you spoil a good piece o' legy'd'main!" He reached up into his right sleeve, pulled down the cigar he had just proffered, detached from a tiny metal eye embedded in the material a tiny metal hook attached to the end of a now-tight piece of elastic, and letting the elastic fly back inside his sleeve and replacing the cigar inside his vest, resumed talking.

"Well now—gettin' back again to the development of our heist—and us!—we read, don't we, up there in the hideout, about the two would-be adminystrators down here goin' to law—and why th' hell not?—adminys-trator's fees bein', in this state, 7 p'cent o' pers'nal property, 7-p'cent is a goddam' fat cut on 100 grand. It's more'n any country jug could earn in sev'ral years. All right. Well, we hear, don't we, about how the dispute is set for hearin' at 9 A.M. on the first day of the first openin' session of the County an' Probate Court of Yocum County—that day bein' yesterday—and Yocum County bein' the county that holds both Cedarville and Brocktown; and we even hear that decision'll *prob'ly* be rendered. Only—*we* know in advance that it's goin' to be—and we know in advance *what* that decision's goin' to be! For, from casin' the whole setup down here in these woods—'r, rather, havin' 'Driller' O'Hare, wit' his oilwells talk an' all, live at the town flop as an oil-scout, an' case ever'thing for us, so's to keep our mugs all in the clear for a poss'ble job—what the hell've we discovered—or Driller dis-covered—but that old man Whitforth's man, Beebles, is a one-time scratch man for the old Mittles Mob—and so we've sent for Beebles, put the press on him, and Beebles—to help us out—*an' him!*—is gonna 'testify' as to *which* o' them wills was writ last. For we know dam' well—from the re-ports of one, 'Driller' O'Hare—and the calculations of one, Al 'Three-Gun' Mulhearn!—that if the Brocktown Bank gets that box—they ain't a flea's chance in hell of anybody, or any mob, snakin' it—but that if this Cedarville Bank, what's only a strawjay at best—with a two-dial vault and not even time locks on it—gets it—it's a perfec', easy, beeootiful an'made-t'-order heist. That is—for a certain Al Mulhearn and Associates!—whose leader has a few 24-carat idees back in his bean about how to git around any an' all nat'ral disadvantages! All right. Well, that decision, rendered yesterday mornin', thanks to Beebles' phony testimony, was that the will that was writ on the pink paper was writ last—and since that's the will namin' the Cedar-ville Bank as adminystrator—then the Cedarville Bank *is* adminystrator—and not the Brocktown Bank. And the decision was that them goods sh'd be turned over to the Cedarville Bank before close o' banking hours of the same day—said hours bein', in *this* hick country, 4 bells in the aft'noon!—and said day bein' that day which now 's yesterday."

"An' provin'," snorted Snipes derisively, "that decision, that the judge was a dimwit. To even order a forchune like that—into a strawjay like that!"

"Meanin', of course," said Al Mulhearn, a bit derisively himself—but, strangely, toward his henchman, "that Hizzoner shoulda named the Cedarville jug adminystrator—but shoulda ordered the gold into the First National Bank o' New York or so'thin', eh? Well, ain't you sort o' forgettin' Law, Snipes—on w'ich guys like Hizzoner operates? Namely, that in this state a man's pers'nal estate has got to be held in th' county where he accumylated it—and where he lived? Why—that's the very basis we worked this whole goddam' heist out on. Th' fact that the gold would hafta stay in th' Cedarville jug *or* th' Brocktown jug—and *we* saw to it it went to the Cedarville one. But let's disregard the goddam' Law just now—and figger out w'ether Hizzoner was th' dimwit you claim he was."

Al Mulhearn paused impressively. Not oblivious at all, however, to the wink that passed between Slim and Scarface, the while Snipes was bending over tightening his shoelace—and its answering wink back again—which said, plainer than words: The boss's givin' the punk all the punk wants—needs—to be 'on high.'"

Al Mulhearn was, indeed, talking directly to the said "punk" at this moment.

"This district, Snipes, is a nat'ral—when it comes to bein' 101 p'cent heistproof. And ever'body, includin' Hizzoner, knows that. 'Twouldn't make much diff, when you come down to it, if they was usin' a paper safe in that jug. In view o' the fact that the safe, as well as the doors and windows o' the jug, are 'lectrically bugged—as *we,* at least, know—and you know too!—to zing in the night, in case entry is pulled, or the v is monkeyed with—in the Sheriff's office, the mayor's home, the telephone exchange, and Christ knows what other spots. But w'en I say 'twouldn't make no diff if they was usin' a paper safe in that jug, I'm not foolin'. For this district, Snipes, is far wors'n that spot that mobmen all over the country call Th' Lousy Spot—yeah, Hot Springs, Arkansas—w'ere th' only way out o' the goddam' burg, sandwiched between them roadless mountains, is by way o' Little Rock, Arkansas—w'ere any mob that's pulled an'thing in Hot Springs is sure t' be glaumed. But this region, Snipes, is a lousier spot yet. F'r a heist pulled on a bugged safe an' bugged premyses, in this district, w'ere no goddam'ed road has any road whatsoever off'n it—an' not on'y all the bug-lines, but all the telephone lines connectin' th' towns an' houses 'r laid in conduits a'most in the bowels o' the earth, from them old W.P.A. days when Uncle S. hadda give these hillbillies plenty o' work—an' hence ain't cuttable, these p'ticler phone lines, like lines on poles!—why, such a heist, Snipes, is as good as cooked before even it's pulled. It's perfessional suicide, Snipes—f'r any mob that tries it. Any mob, that is, but the Mulhearn Mob o' w'ich you got the honor of bein' a val'able member—a mob whose leader has got some plenty bright ideas in his bean about h*ow* to do the imposs'ble.

"F'r what'ell, Snipes, way is there in this whole region to git away wit' the goods in a heist? Not t' mention your own life an' liberty? Now 'spose, f'r instance—you—all by your lonesome—was tryin' to flee this region, in a car, wit' somethin' you heisted, all by your lonesome, from this same jug. Now what moves lays ahead o' you right now? Name me every possible mo—but here!—goddam' it—we're goin' to discuss this affair in chromatic order—and we'll deal wit' all poss'ble ord'nary heists when we get to th' heist itself. Oh, I'll come back to you, Snipes, a'right."

Snipes, who had momentarily and visibly drooped because, presumably, the distinction of having something personally proved to him alone had been bodily snatched away from him, immediately perked up at the prospect that he would again be center of the stage. His thin shoulders braced themselves pleasurably, his colorless cheeks even ruddied a bit. None of which was lost on his chief.

"An' so," the latter was continuing, "gettin' back t' w'ere we left off." He paused. "Th' judge—dimwit as Snipes here calls him—but we'll see about *that* later—th' judge orders that gold into the Cedarville jug before bank closin' hours. Yesterday. An' the which—said jug, I mean!—we can't case no more through Brother 'Driller,' because of the goddam' fool—as us'al—gettin' likkered the day before at the town tavern, an' gettin' in a fight wit' no less'n the mayor, and havin' t' get the hell fast out o' the whole goddam' county or else get stuck in limbergo f'r 30 days and maybe get his f.p.'s sent to Wash'nton. But be that as it may, we follow up jest the same. For Slim Yarnai, our demon driver here—" And Al Mulhearn, indicating the man he had just referred to, and who was just lighting up a new cigarette, seemed almost to be indicating the latter's hands—sensitive yet powerfully muscled hands of a one-time racing-auto driver. "—thanks to havin' slipped down into the district, an' sout' o' town, by walkin' down-country from Tunberry Turnpike, next state up—commences casin' th' Cedarville jug, wit' a binoc'lars, and from that old haunted house a half mile below Cedarville—and acrost the main road—from the moment the decision was give in the Yocum County Court at Brocktown. And only one d'livery was made, wasn't there, Slim, of a heavy box, that had to be handled by two husky men—and accomp'nied by a trio of officials—with appur'ntly hard words passed—and that was at—"

"—at 5 minutes before bank close—or 4 bells—yesterday," said Slim Yarnai, exhaling the fresh cool smoke through his nostrils. "Just 5 minutes before the court's deadline. For—but why do you suppose, Boss, they have a 4 o'clock bank closing hour around here? Instead of the standard 3-o'clock hour? It seems to me—"

"Aw, hick ideas of some sort, that's all," said his superior impatiently. "For ain't this region the hickiest goddamn part of the whole U.S.A.? Hick ideas, that's all. Hicks can't never swallow the idea of a short workin' day. They always have to—but what the hell," he broke off, more impatiently yet, "difference does it make, anyway? Our heist ain't dependin' on no fixed hour. At least of the clock. Not even, b'Jesus, on dark—which comes on 'round 8 o'clock 'round here now. So go on wit' your answer to my question what you int'rrupted yourself on!"

Slim grinned a bit, and obviously at the way that was put. "Well," he repeated laconically, "the delivery of that heavy box, as I was saying, was made 5 minutes before the court's deadline. And no phoney, either—for, if you ask me, the two outfits dam' near came to blows in the signing off. Anyway, the Brocktown outfit cleared away, and went on back. The goods are there now, in the Cedarville Bank, just as we figured, to a 50-50 chance they'd be, 3 full weeks ago."

"To a feefty-feefty chance?" retorted Scarface Scalisi scornfully, spitting out a bit of wet tobacco he had chewed off of his cold cigar butt. "Hall, we know eet to be wan han'erd percant. For deedn' we feex eet to toss eet square into Ce-dar-veel jog?"

"A'right," put in the original querient, the little yellow-haired pockmarked Snipes. "These jays in this neck o' the woods can't act—so if Slim seen 'em gettin' hot under the collar, and all that, the feud musta still been on—and so I'm satisfied that 'twas the real McCoy was transferred. But just 'spose that while Slim slept in that haunted house last night—for you, Boss, wouldn't never keep him awake all night casin' a joint when he was going to drive on a dificult job like this 'un of ours t'day—just 'spose that the box o' gold went out of there *in* the night—toward some big-town connection of the Cedarville Bank. Wouldn't we be saps then to try this heist, and—"

Al Mulhearn raised a hand. "Don't you re'lize, Snipes, that if th' Cedarville jug broke th' probate rules that way—the Brocktown Bank could set their administratorship aside—an', will or no will, get appointed themselves again? Hell, whatcha 'spose them two jugs was fightin' about—but to hold on t' that 7 grand commish? Why—that's the very basis we worked this whole goddam' heist out on. Th' fact that the gold would hafta stay in the Cedarville jug *or* the Brocktown jug—and w*e* saw to it it went to th' Cedarville one!" He sighed. "However, your point's a fair one, Snipes. If, that is, it could be shown that Hizzoner was partial to the Cedarville Bank president—and would never ha' removed him for a breaking o' rules. And to show you that *I* look f'r your interests wit'out you always knowin' I do, I might say that—" He turned to the scarfaced man. "You tell him this, Scarface?"

Scarface shrugged his shoulders. "Well, Snipes, I never no can sleep nighttimes—as you shood ought' know—so Boss here he poot me las' night to caseeng that jog, fram ol' weed-gro' sew'r pipe acrost road an' down leetle-a-bit—w'ile Slim woo'd be snoozeeng. Now Slim—after he come dar 'round town on foot leetle-a w'ile ago, to join us all in theez theeckeet—Slim tol' you how today he bleenked awake at dawn, an' took up ag'an w'ere he lef' off las' night. Well, *I* cased all night teel dawn. An' notheeng— abs'lutely notheeng—cam' out the jog, front or back. So that deeposeet of

100 gran' she eez een there. For what goes een—an' don' come out—eez *een*. An' there ain't no use further av you worr'eeng about eet. You got a beet o' rod-tossin' to worry about."

"Ya satisfied now, Snipes?" Mulhearn inquired, half amusedly. "Al don't let silly errors creep into things. Right now—an' from the minute Slim left the haunted house to join up with us here—the jug is bein' cased by old Beebles himself—and so, up t' the very minute of the heist, we get signals that constitute las'-minute reports on ever'thing. Just like—like Dun and Bradstreet, by Jesus."

"Bot I weel ask wan now, Al," said Scarface, who, whether he had merely contributed to the proper "geeing up" of Snipes, or whether he had actually banished some fears from the latter's brain, had evidently banished not all such from his own. "Soppose that w'an we do make theez heist—by your plan, that eez!—there eez a dommy box een that v'olt—all readee f'r posseeble heist—or, as *they* might call eet, fooleesh attemp' to pool heist! A dommy box weeth the real wan planted onder the bank floor som'ware?"

"Yeah? Well, that box was sealed, when 'twas found, and its contents appraised, at all junctions, by the probate court rep'sent'ives an' th' Fed'ral tax collector for Brock City. Who ain't applyin' *their* seals t' no phonies. So if, my fine Italian fra'n, we don't find seals an' all, what we know are the McCoy, we'll run a clawhammer under one of them box boards—during th' heist—an' stick one of our mitts into them sweet goldpieces, an' make sure. But don't worry! *I* know probate an' Fed'ral tax seals. Sat'sfied?"

"Yes," said Scalisi.

"All—right. Now we go on from where, b' God, we started out—awhile back."

And with a sigh, Al Mulhearn resumed.

"Well, we figger, if I'm not mistaken, that we need 24 hours—after the mazuma is transferred—f'r th' case to cool. But no longer! An' we take it. And no more! F'r we're travelin' on just as rigid a schedule as—as—well, as thar circus outfit that—at least yesterday—was playin' Pricetown, south o' Brock City, and w'ich knew it'd be playin' *that* town—on *that day*—*them* hours—weeks and weeks before, b'God, it even started out on th' road. So we take our 24 hours. Which brings us up to today. Th' time f'r th' heist. And since we still can't start out yet—hardly!—the way *we're* gonna op'rate—I'll step back to what I ain't by a goddam' sight forgot! Brother Snipes here—and his appurrent skeptycism that this region maybe ain't a nat'ral—when it comes to bein' heistproof. By all ord'nary methods, that is. In fact, I'll make him eat his words—about Hizzoner bein' a dimwit—or else. So all right, Snipes. Le's see if you can take it." Snipes could—for he was actually glowing, his cupid's bow lips parted in seeming ecstasy. "So again—as before—an' as a pure example—we'll postylate you alone—travelin', in a distinctive veh'cle of any kind—f'r example, we'll say, a truck wit' a battleship-grey body like ours yonder—wit' or wit'out letters painted on it—it don't matter—'s just an example—an' 'spose you've just pulled a successful heist o' this Cedarville jug in broad daylight—w'ich is the on'y way anybody *could* do it, in view o' them bug circuits—and w'ich daylight heist, in real'ty, you couldn't never pull by yourself—but all this just now is a bit o' chess-playin', and we won't complicate it wit' any details but movin' Mr. Snipes and his goods. Now, Snipes, I'll give you, free gravis, sev'ral things. First, double gas tanks—same's we actually got on *our* truck chassis, yonder—an' wit' the same 350 sure miles of good goin' in 'em from, say, the jug on. I'll give you a stolen license plate—exackly like that hot piece o' tin what's nailed to the end piece of our own scooter yonder—so's you don't have to worry none about bein' traced—*if* you c'n successfully make a getaway. And I'll give you, also, the fact o' the Sheriff o' Cedarville layin' around his house all the time the way he actually is, wit' a foot bound up in yards o' bandages—not that he can't travel on it, no; and I'll not only assume, goddam' me, that they ain't a goddam' car in town that can travel wit' anything like the speed o' your double-tanked truck or what'ell have you, but that the whole town is standin' par'lyzed an' motionless after your heist for quite a while—generous, me, see? I give you ever'thing to go on!—so now what moves—leavin' aside *my* plan—*Al's plan!*—what moves lays ahead of you right now, workin' by ord'nary methods? Name me ev'ry poss'ble move?"

CHAPTER VII

THE COUNTRY THAT WAS YEGG-PROOF!

Snipes appeared to be perilously near to purring, now that he was being made the entire center of attention. He flicked a bit of lint off his coat lapel, picked a thread meticulously off his pants knee.

"We-e-ell," he put in cautiously, "I c'n go northeast or southwest along Cedarville Road."

"O' course, o' course," retorted his chief. "But take one or th' other, will ya, before th' town comes to—an' peppers your guts?"

"Okay. I can go northeast."

"C'rrect! Wit' th' town phonin' ahead—both to Brocktown—an' Brock City at th' end of the road—to wait f'r a gent travelin' goddam' fast in a truck wit' battleship-grey body! In fact, Snipes, th' State Militia at Brock City would start down t' meet you! If you did shoot it out at Brocktown—an' make it—you'd meet up wit' the militia between Brocktown an' Brock City. You like militia, Snipes? Hungry as hell to practice wit' their machine guns? Ever see a Swiss cheese?"

Snipes was coolly reflective, as one who had more than once compared a Swiss chese to the end of his own career. "Naw, I don't like machine guns—naw. I c'n dodge single slugs, Boss—no foolin'—it's a fact!—I get a five seconds' notice before the slug reaches me—a sort of a hunch—to lean away quick an' be where it ain't—but with a Tommy gun op'rating against you, in th' place where the slug you've dodged ain't, another 'un is."

"Boy!" said Slim, grinning between his own 2 rows of perfect white teeth. "Is that putting it pretty!"

"A'right," agreed Al Mulhearn. But to his youthful reincarnation of Robin Hood. "Then you'll go southwest a'right, w'en you leave that bank. But what's open t' you now, Snipes?"

"We-ell," countered Snipes, with the defensiveness of one who realizes that, to keep himself the center of the stage, he must enter—heart and soul—in the argument, "I got t' git to Perkins Junction, a'right, before *anything's* open to me! Then they's lots open. Includin' poppin' off a few banshees, maybe!"

"Don't kid about them banshees," admonished Al Mulhearn darkly. "Old Man Elum's ownin' all that no-good land for miles around that junction—an' believin' the banshees need that there region to dance on nights—an' not puttin' his store there so's the banshees c'n feel free t' use the land—makes that junction o' his one o' the nicest deserted spots f'r a fleein' heister that they is in all U.S.A."

"Am I complainin', Boss?" protested Snipes. "I just put myself there, that's all, at Perkins Junction. But at w'ich point, however, as I said, there's lots o' moves open to me. And none of 'em, in all likelihood, thanks to the goddam'ed loneliness o' the spot—and the fact o' the goddam' junction itself lyin' a bit below the rise what's at the end of ev'ry road comin' into it—watchable by nothing nor nobody—but banshees!"

"What moves is there?" asked Al Mulhearn, through slitted eyes.

"We-ell, I c'n circle right around, over the rise what's to the left o' me, and into and onto East Carthage Road—and travel back eastward—to—"

"T' meet a armed posse—yeah—led by a sheriff, comin' along from Pricetown—which has been not'fied o' the heist, and knows how to head you off from *that* move. And no chanct f'r you to get off—or out o'—that East Carthage Road now'ere, now'ere. No, Snipes, you may as well fergit *that* move—like the previous one where you meet up wit' the militia, an' say 'howdy, boys.'"

"Okay then," Snipes said regretfully, like one whose arguments were being too quickly nipped in the bud. He went on, however, hopefully. "Well, squattin' there all by my majestic lonesomeness in banshee-land—or a cup o' land in banshee-land!—I c'n roar over the rise what's practically facin' me, and dive into th' hills by Old Twistibus!"

"Yeah you can," snorted Al Mulhearn, who, it must be admitted, took a bit of pleasure in this hopelessly one-sided chess game himself. "On'y you better start puttin' on your stir clothes w'ile you're in th' hills! F'r long before you're any distance in, the Sheriff o' Cedarville, foot bound up maybe in a couple tons o' gauze—but hittin' on all fours mentally a'right—him an' a few outraged citizens—'ll be at the junction, an' knowin' def'nitely—soon's one of 'em has hopped out, an' loped over th' west rise on foot, an' inspected the Straightaway barr'er lock, and found it to be intack—that you've either went into Old Twistibus or doubled back along East Carthage Road. They won't worry none about the latter, however, knowin' that if you went that way, th' Sheriff of Pricetown and his posse, coming down that road, will get you sure. And assumin' the Cedarville Sheriff and his good citizens did start out goddamn fast—an' wit'out preparation or nothing—after the heist, and that they ain't equipped at all, at all, for a manhunt in them hills—*if* into them hills it was you went—they'll nevertheless squat there at the junction to see that you, at least—if into them hills you did go—don't come back on out. And when the militia, what's comin' down Cedarville

Road meanwhile from Brock City—an' the Sheriff and his posse from Pricetown—converges there at Perkins Junction, too—completely confirming that you didn't double back—that you went into the hills—an' one or both of them outfits goes right in after you by Old Twistibus, you ain't got—but what?"

"W'y," returned Snipes, so blandly that it sounded almost like a decoy reply, "t' take advantage of my nice time-lead—for you did say, Boss, that when I pulled out from Cedarville, the town was all par'lyzed—and it *does* take time for a posse to come down from Brock City or from Pricetown!—to take advantage of my nice time-lead—and be out of Old Twistibus at Simpson's Junction long before ever the goddam' militia, or th' Pricetown Sheriff, or both, travelin' slower than me by far—'d ever come out. And once out—and headin' northward—toward, at last, that sweet, sweet spot that's been a happy playground, many a night, for all of us!—yeah, Southwest City!—it'd be a walkaway for me to reach the section of Southwest City Road where the crossroads and sideroads begin—and once in *that* maze, it'd be duck soup for me to reach the hideout, on that little road that *we* call—"

"Je-sus!" snorted Al Mulhearn. "Sometimes, Snipes, I b'lieve that what makes you ride high ain't what Slim here says—but that it's gettin' rises out o' me!" He shook his head. "But okay—if that's your brand o' hop. Well, how the hell long, Snipes, d' you think you'd be comin' out o' Old Twistibus? Where that chassis over there couldn't do much better than a spavined mule wit' the blind staggers? Five hours, you dimwit! More if, as I suspeck, that goddam' triple-sized elephant tailin' the circus leavin' Pricetown las' night fell t'rough that flimsy lookin' bridge at Bear Creek. For even if they prodded him outa his beam-braced platform-cart at the bridge, and walked him acrost, the goddam' monster, so I claim, 'uz even then far too heavy f'r *that* bridge. But whether or no, what'ell d' ya think you'd find at Simpson's Junction when you did get out? Why, hours an' hours before you got out, th' Sheriff o' Willis Creek, notified by th' Sheriff o' Cedarville from—say—Elum's store, back of Perkins Junction, that you'd def'nitely took Old Twistibus, and seen same confirmed a hunderd-p'cent by a small scoutin' party sent through to him by way o' th' Straightaway itself, 'd be settin' there at Simpson's Junction on his behind, wit' that Tommy gun of his, waitin' for you t'come out—an' toss 500 sweet plunkos into his lap. F'r Simpson's Junction, don't fergit, is still in an' of his county—even if none of Old Twistibus itself is: Simpson's Junction is just as much part of his county as his own burg o' Willis Creek, or as so much o' that Straightaway as goes up to his side o' the mountain. And ain't there a standin' reward in that goddam'ed county of 250 plunkos for any sheriff thereof what takes a jug-heister alive?—or 500 plunkos if he takes him dead? Yea bo! That baby, Tommy gun atop knees, 'd be there—just to take full advantage o' your havin' t' come out in *his* county! An' if you think he'd have business elsewhere when he heard you was comin' t'rough, then you don't know Bucyrus Duckhouse. An' you're loco in the coco, to boot. For he's the toughest son-of-a-bitch, I tell you, in 40 counties—afraid o' nothin' nor nobody in the world—ex-machine gunner, don't ferget, my fine young hearty, from the World War—or at least such of it he was in—the same bein', they say, on'y 45 days—not long enough even to lose his hick speech—but long enough, a'righr, for t' get a congress'nal medal f'r killin' 22 Heinies in a machine-gun nest, an' capturin' 18 alive—and proud owner of the same goddam' gun—wit' ammunition therefor—what he op'rated in them lively 45 days o' that war. Why, Christ—the time it'd take f'r you to get t'rough an' out o' Old Twistibus, he'd practic'lly have time to send somebody in a car clear down to Foleysburg—what hasn't no phone service—and bring the Sheriff o' Foleysburg back up to help him. Or the Sheriff o' Pricetown c'd easy get clear around, by the Straightaway, to help him. Except'n, o' course, that this Duckhouse bird—accordin' to stories 'round here—don't 'low other sheriffs to even stick their noses into his terr'tory, that is, on sheriffin' business. F'r he, bein' a one-man militia all by himself—an' armed wit' a gun that could shoot right t'rough the very walls of any goddam'ed truck, or truck cab—wouldn't be calculatin' for a single instant to divvy wit' nobody his 500 easy plunkos for the dead driver of a certain truck wit' a battleship-grey body!"

"A'right," said Snipes. "If you, Boss, say this bird is a tough son-of-a-bitch, then his panties sure ain't trimmed with lace. And so I'll assume the Duckhouse duck won't lam out of town on business if and when he hears that a certain damn good-lookin' blond youth tallyin' almost exactly with myself—" And Snipes tossed his pockmarked-faced, asymmetric head challengingly. "—hypythet'cal driver of a battleship-grey bodied truck!—has knocked in the Cedarville jug, and am headin' westward. A'right, Boss. We-ell—" And now Snipes licked his lips hungrily, as one who was backing himself not into a real impasse of any kind, but merely into the end of a very delightful argumentative session in which he was the sole center of attention. "We-ell," he repeated, "there is nothin' left then—in this chess game as you've so wond'fully laid it out, Boss!—there is quite nothin' left for me to do then, standin' there, alone and med'tative, in banshee land—or a cup therein—meanin' Perkins Junction, of course!—in this hypythet'cal heist—but to get over the rise to m' right, blow the lock on th' Straightaway barrier to hell an' gone with a shot o' dinny juice—which same I 'spose you'll allow me in this little game?—if not, I'll shoot th' goddam' lock, say, with my roscoe!—and go down that Straightaway like a shot out o' hell—"

"—into the arms," said Al Mulhearn, chafing at the bit, for it is to be admitted that he too liked the center of a stage when it came to expounding!—"into the arms," he repeated, "a' this same one-man militia, B. Duckhouse, Esquire!—at most any point o' that Straightaway what lies on *his* side o' the mountain—since it's on'y in his county w'ere the 500 plunkos reward offer holds. Not this side o' th' mountain he wouldn't meet an' greet you, my hearty—no!—you could feel very free an' easy, bowlin' along the 37 to 40 miles o' that Straightaway lyin' this side o' the mountain, that no avengin' angel, blowin' smoke an' fire out of its nostrils, 'd come out of that mountain and gun you to hell-an'-gone this side—you, on the inside of the cab, and your four tires on the outside—nowsah!—f'r they's nothin' in the B. Duckhouse pocket did he do so!—he'll be waitin' on his side—and takin' you on his side—after you'd come out o' that curved mountain tunnel; he'll be waitin' on his side, most any goddam' where—if not on the Straightaway itself, then on West Carthage Road what the Straightaway becomes—maybe at the village edge—at any goddam' point, in fact, w'ere he can halt you wit' a chain—either that no-t'orough-fare chain what's hangin' acrost the other end of the West Straightaway end now—or at some point where he c'n toss one acrost, by two trees—or maybe even w'ere he can do that best, an' rig up his Tommy gun, too. Yeah bo! Chanctes are that not long after he got the flash from Cedarville, and knew you'd hit the Junction, he'd have phoned Maw Elum to ride over there on her bike, and case that barr'er lock for him—and he'd know his c'rrect move before even the Cedarville Sheriff and his men got down there. And if by any chance," Al Mulhearn added, almost warming up to the spirit of the thing, "you blew that lock f'r a shill—but took Old Twistibus—it'd be duck soup for him to just squat in Willis Creek, next his place, till 'twas ascertained that it *was* a shill—and that you wasn't on the Straightaway—and then move cas-ally and leisyly around back an' down to Simpson's Junction, an' wait till you come out. And that, my hearty—as I usta say to a certain side-kick who'd don a sailor suit sometimes, and help me pull a certain trick, wit' a coil of rope, before some of my friends!—a lollapaloozer, that trick, providin' you had a helper, an' a sailor suit as a shill—that, my hearty," repeated Al Mulhearn, almost regretfully himself, "concludes, I b'lieve, the sad story of Snipes Spurlock—hypothet'cal heister on an *ord'nary,* everyday, run-o'-the-mill jug heist in this district—and answers—or don't it?—w'ether Hizzoner up there near Brocktown was a dimwit—as *you* called him!—f'r orderin' that gold into a strawjay like the Cedarville jug."

He waited expectantly.

"You win, Boss," acknowledged Snipes, regretfully, but nevertheless an obviously much improved psyche. "The Judge was no dimwit—no! For there just is no way, a'right, to beat the heist-proof setup of *this* region."

"No way," corrected Al Mulhearn, chidingly, "but one. The one that Al—inventor, by the way, o' that same coil-o'-rope trick that's been referred to around here—has worked out! And that one and on'y way is the way I'm goin' to rehearse now—f'r the last time. So pay attention—all!"

CHAPTER VIII

AVOIRDUPOIS

Cecil Mondaine, clad in occult-looking black dressing gown, embroidered with white moons and stars, the upturned ends of his blond mustache newly curled at an alcohol flame in his trailer, and beautifully waxed as well, threaded his way gingerly across the big area devoted to the MacWhorter Shows vehicles. He was bound from the line of trailers, fringing one side of the area, and one of which contained his own bunk and chest of illusionist equipment, to the line of trailers which fringed the other side—and one of which carried, in addition to all the show's clown costumes and fun-making equipment, two individuals—one, Dolly the "World's Fattest Woman"— and one, Florette Smith!

Even as he slightly bridged the space between himself and his objective, he could see a door open in that endmost trailer, and which showed, even at the distance, that it was a special door—extremely wide—triplewidth, in fact, compared to ordinary doors!—fitted into a specially large opening sawed into the vehicle. With some apparent difficulty a gargantua of a woman was wedging herself through it backward; but having evidently stopped to converse with someone still inside, was "stuck," both physically and conversationally!

Mondaine, grinning a bit, in spite of himself, knew exactly where she was bound for; and he slowed his pace carefully so that, when he should safely make that line of trailers, and turn down it toward its endmost one, he would meet this human mountain face to face—and hold certain private and very important converse with her of his own.

The "lot"—rather, that part of the whole devoted to housing all the wheeled vehicles of the MacWhorter Shows—was still in considerable confusion. Garish red and gilt panel-covered wagons stood about, pointed in various directions, and some of the heavier ones had made deep ruts in the loamlike black dirt. Along each side of the square space were the two lines of trailers, known as Trailer Train 1, and Trailer Train 2, each with its powerfully motored engine vehicle in front—and known, those lead-vehicles, respectively, as Old Huff'n Chuff and Old Poof Whoof—and with, at no less than two points in each trailer train, a special trailer with front wheels as well as rear ones—front wheels which, moreover, were turnable by a steering wheel, by a man on a small seat affixed to the front wall of the 4-wheel trailer, so that the whole line of trailers could follow the most devious of roads when either Old Huff'n Chuff—or Old Poof Whoof—turned sharply off one road onto another, or threaded in and out on the same road.

Off a distance from all the vehicles, and trailers too—and resplendent in silver gilt and bright scarlet—the scarlet spelling danger from lights!—and guarded, even now, by a worker, was the tank car which always traveled along, and protected the gas supply for the whole procession; Henry Sinclair, as that tank car was called!

Farthest beyond the area where all this parking had taken place, the Big Top was going up—had gone up, did one judge from the still somewhat irregular mass of brown canvas now magically standing off ground, and Mondaine could hear, within it, the sound of knockdown seats being hastily knocked together. Past—and, indeed, well beyond—the young mountain of canvas, he could see the town of Foleysburg, nestling in the afternoon sunlight, a mere tangle of chimneys and roofs and dirt-paved streets and what not else, and with, beyond and back of itself—and to each side of itself as well—the rich green farming country—country so unlike that desolate region the show had just come through—with many smaller hamlets back within its area which would, in reality, provide the audience tonight. And now bitter reflections entered his mind. For his gaze, shortening itself again, fell upon that smaller "tent" that was right now being erected off to one side of the big tent; the tent for the freakshow—profitable appendage, indeed, to the main show—that merely great flap of canvas, sewed along all its sides with lightweight painted drops, supported on rope-guyed poles, and shrouding completely what it covered, when those drops were tossed over and down—those lying drops which pictured amazing things, such as 3-headed men and living mermaids—things never to be found on land or sea, much less in that interior, the Gall-er-eee of Hu-man Coor-ee-os-is-tees a-a-and In-trig-ing Acts. And Mondaine's eyes, resting on the very drop which described the wonders to be seen in that "tent," as the drop flapped over and into position, grew bitter indeed; for he—an artist, goddamn MacWhorter to hell!—was the fre-e-e attraction to get the rubes into that Gallery of Human Curiosities; he, Cecil Mondaine, Illusionist, being paid 10 lousy dollars a week, and keep—and, by God, taking it!—and so that, after his brief come-on-act, MacWhorter's stooges, bellowing and shouting and threading through the gaping crowd, could sell—for one Angus MacWhorter!—at 50 cents per copy, a certain book on magic which, in New York, at a bankruptcy sale, and in a lot of 100,000 copies, had cost MacWhorter exactly 1 cent apiece. Bah!

But now he had reached the opposite line of trailers—had reached the safety of the midmost one, in fact—and was turning down it. And so well had he timed his progress across the lot that the woman who had been slowly extricating herself from that endmost trailer had now completed that process—had even banged the door of the trailer to with a vicious bang—and was moving like a great battleship—slowly 'but inexorably—up the line towards where Mondaine had momentarily halted.

Now she was nearing him. She looked to be all of the 550 pounds of weight that she was. She was in pink-silk nightgown and slippers, except that a huge half-length cloth coat was buttoned around her torso; and her half bleached, half grey hair stuck up in curlers all over her great head.

Now she was almost upon him. Visible desperation in her harassed eyes. Not even seeing him. Looking, indeed, right through him.

"Whoa there, Dollykins!" Mondaine put out his hand atop her great ham of an arm. "Whither goest, fair one, at this early hour of the day?"

She came to with a snap. Turned her tired hard eyes on him. "Where d' you suppose, Card Riffler? To see Bébé, of course. And after that to look in, once again, on our little Spa—"

"And wherever is our dear Bébé today?"

But Mondaine, now glancing back over his shoulder and about, to see where Bébé might be parked today, while things were getting set up, saw a great snake of a trunk rising gently above a 10-foot-high canvas "wrap-wall"—a wrap-wall being, of course, nothing but a great ribbon of canvas hung loosely about 4 pointed poles jabbed into the earth. He brought his gaze irritably back to the mountain of flesh in front of him. To himself alone, he almost groaned. "Goddamn it to hell," were his words to himself only, "we've got to stand here and discuss that fool Bébé—when I'm burning to ask her for *all* the low-down on what she did for me at Pricetown—and which has put the final, complete and finishing touch on Jim Craney's catching up with *this* show in time to—"

Instead, aloud he said, but placatingly:

"Well, what's wrong today—with our dear Bébé?"

"Don't be sarcastic, Card Riffler," the fat woman rasped.

"You know as well as I that I've got plenty reason to be worried. Why, he's likely to develop blood poisoning where those horrid chains hooked around about his rump, after he—"

"—shook the bridge down?" laughed Mondaine. "My God, Dollykins, but that was the closest escape this outfit ever had! From 3 extra hours of travel, I mean. For I understand that if Bébé 'd been in front—like he was on that Cantertown-Priceville trek—and done the trick he did—we'd have had all of that extra travel to get through. Which—hrum—8 plus 100 plus 550—"

"What the hell are you calculating, Card Riffler?"

He was, to himself, calculating exactly how far from Foleysburg Cecil Mondaine and Florette Smith would be, at and when Jim Craney would have escaped the cunning trap that he, Mondaine, had left for Craney far back in Pricetown, and—

"If you're calculating," she said defensively, "the dislocation to traffic on that damned road that poor Bébé may have caused, just—just forget it. For—for he hasn't caused any—whatsoever! For a native hick nearby there this morning assured me personally that there was a—a tree-trunk bridge 40 feet up that creek—just around that knoll, if you remember?—a couple of tree trunks felled across, with planks laid on 'em. So Bébé hasn't stopped all operations in those damned hills at all, you see. Nor added even 3 minutes to travel through 'em. Besides," she added, with typical feminine logic, "that bridge was a menace—it was better destroyed."

Mondaine could hardly keep his face straight. "We-e-ell," he countered, "that certainly whitewashes our Bébé then." He knew, of course, that Dolly was lying nobly—to protect Bébé's reputation. For no less than the quite simple reason that he himself had walked up that creek, during the delay, around that obscuring knoll—and had seen the creek but grow wider. And tree-trunk bridge there was none, indeed, upon it! But he saw no reason to taunt the fat woman with her lie. For the reason that she would be spreading it everywhere—would already have told it even to Florette—would have—

"But concerning your question," he explained ironically, "of a dozen sentences back, as to what I was calculating, I was merely calculating my huge earnings on this outfit. And—but say, you sure do worry a lot about Bébé, don't you?"

"Good God in heaven, why shouldn't I, Mondaine!" She had melted a bit, when she deigned to call him by his name. "He's so sensitive to—to draughts and things, that child. And that filthy mahout they've got for him doesn't know elephants at all."

"The fellow's hoary-eyed all the time," Mondaine admitted, "on those muggles cigs our Flip fire-eater is purveying. However, he's an old hand at—at mahouting. Was even over Old Twistibus, I understand, with 4 elephants, 20 years ago. Though his memory of the time through it seems cockeyed." He looked solicitously at the fat woman—or at least mockly so. "I can see all right," he granted, "that you're not going to stay on here one minute after you cop a new hookup for yourself and the—er—little boy with the trunk?"

"Cor-rect," she said, in a hard voice. "And MacWhorter knows it, too. But get this into your mind, Mondaine. 'Twon't be show-jumping. MacWhorter can't kick me and Bébé out, under our contract—but *we* can, under it, pull out, any time we wish. And will. Well, I must run."

"To examine Bébé's flanks?"

"To examine? Hell, no." And from a pocket of her nightdress she pulled out a tiny microscopic throw-away sample of Cuticura Salve. "I'm going to treat every one of his dear scratches with this, which I just unearthed in my luggage. And then tell off that chocolate-colored louse that tends him. And then, to Mac's quarters, to tell Mr. Mac that he's got to start, here and now, to doing right by us—or else!"

"Ow?" he reminded her kindly. "You'll have a hell of a long wait. A dozen or more people, always, you know, wanting to see him at each place we pitch—and while we pitch—and you know how he is—with his—er—Scotch justice? Everybody has to take their turns."

"And so what?" she said sneeringly. "I can't stand in line? Well, don't forget there's one footstool in the Universe that's always under my behind—and that's Old Mr. Earth; and there's always one cushion—to put down on it—and I carry *that* cushion with me! So what?"

"You said a pretty mouthful, sweetness," he assured her, sizing up that undoubted cushion she carried. "So good luck. And—but didn't I hear you say you were going to look in 'again' on our young horse acrobat? Meaning—you've already looked in on her. How is the little gal? And how in hell did she stand the trip through Old Twistibus?"

"Like the trouper she is," proclaimed Dolly, speaking of that certain ill member of the troupe riding in the 'sick trailer.' "But I don't like that term 'horse acrobat,' Mondaine, any more than that other term I heard you once applied to me—the Misincarnated Hippo—oh, yes you did! She's an equestrienne, damn your soul, Card Riffler—a talented, trained little equestrienne—operating from a steed that—well, that white horse Arabus has got more noble blood in *his* veins than you'll ever have in yours. And—"

"Cool down, Dollykins—no offense meant to profession and talent. I'm an illusionist—not a magician; the gal's an equestrienne—not a bareback rider; you're a—"

"—circus fat woman," she replied bitterly, "known as the Human Behemoth, and not a damn thing more. But do you care to know how the girl stood the trip through—or don't you?"

"Of course I do," nodded Mondaine, though but like a man trying to make good on his own courtesy.

"Well, she slept like a baby through it—because of the motion. And consequently bucked up a bit—as she invariably does after a rolling trip—and a sleep. Her physician says that her nervous system is so adjusted, from babyhood on, to the nightly pull-out, that it's become a physiolog—"

"Aw come now, Dolly," protested Mondaine, sardonically, "don't call that old booze-nose, Karl the Klown—alias 'Doc'—a physician—"

"And why the hell should I not?" the fat woman defended. "Karl Vanderplanck was more than a great physician before he fell—he was a great surgeon before liquor shook his hand—and gave him a nose so big and red that he doesn't even have to make it up at night. Karl—Doc—or whatever we should rightfully call him—is the best 'buy' this show ever had; those fellows who double in brass have nothing on a clown that doubles in medicine."

"He'll never set *my* wrist if I break it," retorted Mondaine.

"No? Well, he set Silver-Tongue's, don't forget—and it's better than it was before Silver-Tongue broke it!"

"Well, let's not fight about Doc!" said Mondaine. And added contritely, "I never really knew but that that was sheer fakealoo—that he was a great doc in his day."

"Well, I'll tell you something then to disabuse you," the fat woman replied savagely. She was silent a moment. "I knew him," she went on sadly, "I knew him—'when.' For I consulted him in New York—years ago—when I was a young blooming girl, with the world ahead of me, but just starting to alarmingly take on weight. His waiting room was full of the finest people. For he was known to be a great diagnostician. He told me how my fate was decreed by my pituitary gland in my brain—how I could fight it with ovarian extract—but unsuccessfully—and told me to take it on the nose—and to be a good A No. 1 fat woman instead of a—a nothing. He couldn't undo Nature—but he sure did for my mind—and soul." She was sadly silent. "But he was destined," she went on, "to later become disbarred—disqualified, I guess one should call it—because of that drunken operation where he killed that woman—and broken today—a circus clown—because of drink. Unable anywhere to practice—practice for money, that is—but nobody, Mondaine, can stop a disqualified unlicensed doctor from practicing medicine *free!*—as can be proven here. Why—he was such a great man, in his day, Mondaine, that *I*—so help me God!—wouldn't fall so low as to insult him by asking him to look at my own Bébé—no fooling!—that's what *I* think of professional ability. Why, Mondaine, he's the best doctor that little girl could ever have; he has studied her fever, back and forth, with his test tubes—he watches her day and night—he sits in costume in front of that sick trailer between his tricks on the performance—in fact, he says her disease is close to its crisis now—where it'll go one way or the other—"

"Think her folks will succeed in connecting with her here tonight?"

"I do—yes," nodded the fat woman, hopefully. "For after all, you know, this *is* the burg they wired MacWhorter from New York—from the actual liner—at which they could best and quickest break into the itinerary. And they must have had expert help in figuring out the combinations of air, rail, and auto that would put 'em here. But—maybe you know this—and maybe you don't?—the liner had docked before Mac's wire from Pricetown reached 'em—it was reported undeliverable—and so he couldn't switch 'em on to a much better hook-on, like, say, Silver City. So here I'm sure it'll be. Probably by auto from Western City, 35 miles west, which is only 100 miles on a transcontinental rail line from a Great Western Air Lines airport. Maybe they'll come—even—by that jerkwater line that lies off from us a ways."

"Well I hope," said Mondaine, "they take the kid out of the damned outfit. And I hope she rounds her crisis. For Christ, the whole thing—the affair involving *her*—is the strangest damn story I ever heard in my life; I—I wouldn't believe it, Dolly, if I read it in a book. I'd think 'twas stark melodr—but here!—I'm delaying Bébé's anointment—and other things—so we'll continue as we were going—in ways opposite!—except that—" And his voice grew hard—and considerably lower—though he really did not have to lower it in view of the fact that the two trailers alongside which they stood were equipment trailers only. "Come on, now—let's get down to earth—both of us. I got your signal, from your trailer window this morning, while we stood at that country store back of that hills road, that you put it over okay—even your double-signal that it was put over by 100 p'cent. But I want the full lowdown. I—"

"I know you do," she returned quite unblushingly. "But I've been letting you simmer in your own juices for a few minutes. But cool down, my fine romantic knight—without armor." She gazed back of herself, as though to make sure that the trailer each side of them was an "equipment-only" trailer. But she lowered her voice well, as only a woman can. "I slipped the vet your fifty bucks—and your promise that if Jim Craney failed to connect up with the show prior to Hootens Falls, he'd get fifty more by mail. But hell—it was simple enough—seeing I knew the whelp when we were both on the Hagenbark Animal Shows together—and knew he was a gambling fool and never could keep a cent. Why, the fellow can't make fifty bucks in a month there—let alone a hundred—fetching calves into the world and doctoring horses in a gasoline age! He—but you saw all that yourself, when I told you on the platform last night who our prospective lion-kitten accoucheur was." She was silent a moment, almost regretfully so, it seemed. Then spoke again, in a sort of burst of words—but still just barely above a throaty whisper. "So it's all set, you louse! Soon's the kittens are born—for the fellow is a vet first, and a rat, like yourself, afterward!—he's going to slip suddenly out of town, with the garage key in his pocket, leaving the cage-wagon inside—yes, yes, yes, yes, fully protected the big cat'll be—triple ration of milk, red-meat and water—yes!—and the doc won't come back for 48 hours—and then only with some fakealoo about being kidnapped by enemies or something. After which, Jim Craney will have to retrace his course all back around Pricetown, across country to Hootens Falls—and—well—are you set—or are you set?"

"I'm set!" he acknowledged enthusiastically. And from a checked trousers pocket underneath his sun, moon, and star-studded dressing gown, withdrew a sheaf of bills, practically all of which had been earned in night-club work before he had commenced technically "resting" in this circus-illusionist berth. "And I'm going, Dollykins, my sweet, in spite of all your harsh words ag'in me, to make *your* cut fifty—instead of the original twenty-five—here—"

"Keep your dirty money, Card Riffler," she said frigidly. "I did it solely for Florette's sake. She'd never be happy with that damned always dead-broke lion-wagon driver; she will, though, with you, because—louse that you are—you're crazy about her; and, being an artist, you'll always make money. It takes money to make marriage happy; not love—nor brats—nor—nor even chickens! I'd rather have been helping a decent guy—sure! But the point is that you can make mazuma if you get Florette out of here—and her life will be better for it. Selah!"

"Gad, Dollykins, you're—"

"Cut it! I'm making her happy in *my* way—yes—but in the long run my way is *the* way."

"Then—then do a little more, will you? Tell me: is she still ready—to lope out with me—when the show leaves Foleysburg?"

"Hell yes—if he hasn't shown up with that apology."

"Then—"

"My belief," pronounced Dolly, "is that you've spent your money foolishly. For he's so stubborn, he wouldn't have apologized anyway. He just wouldn't have caught up for a few days, that's all. Exactly as Florette already practically knows—in advance. And—but ever'thing's all right," she finished wearily. "When the hour comes that my quarter-ton-plus of poundage starts bouncing and jouncing southward out of Foleysburg, you and Florette can start hoofing westward—and railroadward!—the same. And I shall always be able to remember that I did one mighty good deed for one mighty shortsighted girl."

He beamed on her. "Gad, Dolly, you're Cupid in disguise—God's own right hand. I'll—I'll take mighty good care of that gal, don't you worry. And—well—thanks a million. And so now suppose we start out again now, eh—on our respective ways? Okay. Good luck to *you*. And wish me the same. For as you run lightly toward your various destinations, I shall continue to move majestically onward toward one consisting of that very trailer from which you have just wafted like a new-blown rose petal."

"Nuts," she said, plainly irritated by his never-ending persiflage. And lumbered on.

He too went on, but with a snicker on his lip.

But a half-dozen feet separated from each other, he stopped—gazed back—called to her—

"Hi, Dollykins!"

It arrested her in her tortoise-like flight, for she too was looking back.

"I say, Dolly," he asked, "your charming roommate—is she, just now, decent?"

"Wasn't when I came out," she warned. "So you better knock first."

"Okay," he said, as he resumed his progress, adding to himself: "For knocking—expertly *and* subtly!—is one of my God-given talents! 'Specially knocking homespun lovers. In fact, here goes for the most important bits of the same ever done in my life—first, on the outside of yon trailer barn-door—and then—on the inside. Onward, Rare Artist—to the fray!"

CHAPTER IX

SUPER-PLAN FOR A HEIST!

"Yes," Al Mulhearn, bankrobber, amateur sleight-of-hand artist, and mob-chief was saying as he contemplated his three henchmen—one dressed in striped trucker's clothing like himself—but all seated on stumps about him, in the thicket north of Cedarville, "I'm goin' to now rehearse th' *one* jug-heist that's poss'ble—an' that, b'Jesus, on'y thanks to little Al's God-give' talents!—in this goddam' heist-proof region. So again pay attention, all."

He paused, to see that all were, and with a satisfied glance at that truck, with its battleship-grey body, a short distance beyond, parked on the cleared but curved trail leading out to the roadway, with its black-outlined yellow letters on the truck body side proclaiming: TRANSCONTINENTAL TRUCKING COMPANY—Fast Freight," threw a further hasty glance at that accurate-looking watch on his right wrist, and resumed speaking.

"The 4 of us," he began, "Slim an' me in the cab—Slim at the wheel—honest truckers bot', wit' these here stripet overalls and jumpers an' caps on us!—and Snipes an' Scarface inside the truck—blow out o' this thicket at the zero moment—w'ich we've figgered out to the exact T, I b'lieve!—bowl gently down Cedarville Road to Quarter Mile Turn—¼ mile this side o' Cedarville—7½ minutes it'll take, more or less, wit' easy genteel unsuspicious speed—draw t' th' side o' th' road—and—"

"And Scarface and me," eagerly put in Snipes, of the yellow hair and pockmarked face, "hop out—the second, that is, that th' road is clear between those 2 close turns—and start down on foot to town while—"

"—while you and I, Boss," put in Slim Yarnai, with the thin handsome face and strong tense-fingered hands, lighting up his dozenth cigarette to eventually join the butts all about his stump, "pull out our phoney feedbag, munch away on our sandwiches—and tip our vacuum containers, as though we're swigging Java. Just a couple of—"

"—joost a copple av honest cross-contree crackers," commented Scarface Scalisi, of the black eyes and scar-ridden olive-colored face, holding his lengthless stump of a cold cigar in his fingers in order to speak, "catcheeng late lonch! Joost a—"

"Nev'r mind us," admonished his tall powerfully built chief. "What d' you an' Snipes do now?"

Snipes, of course, was the one who wished to do all the talking.

"We tramp down into town," he said eagerly. "Well apart, though. And take up a position on th' stem, outside the jug. And—"

"I hope t' Jesus you don't mean 'at lity'ally," frowned his chief. "F'r you ain't to take up no positions in front o' no jug as though you're a couple o' cats waitin' round t'—swallow a fat mouse. You're to—"

"Yes, yes, I know," corrected Snipes. "Me in front of th' old drugstore one side the jug—and Scarf—"

"Me seeteeng on long banch in frant av choorch on ather side," put in Scarface.

"Right! That's better. But don't fergit the items in your two mout's— a cig'rette butts in yours, Scarface—f'r a change—a toot'pick in yours, Snipes—so's you'll bot' be just a couple o' lazy loafers. Lazy loafers, see? Wit' no shootin' irons bulgin' nowhere on neither—nor to be found on either, in case of a frisk—because the gats'll be inside the truck, back of the luggage trapdoor in th' rear end; however, they'll be no sheriff to smell around an' ask questions because the son-of-a-bitch is nursin' that gout o' his—and if any rube rubberneck queries who you are, b'Jesus, stranger— Scarface is one o' that crew drillin' f'r oil overland a dozen miles, while you, Snipes, are from Brocktown, tryin' t' get on to the oil survey—soon's some guy like, say, Scarface, can lead you back overland. So now stay there—and le's get back to Slim an' me.

"At the 2-minute-of mark, Slim an' me toss our phoney grub pails into th' bushes—or back into the truck—an' drive on down. An' that's w'ere the fancy timin' has got to be. We got to be at the door o' the bank—will be there, b'Jesus, if you fellows manip'late your Kelly's th' way it's agreed— Snipes' Kelly back on head for the closin'—Scarface's back on head for th' shade-drawin'—we'll be there at the door ½ minute after old Foostum, th' old teller-cashier wit' the Heebie-Jeebies, has drawed them curts o' the bank and door as us'al—and locked the front door f'r th' day.

"O' course," explicated the chief, "it's at this point w'ere we go ahead— or don't go ahead—based on w'ether we've caught th' proper signal from Old Beebles in the haunted house 'way down road, an' visible on'y from the jug—and on'y wit' Slim's farsighted eye. Smoke trailin' out of the chimney means he's seed, wit' th' binoc'lars, that they's been a transfer of one heavy box in th' last 2 hours—which, by God, I tell you, there ain't no chanct of at all—but if they is, however, then Slim an' me case our roadmaps as though we're a cross-country truckin' outfit that's got into the wrong lay-out o' roads—ask some passin' rube w'ether they's any hamburger joints anyw'ere in th' burg—and blow on. Another well-laid plan gone coocoo.

"But if we don't get the backdown signals, from Beebles, we go ahead wit' the heist.

"Which, in turn—at least our entry into the joint for the heist—is the signal for that old wreck of a Beebles to get himself over to the side of the road for a goddam' fast pickup!

"All right! I climb off the seat, an' outa th' cab, and get below our phony d'livery job—the case over there what's screwed, and not tied at all, to the dolly!—and get ready f'r the catch. While Slim, still in the cab, jerks the trick lashin's and lets her down to me. Then him down out o' the cab to—to help me—an' to sup'tend the receiptin' an' all that—but leavin' th' engine runnin' gently. We drag the case acrost the sidewalk as though she was heavy as hell—instead o' filled, as she is, wit' a dozen bricks. And ring the bell. And when th' old boy pulls the door curt aside an' peers out, we say—well, whadda ya say, Slim?"

"'One case,'" called out Slim authoritatively, "'—lead nuggets—from Little Beaver Mine, Nevada—for E. Bull, care this bank.'"

Al Mulhearn grinned satisfiedly.

"Kinda lucky, all right, that they is a bank customer named Ebenezer Bull—and that he's out o' town—and that he's got a lead mine in the West called the Little Beaver! But if they hadn't been, we'd a had some other good fakealoo.

"All right," he continued. "Heebie-Jeebies opens up. We pull her in. No step, nor even t'reshold, to git over, either. He closes the door. An' locks it. And now we're inside. Waitin' to be told w'ere to put the goddam' case. F'r Mr. E. Bull! An' what's confrontin' us, I ast? One empty bank wit'out a single cust'mer in it—an empty bank in w'ich the bug switches ain't ever turned on till Heebie-Jeebies leaves f'r the day—and w'ich don't have no heist alarm—an empty bank wit' a single counter—an' one old two-dial vault that's maybe locked by this time—and maybe ain't yet. An' f'r occupants, Old Heebie-Jeebies—wit' Slim's gat a'ready in his ribs—an' one kid clerk over there monkey-fussin' wit' ledgers, an' on who I've already got the heat. As f'r the pres'dent, Stoeffhaus, he pract'cally ain't ever there at closin' hour—but if he was, he couldn't shoot over his own belly, the flat slob. I'll nick his scalp wit' my silencer-gat if he does.

"All right. We got the heat on them slow-wits that's in the joint. And are back o' curts in th' doin' of it. We make Heebie-Jeebies—in case the vault is a'ready closed f'r the day—open up. After which we gag him and the kid, an' tie 'em up fast. And Fat Belly too, if he's there. We look that gold-holdin' box over damn well—and if we're sat'sfied, from its seals an' all, that it's the McCoy—out wit' the bricks in our case that's atop the dolly—an' into the case wit' the box. W'ich is w'ere a couple o' good strong ginks like Slim and me do our daily hard deed! And after doin' w'ich—good—by! For 'crost the floor we go. Pullin' our box—our case, that is, what's now concealin' the gold box!—on them nice oiled dolly wheels. We let ourselves out. Talkin' back at nobody—and cussin' like—well, what'll you be sayin', Slim?"

"'Hell of a note to fetch a shipment clear across the country and have it refused. Have to charge returns on this. Good—by!'"

"Good-by is right!" echoed Al Mulhearn. "Wit' two rubes gagged an' trussed up inside—an' a door drawed to on 'em wit' a big spring lock!

"Well," he continued, "acrost th' sidewalk we disgrunt'ly draw our load. Our re-fused load! Gangway, rubes—make way f'r a couple o' busy men! And now we got our load und'neat' the rear o' the truck. In direc' line wit' the little hinged trappy door what swings in'ard—f'r boxes and packages. An'—in this case—a certain crate on a dolly! 'Hi, folks—will anybody round here what ain't ruptured give a hand? These lead nuggets is heavy as hell—even f'r 6 men.'

"That 'rupture' stuff, o' course, 'll scare hell out of the rubes. F'r no goddam' rube is gonna rupture his guts helpin' out a couple o' guys who may lay down on him durin' th' liftin.' So the competition against you guys helpin' 'll be less'n zero. But le's see—you got to be invited, don't you? 'Hi, buddy—you wit' the yellow head!—give a hand, will ya? An' you wit' the grey flannel shirt. Lend a finger anyway, will ya?'

"But hell—couple o' good guys like you two wouldn't see a couple o' good guys like Slim and me rupture ourselves tryin' to heist up a heavy box o' nuggets. You've a'ready detached yourselves fr'm your backgroun's, an' come over sheepish-like; an' the four of us, wit' a grunt, an' a heave, an' a ho, swings that bastard 250-pound-'r-so case straight up off th' ground an' into an' t'rough that crappy door like nobody's business. And now, in the twinklin' of an eye, our sweet little transcontynental truck is a gold truck! A gold truck, no less. A gold truck—but no onlooker even dreamin' *that*. 'Thanks, buddies. Have a stogy?' W'ich I poke into your mout's. An' then perceed t' get around—Slim an' me both—to the front. Up into th' cab. Onto our seat. 'Gidda-yap!' And off we go. Except that—"

Al Mulhearn paused. His eyes now narrowed into hard slits.

"Except that," he repeated, "Scarface, still standin' at th' rear o' the truck stupidly smellin' his stogy, suddenly reaches his hand inside the crappy door—pulls out his rod what's been alayin' atop them two nails—Snipes the same—'tother side—an' as we pull off, you two—"

"—are rideeng," put in Scarface, "on the back—weeth wan foot each in angle-iron hook w'at we 'ave bolt on theez day—" He pointed at the truck near-by where, indeed, it could be seen that from each side of the chassis' rear—but apparently by only a single bolt and nut—hung a simple right-angled piece of iron like a step. "—weeth," Scarface was continuing, "wan hand each on hand-greep w'at eez screw' to rear end av crock—"—such also, as he flicked his head toward the truck, were observable, on really close inspection, stoutly, firmly held by screws to that rear truck end—"– geeving each wan of us wan free hand, weeth rod in eet—me the right han'—an' Snipes, who eez lef'paw, heez left one—to—"

"—to pink the leg or wing of the first goddam' rube," said Snipes, rubbing his thin hands ecstatically, "'at makes a move—blowin' hell out of the tires of anybody who even tries to start up his jallopy—and paralyzing the living daylights out of the whole crowd. Jesus, Boss—couldn't I do the whole rearguard stuff by myself? Scarface here always hogs all the sweet shots. I feel 'at I—"

"Don't feel," ordered Al Mulhearn sourly. "Think—an' do. In a job like this, don't feel none at all—if, that is, you're figurin'—as I know you are—to be blowin' 10 grand on all the fat Injun women in Mex'co City, in a couple o' weeks. Well—well, what now, Slim? For you're drivin' right now!"

"That's all," Slim shrugged. "I'm driving. We're down that road, however—and around that first curve—if that's what you want me to certify to—before they've even pulled their hick brains together enough to realize that there has been a heist in broad daylight—under their very snoots. If you ask me, any shots that Scarface and Snipes will have to lay will be nothing but pure evangelistic work. In fact, I say the rubes won't start up a single car; they—"

"W'y shood?" queried Scarface. "W'an tel'phone seestem she at han'?"

"'W'y shood?' is right," mimicked Slim. "W'y shood," he continued mimickingly, "anny wan catch boolet in gots by starteeng op car?"

"All true," affirmed the Chief. "Bot' as Scarface here—an' friend Slim imitatin' him in his own words and own accent!—bot' maintains. And take that sour look off your puss, Scarface—an' that skeptical look out'n yours, Snipes—for Slim here *is* a great actor, w'ether you guys b'lieve it or not—an' should ought to be in Hollywood playin' bits, 'stead o' drivin' cars in jug heists!—except that Slim likes his mazuma in chunks instead of in dribbles. But gettin' back again to your statement, Scarface—an' yours, Slim—what you bot' say is all true. But on'y hypythet'cally true. T'eoret'cally, we'd make th' Junction before a single car would start. But act'ally, you never c'n tell! An' that, by Jesus, is why I inserted Step Number 2 in this heist—"

"But which," pointed out Snipes, dourly, "risks a wholesale bumpoff that'd put us all in the hot-seat—if we got glaumed. I'd druther handle th' pursuit all by pinking wings an' tires. I'd—"

"Goddam' it, punk," half snarled Mulhearn, whose sudden choler was due to the fact that he possessed a deep sensitivity to the subject of electric chairs, "are you tryin' now to get some more high-ridin'—t'rough a fool arg'ment? If you are—forget it! F'r one thing, they got the rope in this backward state—and not the ho—y'know?" Now Snipes winced. "I'll so much as say—before I drop the subject f'r good and all—that fuse is timed to a T. All *you* got to do, t' keep them rubes out o' the blast—and *your* neck out of the rope—" Snipes swallowed hard. "—in case you're ever tied up t' this job, due to shootin' off your mout' too much to one o' them fat Mexican mamas, and she turned out to be an Amer'can G-woman!—is to pop at th' rubes, wit' Scarface here, if any of 'em draws up an'w'ere clost—just to pop away at 'em 'at's all—clost as hell, yes—even if you have to lift a Kelly or two off 'n some beans—or to wing a couple—but not to lay 'em. And that ends the arg'ment. Driller has cemented them 10 sticks o' dinny in that sewer-pipe culvert a half mile below town—dinny at the very middle, an', on the top inside o' the pipe, fuse, helt by bits o' rubber tape, runnin' along the inside top o' th' pipe, a'most t' the right-hand mout', and begin' down there a full coupla inches—all in read'ness; and so we're goin' t' take full advantage of it even if—well, Scarface, think you can find that there hanging fuse end—an' light it—when Slim stops the truck just acrost the culvert—to let you off?"

"Eef nobody poppeeng at me fram uproad," averred Scar-face, "I find eem a'right!"

"Aw," put in Slim, "the rubes, I tell you, won't have a single car started till long, long after we've reached that culvert. Passed it even. So—"

"Then nobodee," pronounced Scarface gently, "weel be poppeeng at me—an' I weel 'ave hopped off—to'ched light to fuse like Boss here theenk we shood do—'ave climb' back on hanging ang'-iron step alongside Snipes, who eez pop-peeng away up road—may-be!—give wheestle t'rough my teeth—an' then maybe in 25 secon's—30 secon's—"

"No maybe," corrected his Chief. "Nor 25 nor 30 either. Twenty seconds *exactly!*"

"Okay, Boss. Twenty saconds later—poof!—"

"Poof is right!" echoed Al Mulhearn. "Poof—10 seconds after we've pulled off—an' they's a crater in the road bigger'n any o' them on the moon. That, by Christ, 'll hold 'em sure till we've reached the Junction. And compel 'em to do all their stuff by phone! Unless, of course, they get around the crater eventually by—"

"But now," said Slim, who evidently didn't like vague hypotheses, "we're at the haunted house—picking up—"

"Beebles!" put in Scarface, with a disgruntled sigh.

"Beebles is right," affirmed his Chief. "For Beebles made this heist poss'ble wit' his phony probate court testimony. And we pick him up—like we promised him we will—even if we have to buy him a sody and a package o' rheumatic remedy on the way!" But this was plainly sardonic facetiousness. And he went on. "Well, here we are now at Perkins Junction. At the barr'er o' the Straightaway. At th' mout' of Old Twistibus. In banshee land. Call it what you want. But—a'right, Scarface?"

"Well," said Scarface, with a gesture of his dark hands, "I 'op out—tak' the leetla nitro-glyc' bomb what Driller 'ave made for us—an' w'at you 'ave tak' out from onder seat there, an' hand down to me—I tak' an' 'ang eet across barr'er lock—light eet—get back on trock—we back off—20—30—40 feet, maybe—and when she go off, 30 seconds after she eez light', she blow whole lock an' bolts right out of barr'er gate. The w'ile—"

"The while," echoed his Chief, unsmilingly, "the rubes o' Cedarville, dammed back on tother side of my moon crater, are phonin' Duckhouse—at Willis Creek—on that very t'eory—and phonin' Pricetown, in case we've doubled back at the Junction—and phonin' Elum's—to find, b'God, that we ain't—and—but go on—go on? Who the hell is drivin' around here?"

"I am—I am—I am," hastily put in Slim. "In fact, I'm going down that Straightaway like a streak out of hell. Providing—as I have to presume!—that Snipes and Scarface have by now hopped out, soon's I've brought the truck up to the blown barrier, and swung that thing—on its rollers—out, enough so's we can get onto the Straightaway. If they have, then I'm going down the Straightaway like a streak out of hell. Sole and only occupant thereof! And knowing—as you've been able to prove conclusively, Boss—that we'll meet nobody—including Brother Duckhouse, the one-man militia!—who'll be plenty busy, however, all this time, figuring to stop us—and gun us!—if needs be!—on his side of the mountain—that juicy $500 side! Yeah, with yours truly at the wheel, we're now going down that Straightaway like—"

"Say, Boss," put in Scarface, "you theenk in theez heist we catch any green money besides gol'?"

"Jesus," caustically countered his Chief, "but you do count your chickens before the rooster has even winked at the hen who's to lay the eggs from w'ich them chicks is to hatch. O' course, we'll pick extry money. We ain't specializing in gold alone, are we? W'y, from all Driller's told us, we'd ought to scoop up a couple o' grand in frogleaves. That's w'y I've got extra loose room inside that case—and a lock what holds the cover down flat and tight. Now carry on, driver?"

"Right," acknowledged Slim. "Well, I can't see that there's anything for *me* to relate. Just zooming along that now-elevated highway, over those deserted lowlands called Frog Gullies, at 50 per—nobody bearing down on us from ahead—nobody inching on us from behind—"

"And to insure which," put in Al Mulhearn, mirthlessly, "is why I fixed to blow that crater in that Cedarville Road. To insure keeping them Cedarville rubes on their side o' the Junction just as much as that $500 reward mazuma—plus county law—'ll be keeping Duckhouse on *his* side o' th' mountain! Why—we'd ought to be diving, like an arrow out o' hell, into that Smoky Ridge tunnel by—"

"Whoa, Boss—slow up!" admonished Slim. "That tunnel, a full city block long, and embracing—at least from points about 50 feet inside each of its openings—a huge and practically 180-degree curve, because of the fact that—"

"Driller said," said the Chief glumly, "that 'twas put in that way to throttle down speeding."

"Well, it'll do that all right, all right!" But here Slim smiled mirthlessly. "Though Driller, I don't mind tipping all of you off, was only wiggling out of telling you it was due to a complicated geological problem—and then having to try to explain it to you when you asked what it was. The real reason for that tunnel's shape is to be found in a peculiar geological fault that lies in this region—rather, diagonally across that mountain. If the tunnel had been put straight through, from east to west, it was in danger of a shear in any fool earth tremor around this region. Whereas, where it lies now—in that granite-encased bend—nothing can ever touch it. It can't—but here, what's the use of my trying to explain geology when Driller wouldn't try?" Slim paused. "But as you say, that arc—that bow—will throttle down speed all right, on that highway. Even when the lights that are to be in the bore eventually are hooked up. But in our case, embracing a curve like it does—and being entirely without lights yet—we'll—"

"Lights?" interrupted Al Mulhearn. "Haven't we got lights? Haven't—"

"Sure—sure we have, Boss—headlights which we're not figuring even to turn on—and electric torches which we *will* use!—but the point is: we don't just dive down on the mouth of that tunnel like a shot out of hell. We slow up on the east mouth—and ease gently in—bending around the curve rightward—using the torches, once inside and around the bend—yes—but—"

"Well, what th' hell's a little slowin' down to us who've lit'rally burned up the mac'dam meanw'ile? What's—but now I'll take up—since this heist was doped out by me—or by me, usin' Driller f'r my right eye. All right. Into the tunnel we go. Into and under our mama's wing—Smoky Ridge Mountain being just now, our mama! Smoky Ridge Mountain Mama— made of stone wit' granite in it as solid an' hard as Snipes' head sometimes is! Into the tunnel we go—"

But here Al Mulhearn stopped. And gazed somewhat quizzically, too, at the 3 visages all facing him. There was a peculiarly grin-like look on each visage.

"I see," he observed dryly, "that our ridin' into a mere tunnel amuses you all?"

"Well, Boss," returned Slim, with a *moue,* "can you blame us?"

"Eet maka me chockle lettla beet an'way," grinned Scarface.

"Boy, I'll have many a laugh in Mexico," said Snipes, gleefully, "when I'm with my fat mamas. 'Bout that tunnel, I mean!"

"I'd sure like," put in Slim, "to see the faces of everybody when they find out—"

"Well, you c'n read all about it," said Al Mulhearn graciously, "later—aft'ward—and at some unknowed time in the fuchure. You c'n—however—any questions?—anybody?"

"Wan," put in Scarface. "Weel we 'ave mak' tonnel, you theenk, Boss, before rubes *they* are at Jonction?"

"I think so," said his chief imperturbably. "Not that it makes no difference. A fat lead is quite all we want. A chance to get there, that's all. If it's that you think they may be in doubt which road we've took, f'get *that*. F'r they'll phone to Elum's, when blocked, and have Maw Elum pedal up to the barr'er on that bike o' hers—and report back to 'em that the barr'er lock is blowed, an' that we've took th' Straightaway a'right, a'right. After w'ich they'll shoot the info, by phone, to Duckhouse at Willis Creek. Questions?"

"How long, Boss," said Snipes, "do you think it will take us to cover that Straightaway from the Junction—to the tunnel?"

"About," said his Chief, "45 minutes. The truck's no racin' car, y' know. But she can hit it up. Will, under Slim. Why did you ask?"

"We-ell, the Duckhouse baby. If he ever came through the tunnel, an' cut us off—"

"Hell-fire," snapped Al Mulhearn, "d'ya think he'd try to do battle on an open stretch o' elyvated highway w'ere he couldn't even put up a halt chain? An' don't that $500 reward business for his county alone, still mean nothin' to you? However, to end this perpet'ally recurrent argyment, he's full 15 minutes himself—even by his own fast car his county gives him—from his side the tunnel. An' it's even possible, boys, I tell you—" And Al Mulhearn leaned forward and emphasized his words with his big forefinger. "It's even poss'ble, boys—from the way Driller figured that that phone conduit *might* cross the road w'ere the culvert is—and the prob'le hookup o' the inter-town lines around here—that the blowin'-up of the culvert will cut off Cedarville by phone from *all* towns. I don't promise nothing—no. But it's poss'ble. And if by luck it happens, then the Duckhouse bird'll never even know or learn they has been a heist. Not even for hours after we've reached the tunnel. Not even—"

"Onless," put in Scarface, significantly, "there woz—"

"Just—a—minute!" interrupted Snipes. "Now that this here discussion is about at the end—except for maybe some 'unless' that Scarface is tryin' to sell us!—it seems to me, lookin' back on the whole goddam' thing, that fully half of it's been about the Duckhouse lug—about his guts—his prob'le ignorance of this—or of that—the kind o' car his county lends him to drive—the length, in minutes, of his travel to his side o' the tunnel—what he'll do—what he won't do—all accordin' to Boss' figurin' here. But goddam' it, when you come right down to it, how about this Duckhouse's figurin'—according to his own style o' fig-urin'! What I mean is: how, Boss, do you have such a complete low-down on him as you claim to have? Driller, so far's I und'stand, never covered the section o' the country that side the tunnel. So—"

"A-a-a-ll right!" groaned Al Mulhearn—but to Slim, glancing carefully at his watch. "Tell him then, Slim—at least what th' hell little you told me!—which, *by* Jesus, was pract'cally nothin'!—and shut him up. I'm—I'm too washed out to explain any more to him."

Slim turned to the youth. "Now see here, Screwball, if you're starting to hop yourself on high again, just by raising some fool issue, I want to warn you you'll get exactly 100 words of info here—and no more. But if you really want the real low-down—okay! I don't usually tell my right hand what my left hand does—haven't even given the Boss a single downright detail of it—but since the Boss says to tell you as much as I've told him—then okay. But it'll be damned concise, Screwball." He paused. "When the Boss commenced to sniff a possible job down here, he needed what he usually needs on any heist job—a good study—a pre-study—made—of the terrain—that's the distances of things and people from this mountain—all that land layout—and the people—including particularly the Sheriff—both sides of the mountain. And so forth. So he sent his—okay, Boss?"

"Yeah, yeah," nodded Al Mulhearn, "I said okay!"

"Well," Slim continued, to the inquiring-faced Snipes, "he sent his moll, Big Edna, to Cedarville. Just a big gal from the city, trying to get a hired girl's job in the country. And about as much chance to do so as a—a flea has to kick over an elephant. But it gave her a week—so the Boss tells me—to stall about the town. And she made a good pre-study of things for Al. And—" Slim Yarnai paused a bit reluctantly, as a man who feared he was being cunningly taken for a discoursational ride! "And Al got me to send my—oh, not my moll—no!—maybe she was once—but she's just my best friend, today—"

"Mollie the Con?" said Snipes. And there was downright reverence in his tones.

"For a chronic question-asker, you sure do know plenty about everything, don't you, Snipes?" Slim retorted, a bit acerbically. "I 'spose you even know Mollie's right handle?"

"Why sure! Marie Delacourte."

"Hell—you don't need this brief story of mine. You—"

"No, no—go on, Slim. Now for the first time I feel as though this job has been really cased properly. So—so you sent Mollie the Con to look things over?"

"Yes, Mollie herself, the smoothest of 'em all, God bless her! And she went down to Willis Creek. After introducing herself, as it were, with an advance letter—to the head peace officer himself. Yeah, the Sheriff! Just a lady looking for a peaceful quiet place to rest up in! Well, to keep this down to that 100 words I said, by God, it was going to be kept to, she got enough dope, in that one week she lay up in Willis Creek, on conditions *that* side of the mountain—just as Al's moll did on this side of it—she got enough dope, Mollie did, on conditions there—and on this rooting tooting so-called fearless fool—plus the driving time from here to there, and from there to here!—plus the fellow's mental I.Q.—wits to you, Screwball!—that—" Slim shrugged his shoulders impatiently. Looked at his superior. "You want me to tell him all, Boss?"

"All?" grunted the individual addressed, and testily. "All is good! If you're applyin' that to what you told me. For you didn't give me one goddam' concrete fact. Though," Al Mulhearn added pointedly, "anything concernin' collie and any deal o' hers that hasn't nothin' to do with this heist of ours, is Mollie's own goddam' private business. And yours—to the extent that you're lending th' lady a loose elbow. So go ahead, Slim. Tell him—as much as you told me. For I want him on high."

"Well, Screwball," Slim said, turning back toward Snipes, and apparently amused himself at the very idea he was about to broach, "Mollie even *took* this rooting tooting fool!"

"She—took him?" echoed Snipes. "Him—a Sheriff?"

"I said so. She even took him double—so far as that goes!"

"We-ell, if she could take him—take him double even!—why wasn't she able, maybe, to get the key from him—or an impression of the key—for that Straightaway barr—"

"Because she didn't try, you damned fool! Wouldn't that have been a fine tip-off—that something was in the wind to be pulled? He isn't quite that dumb!"

"So she took him? Well—does *he* know it?"

"Not yet—no. Unless maybe Sid the Mouthpiece has already put the bee on him, on the bigger take. That may be any time; for it's got nothing to do with this job. It's her own private take, that latter, beween her and Sid. All I'm doing is being the 'join'—and holding—pending the return to Southwest City of your and my good friend Hot-Ice Izzy the Fence, her smaller take, and, against Sid, her fatter take—the sweet thing the Duckhouse bird signed."

"He—he signed somethin'?" said Snipes helplessly.

"Yes, you bull's-eye popping squirt. He not only loaned the gal—the night before she decamped!—and so's she could get an expert opinion for him on what it was worth!—an old-fashioned broach studded with a genuine amethyst, and made out of solid gold to represent a perfect cactus leaf—complete, by God, even to tempered-gold 'thorns' sticking from it—a thing he didn't even own himself—only borrowed it from a friend to get this gal's opinion on whar it might be worth—but, in addition to all this, this rooting tooting Sheriff even let loose of—of a piece of scratchwork! But if you'd never met Mollie the Con—and she started in on you, with that phony helplessness of hers, you'd sign your own death warrant." Slim tapped his breast under his striped trucker's jacket. "Why, if I showed you, Screwball, what I got here—holding for her—but inside a sealed envelope—and that sewed inside my coat lining—you'd catch such a belly laugh you wouldn't be able to shoot straight today. Oh, I don't mean the fool cactus-leaf broach that isn't worth much more than a C note—but the—well, inside that envelope is the very piece of scratchwork Mollie took him for. It—"

"Aw come on, Slim," taunted Al, evidently a deep appreciator of true criminal artistry. "Let us in on it? What is it? Not the piece o' slum—no; I can look at any goddam' cactus leaf an' pertend it's solid gold, an' its thorns tempered gold. But the scratchwork. What is *it?* A deed to his ances-tryal estates?"

"He hasn't any ancestral estates," retorted Slim. "It's—however, but see here, Al, can't I even live up to my own promises to Mollie and Sid to—"

"A'right—a'righr—we don't give a goddam' anyhow. Just the one fact is all we need to know: that the damn fool was able to be took, lock stock and barrel for anything at all, from one dollar to—"

"Well, what would you expect, Boss? And—" And Slim turned to Snipes, whose face was still full of wonderment. "And you too, Snipes? A country jake like that Sheriff—against a world-famous lemon woman like Mollie the Con? Hell, the girl had to keep in practice, didn't she? But let's have done now with these drawnout expositions of everybody. Mollie gave us a regular report on everything about this fellow Duckhouse—his life—his guts—his brains, such as they are. And enough to *know* he won't come through that mountain. And for her work she gets a small cut out of my end of this job in addition to hers and Sid's take from this hick's scratchwork." And Slim Yarnai promptly dried up, though touching his ribs lightly with a forefinger pressed against his striped jacket to feel, evidently, that that sealed envelope, sewed within the lining of some under-jacket, was right where it was being safely kept.

"Well, I am satisfied at last," repeated Snipes, reverently again, "that this job has had a 100 p'cent casin'."

"Oh, thank you, kind sir!" said Al Mulhearn sardonically.

Scarface had been sourly silent during all this. Now he spoke, grumpily.

"Eet seem' to me I woz tryeeng to say sam'theeng eem-portant, when Snipes here he botted een, an'—"

"What t'ell was it?" asked Al Mulhearn quickly,

"Woz theeze. You woz sayeeng, Boss, that maybe conduit she get blow' up, too—in Cedarveele Road—an' eef so, then eet will 'appen that the Duckhouse faller weel never even know or larn there 'as been a heist. Not even, so you said, for hours after we 'ave reach' the ronnel. So *I* say w'at *you* say now eez fack—yes!—*onless*—" And Scarface was speaking very firmly and most significantly. "—*onless* there shood be a weetn—that eez," he broke off, half apologetically, but still as emphatically, "I now ask beegast quastion of all. Mos' eem-portant bastion! Eez theeze, Boss—sillee though she seem. 'Spose—'spose, joost for example—we meet op weeth—you know how eet eez, Boss?—the onexpected she eez often be-com' the actual theeng?—'spose we meet up weeth som'bodee on that Straightaway, mebbe even eenside tonnel, w'ere—"

"And how the hell," asked Al Mulhearn, quite puzzled, "could anybody be on the Straightaway—before *me* blow the lock and open it up? An' after we do, they's nothin' could ever overtake us. So what th' hell do you mean?"

Scarface's shrug was impressive in its noncommittalness. "I no know w'at I mean, Boss. I joos' try cover av'ry poss'-beel'ty. I not even teenkeeng mabee of car—no!—I mabee teenkeeng, say, of man walkeeng—t'rough mountain—or—or on bicyeecle, mabee—w'at he have leeft over barr'er—or—"

"On'y to risk gettin' questioned, on the other side the mountain, by that Sheriff, as to how he got on?"

Scarface again shrugged Latin shoulders.

"I onlee tryeeng to cover hypo—hypo—hypo—"

"—the-siss," finished Al Mulhearn peevishly for him. "A'right then. A man passin' near the tunnel—or even t'rough d' goddam' thing—afoot—or on a bicycle—or—or on roller skates!—so—what?"

"So I ask? So—w'at? Theeza man, mebbe, onlee dirty hobo—sleepeeng een tonnel, w'ere rain no can ger. Bot—"

"A'right—a'right," put in Al Mulhearn. "A fair question, I 'spose—considerin' its poss'bilities. Though the chancts o' an'body bein' on the Straightaway wit' us is abs'lutely less than zero—it sure is—but even if 'twas one in a thousand, why—" And he gave a resigned shrug of his own broad shoulders. "Then o' course we'd have to protect our gr-reat kiss-off. For they's a house, here an' there, down in them gullies, that has a phone. An' who could—"

"You mean," said Snipes hungrily, and leaning forward, "that we could—pop such a witness off?"

"I mean *ezackly* that," granted Al Mulhearn, his blue eyes—though he knew it not—now literal icicles. "They's a law o' corpus delicti, don't never fergit, in this U.S.A.: no man ain't ever been convicted, in the history o' the U.S.A., for bump-off, when the corpse itself was missin'. You happen to pop off one o' them rubes in back of us—and we fry! But if *we* pop off somebody—anybody—at or near that tunnel—on that lonely, Godforsaken Straightaway, that's a diff'ent thing. For we'll do it. We'll lay a slug quick and hearty in his guts—the interferin' son-of-a-bastard—after which, o' course, we'll toss him into the truck, to—"

"—to—to vaneesh—weeth us—een tunnel—"

"Yes, yes, yes," agreed Al Mulhearn wearily. "If they's to be a witness to our play, he's got to go. Only—he goes wit' us! A dead stiff—inside the truck. To be disposed of—when all's done an' finee—in that certain way *we* know how to dispose of a stiff. So that they ain't a square inch of hide—nor hair—left to—"

He stopped, and looked at his wrist watch.

"But here—here!—the moment's here, at last, to pull out—from this thicket. The very exac' moment we figgered out—to the T! So pile in that truck, you two ducks, Snipes and Scarface. And get to the wheel, Slim. Come on, ever'body! Let's go!"

CHAPTER X

"CAT IT IS!"

Jim Craney, standing at the ancient wall phone in Elum's store, on Carthage Road East, the roar of that great lioness, in her red and gilt panel-covered cage-wagon just outside the open door, splitting his very eardrums, making the very clapboards of the ramshackle store vibrate, heard—even louder than the outbreak of the big feline—the dumfounded words of Sheriff Bucyrus Duckhouse of the other side of the mountain:

"A—cat! By the good God A'mighty—a great—big—cat!"

"Damn!" said Jim Craney to himself. "Of all the luck—of all the stinking luck."

Aloud, he tried to stammer forth an explanation of his crime, to this cat-hater of all cat-haters.

"I—I—I didn't say—what 'twas in my wagon, because—because—I heard 'bout you hatin' cats, and so—"

"What!" The Sheriff almost exploded on the wire. "Me—hate cats? What th' devil is the matter o' you? Why—I got two o' my own. And I'm feedin' sev'ral more, becaze—me?—hate cats? Who in hell's bells tolt you that?"

"A—a feller I met up the road—feller, in fact, who told me all about Old Twistibus—feller with ears that stuck out aside his head like—like sails."

"Aw heck, that 'uz Flap-Eared Chesrow. Out'n the east end o' Old Twistibus. Uset to live in Janestown, far west o' hyar—but 'herited a parch o' land in them hills, an' went down thar, th' lazy louse, t' live on it. But how th' hell—and why th' hell he should say that 'bout me is beyant my knowledge. He ain't half-witted by no sight. He—" The Sheriff could even be heard shaking his head on the other end of that 60-mile-long circuit.

Jim Craney's hopes, meanwhile, were soaring. Though even yet he couldn't quite believe his own good luck. It seemed impossible. He endeavored to uncover this mystery.

"Why, he even told me," he explained, "this big-eared feller—how a mountain lion once grabbed your dead grandchild baby out'n its coffin in the middle o' the night—an' loped off with the—the body. And that—that nothin' but bones was found."

"Aw!" snorted the Sheriff, disgustedly, "that 'uz old Sharf Dukkus—o' this town. The town miser! Yes, Sharf *does* hate cats. But by the gods, I never knowed *his* hist'ry an' *mine* was gettin' tangled t'gether in these parts. Sharf Dukkus—Sheriff Duckhouse—hell's bells!—don't people even know how to pernounce they English? An' as fer my grandchildren—" He sniffed audibly. "I hain't no wife—an' hence no children—and ef I did have any o' th' latter, they shore wouldn't be old 'nough to have give me grandchildren—drat that flap-eared idjit." He paused wrathfully. "Well, 'twas true a'right about that mountain cat an' the baby co'pse. And Sharf Dukkus. 'Ceptin' it happened y'ars and y'ars ago—back befo' the town o' Willis Creek got pop'lated—and when this kentry did have mountain cats. But 'twas a hongry cat, plumb crazy fer food. An' ef'n that old skinflint 'd set out his un-et scraps o' food in a pan—fer pore critters like bobcats an' mount'in lions—'stid o' burying the scraps 2 full feet deep whar no kind of a starvin' cat could get th' benefit of 'em, it all 'twouldn't have happened. But it did—so that's that. But what's ser'ous, right now, is that over in that caounty whar you now air, my life hist'ry 'pears to be gittin' tangled up with that old wretch's, an'—my God!—how long's this be'n goin' on, I wonder?—now I wonder ef that old wretch's fallin' in love 'ith a chorus gal 10 y'ars ago is gittin' 'tributed to me too?—by the gods!—well, I shore owe you a favor this day, stranger."

"Then—then," put in Jim, finally convinced that the last obstacle toward cutting off the miles and miles, and hours and hours, of Old Twistibus, had completely evaporated, "you will, then—let me throu'gh—by that Straight-away—so's I can get to Foleysburg—before my show closes?"

The Sheriff did not answer that question, however. Instead, he asked, and somewhat soberly:

"Has this hyar cat jest had young 'uns—like you claimed the critter you was transpo'tin' had?"

"Now—what?" said Jim to himself only, and uneasily. "What the devil would that have to do with things? Turn us into a—a travelin' zoo, I wonder? Hm?"

Aloud, however, he said:

"Yes, Sheriff. Five beautiful kittens—prettiest things you ever see." And now Jim Craney, sensing the existence, in this man on the other end, of some deep, even if wavering, feeling for new mothers, human or animal—and having played cards a-plenty in his life, saw that here was the moment, if ever, to press his plays. "And," Jim followed hastily up, "I—I got money, too. I'm—I'm authorized by Mr. MacWhorter to pay it out—when an' as I *have* to. Now if $10, Sheriff, would—"

"Now stop that," ordered the Sheriff gruffly. "I don't know what kind o' p'lice officers you circus fellers come up ag'inst 'round the kentry—but you may as well know that yo've met up with one that's honest. And who don't let his palm git crossed. At least," added the Sheriff dryly, as one who felt that inordinate honesty *must* be explained to some people, "—not fer no paltry $10! An' I take it yo' haven't got no big money—such as *I* could use!—to fix me with, heh? Sence—whar's 'at, Lucy?" Evidently the local Central had come in. "No, still on, gal." A click, and the two men were apparently alone again on the circuit. "I ain't lettin' circus car'vans," the Sheriff went on firmly, "through that thar new roadway not fer even one honderd dollars. But now a single cage—with jest a single pore cat—hm?—now let me think a bit, Craney—I—"

"You like cats pretty much, don't you, Sheriff?" For Jim, being a cat-lover of unmistakable hue, had detected that something in that phrase "pore cat" which only a profound cat-lover like himself could have ever put into it!

"Too danged much, I reckon," said the Sheriff laconically—and apologetically. "Guess I'm one o' them cat-lovers a'right. 'Specially of cats what show a leetle bit of affection."

"Affection?" Jim saw something to press hard on. "This creature's a Nubian lioness, Sheriff—same kind of creature they had in Egypt in Cleopatry's day—and the only kind of cat in the world that can be made into a house pet—pro-vidin' there's only one other person in the house: its master! This one, as a matter of fact, loves two of us—Mr. MacWhorter and me—so much that I'm certain if we let her out of her cage and nobody else was around, she'd likely rub herself up against one or the other of us so hard that—that she'd knock us down. But of course," Jim qualified, for he was no nature-faker, "they's other people in this world—that she don't feel that way toward—and so we couldn't very well let her out. But I've been in her cage lots of times—only, of course, after she's had a good feeding. For before these big cats are fed, they get a—a bit flighty, sometimes. Right now, with her kittens, I wouldn't go in either. 'Cause she's all 'cited over what Mother Nature has brung her."

"I don't hardly have to ask," commented the Sheriff dryly, "whether you like cats?"

"Always was crazy about the fool creatures," admitted Jim blushingly. "Big ones—little ones—an' kittens to boot!" Now he became practical. "So, as one cat-lover to another, Sheriff—and in the face of this—this poor cat with her—"

"Now wait," interrupted the Sheriff helplessly—though obviously a new man entirely now that he was on the wire with one who felt, about cats, like himself, "I aim to be hooman'tar'an—shore—and to do right—but I got sartin implied obligations to—now wait'll I think—I want to try to do ye' a favor—ef it's poss'ble—'caze oncet in a circus, when I 'uz a boy, an' thar wuz a fire an' a panic, a clown he he'pped me out—but you see they's plenty people will criticize me fer bein' inconsistent. And so—"

"Yes," put in Jim eagerly, "but when you tell 'em that this is a beautiful, valuable living creature—of a mighty rare specy—and an abs'lute perfect example of her specy, to boot!—and worth a lot o' money—even without her young—which'll be worth $100 apiece if they ever reach 5 months old—the people'll understand."

"Yeah," grumped the Sheriff, "and they's plenty what won't, too!"

He was silent. Doing some problem—or even problems!—in mental logic. And now some of his ratiocination became audible.

"No," his words came over the wire troubledly, "any danged fool'd know that ef our office wouldn't let a circus through—fer a ondoubted piece o' money, I—I wouldn't be takin' a fool 5-spot 'r so fer jest lettin' one car through. Co'se they would! But my obl'gations to this cent'narial openin' date now? They—"

He was silent again. Indeed, Jim Craney could almost hear the other thinking. But knew that a very decent sort of a white man—and an honest man, of all things in the Universe—was trying now to find a watertight excuse for being decent. Decent, that is, to a cat! And it appeared, from that same honest man's sudden and next words, that the latter had, indeed, found a complete way out of his dilemma.

"Wa-all," he was saying—and quite emphatically now, "I cain't see as how they's any arg'ment poss'ble that them pore little kittens should be shookened up by—by totin' 'em all in an' out an' over that hills road fer hours an' hours—yes, 'at's jest what I don't. Them's new little things, and they shouldn't ought to have that so'te o' baptism. No, they shouldn't. Bein' bo'n is bad 'nough—but when yo're bo'n blind—and on a milk diet, to boot!—a—a special milk diet, at that—Nub'an li'ness milk!—yo're in one hell of a ticklish state. Pure hooman'tar'an princ'ples alone 'd dictate 'at—yes—guess they ain't ary arg'ment whatsoever kin be raised. And so, Craney, yo're p'tition is granted! And so now I'm goin' to tell you how to git past this hyar locked barry-cade lyin' up ahead o' yourse'f. Fer—air yo' listenin' clost?"

"You bet I am, Sheriff!"

"Wall, fu'st thing of all, the key t' that barr'er is hid—but wait!—sence you're at Elum's store right now—and comin' thisaway now—ever'thing's right in the bag fer me to git me so'thin' to read. Fer I heerd tell, day befo' yist'day, 'at Elums 'z puttin' in a lendin' liberry thar—God he'p 'em, fer I doubt ef anybody in that kentry whar yo' air kin even read. That I do, b'God! But anyway, I want fer you to do me a very small favor. Y'see, I've read ev'ry danged novel that we got in this two-by-fo' lendin' liberry of our'n at Willis Creek, an' so I'd like fer you to fetch me 'long a novel out'n Elum's line-up o' books, an' drap it off to me hyar, this side th' mountain—say, at the do'step o' my shack what's 'long-side the road, jest 7½ mile east o' town—or 2½ mile west o' this end o' the Straightaway—or full 15 mile this side th' Ridge. An I kin send th' book back by someone travelin' east'ard atter the Straightaway is 'ficially opened. Will you do that leetle thing fer me?"

"Sure will, Sheriff! But what kind of a novel would you want?"

"Hell's bells—any kind—I read an'thing or ever'thing."

"Then hold the wire, will you, Sheriff?"

Jim Craney turned to the drab calico-clad woman with the topknot on her head, and the snuff-dipped sweetwood stick in her mouth, who had dusted her way by this time clear up to the front of the store.

"Sheriff Duckhouse, up ahead," he told her, "wants that I should fetch him along a novel from your new library. He says he's read ever'thing they've got in his town, and that he'll send it back next week—with, I 'spose, the readin' fee."

"Readin' fee?" expostulated the woman. "Pshaw! An' off'cer of a caounty up-a-ways from our own wouldn't have to pay us nothin'. But trouble is, them 25 books what was to be the liberry hain't come yit—and so ef'n it's a book he wants, I hain't nothin'—but wait!—they is a book onder this counter som'eres what some calico drummer left ahind las' week. He kin have it, I reckon."

"What might it be?" asked Jim, troubled at having to be a literary arbiter for a country Sheriff. And in the phone explained the matter to the Sheriff.

"Sheriff? The library isn't delivered yet, but there's a book here what the lady says you can have if you want it—one left behind by some drummer."

"What so'te o' book?" asked the Sheriff anxiously.

The woman was extending to Jim a bright scarlet book, without a jacket. Stamped in its cloth cover, in Chinese-like brushstroke-like letters, was a title.

Jim did not bother to open it. Since, from that title, and the elaborate lettering, it plainly was not technical.

"It's some kind of a novel 'bout life in China, judgin' from the cover. Or—or a problem novel, maybe, with a Chinaman in it."

"Okay," assented the Sheriff graciously. "Whether it's laid in Shanghai or on Broadway, it'll do plenty fine fer a readin'-hongry man."

"Shore—take it," the woman at Jim's elbow was saying. And starting to shuffle back toward the rear of the store. And Jim, so that by no manner of means would he forget it, drew in his stomach and slid the book firmly inside the broad belt that held up his red-striped-edged black trousers, close to the short bullwhip which was part of his flamboyant costume. Rendering himself, though he didn't realize it, more chromatic than ever, with the brilliant scarlet book against the vivid green flannel of his short-sleeved shirt, and the thong-laced shin-high yellow cowhide boots. He tilted back that most troublesome part of his official costume—that Australian-like grey felt hat whose unusually broad brim kept getting nudged by the rear of the transmitter arm, and continued talking.

"All right, Sheriff I got your book fast and tight—right in my belt—and it'll be a simple case of my droppin' it off to you—wherever you'll be. Not that I'm sure you'll like it. For those Chinesy letters look to me sorta—"

"Wa-all, what's the name o' th' book?"

"The Way Out," explained Jim.

"Whoops!" exclaimed the Sheriff delightedly. "A mystery story, o' co'se! Better'n ever. A mystery story 'ith a whole passel o' Chinamen in it, includin' mebbe Fu Manchu. That's fine. And so now fer the impo'tent part o' this call—an' I'll let you go—and myse'f too. Just how now I wonder—hm?—are you an' me goin' to prob'ly connect so's I kin get my book, an' also see yore cat an' her kittens, an' also—ef, that is, you don't object—hold my own fool cat, Tobias, up to some hole or so'thing so's *he* sees yo're cat, too—he's such a strange cat, Tobias is, that I'd like to see ezackly what he'd do in a case like that!—now le's see—I—"

"Why, I'll stop right at your shack, as you called it," offered Jim, "providin' you hang out somethin' so I'll know which it is!"

"Ha!" returned the Sheriff. "You ain't next to the fact yet, air you, that this is a kentry 'thout many people in it. At least atween towns. Why, they ain't but three houses 'tween this side th' mounuin an' Willis Creek—and the one that's a goddanged shack is mine! Howsomever—" But the Sherif's subsequent words were to prove that he was but being jocular. "—ef yo' insist on some kind of a signal flag, I mought hang out this new hick'ry shirt I'm wearin' t'day—fo' it seems t' me its black-an'-white checks air a right-smart bit bigger 'n I see in mos' hick'ry shirts." He became serious again. "But all jokin' aside—and I've heerd plenty t'day 'bout this hick'ry shirt o' mine—the p'int is, Craney, that right now I'm talkin' to you from town—you see, I have my calls switched to whar'ever I happen to be—an' right now I'm still in Willis Creek, atter gittin' in hyar at noon from Janestown—in fac', I'm talkin' from a leetle barren room in the jail-buildin' what's giv' me fur a town office—'tain't a office; it's jest a so'te o' hangin'-'round place, that's all!—but I aim now to git out home to my 'ficial office—which is my shack, o' co'se—fur my cats hain't prob'ly b'en fed a durned mite by my dep'ty sence I b'en away, and—"

He stopped, reflectively.

"Yes," he resumed, "we'll hatter 'range—you and me—our mutual movements so's I'm back at the shack by the time yo're through the tunnel—through the tunnel, that is, an' passin' the shack."

"I'll wait there, Sherdf, gladly. However—is it time *you* need? For I could use up some myself."

"Yes," admitted the Sheriff; in response to the direct query. "I need time fur to see a confounded pris'ner in this jail—shouldn't take me but a few minutes—and then I hatter pick up any mail that there may be for me, over at the post office—and then I kin start drivin' out east to'ds my place—but I aim also to stop in on m' way, and see ef my clostest neighbor—" Jim was confident he felt the Sheriff's blush over the wire. And surmised that the Sheriff was combining some official chicken-thief business with romance. "—to see," repeated the Sheriff musingly, "ef my clostest neighbor has got back from Southwest City—whar her husband is sick in a hospital."

"Aha!" said Jim to himself. "A triangle of some sort!" Aloud he asked; "How much time would you want, Sheriff? Since you're lettin' me through by that Straightaway, why—hell-fire!—" this was possible thanks to the fact the woman had vanished into her living quarters "—I got time galore—hours galore, now!—that I can fritter plumb away."

"Wa-all now, le' me see? Le' me figger on this a minute."

Jim was acquiescently silent. From outside a gentle sub-roar wafted into the store. It was suggestive only of what it might have been—had it come full force! Princess must have had, at the moment, to reach out far—very far—with her great paw, after one of her young blind hopefuls. The roar subsided promptly; she doubtless had her kitten again.

But now a real interposition—instead of a mere sound—came in to perhaps interrupt the Sheriff's thinking. The voice, in fact, of the girl Central—or one of the two who must have made this connection.

"You folks still on?" she inquired.

"Yes, yes, yes," the Sheriff replied testily. "Shore we're still on, Lucy. And on very impo'tent bus'ness. Why?"

"Well jest," the girl replied troubledly, "that a party roundabouts hyer—I cain't say who they are—is waitin' f'r a London c'nnection. And I—"

"London, heh? And I know why! Some mo' cattle spec'lation. Gittin' the price o' beef on the hoof at Liv'pool, then phonin' in quick to Omaha to buy or sell. It's gamblin', that's what it is. And ought to be stopped. *I* even know who 'tis. It's old John Hickleberry, who—"

"I—I didn't say 'twas," the girl objected anxiously.

"Nobody said you did. But I kin think for myse'f, cain't I? And—but see hyar, you kin put Old John onto London 'thout us goin' off—you know you kin. This is a multiplex circuit—ever sence 'twas c'nnected up to run through the mountain, and—"

"But," the girl replied, "talkin' on it is always clearer when—"

"But nothin'," the Sheriff said firmly. "This is a multiplex circuit, I tell you, guar'nteed proof 'g'inst list'ners—at least outside o' any who mought tap in 'long the Straightaway—an' guar'nteed to be usable by two or even mo' parties at th' same time. So this gentleman an' me ain't int'ferin' a single bit with old John's spec'latin'. So git back to yo're dispatchin', an' I'll buzz yo're bo'rd when we're done." A downright angry click in the circuit announced the girl had departed it. The Sheriff spoke. "Craney, you there?"

Jim acknowledged his presence with a single "Yep." "Wal, hold ever'thing," the Sheriff commanded. "And le' me go on thinkin' a bit fu'ther."

Again silence. Now the Sheriff spoke. To the politely waiting Craney.

"You say," he inquired, "that you got so'thin' you kin do thar?"

"Sure have," agreed Jim. "I'd like for to spread myself out on my seat here a can o' beans, some sardines, and a can o' peaches—if Elum's have got any. And to eat 'em—for a change—while standin' still. And so far as the cage-wagon itself goes, I'd like even to change a tire—and get the full benefit of that sweet stretch of macadam you're giving me."

"Okay, then," assented the Sheriff. "That makes it fine. All but the movements. W'ich—now le's see?" He was doing some extreme calculating, all right. "How air you fixed—say—to start out from whar you air at 4 'clock sharp?"

"Better'n that. I could snatch me a full 30-minute hunk of sleep in the seat—the lady here could wake me right on the dot."

"Okay, then. Then make it 4 'clock—fer yo're start. An' now I'll give you yo're di-rections 'bout that key. An' yo're schedule, as well—startin' out from thar at 4. Said schedule bein', of co'se, not on'y yo're complete an' perfec' guide to comin' through 'thout no troubles—but yo're timetable, as well, fer every p'int yo'll be passin' on yo're trip through the mountain!"

And which same the Sheriff, with the familiarity of a man who knew every inch of the road between Elum's store and Willis Creek, proceeded now to give minutely and completely!

CHAPTER XI

EPISODE IN LONDON-TOWN!

Jarrold Wynstaby, Fleet Street journalist, thoughtfully surveyed the tarnished brass sign which confronted him at the side of the dingy doorway in Mile End Road, London. Its sunken reversed-embossed letters, most of which were minus their black filling, read

MADAME MILLY WHITE
TRANCE MEDIUM
Ring and Walk up

After which surveyal, he put out the paper match by whose light he had been examining the sign—for it was, at this moment, in London, exactly 10 o'clock at night, just as in New York City, America, it was 5 in the afternoon—in Chicago, 4 P.M.—and in Denver, and other points of America's West and Southwest, but 3! And now Jarrold Wynstaby prepared to ascend the inside steps of this dubious-looking portal on what was to be the last of his series of expose articles on London's fortune-tellers and trance mediums, the first article of which would, within but a few more hours, be on press in the early edition of the *London Telegram*.

Of this woman upstairs he had heard several amazing, though highly disparate things: one, from an Indian Yogi in the West End—that she was a genuine psychic; one—from a drunken lorry driver in a far East End pub—that, by the aid of the telephone in her bedroom, she was a go-between for international criminals, and her mediumistic stuff all a front; one—from a landlady Wynstaby once had had, on Guilford Street, that Milly White was but an arrant quack, capable of portraying spurious trances, supporting herself on gullible people. And the curious thought occurred to Jarrold Wynstaby, as he thrust aside the door, that if she were any one of those three things, she might be able to see, underneath the keen-faced bowler-hatted gentleman, of 44 or thereabouts, with cutaway coat and stick, about to ascend her stairs, the real Jarrold Wynstaby who, in Fleet Street, affected a soft black felt hat and a black Windsor tie: the journalist!

The stairs inside, though wide, were dingy and carpetless, as he could see, thanks to the fact that a streetlight outside, which had been oddly dark when he had come here, had blazed suddenly and miraculously on again, and filtered over the transom. A smell, which held in it unmistakable boiled cabbage—and cheap gin!—pervaded the hallway. But at this point the hallway became lighted up by the opening of a door—one of two fronting the street-level entrance—revealing a dingy sitting room with a painted porcelain lamp, and a huge Cockney laborer of some sore, unshaven, with a striped dickey on his neck, saying good-by to someone inside on his way to some kind of night-shift work. For he was saying, to a woman knitting: "See yer at 6 A.M." He threw but a glance at Wynstaby.

"She's at the top o' the flight, guv-nor—the left door," he announced, without asking Wynstaby who he might even want. "An' she'll charge yer 6 shillin's!"

"And how," asked Wynstaby, nettled, "do you know whom I wish to see?"

"'Ow!" The Cockney, by the light from the open door, looked up and down Wynstaby's clothing. "Toffs like you, guv'nor, downt—but 'int Madame's vis'tors 99 p'cent o' everybody 'oo comes in 'ere?"

Visitors! It sounded like Madame Milly White did not starve to death. Or else—And Wynstaby was frowningly thinking of that strange thing he had heard about her: that she was the "front" for a band of international—

"What—er—kind of a psychic is the lady?" he asked. He stuck forth a shilling. "Here, have a cigar, will you?"

"Thanks, guv'nor." The Cockney had grabbed the coin.

"H'Im sorry to s'y I downt know—because I just come 'ere meself, from Whitechapel 'igh Road, to live, larst week."

"Oh?" said Wynstaby. "Well thanks, anyway." And he trudged up the stairs. As the dickey-clad man, with a final, "Watch th' byby well, Tottie," went out onto the sidewalk.

Now Wynstaby was at the head of the stairs. At the left door, in fact. A knocker was on it. He operated it. There was a long pause. He heard an inner door being closed. Then this hallway door opened. Almost simultaneously with a light being snapped on, in the ceiling above Wynstaby's head. So that, no doubt—so he estimated—he could be well scrutinized. which light, however, gave him equal opportunity to scrutinize his examiner! She was a tall and very tired-looking woman, about 38 years of age, with pale, almost colorless, blue eyes, faded taffy-colored hair, and dressed in a soiled dress. The room back of her, thanks to a dirty electric ceiling light, could be seen to be but a sitting room, looking out on Mile End Road—except that its front shades were drawn tight, with a knobby spreadleg table stand near one corner, a thin, even badly worn carpet on the floor, a bookcase with a few books in it and no glass whatsoever—and a huge ebony-based crystal globe, fully 1 foot in diameter, on a mantel. A door in the wall opposite suggested entrance to a bedroom—to anything.

"You are—Madame White?" Wynstaby asked, in his most suave tone.

"I am." Her voice was curiously toneless, colorless, like herself. She surveyed him intently. Almost suspiciously. So much so that it occurred to him that perhaps the word had leaked—as such things do—even out of the offices of the *Telegram*—that a mediumistic exposé was shortly to be published.

"I am anxious to obtain a trance seance," he said simply. She looked him over approvingly.

"I charge 6 shillings—and whether or no."

"Whether or no—" He was bewildered by that.

"Whether or no—I touch your own problems."

"Oh—yes, yes—quite all right. I'll take my chance."

But he frowned—with perplexity. For every other one, of this category, were ready and willing, with their cards, their globes, their what not, to illuminate his whole life, past, present and future; moreover, did so prove to do so!—by mention of "dark women" whom he might recognize—"blonde women" the same!—his "financial" affairs, which were financial, even if they were skimpy! This was an odd one, this woman, with her "whether or no."

"Come in," she said in that toneless voice of hers.

He did so, and she was now closing the door behind him.

"I trust," he apologized, amiably, "that I did not—ah—interrupt you?"

"It is nothing," she said. "I was just—telephoning. As you knocked. Long distance."

"Oh? Pardon me! Well, I'll be glad to wait, till you've—"

"I had finished," she said tonelessly. "As you knocked."

Which may or may not have been true. So far as he was concerned. For since he saw no phone, it could—or could not be—in that farther room.

She had gone on speaking. Seemingly explaining. But expressionlessly quite, however. "So—if I use accidentally a Lithuanian word, please overlook it."

"Lith—" He was twiddling his bowler, for she had not even asked him to set it, nor his stick, down anywhere.

"I had been talking," she said simply, "in Lithuanian."

"Oh, you are—"

"No, I am British. Brought up, merely, in Lithuania. As a child."

A frown on her face at this juncture indicated she was irritable with herself for discussing her own life with a stranger, a mere client.

Indeed, she was already sliding over the knobby-legged table stand. Which moved so freely over the carpet that it was plain its castors were oiled. She moved it, in fact, to where an overstuffed tapestry chair, much mended and much darned, stood near one wall. "Sit there," she directed. And taking down her crystal globe from the mantel, brought it over to the table. Setting it meticulously in the middle.

"Be seated," she said, a bit irritatedly. Was now, in fact, dragging over a stiff wooden chair. For herself, obviously.

He was seating himself. Setting his bowler and stick on the floor.

She too, now was seating herself.

But she hadn't even yet asked him, however, for his 6 shillings. Nevertheless, from a handful of silver which he brought up from one pocket, he extracted the entire 6—bright coins, all!—and laid them, in a pile, politely on the edge of the table.

She ignored the pile completely. Allowing it to stand just where he had placed it. Not even counting the coins. The other women he had consulted had always tucked the money swiftly into stocking or bosom.

She was looking at him, a bit inquiringly.

"May I ask, sir, why you came—to me?"

"Well," he countered, "I heard you were extremely psychic."

"May I ask—from whom?"

"An—an American," he lied gracefully. "Whom I met—in Liverpool last week."

"An American?" she said. "How odd! I have not had an American client, I believe, in all my practice."

"Oh, this chap's wife—his English wife," Wynstaby lied, "had consulted you. While home here—on a visit."

"I see." She was thoughtfully silent. Contemplatively, regretfully so. "How nice it must be—to be able to go back and forth—between countries. I—" She sighed. "I wish I could see America. Could even go there. They say—they say that professional psychics are properly treated over there. Here, with my powers—such as they are—I live like—" She waved a hand. "You're a gentleman. And can see—and smell—for yourself! My parlor—" She waved a hand at the door back of her. "My bedroom. And one dark kitchenette beyond."

"I'm afraid," said Wynstaby, "I know nothing about America myself." Which was the truth.

She was speaking again. In that curious toneless voice of hers.

"Have you ever had a globe-reading trance seance before?"

He knew he had better be honest here.

"Yes—several of them."

"May I ask—if you were satisfied?"

"Well," he said—and did indeed tell the truth here!—"my chief objections have always been the vagueness—oh, the extreme vagueness!—of the things seen by the mediums."

She smiled faintly. "I see," she nodded. She was silent. "Such things as *I* see, I see—to the finest detail."

To himself only, Wynstaby said:

"Well, come on, old gal—and dish it out!"

She may, or may not, have read his thought.

"Well, I think we may as well begin," she said. She was ignoring the 6 shillings altogether. She moved the globe—a trifle closer to her. But looked at him, almost plaintively.

"You understand now, I hope, that with a genuine psychic like myself, what I may see may—or may not—have a bearing or bearings on your own life, your past, your future?"

"I don't exactly under—"

"I mean," she explained, "that what I see may be something involving only the lives of others. For you see there is, in the world of telepathic vision, possibilities of—"

"—of cross connections?" he retorted. "Like on telephones?" He thought he had best help her out.

"As nearly as one can put it," she nodded, "that is it."

"I am content," he assured her, "to take whatever the gods send."

"The gods send nothing," she corrected him dignifiedly.

"Vision merely tells. That is all there is. Well—we'll see."

But still she lingered—with her performance-to-be.

"And so," she queried plaintively, "you have been annoyed, in other readings, with the extreme vagueness of the things seen?"

"My God yes," he said disgruntedly. "A medium would see a man—bur he would be just a man—nothing more—a man—she would see a room—it would be just a room—why, there are fifty million kinds of rooms in the wor—but I am being frank."

"Quite every bit of all right," she acknowledged. "To be frank. The field is full of frauds. Who think nothing of—but now I believe I am prepared."

"You ought to be, old gal," said Wynstaby to himself.

"I've sure given you lots to go on!"

She was staring troubledly at her globe. She moved it even a slight bit closer to her. She paid no attention to Wynstaby now. Indeed, she stared so fixedly at the ball of crystal, that he had the illusion she had passed away from his ken—from a point, that is, of realizing that anything—him included—was in that room. He had the strange, eerie feeling of being entirely alone, with a disembodied spirit—rather, should it be said, a spiritless body. Now she was speaking. Like a woman in a dream.

"I see—I see a man—a thin—almost rangy man—though not unhandsome—no!—sunburned—windburned, too—a man bronzed—by much sun and wind—being given—being given minute instructions—on a telephone. I cannot hear the words—for I can but view only—but this man—this man stands in a strange shop—but not a London shop at all—no!—for biscuits—in open barrels!—stand about—uncovered—there are signs on the wall—they refer, all of them, to tobacco—tobacco to chew—but only to chew!—there are some square red cans near a corner—there are tinned goods—on shelves—but all this is not in London—nor Liverpool—so could it be—in Australia?—for there is so much—about it—the man's hat, for instance—that suggests Austr—but no!—the sun shines in this shop—the afternoon sun—the sun—of mid-afternoon—and all Australia—at this second—is blanketed with night, so—why—America—of course!—America, in those wild regions—of—of its West or its Southwest—but what does it matter?—he is a man—receiving directions—his eyes squint—his face concentrates—it even moves, with each direction—a simple man, for—ah!—I see both now—him—and the man who gives him the directions—the man—on the other end of the wire—an older man—a man wearing—great heavens!—a shirt—like a black-and-white checkerboard—who, in all England, ever heard—of a shirt—like a checkerbo—but what is this?—these men—are not alone—that is—there is a third party—an elderly woman—overhearing their conversation—on the telephone circuit—she holds—a receiver to her ear—even more—she is taking the conversation down—she—but now I see her more closely—but good heav—she is not a woman!—she is a man!—a man—in a cotton dress—with a grey wig—and silver spectacles—on his big nose—one lens cracked—gold tooth—he—this creature!—must have been taking notes—of this conversation—for written—on a piece of paper in his hand, near the phone—oh, dear!—the picture—not big enough—in the globe—for me to see mere handwriting—on a scrap of paper—besides—so difficult—so difficult to hold—three persons—all at the same ti—but perhaps—if I bring—the writing to my eyes—I might see—might be able—to rea—"

The woman, apparently gone from this world, actually moved her head so close to her crystal ball that her nose almost touched it. While Wynstaby, cold shivers passing over him, gasped. For she was seeing—or presumably so!—that very imaginary writing—judging from her words. For she was reading—as from something tremendously enlarged in her mind's eye.

"Ah—now I can read them!—the words written on the paper held by the old woman—man, that is—it says—it says—it says—'Whoever enters The Tunnel—between 5:26½—and 5:39¾—in the afternoon—does not emerge.' Strange words, those! Could I—have made an error? 'Whoever—enters The Tunnel—between 5:26½—and 5:39¾—in the afternoon—does not emerge'—it sounds so—so cryptic—but even more, sinister—for it seems to relate—to the conversation being held—hence, the man who is receiving directions—must be receiving directions—about entering a tunnel—and the man—the man who is giving the directions—must be giving directions—about entering a tunnel—perhaps—perhaps the time—when the tunnel will be entered!—and the third party knows something which neither of the others know, and—oh, if only I could hear the words being spoken—how awful!—that three persons I can see so clearly can hear what I cannot hear at all—and that I sit—so helpless—seeing three people—their lives—their destinies—apparently being written—in matters of hours—and minutes—arrivals—departures—and two not knowing—of the third person—nor of the strange figure 5:26½—nor the figure 5:39¾—which means—but what can it mean?—I say!—you!—you who are receiving directions—and you—you who are giving them—cannot you see?—that another listens?—to your words?—takes down your words—wake up!—wake up!—God, wake up!—wake—"

But it was the woman herself who, to all intents and purposes, came awake—for her mental observations had ceased completely—and she gave vent to a staggering little cry.

"Oh—I'm so sorry," she said, again in that toneless voice of hers. "I seem to have awakened myself in some way, but from an uncompleted dream. But a dream, unfortunately, of which I have no recollection. I do hope, though, that it was at least detailed—and that it told you *something* touching upon your own life?—or your own activities?"

"It surely was, Madame White," said Wynstaby, reaching for his stick and bowler, and rising from his chair. "And did! For you told me enough—gave me enough—for at least a complete column—at 3 guineas a column! In fact, what you've given me here tonight was so bizarre and so colorful that I shall use this episode to start my series with—instead of to end it. And now I bid you adieu—and watch your step with the next client!"

She was gazing at him, as he spoke, with a helpless hurt look. And was still gazing at him, his 6 shillings even still untouched, as he went out the door, somehow hating his journalistic work. For he would have sworn he had slapped the very soul of someone who had really seen certain weird, cryptic things—things happening in faraway places—who had really been in a state of transcendent vision of some sort—instead of having been the faker he was going to have to make her out to be.

And he was still thinking uneasily, troubledly of the whole eerie episode, as he waited for a city-bound bus near the corner of White Horse Lane. Scratching his head puzzledly. Harking back to the amazing detailedness of her "trance"—its hyper-objective reality—a thing about which, however, that detailed "objectivity," he was to learn much—a surprising much!—if not everything!—when, tonight, after his first article should roll off the 1 A.M. presses, her place would be raided by the police, and they would find—

And now, like a tidal wave, strange unconnected bits of information and hearsay he had acquired during his long journalistic career were flowing together in his brain—examples of strange and unexplainable psychic phenomena, said to have occurred in India—in history!—examples of "vision" which transcended ordinary vision; examples of—

Indeed, because of the very spell he was casting upon himself at this very second, and because, also, so vivid and real was the picture Madame Milly White had conjured up—if not in her mind, then in his!—that, as he waited for the bus to come along and take him back to his typewriter in Fleet Street, he said aloud—but to absolutely nobody at all:

"Watch your step, Chappie!—whoever you are—wherever you are—your movements are being recorded—and don't—don't—whatever you do—enter that tunnel—between 5:26½ and 5:39¾. *Don't!*"

CHAPTER XII

HOW TO APPROACH A MOUNTAIN!

Jim Craney listened attentively as the Sheriff, on the other end of the wire, detailed the steps that must be taken—to get through the mountain.

"Yo'll be at Perkins Junction," the Sheriff was saying, "on such a start as yo'll be makin'—same agreed now atween us to be 4 'clock!—at 4:15 or thar'bours. Fur outside of its outside edge—what makes a good bicycle path, anyway—fur Maw Elum!—that leetle stretch o' road 'tween Elum's and Perkins Junction is bad—an' reason 'nough: it's a fo'-taste o' Old Twist-ibus! You cain't mistake the junction, o' cose. Fur it's whar three roads all comes t'gether—two, thar is, into an' onto the one yo're on. Trouble is, that th' junction cain't be seed—in a'vance—from any one o' the roads goin' into it, 'caze it lays beyant—an' below—a rise what's in evv'y danged one of 'em! But you'll know it a'right, by the 3 roads.

"The rise what you'll have jest came over yorese'f to git onto it, how-ever, is the least-most of all them 3 rises facin' it. So it hain't told you noth-in' 'bout what's back on the two other roads. And so thar you are—'ith 3 roads facin' you! The left 'un, whose rise lays plumb atween a couple o' low knolls, with more and bigger knolls beyant them, an' actual hills beyant an' back o' them, is a road what, once past that thar rise, gets lost immedi'tly an' completely, in hills—hills—and mo' and never-endin' hills—keereckt!—Old Twistibus itse'f. The right 'un is a road what, behint the rise in *it,* what's also blockin' yo're view, comes down from a town called Cedarville. A town actual' above an' back o' you—but the road she has veered 'round a bit, and comes in very deceptive-like. Don't mistake sech of her as is atween the junction and the rise in her, as th' lead into the Straightaway, jest 'caze she's sech a good road! She's so good, in fact, that Cedarville, what's many miles from the junction, is no mo', in sheer drivin' time, than yo'll be from Elum's. A fact!

"You go right on ahead—on the road yo're on—the mid-road—w'ich is risin' quite steeply—very steeply—but is, so t' speak, now the Straight-away. Sence it's th' lead tharto! An' th' minute yo're eyes is level 'ith the crest o' *that* sho't rise, yo'll see the Straightaway, th' actual Straightaway, commencin' jest a few rods beyant it—jest a beeootiful stretch o' macadamized roadway, atween low concrete guard-rail-walls risin' right up off'n the ground on concrete pillars—ruther, let me put it, the ground drappin' sharply away onder it to form Frog Gullies.

"And thar, 25 feet or so beyant whar the macadam an' all commences— whar the highway, in fact, is a'ready 7—8 feet off'n ground—is the barr'er— a huge structure of cross-laced 'luminum beams mounted at var'ous p'ints on ball-bearin' rubber-tired wheels so that the hull thing kin be swung aside by one pusson. It's hinged to a brick pillar at the futhe'most lef' side o' th' roadway, an' locked tight to a fixture in a like brick pillar at the far right side o' th' roadway. Now the key—"

The Sheriff's voice lowered.

"The key, Craney, is stuck, by a couple of gobs of chewin' gum, to the onder side of the stone copin' of that brick pillar—but of the edge opp'site to the pillar's face. You'll hatter feel fur it. Clar 'round th' pillar. Pluck it off. *It fits two things on that pillar.* One bein' the lock o' th' barr'er. An' the other bein' a so'te of small door in the pillar's hint face—a door cemented over with thin brick sections so as to look like—like jest bricks—oh, it's cunnin' as hell—anyway, inside of it's a niche 'ith a phone in it what kin git anything or anybody in all Amer'ca—jest like the one yo're on now. And cain't never git out o' order, 'caze the conduits carryin' its wires—at least in this direction—is built deep into the concrete of the Straightaway. Don't bother, however, atter yo' are inside, tryin' to call me on it, 'caze I won't be on no phone connection at all by the time yo're thar. Travelin', thar is, on the schedule we've laid out fur ourse'ves.

"Jest onlock the barr'er with the key. It swings beeootifully out on the macadam. When yo've made room 'nough to git yo're cage-truck through, swing her back. 'Twell she locks tight. Automatic.

"Don't fetch the key 'long with you, 'caze it has to stay thar count of 'mergency. Whar like, say, th' Sheriffs o' Cedarville or Pricetown, havin' to come through—or t' use that phone—could do so. Jest stick th' key back 'g'inst the chewin' gum gobs.

"Now you kin drive out on that Straightaway. And you'll be lost to sight, so fur's the p'int yo've started from goes, in one minute—"

"How—how is that?" asked Jim Craney, puzzledly.

"How? Why, in one minute you'll have kivvered enough part of a mile that the light mist what alluz lays at that end, 'count o' the gullies thar not bein' co'pletely dry yit, will screen you from—well, from all but th' 'casional hab'tations what lays on some o' th' higher spots in them gullies. It's a 50-mile Straightaway, don't fergit!—and you'll have 37½ miles ahead o' you on that side the mountain only. Don't try to burn it up, 'caze, in my estymation, a truck like yo're'n, whose body overlays its wheels, is a mite on th' top-heavy side—so *I* think, anyway!—and, again in my own estyma- tion, that concrete guard-rail wall 'longside the macadam ain't near high 'nough to keep a top-heavy—or near-top-heavy—cage-wagon from hurtlin' over into them gullies ef'n it evah got outa control—and they's 'nough distance down to terry firmy that yo're cage-wagon an' you—and yo're cat pussies—would be jest a mixture o' gear wheels, boot-leather, cat ears and kitten paws. No foolin'!

"In fact," the Sheriff suggested, "I'd take it easy ef I wuz you, with them kittens an' all—figger to give to that stretch—oh—'bout a hour or—or even a hour an' a qua'tter—to put yo'rese'f to an' in the tunnel at 'bout a quatter atter 5 to five-thutty.

"You'll see Smoky Ridge, however," the Sheriff amplified, "long long afore you git to it. 'Bout—"

"Through that mist?" inquired Jim.

"Hell-far—mist'll be all ahind you atter yo've went 5 miles. The gullies git dried out as hell. No, you'll see Smoky Ridge a'right, and jest afore you run into th' tunnel openin' on yo're side, you'll see two houses—such as they air!—down below. One, th' Shattuck's place, a ramblin', unpainted house, 'bout 150 feet off, to yo're right, from th' Straightaway pillars. The Porch-Sittin' Shattucks, we call 'em, 'caze the lazy no-good things are always settin' out, mornin', noon an' night, on their front porch facin' the highway—an' so they'll prob'ly wave to you. The other house you'll see, jest as yo're 'bout to enter the tunnel, 'll be Gran'ther Fiddlecroft's shack, made o' logs. Pore old feller! You won't see him, prob'ly, 'caze not on'y does he live alone, but he's inside the 'arth half the time buildin' his bom'proof subcellar 'g'inst the time Amer'ca gits invaded by the Germans!

"Now, however, yo're enterin' the tunnel. W'ich, in a manner o' speakin', may be said t' be th' thing w'ich has jestified all these detailed instructions! Don't go into it like a shot out o' hell. 'Caze it's a curved tunnel—it twists to th' right, 'bout 50 feet in—and runs in a great curve, nearly a block long—and comes out later straight ag'in. An' it hain't any lights in it, yit. They air strung—yes!—but hain't c'nnected up yit. And they ain't even a warnin' sign on that tunnel mouth to tip a driver off to what's inside. Yo'll have to coast very keerfully 'round the bend inside. With, say, one headlight an'way on—or half on.

"Now yo're round it—yo're out—yo're into the daylight ag'in! More gullies onder you, ag'in. But no people atall livin' down in these 'uns. They's a pile of colored-rock boulders next the openin'—stuff what's t' be cemented 'round the tunnel mouth later fur orn'mentation—but 'twon't block you nohow, an' in noway. Fur it's all to yo're left, piled up 'g'inst a brick pillar like them others I described, an' with a phone in it, too. No barr'er hyar, nor nothin'.

"Now yo' got'zackly 12½ miles o' Straightaway to kivver! Atter w'ich yo're on hard dirt ag'in—on level ground ag'in. By merely onhookin', that is, a chain what sep'rates 'em thar. Hook it to ag'in, please, after you pass it.

"Now yo're on a dirt section o' this whole road whur onct was a dead-end stretch. This is the section whar I live. And two others,' on'y.

"Yo' proceed to kivver 2½ miles o' this. At w'ich p'int, b'lieve it or not, yo're at my shack! Built 'longside th' road on a spot o' ground w'ich, God he'p me, 'longs to me.

"And I'll be thar—on the step—to git my book. And to see yo're kittens and yo're big cat, too. And t' show my Tobias so'thin' in the cat line! Atter w'ich, I'll let you be moseyin' on. Yo'll be passin' th'ough Willis Creek 7½ miles later—you'll be at—"

"Any detours 'round the town itself?" asked Jim hurriedly. "For where towns are, people stop a circus-wagon driver on more fool pretexts—all calc'lated just to give 'em a chance to ask questions 'bout what's inside his wag—"

"No detours yo're way," was the Sheriff's prompt and frank rejoinder. "They's a secret un'ficial detour what *I* only could give you—what would carry you only, however, to'ds the Southwest City region—bring you out, that is, on some road leadin' into Southwest City Road far, far no'th of us—it's by *way* of a dried creek bottom!—an invis'ble gap atween a pair o' low hills!—a mesa!—and a long huge stretch o' Dead Woods w'ich have b'en dead sence the first dog was a woof in his father's bark!—a dead woods with a single broad trail through it—and a single Injun in it!—the Injun wouldn't scalp you, no!—he'd on'y pester you fur fire-w—but hyar, what the devil air we talkin' 'bout no'thwu'd detours when *yo're* bound sout'wu'ds?—an' not no'thwu'ds? We—"

"'Twas only," explained Jim, "'cause o' my bein' pestered so much in towns by people askin'—"

"Oh, yes—yes—well, don't worry 'bout the folks here pesterin' you none—fur I'll start the word, as I leave town—by a few of th' longest tongues what we got—an' all o' w'ich kin be found in the public square right acrost from this place!—that the 'last wagon' is comin' through thisaway—car-ryin' a—a—a well, a lioness what's got newborn kittens—what else but the truth is necessary?—and I'll say I don't want you delayed nor pestered. So that's that! And so—as I started out to say 'way back thar—you'll be passin' th'ough Willis Creek 7½ miles atter yo' pass me an' my place—yo'll be at Southwest City Crossin' 10 miles atter thar—an' yo'll be down to Simpson's Junction 'bout 15 minutes atter that—thus reach-in' a p'int w'ich, did you try to reach it by Old Twistibus, 'd have tu'k yo' full 8 hours drivin'. Now air we cat-lovers stickin' together—or air we not?"

"We shore ai—hrmph—sure are," said Jim.

"Okay, then," said the Sheriff. "Then I'll per-ceed to get ready to hang up. Now is ever'thing clear?"

"Quite," responded Jim, anxious to eat, to change that tire, and to get that 30 minutes of sleep.

"All right. I'll go by yo're movements on my own watch hyar. An' o'clock is yo're startin' time. Got it!"

"Right! 4 bells—on the nose—bank-closin' time, if I'm not mistaken, around here?"

"Keerect! Bank-closin' hour ezackly. And—but one last injunction."

"Yes, Sheriff? What?"

"Don't try to speed in that tunnel! Ef you broke yo're fool head in that tunnel—or got hurt any way in it—I'd—I'd be on the 'ficial spot. Fur lettin' you through it. Them walls is moughty danged hard ef you don't take 'em on the 'zact curve they was cut. I seed 'em carved out by steam hammers—and I assure you they lay in the toughest kind o' hard rock they is in 7 caounties. Watch yo're step!"

"I will," said Jim Craney. "But that won't be hard. Since I'll be the only passenger this afternoon on the whole elevated highway. Good-by, Sheriff, and, on behalf of Princess and myself—our thanks!"

BOOK II

CHAPTER I

BAD NEWS FOR A HICK SHERIFF!

Sheriff Bucyrus Duckhouse sat, reading a letter, in the big-handled chair drawn up to his kitchen table, by the open door of his 2-room shack on Carthage Road West. And though he did not know it, the Sheriff looked, at this moment, exceedingly sick about the gills; the flesh under his eyes actually sagged, and he gulped spasmodically as he read. For the letter, which was from Southwest City, and which was long and typewritten, began:

Dear Buce:
   I'm sorry as hell to have to tell you that that city woman you befriended down there was a cunning and ingenious swindler, and has got you! For forgery—no less! Twenty ways across the board—and where the hair is short. And because of what she and her outfit—including a certain crooked lawyer here in Southwest City—figure to do, if they can't get your money, will mean not only that you will be "out" as Sheriff, but will be serving time in Southwest City's Northern State Penitentiary as well! Yes, Buce, they've got you bad—by as clever and Machiavellian a rope-in of an unsuspecting country sheriff as has ever been pulled off. And it'll cost you—

The big fly-specked wall clock ticking away on the wall behind the Sheriff showed the time to be 4: 10 in the afternoon. The bigness of that very clock, the rickety telephone standing atop the practically empty kitchen table, and the powerful Yale-locked metal wall cabinet which overhung that table, gave to the room a sort of office-like aspect; though, on the other hand, the rusty woodburning stove which lay across the splintered softwood floor, alongside a rack of none-too-clean pots and pans, indicated also that it was a kitchen—and a bachelor's kitchen at that!

Outside on the roadway, beyond the shack a slight way mountainward—and pointing mountainward!—was parked the splendid purple Durlex-Spinay high-speed car, the free use of which the County allowed the Sheriff, though habitations there were none across the road from him; nor, for that matter, any in view on either side of him! There were, indeed, no habitations whatsoever between his place and the mountain, just as there were but two—and both on the other side of the road—between himself and the village of Willis Creek, 7½ miles distant. At this hour of the late, though bright, afternoon, he knew that the town's loafers were out in full force, lounging on the benches in the grassy tree-studded square that fronted this very road at that point, some idly watching the line of store fronts facing them from across that road, others merely the hens that now and then quacked across the ribbon of hard dirt.

The Sheriff's homespun brown coat, hung across the back of the chair ever since he got in here—and which was but 5 minutes ago—revealed the resplendent checkered hickory shirt that encased his lean but tough-muscled form, with its attached black leather wristlets, matching the high thong-laced legging-like boots. His broadbrimmed black hat, with its tall conelike crown, sat back upon his head, while he fastened on his letter a pained gaze from a pair of eyes, set in a round red face, which eyes were every bit as cerulean blue as they were on the day of his birth, 45 long years ago.

Near by him, on the kitchen table, his front paws curled in under him, slept the Sheriff's favorite cat, the brightly striped Tobias; Sebastien, the Sheriff's other cat, the black one with the white bib and white left ear, was at this moment out "catting" for stray countryside Marias; and the kittens of one of those very Marias—though not by Sebastien, whom the Sheriff had not owned long enough—were under this floor at this very moment, some faint high-pitched mewings apprising the Sheriff that their mother was gallivanting—beyond any doubt with the fascinating Sebastien himself!—and it was time for him, the Sheriff, to shamefacedly crawl in under the house with a clean pan and a bottle of hot milk made of $^{11}/_{20}$ths can Carnation Evaporated, $^{9}/_{20}$ths same can boiling water, and 8½ drops of lime water.

But the Sheriff's tender heart, beating methodically away under the very gleaming five-pointed star pinned to his checkered breast, was, at this moment, in temporary abeyance as a font of kitten-sympathy, due to this letter which he, uneasy because of possible bad news it might contain, had brought unopened all the way from town. But which now, in the more comforting shadow of his own home precincts, he had opened. It was from Walter Ferrebee, a buddy of his back in the Great War—a man who visited him now and then, once a year or so, for a day or so—now an attorney in Southwest City, and, from where the Sheriff's eyes were now resting on it, the letter continued:

> You are, Buce, beyond doubt, the bravest and most reckless gink in all America—your capture, a year ago, of that Willis Creek County madman, yourself unarmed, and him armed with a bundle of dynamite, proves that. As even does a certain other little exploit of yours, of 8 years before that, of shooting it out with those 3 drug-crazed gangsters who drove through there, and who blew their fool tops; and your killing two and capturing one. And even Uncle Sam has proclaimed something like I have just

endeavored to say, as per a certain medal he gave you, and with which you today prop up your coffee-pot stand. And *I* can well remember—even today—25 full years after!—the day you came across No Man's Land, driving—my God, a mere gangling kid you were, catapulted straight into the trenches from a training camp, and insisting on wearing your coonskin cap on your head instead of your tin helmet!—but as I was about to say, I can well remember that day you came across No Man's Land driving ahead of you what seemed, by God, to be the whole German army! But at the same time, Buce, you are—were then, and are now—the biggest and damndest fool, in a certain 2 respects, on the entire globe!

One being rendering courtesies to women.

And the other being cats!

And so, Buce, I've gone thoroughly into this jam you've gotten yourself into. And which, believe it or not, is forgery. Without, strangely, forgery having been committed!

Tie *that* if you can!

For—but before I forget it, Buce, I just rang Oakhaven Hospital here to find out how Hosea Finfrock was. And I was shocked at the news I received. For I was confident that, coming up here, as he did, from Willis Creek, and entering a big-town hospital, he would pull through. But he didn't. For he died, Buce, 5 minutes ago. So M'lissa is free! Poor girl, what a life she led with that elderly drunken wretch; what a price she paid, in marrying him so that he couldn't foreclose on her crippled father. But Fate has freed her now. And now, Buce, the field is clear for you to claim her. And get some happiness yourself, out of all these years of frustration. Except of course, Buce, if you don't solve this damned jam you're in—*by* digging up the pay-off mazuma involved—you'll not be claiming anybody! For, if you're not shortly doing the lockstep in Southwest City's Northern State Penitentiary with lots of city crooks whom you've held there in Willis Creek till Southwest City authorities could come down and get 'em, you'll be fishing for a living! And—

Oh, by the way, I talked to M'lissa. On the phone. For she was at Hosea's deathbed. She tells me she will be taking the train to Janestown tomorrow morning. And will arrange for somebody there to bring her on through Willis Creek, and out home. But is, she says, going to go on beyond, as far as your place—in case you're not in town—to tell you the sad news first. And then will go on back home. She ought, she figures, be at your place at about 4:30 or so. Be thoughtful of her, Buce, and don't even try to talk affection to her right now.

And now for the sad facts which I've unearthed, and which, disagreeable as it is to me, I shall have to call "The Story of the Sap of Saps."

The Sheriff groaned. Rose and went to the open door. Looked down the road westward. M'lissa, according to the schedule set forth in the letter, ought to be along almost minute now if as was almost certain, she got somebody in Janestown to fetch her out. But there was no vehicle in sight in that direction—yet.

And so he went back to his chair, and his letter, and proceeded grimly and wryly to re-peruse what Walter Ferrebee had ruthlessly called "The Story of the Sap of Saps."

CHAPTER II

THE SAP OF SAPS

"Now *[continued the letter from Walter Ferrebee]* as things stood when you wrote me 3 days ago, a lawyer named Sid Nudelman of Southwest City called you up, by long-distance, and said that a check for $1000 which you had presumably issued to a client of his, one 'George Yarnai,' presumably for gambling losses you had incurred to the latter while up there in Southwest City retrieving a prisoner—and which check had been endorsed over to him, Sid Nudelman, for legal expenses—had been returned from the bank as a forgery; and that the client and himself both wanted the check made good—*or else.*

"And so, knowing there was some weird mistake, you wrote to me—detailed to me fully the only circumstances under which you had ever issued a check of that denomination—and I investigated.

"Well first I was able to pick up the info that George Yarnai is a criminal of some sort, with various subterranean connections with criminals, and was once associated with a moll whose description tallies pretty accurately with that of this woman, Mrs. Marie Delacourte, who has duped you.

"Nudelman is a criminal attorney of sorts. A shady sort. Has made the defense in a couple of bank robberies performed up here. But has never been even remotely involved with having engaged in any actual criminal deals.

"And now we get to this woman herself—this adventuress, Buce, for that I'm able now to say is what she was—this woman who came down 3 weeks or so, or thereabouts, ago to Willis Creek for a rest, after you were kind enough to write her a letter, in response to her query about the village, and tell her a-a-a-all about it, and who then proceeded, after she got there, and rented a house, to *take* you for a nice ride!

"Why she ever selected Willis Creek will have to remain a problem; probably she just stuck a pin in a map, and said, 'There's a sucker in every town—and here also will be one!' But one thing I do know, Buce: before coming down there, she deliberately opened a checking account in the Southwest City Trust—but under a signature which she evidently made to be a fair facsimile of your own. By following your handwritten letter, of course!

"She brought Sebastien with her to Willis Creek, guessing from some guileless thing you dropped in your letter that you were a cat-lovin' fool. And knowing that Sebastien would be a splendid entree for a friendship. Sebastien, as it appears, however, is no blooded cat as she described to you; he's nothing but a damned alley cat—one of several hundred or so cats with white bibs and left white ears, roaming the Little-Hell section of Southwest City. All, the descendants, as I have found, of some grandfather marked in that identical way who evidently felt it his cat-duty to populate all Southwest City with white-bibbed cats!

"Whether or no, this woman, as it appears, made immediate friends with you—by and through Sebastien—whom subsequently she even left on your hands—and during that brief friendship—yes, yes, Buce, I *am* writing out here what you already know, but I'd like for you to see exactly how it looks in cold, hard print!—all right—well, during that brief friendship, this woman insisted one day on giving you power of attorney to sign her name, so that during a time when she expected to be away and have to do some business with a certain 'European art-agent' who would be coming to Willis Creek to see her, you could transact it for her. Her story, which she made confidential, and got your promise not to reveal, that she wanted you to pay anywhere up to $250 which this man might ask, for an option on an Egyptian ring—oh, Buce, and *you* a fiction reader, of sorts! Be it so, after later filching the power of attorney out of your quarters—for it's gone, isn't it?—oh, you w*ill* show city ladies about a country sheriff's domicile, and leave them there while you go out after a drunken nigg—anyway, after getting the paper back, what does she do but conveniently 'burn' both of her hands—bandage'em, anyway!—and then, in order, as she put it, to get an immediate check off for $1000 to pay off a mortgage against her in Southwest City, held by a Mr. George Yarnai, she has you make the check out—under your power of attorney to sign her name—because you, with your good hands, could fix it up and sign it—and she, temporarily, couldn't. For said she, said she, she had already notified her bank of this power of attorneyship. So everything was quite hunky dory! And—

"And right there, Buce, is where she got you. In 2 different ways. First, in having you make it out to yourself and endorse it on the back to this fellow Yarnai—under the plea that she wished this 'cruel bad man' to believe she had a legal defender, counselor, and friend watching over her affairs. How you must have thrilled to that, poor sap!

"And right there, Buce, again she got you. For she gave you an outsized check to sign—one a half-inch deeper than the standard Southwest City Trust check. I know she did! For I find she once knew a printer in the plant that prints checks for this bank. Now, however, unfortunately dead. But who evidently once gave her a small stack of outsized ones, for just such a possible future con game. And so, after you made out this check to yourself, and endorsed it to this Yarnai, and signed her name in your writing (and nearly hers!)—and then, in the generous space underneath it—as she showed you how to do!—

Per Bucyrus Duckhouse, as per powers and
rights granted under power of attorney,

They sheared the check off at the bottom in a paper shearer. Sheared off that entire explanatory matter. Leaving the check standard size. And bearing *her sig* in *your handwriting*—virtually.

"It was then, as I have been able to find out, endorsed to Sid Nudelman, the lawyer, by the fellow Yarnai. For 'legal expenses.' And put through to the bank. From which it came back promptly repudiated—even stamped 'Forgery.' Even worse, carrying a full statement of the bank president below the signature, signed and all, that the account holder had repudiated the signature.

"Now the lawyer, Nudelman, says he and his client—which of course is the said George Yarnai—for the woman has disappeared—want that check made good. Note that well, Bucyrus! Just *made good.* (No blackmail there, you see!) *Just make it good!* That takes it 100-percent out of the field of blackmail.

"Nudelman definitely does not have the check in his possession, that I know. For I tried him out by saying that if he would show it to me—front and back—I would immediately recommend to my client its immediately being made good. Even with that fat bait, he couldn't show it to me. Could only describe it in full detail. He says it has temporarily gone back to his client (who, I take it, doesn't care to have it knocking around where Nudelman might make a personal deal on it and doublecross him; who may even want to use it for 'fall money' to pass to Nudelman in case some job he's on fails). But, Nudelman says, he can get hold of the repudiated and forgery-certified check whenever you are ready to make good on it.

"And which, he says, will have to be within 3 days from now. Or else it will, he says, be sold for whatever it will bring to old Jarg Hickey—your honorable town tavernkeeper, who always runs against you, but who with all his wealth it appears can't get the distinction of the Sheriffship against the world-famous Bucy Duckhouse. Nudelman has even, it seems, held some kind of a powwow on the wire with old Jarg Hickey, and gotten some sort of an assurance that mazuma aplenty will be paid for a bit of paper like that. And so, Nudelman says, the check will probably be sold to Jarg, if you don't make good on it. It will even, Nudelman says, be endorsed over by him to Jarg, on such sale, giving Jarg full rights to prosecute under it. And Jarg, being a third or fourth party, and a quite innocent one, will be in a position to give you the works—without one of the intermediaries being in the picture, or on any witness stand to answer questions! Why—Jarg, with that check, carrying your signature of another person's name clumsily 'forged'—and payable to yourself for $1000—could knock you legally out from even re-running for Sheriff, by merely indicting you only for forgery; could lick you hands down in the next election, even without sending you to Northern State Pen. Which, if he did, you'd hardly be marrying M'lissa, I take it; and, if by some miracle he didn't, you still wouldn't, I take it, be marrying her, either. For you're hardly the man to try to support a woman by fishing!

"Under the circumstances, Buce—your deep feelings for M'lissa, and all—the only thing you can do is to raise the money and buy the damned check back. For you haven't a solitary thing in the world to prove your story—or the tiniest part of it; it's almost a miracle, Buce, that *I* believe it, for now, on rereading my own letter to you, I even find myself wondering whether—but oh, skip it! No offense meant. I cite it more to show you that if it looked as bad as that, even momentarily, to your own old friend, what would it look like to a hard-faced Southwest City Judge—before whom it would be tried, since forgery is now tried at the place where the forgery has been paid over; or what would it look like to a jury of smart-aleck city people, quite unsympathetic to a hick from the country? Indeed, in the face of all this, Buce, you must buy the check back. I wish I could throw in something toward your doing so. But being just in the process of passing through bankruptcy because of that deficiency judgment recently closed against me, *my* $123.23 cash assets are in the hands of the County Court here. I'm as broke as the day I was born. But you'll have, as I say, to buy the check back. For it'll ruin you, Buce, for all time to come. Buy it back somehow. And let it all be just a valuable lesson to you to never again sign, under a power of attorney, on the bottom of a too-deep check—made out to yourself and all that. Especially for a person whose handwriting you don't even know! Live and learn, Buce! Whenever you get the money together, I'll be glad to act as intermediary—for Nudelman says he can contact the client Yarnai.

Sincerely,
Walter."

CHAPTER III

THE WIDOW

The Sheriff, coming to the bottom of the letter, groaned aloud. For the reason that—

But there was a P.S. And moodily he reread that:

> P.S. The meanest thing that woman did to you, Buce, was to wish onto you Sebastien! For Sebastien, as I learned from Hosea, during his last lucid day before he died, has set himself the project of becoming the husband of all the lady cats in Willis Creek County—as least between the mountain and the village; and, with your peculiar sense of moral obligation, Buce, it is easy to see that your life will eventually be consecrated and devoted solely to taking care of white-bibbed kittens with left white ears, rapidly filling the county in geometrical progression.
>
> For with Sebastien so fascinating to lady cats with kittens that he can draw them right off their nests, it is easy to see that you are destined to be mother and father both to a huge white-bibbed tribe. A sad situation, Buce.

Thus, completely, the letter which was causing the hungry mewings of a flock of kittens under the very house to go unheeded.

And the Sheriff, heaving another great groan, rose and moved miserably over to his waterpail, underneath his rack of pots and pans, and from the tin dipper within it quaffed deep and gulpingly from the tepid water it contained, as though he would drink this problem into oblivion.

But there, quaffing thus deeply, he heard, coming from the west, the sound of a somewhat asthmatic motor car. Dipper in hand, he listened intently. M'lissa?

It was, evidently—for the motor car came to a stop. Somebody climbed out. And the individual's shadow darkened the open door even as the machine appeared to be turning itself around preparatory to going back the same way it had come. Except that it evidently stood, with engine now silently rumbling.

M'lissa, appearing in the open doorway a second later, even as the Sheriff was tossing back his tin dipper into his pail, was dressed entirely in black, which she must have bought hastily there in Southwest City. Though 35, she looked not a day more than 25. Slender in build, her cheeks were like roses, though her blue eyes were saddened and hurt. He was across the floor, to her, in a second, aching to take her in his arms. But held himself. He could not help but note, however, with a momentary feeling of gladness—for her sake only—the first concrete sign of M'lissa's freedom from the tyrant who had ruled over her for 10 long years. For she had bought a necklace of beads—great marble-like beads. Black beads, to be sure; M'lissa would never do anything to offend convention—but—they were beads! Anathema, such things, to Hosea. And they looked, the Sheriff thought at that moment, beautiful on M'lissa's still white firm throat.

But she was speaking to him. Sadly.

"Yes, Bucy, Hosea died yest'day—'bout noon. I—I cremated him this mo'nin'—'zackly 'co'din' to his wishes. He died broke, Bucy—if it int'rests you any; he never had any of that money what people credited him with. In fact, I spent the last of his money—burnin' him up." Purely unconsciously she made a nervous gesture with her black-cotton-gloved hands that showed plainly what was in her subconscious mind: it was a gesture of washing—washing away from her life an era of pain and unhappiness. She continued explaining. "Then—then I left Southwest City, soon's thereafter as I could, on the M.S. and S.—and got into Janestown late this aft'noon. Mist' Cravey he fetched me on out. I told him to please go on this fur—so's I could tell you all 'bout it."

"Jup'ter Priest, M'lissa, I—I—I—"

"Yes, Bucy, I know what you want to say—and what you think. You think: Thank God M'lissa's free! Well I *am* free, Bucy. An' I know that you want to say that you love me and have b'en starved for me for—"

"Y-y-y-yes, M'lissa, that's right. I—I—I—I—"

She smiled sadly. "Pore Bucy! Abs'lutely the bravest and fearlessest man in the world—"

"No!" he retorted firmly. "No—"

"Yes," she echoed, equally firmly. "Afraid o' nothin'. So afraid o' nothin' that someday he's goin' to get famous all over again by doin' some fool reckless thing that's never been did befo' in arrestin' people. He's afraid o' nothin'. Except—tellin' a woman he loves her. So that sich woman—has to read it—all out of his eyes. But I honor you fur that, Bucy. An' right now it's the on'y way sich a thing could be handled. Fur I'm in widow's weeds an' all, now, Bucy—Death has struck!—and I got to do right. They's—they's consid'ations has to be lived up with. All that. But Bucy—"

"Yes, M'lissa?"

"Will you tell me all them things that 'uz tremblin' on yo're lips a minute ago—in 'bout a month?"

"Goddang it yes, I will, M'lissa. I—"

"That's all I want to know, Bucy. So I'll go on back now."

But she waited, in an odd uneasy manner.

The Sheriff knew she wanted to ask him something—or ask him about something. So he helped her.

"Yes, M'lissa?" he said kindly.

"Well, Bucy," she explained, "in sayin' Hosea died broke, I should oughter excep' th' one thing his estate consists of: th' cactus-leaf gold pin what you borried to show that woman. Anyway, Hosea, as it now seems, from th' will we found und'neath his pillow, lef' that pin to Southwest City's famous Jewelers Mooseum, who 'uz always eager to get it, 'count th' pin bein' 'purrently the on'y example of its kind whar a cactus leaf was act'ally did in gold—soft gold fur th' leaf an' hard gold fur the thorns. I talked, on th' long-distance phone, to Phil March, the Willis Creek town clerk, from Southwest City, right atter Hosea's death, an' Phil drew up all my estate papers fur me, and so, goin' through a while back, I stopped off, filed Hosea's will, filed my inventory consistin' o' that one pin, and signed it—an' cotched my letters of admin'stratorship an' all that—and now—ah—ah—we'll turn it over t' th' Mooseum, git their receipt fur it, an' then I'm—I'm clear with th' world." She waited expectantly.

The Sheriff was a fiery red—all over his face and neck an'd ears—and, worse, knew it.

"Th'—th' Mooseum," he hemmed, "wouldn't want—I 'spose—th' money equiv'lent fur the pin, o' co'se?"

"Indeed no!" she retorted, and with such firmness he was startled. "I talked to 'em there in town—an' they want it as a curoo. The quicker th' better. But who on earth, Bucy, 'd ever want t' give money fur th' foolish thing?"

"Hrmph—yes—of co'se. Well—uh—now—gosh, M'liss—what would they do to you ef'n you didn't have it?"

"Send me to jail, of co'se," she said quite simply. "Sence I've listed it as in my p'session—signed fur it—yet wouldn't have it to turn over. Yes, they'd nat'rally do to me th' same's they did to that feller in Chicago, who 'uz holdin' a brooch left to 'em—and gambled it away. Send me to jail. Fur contempt o' co'te. When the circuit co'te kivvers Willis Creek. At least send me there till I perduced th' pin. An' which, ef I didn't have it, I couldn't perduce it, could I?" She eyed Bucyrus Duckhouse gravely, queryingly.

"Yes, yes," nodded the Sheriff, musingly. "Yes. Seein's you've listed it, and receipted fur it. Hrmph? Yes." He stroked his chin fiercely.

But she was waiting. An expectant look on her face. And so he answered her, looking violently away and around, as for his other cat.

"I'll—I'll be fetchin' it over to you, M'liss—atter—hrmph—th' grievin' days air over. So's—so's you kin make good on Hosea's will 'ith them jew'ler fellers. Yes I—I got it—hrmph—the pin, yes—but so—so durned locked up jest now, under—under lock and key—practically under th' floor boar—that is, up above in the attic—rather, I mean, back inside th'—"

"That's all right, Bucy," she said with great haste. "Don't 'splain! I jest wanted to hear from yo're lips that ever'thing was all right. I was so'te of afraid, mebbe, that that woman wan't all she—but no, I wan't afraid o' nothin'."

"G-g-good," choked the Sheriff.

Now she spoke again.

"Well then, Bucy," she said with quiet dignity, "I reckon I *will* go on back now." She called down the road a short distance, "Yes, Mist' Cravey—I'm comin'."

And she was gone. Was climbing, a few seconds later, into the car. And it, now, was chugging down the road.

And the Sherif, with a sudden glance at his clock, whose hands were now at 20 minutes of 5, went back to his table.

And heaved now, aloud, the greatest of all the groans he had been heaving.

For not only would he soon—if not sooner!—have to tell M'lissa that he had been 4 kinds of a soft-headed half-wit and gotten her into a distressing snarl with the courts and the Jewelers Museum, but, on top of that, he himself possessed quite nothing in the world to buy back that damned $1000 "forged" check with! Not even his salary of $50 a month to the end of his term. Now but 4 months distant. And all of which salary he had drawn, in advance, to wipe off a debt of his own deceased father's which had come to light after many years.

And so now Jarg Hickey would get the $50 a month. And the distinction of being called "Sheriff Hickey," which, to Jarg, with his wealth and his tavern, meant more than anything in the world. While he, Buce Duckhouse would—if by some remote miracle of miracles he were not then doing the lockstep in Southwest City's Northern State Penitentiary—would be stranded in a locality where no work was available—a once-upon-a-time ex-Sheriff demoted, de-starred, because of crooked dealings—having, b'God, to fish for a living. Except that—the creeks in this part of the country, and the gullies, too, were all dried up today—and there was no fishing! And so—

Damn these cunning slickers from the city. Doubledamn all of 'em to he—

But right at this second the telephone on the table in front of the Sheriff rang. Rang so long and continuously, and without a break, that the Sheriff knew immediately that there was trouble—of some strange sort—in Willis Creek County!

CHAPTER IV

"WATCH THE ROAD!"

The Sheriff had the receiver of the phone to his ear in a minute; the transmitter to his lips.

"Sher'ff's off—" he began, in his most official voice, but that was quite as far as he got; for an immediate reply was literally pouring into his ear from that receiver.

"Duckhouse? Sheriff Bill Jeth speaking—yes, Jeth of Cedarville—listen, Duckhouse, the Cedarville Bank was just held up—by a gang o' four men—'bout 40 minutes ago—it's no more'n 32 minutes or so since the holdup that the robbers drove away—we've trailed 'em far's Perkins Junction—President Stoeffhaas of the bank is with me—also 8 citizens with shotguns—and we've found that the holdup gang has went onto the new Straightaway, and is headin' through f'r Willis Creek."

"What makes you think so, Jeth?" said Sheriff Duckhouse, pulling his broad belt to with his hand, then reaching, even as he talked, into his kitchen table drawer where, on arriving home, he had deposited his holstered .38.

"Because the lock's been blowed to smith'reens, Duckhouse, an' the gate's half ajar. I'm callin' right now from the phone in th' brick barrier pillar. They ev'dently didn't know nothin' 'bout a phone bein' in here."

"'S the key thar, onder the west aidge o' th' pillar cap, ag'in the gobs o' chewin' gum what—"

"Course! It was right where you told me an' Sheriff Gaines of Price County it would always be. In case of emergency. That's how I onlocked this here brick-faced door o' the pillar. I—"

"Now wait, Jeth!" And as the Sheriff talked he expertly hooked the holster of his .38 to his belt, and opened its flap for use. "How you know they hain't blowed th' lock f'r a stall, but went into the hills by Ol' Twistibus? Or doubled back 'long Carthage Road East? Or—hyar th' most impo'tent question fur me to axe hyar and now is this: 'zactly how fur ahind 'em air you?"

"No more, b'God, Duckhouse, than—than 'bout 15 minutes. At th' most. Except that we're all traveling in a car what's got both of its front tires shot! And can't poss'bly overtake 'em. They blew a gi-gantic hole in th' roadway shortly after roarin' away from the bank—an' killed the whole

Cedarville tel'phone system 'count the conduit crossing there—nary a car could git by—but my car, y'see—listen, Duckhouse, this's somethin' that can best be told you later. Jest now—"

"Take it easy, Jeth! If yo're that close ahind 'em—15 minutes!—ever'thing's in the bag—no matter *what* way they went. Even ef they're on th' Straightaway, it could be fully a half hour yet afore they'll even strike the mount'in. An' then they's still more Straightaway for 'em this side—a'most to this shack o' mine where I am right now—settin', b'God, right in their path! At least—but an'body git thar license number?"

"Hell—yes! 888,001; this state. And tain't likely they'll have no chance to switch it, since the license plate was nailed, folks say, by pow'rful strong nails to the back end of their vehic—but it's a stolen license plate, of course. For they made no effort to conceal it, folks say. Even had nary mud on any o' the figgers. 888,001."

"Shore it's stolen then," nodded Bucyrus Duckhouse. "888,001, eh? An' this state? Must be then, if it's nailed down so plumb tight as all that, that they ain't nary hopes fur 'em to throw no dust in nobody's—but hyar—what'r they trav-elin' in?—a 6-pass'nger?—flivver—"

"A truck. It's a—"

"A truck? Shucks! They cain't make no mo'n 50 in any truck! That puts 'em def'nitely full 45 minutes off yit. Now pipe down. We're 45 minutes to the good on 'em, I tell you. Now I want th' full facks. And the whole time-scheme, sence—"

"Okay—okay! Guess you're right about them bein' set for a while. Well, all I had to say an'way was that by good luck my car was parked beyond that godawful crater—I was in Doc Kinsey's gettin' my gout pre-scription changed, and my gouty foot re-wrapped—I heard the explosion, and I also see 'em roar past, from Doc's window, and knew they must a b'en a holdup—but they peppered hell outa my front tires as they roared past—well, I kep' waitin' for the town cars to come up, so's I could get a good fas' machine—like, say, Sam Turner's the hardware man's—then the fellers from town, Sam an' all, come up on foot—with shotguns—told me what that 'splosion was, and had did—and off we all went in this car, on flat front tires. Now, Duckhouse, we—"

"Now wait, Jeth! Take it easy. Ain't I settin' right hyar in them fellers' path? An' you know they ain't no way off the whole Straightaway, what-so-ever—onless a man kin fly!—and they ain't a way on earth to leave this road, neither—'twell it hits Southwest City road tother side Willis Creek—so take it easy. Now, fu'st of all, how—how you know they didn't blow the barr'er lock—f'r a stall—then back 'round and into Old Twistibus? Shorely they'd never a risked a ambush at Will—"

"Hell-fire, Duckhouse, don't you 'spose I checked on that myself before I called you? Even as we pulled up here, Paw Elum, ridin' on Maw Elum's bicycle, drove up too—and was able at least to let us know the gang never doubled back on Carthage Road East. So I made a quick call first—while the telephone girls were a-gettin' you—to make sure the gang *did* roar out onto th' Straightaway."

"Who'd you call?"

"I called the Wanties, who live in the north gullies, 'bout 2 mile from here. And—"

"And what'd they say?"

"They told me, without my even givin' 'em any de-scription, that they'd seen a battleship-grey bodied truck, with the words on it, in bright black-edged yellow, 'Transcontinental Trucking Company, Fast Freight,' bowl past, on the Straightaway above their heads, goin' 'bout 50 mile an hour—"

"Battleship-grey bodied truck, heh? Is that what the gang is usin'?"

"Right, Duckhouse. With that there identical letterin'. It's—"

"I know the truck—kind o' truck anyway. Have seed one makin' de-liveries in Janestown. It's a stolen truck a'most cert'nly. All right. I got the full de-scription. Go ah'id—but no, wait? Give me th' de-scription now o' the gang? How many gun-tossers in it?"

From the manner in which Tobias, at that instant, at the sound of the word "gun-tossers," sprang off the table and flew out of the door, it would seem that Tobias at least had sensed, in the very air, impending action and noise. Anathema both, to cats!

But Sheriff Jeth was talking.

"Goddamn it, Duckhouse," he was saying, "we shouldn't ought to waste time discussin'—but a'right. The driver and his helper, who pulled the ac-tual holdup, was in striped trucker's suits. Handsome duck drivin'—and a big thickheaded sort o' lunk helpin'. Two gunmen covered 'em from behind, each standin' on a hangin' angled iron step-like bolted t' th' chassis, and hangin' to a handgrip screwed into th' end piece o' the truck. Now that the getaway's been safely made, however, they've unbolted the hangin' steps so's that no kid, at some temp'rary slowdown, can hop up and travel along with 'em; and they'll be doin' their shootin'—if any!—from now on from the rear end. They—"

"How you know all that?"

"Because we found the hangin' angled steps, and the bolts, no more'n 1/8th mile from the junction here, layin' right in the road."

"Oh, yes, I see. An' you got things right, too. They don't want no snot-nose kids climbin' up ahind, at some slowdown, and maybe listenin' to some o' their plans. But now these here gunmen—they come out o' th' truck at th' time o' th'—"

"No. They was loafin' in town near the bank, waitin' the exact moment. One was a little yallerheaded guy; the other a scarfaced guy. They—"

"That's 'nough fur me. I got it all. Now go ah'id?"

"Well, the Wanties seen the truck bowl past 'em on the Straightaway above their heads no mor'n 'bout 5 minutes afore I called. The whole fambly was just pilin' into the house for a snack, at the time. And wondered what 'mer-gency could a-b'en up. Was all at the table talkin' 'bout it when I called up. So you see, Duckhouse, the gang and its truck *is* on th' Straightaway—even if they can't be seen a mile away from themselves in the mist o' this end. And—"

"Good! Goddanged good—ef you ask me? We got 'em! We—but hyar, what did they git? Shorely not the—"

But here a new voice came on the phone. A sort of thick German voice.

"Duckhouse? This is President Stoeffhaas—yes—of the bank. Listen, Duckhouse, those men got that box of gold that we were trustees for, and—"

"Good Christ!" ejaculated the Sheriff. "That hundred thou—"

"Yes, Duckhouse. It's—it's ruin for us! Our—our legal fees alone for being administrator of the will bequeathing that gold, would have been $7000. Duckhouse, we can't possibly get 'em—traveling as we are on flat front tires—but you maybe can—or at—at least can turn 'em back—now, Duckhouse—and I'm saying this in front of 8 witnesses—if you can turn that gang back alone, so that we can get 'em here—for Jeth has a machine gun—your reward will be $1000; and if you can get 'em, it'll—it'll be $2000."

"A—a thousand—if—if I turn 'em back?—two thousand if I—I get 'em?—it's a deal, Mist' Stoeffhaas—now you-all squat there, fur—"

A change of voices again. Sheriff Jeth was back on the wire. Duckhouse gave orders now like a general.

"Listen, Jeth, we-all—a-workin' together—have got them fellers in the bag. Leastways the way *I'm* goin' t' handle this! Yes, we have. But you squat right there, will you!"

"'Course we will. We got arms an' ammunition a-plenty even if we haven't a decent car. And me, though I'm pract'cally walkin', by God, on a pillow, I got a 1940 Tommy gun that—"

"Then squat right there—ahind an'thing an' ever'thing that'll give you protection. Them pillars'll be perfect. Yo're car, likewise. Rope or wire up that barr'er gate to that brick pillar—so that they can't get back 'thout at least rammin' it. We got 'em, Jeth! Fur I'll stop 'em this side th' mount'in ef—ef I have to blow 'em to hell—I'll—fact is, though, they're shore they've kilt all commun'cation—an' they'll turn tail immediately they find they're gittin' headed off—I may even have to chase 'em—but no, I won't work out o' my county, 'caze thar's a little 'ditional reward hyar fur—however, I'll drive 'em back, be shore o' that, so's you folks kin do what I'd like to do. Stick tight thar, now."

"We'll stick here tight, Duckhouse. We'll even be working on the tires meanwhile. Good luck."

"To hell 'ith luck! I only hope t' God I kin get 'em at a sartin p'int whar they *cain't* turn back! But I got an idea on *that*. Stick thar, now, 'caze I—I may be callin' back—thar—later. Fu'st of all, however, I'm goin' to check their prog'ess at—say—12-Mile P'int—that's a even one-third way to the mount'in—then I'll—"

Sheriff Bucyrus Duckhouse did not say what he was going to do. Indeed, he hung up. Rattled the phone. About 2 rattles—that was all—for service was speedy *this* day!

"Lucy, git me 'mediately the—the Billians' cottage—tother side th' mountain—no, no, the gulley Billianses—at 12-Mile P'int—then, w'ile yo're gettin' them, be gettin'—yes—Glos Mandivey—in the same gullies—at, I think, Glos is, at 12-Mile Pillar. Quick now. Bankrobbery—as yo' must know. Quick!"

It was amazing the speed with which the Sheriff was put onto the Billianses' cottage which lay just 12 miles this side of that east Straightaway barrier. The Sheriff recognized the unmistakable drawl of Job Billians who, though deaf, *could* hear through a telephone.

"Billians—this is Sher'ff Duckhouse—o' Willis Creek County—yes, Job—say listen, Job, have you folks seed an'thing go past, up thar on th' Straightaway, in the last few min—"

"Folks? Folks is all away, Sher'ff. To their folks—in Hustane County. So I'm takin' 'vannge o' they bein' gone, an' puttin' up a new backhouse. However, but 5—6 minutes ago, as I come 'round the side o' the house, to retrieve my hammer, what I'd lef' thar, I seed a grey-bodied truck with yaller letters, Transcontynental Something or other—two men in stripet jumpers in th' drivin' cab—"

"Okay, Job! That's 'nough."

"Wait, Sherif. I—I shook m' fist at 'em—befo' I went back to m' backhouse work—figurin' they had no right to be up thar. I—I even made motions like as if I was holdin' a telyphone receiver to m' ear—"

"Oh-oh? Showed 'em poss'bil'ties o' phone c'nnections what they hadn't de-stroyed! Now I wonder, will they try to talk their way through—or shoot it through? Or even, mebbe turn back, an'—good-by, Job."

The Sheriff was off, so far as Job Billians was concerned, but was on—by the expert work of Miss Lucy Higgins—to no less than Glos Mandivey, lone widower. Indeed, the Sheriff' recognized Mandivey's high-pitched voice.

"Sher'ff' Duckhouse, Mandivey. Say—has an'thing passed yo're place yit? Up on th' Straightaway? Yo're the last poss'-ble place I kin find out anyth—"

"On the Straightaway, Sher'ff?" piped Glos Mandivey. "Why, yes. Yes. I b'en hoein' in back the house, an' jest as I come 'round to whet my hoe, a few minutes back, I see a circus wagon a-bowlin' along up thar, an' as she hit a pebble or so'thin' she bounced, an' the critter inside give a roar like all get-out. A lion—ef you ast me! God, it skeered hell out'n me. Lions—lions kin leap down long distances—even 's much as the 20 feet from the Straightaway to the gullies hyar—an' ef that circus wagon should tip over, so I figgered, it—well, I skun 'medi't'ly fur my cellar—whar I b'en 'twell yo' jest rung."

"And seed no more," grumped the Sheriff. "Okay!" He hung up. Without even bothering to put on his brown coat, he leaned across the table, hurriedly unlocked that overhanging powerful metal cabinet, and almost into his arms tumbled the well-oiled machine gun in which, at this very moment, a strip of cartridges was in place—all in readiness. Gun in arms, he toted it through the doorway, into the seat of his high-powered Durlex-Spinay racer—pointed conveniently mountainward!—and climbed into the seat itself.

"God," he was musing, "they're both on th' Straightaway—Craney an' them gangsters—one ah'id o' the other—yes!—but which? This *is* a complycation—an' how!" His engine roared into action. "Wa-all, I hope nothin' happens to Craney an' his cat! Fur—but that's *his* lookout now, I reckon. Fur my job now is goin' to be—at the very leas'—t' turn them fellers back! Fur a thousand dollars is wu'th the havin'. An' how! And two thousand—good God!—"

And throwing in his clutch, he shot forward, at high speed, toward Smoky Ridge, 15 miles distant—Smoky Ridge and the west Tunnel entrance, which, by the grace of God, was in Willis Creek County! And where—as he happened to know—he had the actual capture of this gang in the palm of his hand—*if* and providing he got there first!

CHAPTER V

SPEED!

The Sheriff, roaring up the lonely sun-baked roadway at almost his very topmost speed, the entire ribbon of dirt his alone, because of the non-existence of habitations between his place and Smoky Ridge—hence, no vehicles—and hence, no pedestrians!—kept his eyes grimly on the line of way stretching ahead of him. Not, however, because he had any qualms whatsoever that his quarry, sighting him, might turn out, and detour via the very countryside about him. For that was a thing utterly impossible; since the road here, all the way to where it became literally fused to the end of that part of the Straightaway lying this side of the mountain, was hemmed in, each side, by a deep trough that once, in the long ago, had been a ditch, emptying into the gullies farther on; but both ditches now permanently dried out. No machine without, perhaps, caterpillar treads—and wings to boot!—could leave *this* roadway between his oncoming car and that mountain; and, did it do so by a miracle, it would have but found itself on rocky, hillocky terrain over which, a quarter mile back of the road each side—and parallel to the road—ran a small continuous ridge so steep and precipitous that a car, to get over either ridge, would have had to be literally lifted over by the Dirigible Eckener! No, there was no chance whatsoever to leave that Straightaway crossing the west lowlands—and which very Straightaway end—marked by a light chain suspended from two pillars—was rushing toward him.

Indeed, the blazing, though now-reddening sun at the Sherif's back along the road, about $^2/_3$'s the way to the horizon at this still very bright hour of close on to 5, gave the Sheriff all the advantage; he doubted very much whether any vehicle coming toward him could see him anywhere as near—as quickly—or as well—as he could see it. At least in time!

The fusion between dead-end roadway and Straightaway end was abrupt indeed! The land, each side of the fused roadways, came to a precipitous stop—simply broke, and looked down now into the gulley bottom; the two ridges that had been running parallel to the roadway also broke off abruptly—and became space; the two ditches, which in the long ago splashingly poured water down into the gullies, broke off, too—all so abruptly that, had any luckless driver—prior to the days of the Straightaway—ever essayed to keep on driving at high speed, from that point, he would have volplaned into Kingdom Come! As it was, the pillar-supported Straightaway literally seized from the road its duties, and seemed to proclaim that level was going to be maintained along here, even if Uncle Sam had spent the whole Treasury at Washington, D.C.!

Across the road-Straightaway junction hung a light chain, supported by two red brick pillars each side, a sign, hanging from its pendent are, reading *"No Thoroughfare."* The Sheriff did not even have to get out of his car to get this out of his way. He had slowed down, close to the rightward pillar, to nose up against the chain. He merely leaned out over the side of his car, unhooked the chain; its sagging weight dragged it out of the road in front of him—and he was off again. Of no utility that chain, he knew, even to hook up again, as it could be rammed—snapped—by anything.

Now his car was purring—and, at the same time, zooming like a bullet!—over the fine smooth highway, the while he cast only the slightest of occasional glances down, over the low concrete guard wall, to the extensive lowlands far below, all of which had never yet dried out properly, underneath their topmost layer, for human habitation. Though of mist or haze there was not the slightest trace. He forced his car up a bit faster. For that was a bare and cheerless terrain down there, he well knew—and one from which—if a man were shot in a gun battle, and left dying on this stretch of highway—not a scintilla of help could be summoned. Whereas, at the mountain was a phone—a phone which—

And now that very mountain, Smoky Ridge, far up ahead of him, began to definitely evolve from a low brown blur, covered by a blue-black haze, against the bright sky, into a mountain—of sorts. The very great black hole in the brown rock, marking the tunnel, and visible for some reason as such in the brilliant sunlight falling there, grew, implacably, before the Sheriff's very squinted eyes, like the expanding shutter-hole of a camera. The pile of coruscating green broken rock at the right side of the road, as it faced him, dumped there some time back for later—and probably long later!—ornamental facing of that tunnel mouth, was growing too, from an irregular greenish patch, to a definite jumble of rocks. While the red brick pillar, around which, and beyond which, those rocks had been dumped—and which pillar contained a phone!—commenced to materialize out of the greenish blur in the form of a narrow bright red perfect oblong.

Now he was there! Shooting his car up as close to that pillar—and that heap of broken rocks—as he could. To make all—car, pillar, rocks—a continuous breastworks of sorts—for a running battle—if such was to be.

Of nervousness, at this moment, Sheriff Bucyrus Duckhouse had absolutely none whatsover! Indeed, the very call of battle was making his nostrils actually distend. And any unease he had had—concerning purely certain elements of what he had figured to do—was gone completely. For he had made it! Made a vantage point—and a telephone wire!—from which, with his loaded and ready machine gun, he was king of the situation. He sensed, however, that he had an extremely short time—perhaps minutes at most—to do what he had to do; indeed, he knew it—as he jerked out his silver turnip, threw a single glance at it, and saw that its hands stood at 5:16. Now, with the machine gun in his arms he was hopping out. Leaving the very car door open, to save seconds. He lugged the gun, cartridge belt flopping, up onto the rocks to exactly where the several-foot-long crest of the pile was—some 6 feet from the brick pillar. Shoving away, and down on the farther slope, one large rock that helped to make up that crest, a natural yet perfect slot was left; and into that slot, with a satisfied grunt, he dropped the machine gun. Not entirely satisfied, however, he poised an additional rock each side of the machine gun. Making it relatively to lie in a deeper slot yet! Now it was perfect. He dropped down—as best he could—on all fours—sighted his gun roughly from behind that crest—tossed a few rocks out from under his torso—kicked a couple more away with a heel—nudged one away that was too close to his elbow—and lo!—he now had a perfect bumpless slope of rocks on which to lie—to sight his gun—to sight his gun, indeed, against that very tunnel mouth and the 20 feet or so of glistening roadway between it and his position. He licked his lips eagerly, hungrily. Perfect! Come on—the whole German army!

He was already on his belly, flat on that prepared slope, beautifully and completely covered by the rising crest of rocks in front of him, yet withal able to see everything—through chinks—crannies galore—between the poorly piled topmost rocks. Jerking his hat off, he sighted his gun— then manipulated it lovingly in its perfect emplacement. It was beautifully swingable, side to side—perfectly tiltable, up and down—and its operator shielded from any and all shots that might come from roadway or tunnel mouth. The lust of battle that was in the Sheriff's soul at this minute was such that personally he would like to have had it out in the open—shot for shot. Such goddanged sneakin' methods as this were low'rn, b'God, than a nigger's heel. But—there was M'lissa now—at long last!—and there was that other hateful factor that always haunted him day and night: that some-day some louse of a city gunman might get the opportunity of bragging, in some underworld big-town hangout, that he had killed a small-town cop. And the Sheriff, being a sensitive soul, was willing to lean over a long ways backward to prevent *that!*

He lay there now, the hot red lowering sun beating fiercely against his left cheek—as well as against his left forearm whose fingers were loosely holding the machine gun's handle-block—licking his lips appreciatively.

He could feel his silver turnip under his ribs, and so proceeded to time matters again—though without actually rising up on all fours and seesawing it out, lest those gangsters, rolling perhaps quite unexpectedly out of that tunnel, might spray his spine with lead—and investigate afterward! An' what a disgrace that'd be! Instead, lying flat and heavily on the timepiece, he managed to work it forth from the somewhat tight pocket which obdurately held it, and transferred it adroitly to his looser right hip pocket, but with a careful glance downward of himself at it as he did so. 5:21! He glanced lovingly at that brick pillar, too, some half-dozen feet to his left—and to which he had the key—and wished he had time to call the posse waiting at the other end of this Straightaway—and tell them to start counting dead gangsters on their fingers—but, as in the case of the open and clumsy withdrawal of his timepiece which he had avoided, he dared not create a setup that might ultimately be tallied as "Dead Sheriffs…1." Not yet, anyway!

With immense satisfaction he knew that when this gang rolled out of this tunnel, they'd have to come mighty slowly—because of the huge curve which lay back of that 25 feet or so of straight approach to the tunnel mouth; indeed, he himself, able, by turning his head properly, to face that tunnel mouth, could not, right now, see further back in it than that 25 feet. Because of the further curve setting abruptly in—and the darkness back where it did set in. And, with greater satisfaction yet, he knew that, coming out of that tunnel, those gangsters practically couldn't turn about! And if they tried—on sight of his standing empty car—and the sound of his "halt," which he *did* intend to render them!—to leap forward into high, he knew he'd have that truck looking like a traveling cheesebox with these steelnosed bullets; the drivers themselves likewise perforated through but two thicknesses of wooden truck wall—all the tires, bar none, flat; indeed, he could visualize the truck, driven by dead or wounded men, catapulting over the very low guard wall into the gulley. In which case he'd have 'em all!—for if any one so much as crawled out from that wreckage, gun in hand—he, The Sheriff, up there on the high road above that man's head, with his machine gun—awrr—too easy! Too—

Thus, nevertheless, as he lay there and waited, the quarter minutes ticking away, he built his plans, and efficiently too.

He even rehearsed the exact degree of the palaver he would hold with them when, at sight of that machine gun, and his yell of "halt," and perhaps an admonishing half a dozen bullets spitting harmlessly into the macadam, they stopped dead—crouched in their seat—hands trying to get to guns. For slowly the idea was seeping into him that to drive into Willis Creek with four bankrobbers lying on their faces, with their hands bound behind them—for there was rope a-plenty in the car!—and their ankles wired together—for there was some wire and a wirecutters too!—was, in the face of a certain $2000 reward earned thereby, worth more than $500 additional reward available for potting one—toward the re-election of one, Bucyrus

Duckhouse. Such a colorful performance as that might even make the papers all over the world, an'—

He took another glance at his watch, looking down and along himself toward his hip pocket and the hand which held the turnip partly forth from its new site.

5:24!

He slid the heavy silver timepiece back in without varying his position a millimeter.

But now, suddenly, the resonant air of the tunnel mouth became a font of music—a gay whistle was tromboning out of it—a lilting air that bespoke Circus—circuses all over the world! And almost before the Sheriff had tightened his finger on the trigger of his machine gun—though frowningly—the whistle took on, with itself, a rumbling, crunching sound—tires grinding against small unswept particles of gravel.

And almost before the Sheriff had had time to put 2 and 2 together—and realize what might be happening—a resplendent red-and-gilt circus wagon—one headlight burning at half-brilliance, evidently for guidance back in the gloom—its driver lolling in the short squatty open cab plastered against the garish front end of the circus wagon—the gay whistler himself, in fact, dressed in short-sleeved green flannel shirt, red-edged black trousers buckled into shin-high thong-laced yellow cowhide boots, and Australian-like grey felt hat with a side turn to the brim—came rolling forth. Tucked under his arm—and which evidently he had been looking over somewhere back on the other side of the tunnel—was a bright crimson book—though the thing that really struck the Sheriff most forcibly at this moment was, strangely enough, the short bullwhip hanging from the driver's side—of all things!— a bullwhip—for a driver of a motorized vehicle!

The whistle had stopped dead. The lower jaw of the driver had fallen open. For he could not fail to see the machine gun covering the roadway. He had, indeed, even drawn to a complete stop—a stop so sudden that it swung his body forward, momentarily, out over his driving wheel. So sudden, indeed, that two-thirds only of his vehicle protruded from the tunnel, and one-third remained within.

And thus was the bizarre manner of arrival in Willis Creek County of one, J. Craney, bound for points west!

CHAPTER VI

DISCUSSION ANENT 4 MEN IN A GREY TRUCK!

The Sheriff's head was already above the crest of rocks. And he was gesticulating violently, even as he was blinking a bit, too, because of the manner in which some of the rays of the low sun were being reflected almost straight at him from the bright gilt-tipped convexities in the intricate relief-work on the wagon's front, showing at both sides of, and above, the black cab. He was shouting as he gesticulated.

"Craney—it's me!—I'm—"

"Why—you're Sheriff Duckhouse—who I was just talk-in' with," the other called out helplessly, over the short bridge of space. "I rec'nize your voice—and then—then there's that shirt o' yours! But what—what in hell's bells, Sheriff, is goin' on he—"

"Draw over thisaway, Craney, will yo'?—I got to stick right whar I am—nose yo're machine—ef'n you kin do it—ag'in these rocks hyar—but to my lef'—so's I kin ask yo' a few things, an' you'll be cl'ar o' that tunnel mouth. Hurry now, man. Hurry!"

The other, obviously not lost to the tense tone in the Sheriff's voice, manipulated his pedals and wheel skillfully. Turned abruptly at almost right angles, as he drove out of the tunnel, and nosed up to the very further edge of the rock-pile base, his vehicle now at right angles to the road width, its front practically bridging the space between the Sheriff's left elbow and the brick pillar; the driver looking down on the Sheriff now from a convenient point only 6 feet off. This position brought the machine not only completely out of the way of the tunnel mouth—but out of the entire area in front thereof. The Sheriff, with a hasty glance rightward, saw that he had his vital area completely covered again. For good measure, he manipulated his machine-gun handle block again, found that he could swing the weapon easily leftward, and entirely past the waiting red-and-gilt wagon and, as before, cover the entire roadway almost as far as the eye could see. He brought it back to its original position. But now the driver of that vehicle facing him was speaking across the 6 feet or so of vertical and horizontal space separating them.

"What—in—hell's bells," the latter essayed to say, half jocularly, and then—suddenly: "Sa-a-y—are you—by any chance—gunnin' for a party o' 5 men travelin' in a grey tru—"

But at this juncture a low rumbling throaty growl inside the vehicle rose to an ominous pitch.

"Quiet, girl—quiet!" the man in the cab said, turning completely about to peer through some crack or something. And, throwing a look back to the Sheriff', added explanatorily: "Stoppin' dead—after you've been clippin' along right lively—gets these cat-critters all alarmed!"

The growl had obviously been allayed by his words. He faced the Sheriff again. Expectantly. And the latter at last explained his own strange position.

"I *am* waitin' for 4 men, Craney," the Sheriff said. "Which you now make to be 5 men. But 't must be the same party; they must a had a fifth— an'way, yo're ev'dently the one man who kin tell me e'zackly whar they—"

"Are they ridin'," the other asked, "in a Transcont'nental Truckin' Company truck? With yellow—"

"Yes, yes," said the Sheriff. "But le's not waste time—"

"Take it easy, then, Sheriff," cautioned the other. "They're full 10 minutes behind me. Fully so—if not more. 'Count of a wheel-changin'—or mebbe a tire-changin'—they was doing. So—"

"Full 10 minutes, eh? Good! You passed 'em then, Craney?"

"Yes—sure. They musta been the guys who jimmied your barr'er lock. For when I drove up there, 'bout an hour—or a little more'n an hour ago— the barr'er was 'way open. An'—"

"You didn't have to use the key, then?"

"Hell, no, Sheriff! I simply rode right in. Leavin' it, however, the way 'twas. We-ell—you're layin' for 'em for *that,* eh? Well—"

"Not in a pig's eye," grunted the Sheriff. "I'm—but listen—give me the full de—what's that?"

For the other was holding up a bright scarlet book.

"Your book—which I'm fetchin' you; but it's only a—"

"Ne' mind the book this second. Tell me what them fellers was doin', and ezackly whar you passed 'em?"

The Sheriff was tense; but the answer—as was to eventuate a second later—which was to emanate from this vehicle which was carrying one, J. Craney—of points many and various—out of Smoky Ridge Mountain, at 5:25 in the afternoon—and which said Craney was even at this instant mopping off a dusty wet forehead with a soiled bandanna handkerchief—was to contain reassuring information to one, Bucyrus Duckhouse!

"Oh, I can't tell you exactly where I passed 'em, Sheriff," the man on the seat was saying promptly. "For all that terr'tory under the highway looked 'bout the same to me. But 'twas about 10 full minutes back o' the tunnel, accordin' to my drivin' speed. Which, because I was traveling too leisurely,

I'd jest shoved up. The driver and his helper—fellers in striped clothin'—had jest took a wheel off, to do something to it." He frowned speculatively. Though the bandanna that had just wiped Mr. J. Craney's forehead, and had been restored to a pocket, was not part of this picture, at the second, the picture was by no means devoid of such!—for the Sheriff was withdrawing from his own pocket the biggest, reddest bandanna that probably had ever been seen in Willis Creek County. Was wiping his own forehead off for the first time. The brows of the man in the driver's seat rose almost enviously. He went on, however, answering the Sheriff's question. "The two fellers in striped clothing," he continued, "had took the wheel off to—I guess—fix a tire. Though damned if I know exactly. An old feller with grey hair, lookin' a bit jittered, leaned against the end o' th' truck. One feller—a pock-marked little snot with yaller hair—was stationed down the road from the stalled truck about 30 feet; and another, a scar-faced feller looking like a dago, up the road th' same distance."

"Coverin'! They look at you hard?"

"Did they! Bad actors—if you ask me. For—quiet, girl—" for a low impatient growl was emanating from inside the vehicle.

"Didn't try to stop you, eh?" the Sheriff was continuing.

"No. They kep' their free hands—the ones which didn't hold watches—kinda near their hips like as if—but they just sized me up, with black looks—I give 'em a cheerful flirt of my hands, like, meaning 'Howdy, boys'—and rolled on. If I'm any judge o' repair work—and standard reasons for takin' a wheel off!—I calculate that right now they're only screwin' back the nut on that wheel!"

"Well," commented the Sheriff significantly, "we've used up 2 o' that there 10 minutes gassin'." He gazed longingly up and along the vehicle, then at the tunnel mouth; then at the vehicle again. "I'd shore like to hop up there 'ith you, and take a gander at that cat and her kittens, through that crack or whatever that you jest looked through—but t'would jest be, then an' there, that at that very moment them feller's 'd roll out yander tunnel—and where the hell'd I be?—fur stoppin' 'em' Blocked co'pletely off'n 'em. No, I—"

"They're 10 minutes back, I tell you," assured the other.

"Yeah," observed the Sheriff troubledly, "but they may ha' put that wheel back on a leetle sooner'n yo' think—an' they may have jest burned up th' road atter they did start up—no, I cain't resk it."

"You're the doctor," said the other. "Anyway—catch!"

"Ca— oh, the book—yes!—"

The Sheriff caught it deftly as it was tossed to him. Saw that it held black Chinese-like letters on its cover that read *The Way Out*. The other was speaking.

"But 'tain't a novel, Sheriff; it's jest a c'llection o' Chinee wisdom—proverbs!—from Chiny's ancient days—'sposed to be the answer to all questions in the Universe."

"Nuts!" barked the Sheriff. "Fur how could ancient wisd— but skip it. Now listen, Craney, you better pull th' hell out o' here now. Them fellers is bankrobbers, an'—"

"Bankrobbers? The—hell!" The driver gazed back fascinatedly at that tunnel mouth which had just been announced to be a possible source that might any minute vomit forth bankrobbers. Then looked helplessly at the Sheriff. "S-aay—shall I git down there with you?—you got a extry gun?—you—"

"No."

And the Sheriff swallowed hard. At the picture of having to take help—after he had accomplished the most perfect gang-trapping setup in all history. Though part of his swallowing was at the picture of dividing either one or two sweet thousand dollars two ways, with a man who had risked his fool life. Indeed, he put a stop to that rapidly!

"No, I—I cain't be 'sponsible for you. Yo' git away from hyar, now. Ef'n you wan't killed yo'rese'f, yo're cat and all her kittens is shore to be. And mebbe I'd have to spend all my rewar—hrmph—salary—t' pay for their deaths. Now you git on as fast as you kin. That's what you kin do fer me."

"But Jesus, Sheriff—"

"Don't Jesus me," snapped the Sheriff. "Git, and keep gittin'! I—I know my business. An' 'zackly what to do in a gun battle. Yo'd on'y be the extry cook to spoil the broth. Ten minutes, yo' say, ef they was changin' a tire—but that makes it now 6 minutes—go now, Craney—Jim—please—"

"Okay, Sheriff." The other seemed a bit hurt. "You're the doctor—in your own county. Thanks for ever'thing."

"That's a'right," said the Sherift "But havin' let you through, I—I want to git you through safe. Shove now, feller!"

The other had his foot on one pedal, he had started his engine to purring; he was ready, indeed, to draw out backward and turn.

"Attaboy!" urged the Sheriff, nervously watching the vehicle and the tunnel mouth both at the same time. "Go like hell when you start up the road—to git out'n bullet range—in case—"

"Okay." The machine was drawing out backward; nosed to a stop. The driver was swinging his great wheel.

"Cra— Jim, a minute," admonished the Sheriff. The wheel turning stopped. "You say them fellers—both up road an' down road o' the stalled truck—had watches—in their hands?"

"Right."

"Why?"

"I dunno."

"But why should—say, listen—was that a bonyfide repair job they was doin'—or was it maybe a stall to let so'thin—anythin'—they sensed was back of 'em, pass 'em?"

"Search me! But since you speak of it, it kinda did look like that at that. I seen no tools. Then, anyway. Fact is, if they was watchin' watches—but I give up."

"So do I! But git on now, old man—and fast."

The bullwhip-equipped driver of a 20th-century automotive vehicle completed the turning of his wheel. Looked helplessly back at the Sheriff. Whose eyes were literally riveted now on that tunnel mouth. The engine came on full speed; the red-and-gilt wagon drove away, putting on speed as it departed.

The Sheriff could not, of course, see the puzzled look that, at this very minute, was on the face of Craney who but a short while back had been contemplating him from the short distance of 6 or 7 feet. A Craney who was puzzled deeply because an offer of help to capture 5 bankrobbers had been stoutly, crudely, firmly refused. Nor could the Sheriff see the gesture of one hand made by the same Craney which said "Well, it isn't my funeral!"

Indeed the Sheriff could not have seen anything at this identical second, for he was again sneaking a quick look at his watch, and ending the time to be now 5:33.

In fact, the Sheriff, after the departing machine had vanished well up the road, the gold and black of its Federal interstate license plate fusing swiftly into the gilt-and-red substance in which it had been tacked or set, gave vent to but two words. And which were:

"Thank—God!"

To which, a quarter second later, he added fervently: "M' reward— whatever it's t' be—is safe now. Think of havin' to divide—"

He stopped in his words. Crawled flatter than ever. Convinced, at that second, that he heard, 'way inside the tunnel, from its other end, sounds— faint sounds—sounds that might have been wheels rolling against gravel dust—or echoic resonances thereof—though it all might, he knew, be but the buzz of some curious evening insect a few feet back of his ears—the chirrup of a too early cricket. He cocked those ears, however, waiting to hear the rising din of the battleship-grey truck rumbling through.

And he was still waiting thus—one full hour later!—the sun now very close to the horizon—when he realized, at last, that the truck, its bankrobbing crew alarmed because of that circus wagon thar had passed them, had turned back—was already in the hands of Jeth and his posse—and that he, Bucyrus Duckhouse, had lost the credit of even turning the gang back—and thus winning $1000.

And reasonably convinced now that nothing, at this late though still bright hour, was going to emanate from that tunnel mouth, he prepared—on a forlorn chance—to call on the phone that lay inside that brick pillar but 5 feet from his left elbow.

CHAPTER VII

ACCUSATION—COUNTER-ACCUSATION

Keeping his eye ever on that tunnel mouth—just on general principles!—the Sheriff rose to his hands and knees—to his feet—moved sidewise to that red brick pillar—opened, with the key that was on the ring of keys in his trousers pocket, the brick-end faced door in that pillar, and seized the phone that stood on a shelf inside. And reflecting right here that nothing was certain in this Universe, and comparing the two possible positions—in back of that pillar—and behind that machine gun—he carried the phone, its long flexible cord letting out after it, back to his original position, where, but squatting now, he raised the receiver.

Immediate answer came when he did. It was Lucy Higgins, the Willis Creek County operator.

"Give me th' East Straight'way end phone, Lucy—quick!"

"Yes, Sher'ff." A clicking, and an immediate answer—in, of all things, the eager voice of Sheriff Bill Jeth.

"Duckhouse?" the latter said. "Yo're gal told me 'twas you. I 'spose you've captured 'em all?"

"Captured—'em all?" echoed Bucyrus Duckhouse, sinking to a more stable position on his heels. "Captured 'em?" he repeated. "Yo' mean—they ain't—back, yit?"

"Back? Back where? Hell no! We're all still posted here at the barr'er—gate wired an' all—an'—"

"Jup'ter Priest!" Sheriff Duckhouse ejaculated. "Then—then it means they're on the elyvated highway yit—and we got 'em penned in atween us."

"You mean, Duckhouse, they ain't come up yet—or through—at all?" queried the other county police officer.

"Hell—no! I b'en hyar—an' I'm talkin' from the west-tunnel-end pillar phone—I b'en hyar practically ever sence I got yo're call. With my machine gun all set in position to gun 'em. And—listen, Jeth, they cain't get rid o' their truck at all—their gold truck, as 'tis!—but they can escape—yes—they kin shin down one of the pill—— listen, Jeth, I'm all alone—but got my machine gun set up in a de luxe po-sition from w'ich I could capture the whole German army—now ef you got a posse—but yo're car is flatted, ain't it?"

"No more, Duckhouse. Two boys b'en workin' on it. The front tires has jest now been rizzed with a handpump. We kin git an'where."

"The hell you say! And all o' yo' air armed, yo' say?"

"Hell, yes. We—"

"Well then we're sot! We got 'em atween us. And got two full hours of danged good daylight yet, to boot! Now I'll gu'rantee they'll never pass, whar my gun is set up, alive—ef you kin gently drive 'em—urge 'em—by lots o' noise an' whistlin' and yellin'—but p'tic'ly a display o' force!—on to drive th'ough to me—on this side the monnt'in. I—"

"Hell, Duckhouse, that's easy. They know *we're* a posse—and you—I don't know what they know 'bout you. Okay. We're startin' 'long the Straightaway now—so's I kin make time, I'll take on'y 5 men with me in the car—and leave four to squat here at the barr'er so's to—but listen—where 'long there is your gun set up?—listen—don't unsheath yo're art'llery till you know abs'lutely what you're shootin' at. For—"

"D' you think I'm a goddanged fool?" grumped Sheriff Bucyrus Duck-house, forgetting in his own ire to say *where* his gun was set up. "Do you think—bah!" he broke off disgustedly. "Listen, Jeth, you drive 'em on th'ough—and I'll—ne' mind what I'll do—you-all drive 'em th'ough."

"And—how!" said Jeth, the sound of his teeth clicking together coming through the phone.

It was a mutual hang-up. Though so precipitate that Bill Jeth had failed to learn whether that machine gun was set up a mile from the mountain—two miles—or even only a half mile! Nevertheless, with great satisfaction Bucyrus Duck-house regained his position next his machine gun—in actuality but 22 feet from that mountain. On his belly again.

And waited.

Waited, while the minutes drove inexorably by.

And knowing well that splendid highspeed car that Jeth of Cedarville had—and the fact that its front tires had been put back into commission—Sheriff Duckhouse was almost able to follow, in his mind's eye, the events that now were taking place on the other side of the mountain, miles away.

The big green car, one man probably riding on each of its running boards, was speeding, bounding toward the mountain—though probably, at this second, not even glimpsing yet the crew of vicious gangsters who were waiting for—but waiting for what? Nightfall? Or a decision between themselves—whether to go ahead—or turn back? Or—

Sheriff Duckhouse looked at his watch. Twenty to 7, now! The red ball of the sun, thanks to daylight-saving time, was not even fully half below the horizon now. The sky above him was bright and cloudless; would be a font of powerful daylight for at least an hour and a half yet.

He continued to wait. Visualizing events, the other side of the mountain, as best he could.

Now—perhaps now, anyway!—the big green car, by now out of the semi-misty belt of the East Straightaway east end, had sighted the gangster mob—a mile or so away. And, of course—was being sighted itself—for exactly what it was: an armed posse! Probably it was slowing a bit now—in accordance with the plan—but putting on a great show of noise—whistling—yelling—banging. And the cowardly rats ahead of it, skulking there at some point of the highway above the lonely lowlands, their truck still turned toward the mountain, and unknowing quite that they were hemmed in by telephones in cunning brick pillars each side of where they stood, were hopping into their truck—were stepping on the gas; or if, on the other hand, their truck had for some reason been turned about, meanwhile, they were turning it about again—to head for the mountain full speed!

The minutes ticked by.

He looked at his watch again.

4 o'clock!

Quarry—and pursuers—must both by now be close to the mountain. Since quarry had not yet emerged—and pursuers themselves must be about there. The quarry no doubt at this moment was being urged closer to—if not into the mountain. Bucyrus Duckhouse wished devoutly he too could go in—from this end—and help. But, he realized also, he was the only living soul to cut off flight completely west of the mountain.

And besides—a dead bankrobber was still worth $500 on this side of that hulk of brown stone; nothing on the other side; and probably nothing within—thanks to the fact that this particular mountain face was said to mark the county boundary.

So here he must stand.

More minutes passed. He strained his ears. Had the quarry wormed into the mountain?—into the very black hole that constituted the tunnel?—and were making a stand of it? With the posse afraid to go in after it? That—that wasn't like Bill Jeth. Nor the undoubtedly furious citizens he had with him. Who certainly had lights to flash ahead over such of the curve as was untenanted; guns to fire—if so much as one foot hove into that arc of curve.

Bucyrus Duckhouse wondered.

But suddenly he heard men's voices—voices which, resonating peculiarly, were yet curiously dampened; their pitch indicated they were yells, and were accompanied by shrill whistlings of the kind made by putting two fingers in a mouth—there were even hollow but strident bangings of gun barrels, or monkey wrenches, against tin pans or something—now he even heard *wah-wah-wah-hoo* yells such as Comanche Indians gave out—now the whole medley of sounds was louder—and catapulting hornlike out of the tunnel mouth—the posse!—but where?—where was the—

Louder and still more resonant grew the medley of sounds. It grew to a din that—

But now, Bucyrus Duckhouse, hand gripped on his machine-gun handle block, saw, rounding some bend back in the tunnel, a pack of men, armed with shotguns—two were obviously carrying brilliant flashlight torches, held pointed ahead of themselves, for the reflectors of the torches burned through the tunnel gloom like locomotive headlights—now came into view, in someone's hand, a flaming torch, the clouds of oily smoke emanating from it showing that it had been made by tying oil-soaked rags in a knob around the end of a long wooden-handled monkey wrench—the entire pack were whistling—yelling—banging on metal objects of some sort—tramping forward all in unison. All on foot. No car whatsoever.

But as they emerged out of the blackness entirely, Bucyrus Duckhouse saw Sheriff Bill Jeth, a stocky short man with red hair, in a wallpaper-like shirt—Jeth was limping apparently painfully on a foot bound up in gauze so that it looked like a pillow—Bucyrus Duckhouse saw even Hans Stoeffhaas, the Cedarville banker, big of belly, with moonlike face, with square black beard, carrying a .45 in each pudgy hand!

Sheriff Duckhouse rose—from behind the rocks.

"Here—Jeth!—folks!—here I am!"

The Sheriff of Cedarville County stood there, at the very portal of the tunnel, a light modern machine gun in his two hands, his somewhat sallow face puzzled.

"Good—Christ!—so it's *here you* were stationed, Duckhouse?—we b'lieved 'twas maybe a quarter mile down, or we'd never have barged out of here like—but—but here we are—and where—where is the truck?"

Bucyrus Duckhouse, who, meanwhile, had been clambering up over the rocks and down on the other side, felt as though he had collided head on with Bill Jeth's last words.

"Truck?" Sheriff Duckhouse ejaculated, stopping dead in his tracks. "Truck?" he repeated. "Why—goddang it—no truck—no truck came out'n this mountain. No—"

"No truck—came out o' this mountain?" There were 5 men now, including the fat-bellied Stoeffhaas, clustering about Jeth's shoulders. Two wore hickory shirts like Bucyrus Duckhouse himself, two wore white collars, two carried brand-new tin dishpans, the explanation for such implements—as well as perhaps the electric torches—being provided by the presence of still another freckled lanky individual, Sam Turner, the hardware man, who must have been actually dusting stock at the moment of the bank robbery. All, without exception, had tense strained faces. Jeth was continuing. To the man now facing him across but 7 or 8 feet of space.

"Why, goddamn it, Duckhouse, do you take us for—"

But here the fat-bellied bank president with the square black beard spoke up. Raspingly. And with a touch of German gutturalness.

"No truck can leap off uf a raised highway ant disappear. So that truck must—listen, Duckhouse, do you mean to tell us that you'fe gone crooked. If—"

"Crooked?" ejaculated Bucyrus Duckhouse. "What the—no, by God, I hain't crooked—and you know it—what th' hell you mean by say—"

"I mean," rasped the President angrily, shifting his two .45's to one hand, and pointing a pudgy finger at Bucyrus Duckhouse, "that those fellows scooped up $2000 in bank-notes when they lugged out that gold—and by God, they've—"

"Now—now stop that! I never let them fellers through hyar—ef that's what you mean. And I b'en right hyar, too—ever sence I las' phoned. I ain't taken a cent. But I shore oughta smash you one fur—fur that. I—but ef yo're that crazy, search me! Go on—search—"

"Bah," snorted Stoeffhaas, "you'fe had bract'cally a full 2 hours to stash whateffer you took into a gopher hole alongside the road anywhere between here and 15 miles up; or unter a rock, the same; or—"

"Yo're crazy as hell, Stoeffhaas—yo've lost your—"

"Crazy, am I?" raged Stoeffhaas. "Well, maype I'm crazy when I listen by rumors! Which from now on I will. And barticularly to one apout you— from Jarg—bat ne' mind—that you forched a big check on some big city bank—"

"It's a lie!" shouted Sheriff Duckhouse, though inwardly he winced. "Show me the check," he demanded. "Show me—"

"Easy, Mister Stoeffhaas," cautioned the freckled Sam Turner. "That Jarg Hickey, of Willis Creek, who you ev'dently refer to, is knowed to keep that French drink, absinthe, on his premises f'r his own use. And to drink it! *If* he does, then nothing he says can be relied on. And Sheriff Duckhouse here could maybe get you for libel on anything like what you just said—*if* you can't produce the che—"

"I withtraw any implied aggusations," said Stoeffhaas quickly. "I but sait I heart a rumor. And nobody can't prevent me from say—"

"Wa-all, it better be no more'n that," retorted Bucyrus Duckhouse. He gazed about him at the circle of belligerent, challenging faces. "But see hyar, folks," he said plaintively, "you folks have gone a bit crazy with 'cite-ment—and now I'm goin' crazy myse'f in turn—for a gold truck—disap-pearin' between yo'-all and me—on this raised highw—"

"Well, I'll ask one now," interrupted Bill Jeth, with cold meaningful-ness. "And 'twon't have to do with damfool forged check rumors. It—" His brown eyes bored into Bucyrus Duckhouse's face. "Duckhouse, I talked with your local op'rator, Lucy Higgins—from that pillar phone—durin' that long wait. To see if they was any undue activity up her ways on the tel'phone circuits before that bankrobbery. She said no—which proves it 'twas all planned ahead—she said there was only one c'nnection, even, acrost the mountain today—an' that atween you and somebody askin' directions 'bout roads and distances—'bout the drivin' time, I guess 'twas, through Ol' Twistibus—a circus driver, if I ain't mistaken, who was trailin' his show—a c'nnection in which, however, you was sayin', once, jest as she come into it for a minute—"

"Sayin'—what?" demanded Bucyrus Duckhouse.

"Saying—" repeated Bill Jeth incisively. And now, with eyes staring unseeingly, in obvious recollection, he was palpably repeating what he had heard: "'—not for no paltry $10. And I take it you haven't got no big money—such as I could use!—to fix me with, heh? Since—'" Bill Jeth snapped back to reality, and turned to a weatherbeaten, leatherskinned man. "Wasn't that, Hennery, what my own cousin Lucy Higgins po'red into my ear?"

"Shore was," said the leatherskinned man. "I heered ev-ry word of it squeeakin' out th' receiver. E-zackly that. I mean," he qualified hastily, "as it come from the gal."

"Aw," snorted Bucyrus Duckhouse disgustedly, "that's a—no, it ain't a lie—I'm not even claimin' that—I was jest bein'—"

"Ee-ronic," said a short man with a double-barreled shotgun.

Bucyrus Duckhouse looked from face to face of the sextette in front of him.

"Seems I hain't ary friend in Cedarville, a'right," he declared, bitterly. "An' I hain't nary witness to nothin', neither. About, I mean, whether or no I let that there mob go through hyar. But, fo'tunately, I'll be able to prove my words—atter you folks 'quire from M'lissa Finfrock—then Gran'pa and Gran'ma Josephs next—then the whole danged town o' Willis Creek— w'ether any truck passed—"

"Come, come, come, Duckhouse!" protested Jeth sarcastically—and wearily. "Don't insult our 'telligence. A man lettin' a gang of robbers through for hard cash 'd have to show 'em the way to sidetrack all the people what could later prove he done so! And you cert'nly ought to know that we know that you know 'bout that 20-foot-wide dried flat creek bottom leadin' gently off this very road—rightward an' northward—no mor'n a city block beyant your shack—yet a full half-mile ah'id o' the first house next—Hosea and M'lissa Finfrock's—ah'id, in fack, o' any houses and livin' person—and far, far, far ahead o' town, so far's that go—"

"Aw," Bucyrus Duckhouse endeavored to put in, but the other drowned him out by the very force of words.

"—that dried creek bottom," Jeth went on relentlessly, "what—if you take the unpromisin' thing—leads straight through them low hills lyin' north o' Carthage Road, an' up onto that sun-dried mesa behint 'em—an' acrost which—"

"Aw!" Bucyrus Duckhouse interpolated again, but was again cut off by the incisive description.

"—acrost which," Jeth pounded on, "is the end of that old wide-gauge Ind'an trail—leadin' through that deadwoods country—that trail what's never less'n 8 feet wide—t'day a reg'lar ribbon of hard-caked mud windin' through dead lifeless trees—nobody livin' on it—an' goin' clear to Southwest City Ro——or no—goin' t' one o' them godforsaken roads what lead into Southwest City Ro——hell, fire!—it's b'en fully two hours now since them gangsters musta come th'ough here—and since they was on'y 45 minutes from Southwest City Road by a legit'mate way like this, they ain't failed to make it by that ill'git'mate way in far less'n twict that—why, hell!—they're long since into it by that there foxy buried trail—they're safe, by Christ!—safe in that goddamned tangle o' roads lyin' south of the city, with gangster hideouts a-plenty studded amidst'em—and gangster friends—they're—"

"'Zamine th' creek bottom," demanded Bucyrus Duckhouse fiercely. "An' th' mesa—an' the trail—fur tireprints. An'—"

"Bah!" snorted Bill Jeth. "It's a mess o' tireprints today. Thousands of 'em—printed in on days when the mud was dampish. Hain't I shortcutted myself thataway mor'n once? An' seen fer myself? Even met city folks—an' spooners—what acc'dental' got onto th' detour trail up north there, an' were drivin' hard an' straight on, t' git out someway ag'in—"

"Why, goddang it, Jeth," raged Bucyrus Duckhouse, "them gangsters 'd never in Christ's world have trapped theirsevves atween that one creek bottom 'out'—and that Ind'an trail—that'd be as in-sane as divin' into Old Twistibus!—an' they shore wan't insa—— but the fact is—you know it—an' I know it—that they couldn't even know 'bout the 'zistence o' that crazy detour, ef fur no other reason 'n 'at they's a opt'cal illusion when you look 'long the creek bed thisaway, like—like as ef it ends flat ag'in' that biggest hill—an they's a live leafy thicket, they say, on the end of the Ind'an trail w'ere it empties out into—"

"Course they didn't know 'bout it," retorted Bill Jeth. "Till, that is, they were told."

Bucyrus Duckhouse threw up his hands.

"Now see hyar—see hyar!—them fellers didn't and couldn't—have turned off ef—ef they was 50 creek bottoms wide 'nough fur truckin'—and with signs on 'em act'ally sayin' THROUGH ROAD—sence I 'uz atween 'em and ev'ry mile o' this road now behint me—but oh, yes—I fo'got—you do say that I fixed things f'r 'em to git through—tolt 'em all 'bout that de-tour—guar'nteed 'em they'd be no pu'suit hem-min' 'em in on the mesa—or the Ind'an trail—though, come to think of it, the stolened money they'd have passed me would a-b'en its own guar'ntee, wouldn't it?—fur ef *they* got cotched, *I'd* a-had to kick back the pass money!—oh, yes!—o' co'se—but now listen—listen hyar!—listen, all o' you—I hain't taken a cent, I tell you—I hain't seed no robbers—I hain' seed no truck—I—oh, Christ, a gold truck—disappearin' on the way. Why, goddang it, you fellers yo're-sevves know—"

Sheriff Bucyrus Duckhouse stopped. For he realized he was facing the 6 most sternly unbelieving faces he had ever confronted in his life. Bur he was facing something even worse—in himself.

"I am goin' crazy," he said simply. "Becaze—"

Bill Jeth interrupted. He was, indeed, motioning his entire posse peremptorily back into that tunnel.

"All right, boys—out an' back. To th' tother side—where we got our car standin'." He turned to the square-bearded man. "Pres'dent Stoeffhaas, I'm out o' my county here—out of it by at least two counties—considerin' that Frog Gullies, back of us there behind the mount'in, is really the north edge o' Dan's Boone County—and so far's havin' any author'ty here, I haven't got no more than a—a damned fieldmouse. So I'm gettin' back to my own county—*and* pronto! But my advice to you is to indict this fellow th' minute the Willis Creek County Grand Jury sets—indict him with all *our* test'mony—and those forged check rumors, too, if the judge will let 'em in!—and my cousin Lucy Higgins' test'mony—and the test'mony, too, of the Wanties at 2-Mile Point, who seed the gangster truck roarin' for the tunnel—and give this fellow what he deserves for lettin' a whole God-fearin' community be took—be kicked in the face. Yes, Pres'dent Stoeffhaas, give him 10 good years in the pen'tentiary. For he let them gangsters through—there's no doubt what-so-ever about it—for they and their gold truck never dis'ppeared into thin air—not on *this* raised highway. No—sir!"

Stoeffhaas gazed bitterly at Bucyrus Duckhouse.

The rest of the posse were already turning angrily back into the tunnel.

Then the fat man, too, turned.

"Okay," he said, though to nobody in particular. "I'll do it! For the Willis Creek Grand Jury sits day afder tomorrow. Yes, by Gott, I'll do it!"

CHAPTER VIII

by Hazel Goodwin Keeler

SPANGLES

That evening found the performers of The MacWhorter Shows in a blaze of excitement!

For The Scandal was to reach its culmination this night!—an incredible culmination not foreseen a dozen days earlier, when Bella, the bareback rider, had been brought in dead—not from a fall off her horse, but strangled through the very bars of its cage, by the dwarf gorilla. Not ten minutes later, the secret about Spangles had come to light, and gone the rounds of the entire troupe.

They had never suspected anything of the size of this, however! They had done a lot of speculating, to be sure. Performers attached to a small traveling company like MacWhorter's, would do nothing else. An exquisite little creature like Spangles, the "equestrienne," could never have been born of Bella the bareback rider! But that the girl might have been stolen from so ancient and eminent a family as the Mainwarings of Ashton-under-Tyne, England, would have been too fantastic a thought!

Yet there was no disputing that evidence found on Bella's stilled body: the small, flaky bundle of yellowed clippings and photographs, and Spangles' baby locket, imprisoned for over a decade in the darkness of Bella's bosom: preserved, perhaps, in the deferred hope of collecting ransom.

Of course the Mainwarings of Ashton-under-Tyne, England had been cabled at once. They were, in fact, due to arrive in Foleysburg this very night. And there lay poor Spangles in her little bed, desperately ill and supremely unconscious of the events of the past two weeks—not only of the impending Mainwarings, but even of Bella's fatal encounter.

* * * *

As for Charlot, he was desolate: as desolate as a dark-eyed, slender boy of seventeen could be. Spangles was entwined in his whole life, like a grapevine in its trellis. Ever since he was seven and she, six—when Bella had brought her from Europe—he and Spangles had been like brother and sister: drawn close by common tears and heartbreak. They had planned to marry in two more years: just as soon as she was eighteen.

But now—

It was already dark as Charlot, ruminating on all this, came up to the sick-trailer in which Spangles lay. There were fully twenty minutes before he was to go on, in his prelude, for the seating of the evening show crowds. Dr. Karl the Klown was sitting on a low stool just outside the sick-trailer. Only the white patches of his parti-colored costume of black and white, glowed feebly. The low light from the open trailer door glinted on the steel rims of his spectacles. He watched over his patient just as earnestly as ever he could have watched over her in those earlier days, when he was still "the noted Dr. Karl Vanderplanck," most successful diagnostician in the East. That was evident!

"How is she?" Charlot whispered.

Dr. Karl threw back his head; looked up. The incongruous triangular patches of black grease paint that hung under his eyes were like enormous tears.

"We can't bring her out of the fever," he complained softly. "Swamp fever has to break before the fifteenth day—or it's a bad sign, boy. And this is the fifteenth day, and there isn't any sign of its breaking!"

The talons that had been tight around Charlot's heart for days, grew still tighter.

"'Swamp fever'?" he echoed, in the peculiar, soft accents of the inland South, so different from the hillbilly-like vernacular of the region through which the show had been passing.

"Swamp fever's only the popular name for it, sonny. If I told you the technical name, you'd only get a word a yard long."

"Yes, sir," Charlot answered: "I reckon that's so. I know what you mean. It like when Mr. MacWhorter done ask me if that was George and Maggie di—di—dissentin' all night—and I told him I didn't know 'bout that, but I did know that they fit, and they fit, and they fit, clean through to sun-up."

He went back to the subject of the favor he had come to ask.

"Please, sir, might I go in see Miss Spangles?"

Karl looked at the other; speculated.

"Why—I guess so, sonny—if you think you can do it without her hearing you."

"Thank you kindly, sir."

Charlot hesitated, however.

"Dr. Karl—how come they tote a girl like Spangles all over the roads, night after night, sick like she is? She like to die, being toted around that-a-way, ain't she?"

Dr. Karl took off his glasses, and Charlot could see him in the dim light lean wearily forward, his elbows braced upon his pantalooned knees.

"Don't you worry about that, boy! Not in this trailer," he answered. "Trailers like this are made especially; by an ambulance company. The springs are so fine and delicately balanced—why they run all through the thing—in and around the trailer body, and the bunk, and the mattress and the special box spring—Spangles is just like a baby in her own cradle. Just a gentle rocking, that's all, Charlot. And that seems to soothe her, rather than harm her. She got used to it so young, you see. She really perks up after each long haul—"

"You mean even after that jump through Ol' Twistibus, she perked up?"

"Yes, even after that! Even more so. But the fever's keeping up over-time! I don't like it."

"Maybe it'd do her hurt if I went in again. Course I'd—only just look at her—I'd be right careful, thank you kindly—"

"I'm sure it wouldn't hurt her, Charlot. Just slip in softly and don't talk to her—don't even whisper, you know. But please be careful about making any sound?" cautioned the doctor.

"Yes, sir, thank you, sir," answered Charlot.

He had a quarter of an hour before his act. He still had to make up. And he hadn't had the usual pre-performance snack. But a cup of coffee was all he'd be wanting, and he could make up in five minutes. He climbed quietly into Spangles' trailer. His heart was heavy. For he realized that, even if Spangles were to recover, this would undoubtedly prove to be the last time that he was ever to see her.

For the Mainwarings were coming this very night.

* * * *

An oil lamp hung just within the trailer door. The light from its restless flame flitted over the space with its white wooden floor and the uncompromising front surfaces of the chromium-plated wall compartments.

It was a barren place, at best. At a short distance from the bunk stood Spangles' small trunk, thrown in, undoubtedly, the day she was taken ill, to make available, to some other occupant, the sleeping-trailer space she had vacated.

Upon this trunk had been hastily tossed all the mysterious accessories of Spangles' art: a swansdown powder puff, huge as a nesting heron; black, red, orange and mauve grease paint; eye shadow and mascara; a spangled fan; a black satin masque; all in reckless confusion. Gauze tights lay among them in a silvery pool, with one leg of them darting like a waterfall over the edge, bright against the shadows behind. Upon the floor, close to the trunk, a white ballet skirt had tumbled, all crispy little angles, its sheer tulle—and brilliants sparkled through it like dew. New moons of ballet slippers and a white buckskin and silver tambourine gleamed up neglectedly beside it.

Small and white, in the fitful light, lay the little proprietress of this glittering ruin. The challenging little face was motionless; the grave, grey eyes were brightly open, but unseeing; they seemed larger than ever: almost enormous, as she lay there. The short, bright corn-colored hair glinted with a thousand writhing sparkles, to the mood of the flame of the oil lamp.

Charlot knelt down upon the floor beside the bed, and gazed long and intently upon the little face he loved.

Suddenly, as he gazed, her eyes dilated, and slowly focussed themselves upon his face. The slim eyebrows lifted, and one hand, as it lay along the quilt, made a little darting movement toward the trunk.

Charlot understood. Turning cautiously upon his knees, avoiding the slightest sound, he crept to the trunk. Carefully removing the objects there, and laying them upon the floor beside it, he opened the lid; found, and withdrew, a handful of peculiar little water-color paintings—scenes that depicted stage settings, done on coarse, ruled, writing paper.

When he went out, a kiss lay upon Spangles' hand, and the painted sets hung in silent display on the wall opposite her eyes.

The boy left the trailer and walked out into the perfumed velvet of an Indian-summer night. The show tent rose close before him like a great, parchment lantern, with silhouetted figures never still. Hugging the rear of the show tent, the pearly splotch of the ambulance trailer could barely be distinguished.

An evening breeze swept along the lot. It smelled of damp oak leaves, and dogwood blossoms, and fall-blooming violets. These gentle, familiar things, however, were suddenly filled with mockery and silent heartbreak. Charlot's mind was staggered before the crushing force of Spangles' danger.

He had lived for Spangles: lived for the day when he could release her from the narrowing chains of the circus: when he could take her away from it, and out into the world of normal people. He had had dreams of her in cool, far gardens and spacious halls: dreams of a sheltered life for her; dreams of bright-eyed, fresh-faced little children. And mingled with these, and giving substance to them, were dreams of creation: of bringing into being such exaggerated beauty and line as had never yet been seen on the stage; such hues and lightings as had never before been combined: weird, woodland scenes; baronial halls; South Sea Island glades; ice castles at the North Pole; towns on the Moon: such things as he had sketched, crudely to be sure, with his small box of water colors on his pad of pencil paper.

Spangles had always said that to watch him paint them was better than real traveling could be—since there were no castles at the Pole, really. And tropical air could never be as soothingly languorous as that which shimmered under Charlot's brush!

"Well, what's ailin' you?"

It was a harsh, feminine voice. Charlot realized he had been standing for some moments outside the open door of the kitchen trailer. It was a gloomy place, after nightfall. Maggie, the cook—a thin, black-eyed, gypsy-faced woman of the South, in her late forties—was making the air thick with the frying of fishcakes for her own and her husband's supper.

Charlot watched her idly, for a moment, as her wiry, sunburnt arms flew too energetically about her task. Trapeze performers, before rheumatism had reduced their status, Maggie and her husband George were the only parents the boy had had since the death of his own mother. And that had been years before. These foster parents, however, were finding it impossible to realize that their charge was growing up.

"Give me m'coffee now, Maggie?" Charlot asked, going into the kitchen vehicle, unfolding a camp chair that had been resting against the wall and sitting down astride it. "Medusy done bit me again and it clean took m'appetite."

"Where's George!" the woman demanded, irrelevantly, pouring a black tincupful from a huge, coverless pot on the stove, and setting the cup down with emphasis upon the bare, chipped table ledge before him. "I'd give a pretty to know where that lazy houn' that calls himself my husband lays up wheh there's totin' to do. Assistant cook and handy man around here, is he? Why, hell-fire, that tonic-head!—he never so much as made a hoe cake in his whole good-for-nothing life! Nor tied a pole nor driven a stake! But that li'l ol' boy sure fixin' to slink in for his supper right smart—d'rec'ly the work's done!"

Charlot took up his tin cup in silence and swallowed some of the murky and bitter stuff, allowing as polite a pause as possible to follow Maggie's outburst.

"Do you reckon Spangles going to get well?" he finally ventured.

An ominous silence greeted this query. Then the woman slammed a kettle upon the stove with a tempestuous bang, and wheeled sharply about. There was menace in her beady, black eyes.

"You listen at me!" she cried. "You go in that sick car of Spangles' and catch the swamp fever, and I'll wear you out! You ain't none too big yet to have your hide tanned. Doctor Karl saying, a little ago, Spangles going to die! 'Cause he cain't fetch her out of the fever. But it's not enough that I been fotchin' and carryin' for *her*, day and night, like a nigger mammy, but I got to do it for you, now! Well I ain't aimin' to go through *that* all over again.

"God!" she cried, as if to strengthen the argument.

"But she done been wanting me, Maggie. She'd feel strange-like—"

At this, the woman spun around again, and with renewed ferocity, seemed on the verge of launching into an even more violent stream of threats. But evidently finding it would require more strength than she had left, she heaved a sigh, instead, and turned back to the stove.

Charlot drank gravely from his cup.

"So the old gorilla bitten you, did she?" Maggie at length deigned to say.

"Yes'm! Right through the canvas of the tent, when I accidentally knocked m'elbow through the little old bars of her cage, from th' outside."

"Humph! Done you right! You should knowed better, after her killing Bella that-a-way. You knowed she done gone plumb crazy since that other ugly-looking critter died—that ornery Cheng!"

Charlot, having finished his coffee and, to a degree, placated Maggie, arose.

"Yes'm, it sure did take Cheng to keep Medusy cowed," he agreed. "Mr. MacWhorter saying Cheng done bit Medusy right powerful, once—like to tore her cheek clean off; before he turned her loose. I reckon she's as glad he died as th' orangoutangs are. She won't be studyin' about wantin' no more mate, I reckon!"

He looked out at the black sky gloomily.

"Well—guess I'll go make me up," he concluded.

The odor of damp, unpainted pine, and of horse liniment—that panacea for all human aches and pains among circus performers—drifted out from the open flap of Charlot's makeup tent. This tent was a relic from old, pre-trailer days. Small, capable of being pitched or taken down almost with a turn of the wrist, it was the one thing he clung to with all the characteristic "love of the familiar," so common to the darkeyed races. For, when he was a very small boy, he had shared this tent with his mother.

A gasoline lamp, twisted and battered by years and miles of travel, hung at a weird angle to the center pole inside the tent, revealing that the drum-shaped, black metal box and long, black stem were not too well supplied with fuel. He lit the nozzle. A restless flame sprang forth like a bright, reaching starfish.

Performance would be starting in no time. The make-up for Charlot's act, however, was easy. Stooping over an old trunk, he drew from it a dwarf-gorilla skin, complete except for hands and feet. He took off his shoes and socks, climbed out of his clothing, and put his bare feet through a gap in the side of the hide, With a contortion, he drew the upper part over his head and the rest of his body, adjusting the elastics under the chin and about the forehead, so that the holes where the eyes had been, in the monkey-face, exactly and firmly rimmed his own brown eyes. Drawing the arms and legs up above his wrists and ankles for a few moments, he filled a washbowl from a pitcher of water, and emptied into the basin brown powder from a cardboard container, stirring it with a stick. He plunged first his hands, then his feet, into the solution. They came forth dripping, and stained as dark as the fur of the hide he wore. Standing upon a mat of rubber mesh, he waved his hands about in the air and kicked his feet, to dry them.

This night, for the first time, he realized that life in the circus had not been unhappy at all: it had been all sunshine and gold—if he had only known enough to take the scales from his eyes! Why had he not been able to see it before Fate indulged in this shattering caprice? He had had Spangles, all along. What more, dear God, could he have asked? Life had long ceased to be cruel to them, too. The memory of the days when Bella, and George and Maggie, had superintended their waking hours with a cat-o'-nine-tails, and the inexorable decree had been to "do the trick"—all this had been relegated to the scrap-pile of forgotten things.

It had been hard in those days, to be sure. Life had been without compromise. Eight or ten lashings had been nothing for a morning, and often, when he and Spangles had been particularly terrified, there had been more. Spangles' brave linle face had always been streaked from crying.

But that was past! They had each grown as supple and agile as the best. She could dash through a hoop and back upon the haunches of her white, pseudo-Arabian charger as quick as one could wink. And as for Charlot, backward, intra-trapeze somersaults had become as simple a means of self-expression as a mere lift of his eyebrows.

The wish to take Spangles away from life with the circus had not diminished, however, with these cruelties. Forgotten though they were, their scars had remained. The experiences, received so early in life, were deeply rooted and traumatic. Charlot, ever since his seventeenth birthday had loomed upon the horizon like a red harvest moon, had been laying very definite plans. In two years—on Spangles' eighteenth birthday—they would be married, and flee. He had determined on New Orleans. There he would get a start: find a nook and a berth: do any sort of routine work during the day, and work nights upon his stage setting designs. Then, when they had enough money saved, they would go to New York or Hollywood and interest some great producer. But now—

His eyes blurred.

The stain had dried, at last, on his hands and feet. He shoved down into place the elastic binding that terminated the wrists and ankles of the hide. It was the skin of the huge old dwarf-gorilla Cheng that had recently died. With the aid of side and neck padding, it had been made to fit Charlot. He smoothed the fur down, absently, hung his clothes upon a ten-penny nail, and walked out again, into the night.

* * * *

The Foleysburg crowds had come out early. The benches in the great show tent were rapidly filling with throngs in a holiday mood. Clowns were rumbling and capering about on the carefully raked sawdust. Goober-Jim and his crew of peanut venders were noisily waving their wares. Brightly colored popcorn paper already littered the place, and children blew raucous, cardboard horns.

Charlot, in accordance with his custom, went to the side of the tent along which stood the great cage-car that held the monkeys. Not far from this cage, in the canvas wall, was a series of ascending rungs, fastened into the stuff of the canvas. Up the canvas walls, they went, then continued on up the slant of the ceiling top, to the very center.

The boy climbed these to the struts of the upper framework from which the trapezes hung, ran over this framework until he reached the clean, stiff ropes of the trapezes; slid down one of the latter, and at once began his performance, going lightly through his antics.

The circus was a two-ring, or two-arena one. Across the diameter of the opposite arena hung a series of polished, wooden rings, each about the size of a barrel hoop. These rings depended by ropes at intervals of a few feet, and at consecutively increasing heights—like printed half-notes in an ascending musical scale. The lowest hung within ten feet of the ground, at one end of the row, and the highest, within twenty feet of the tent top, at the other end.

But the arena in which Charlot did his comedy pantomine, was the one which contained the trapezes which, at the beginning of performance each night, hung particularly high from the ground. They were kept drawn this way until later, when the regular trapeze troop came on. Charlot's first act, which was a sort of curtain raiser, took place in this latter arena. His act was informal, and designed to entertain those who were already seated, while the rest of the audience was arriving and filing into place.

The three sides of the amphitheater were already three terraces of human heads. Only because everything about him was proceeding as usual did Charlot know that his performance was progressing according to schedule. For while his body, through long habit, twisted and flew and vaulted, his mind stood motionless at the brink of a great, bottomless, black pool. If Spangles were taken away! If kind God could let his little Spangles die! Why, if only He would let her live and be happy, Charlot would never ask for anything again: not even to see her. Just to know she was somewhere on this earth with him would be happiness enough—if only she didn't die. For if there were no Spangles on earth with him—no Spangles in life—

His body continued to career and whirl; somersault through space; caper and spring. And the spontaneous bursts of laughter continued to rise from the crowd below at the usual places in the routine. At length there came his particularly high leap. Subconscious messengers warned him to the needed alertness. He paused in his tragic thoughts to compute the distance. Before he could relapse, however, his eye fell upon the great cage-car where the dwarf-gorilla Medusa and the other simians were kept. Medusa was separated from the rest of the monkeys by a partition of bars placed about a third the distance from one end of the cage. This smaller compartment she had to herself. She hung sullenly close to the gate in this partition, and snarled at the orangoutangs in the larger compartment. But what caused Charlot to catch himself on the brink of his leap and cling instead with a jerk to the bar and swing back with it, was the figure in filmy white which stood in front of the orangoutangs' compartment. Though it was countless yards below, Charlot could see it was Spangles. She seemed to be doing something to the cage gate, unobserved by the spectators, who, as one mass, were intent upon Charlot.

Before he had time to leap forward to the next trapeze, the girl had swung the gate wide open. She calmly walked into the cage and went falteringly down its length, past the orangoutangs that sat in various attitudes, blinking in surprise at her, until she reached Medusa's partition.

With one terrific cry, Charlot tried to signal the crowd. It would be certain death for him to leap to the ground from the height at which he swung, but he shouted again and again, pointing frantically, with wide gestures, toward the cage-car. The crowd merely laughed at him, taking it for one of his tricks, while Spangles, unhindered, undid the lock of Medusa's gate and pushed it open.

The explanation came to Charlot in a sudden, dizzy wave of realization.

"God!" he told hunself. "She thinks Medusy's me!"

The gorilla, which had been clinging to the bars with its hands, now turned to the gate as it opened, and snarled.

In Spangles went, and up to the animal fearlessly, and put her hands upon the great, hairy chest. Medusa pounced upon the girl, crushing her to the floor; then drawing her up under one powerful arm, vaulted with her, out of the gate of the smaller compartment, down across the floor of the orangoutangs' cage and out through the outer gate. The orangoutangs, not slow to be roused out of their first stupefaction, leaped up from their squatting postures and started out after the dwarf gorilla in hot pursuit. Over the sawdust they swept like a comet and its tail, Medusa in the lead; she made for the ring arena opposite Charlot's, sprang to the lowest of the row of hoop-sized rings that hung there. From ring to ring of the ascending series the gorilla went—leaping in a sickening sequence of jerks, clasping the limp white clad form tightly to her coat. The bright head of the unconscious girl rolled loosely against the rough ape-body and the slender little feet dangled lifelessly.

The orangoutangs that had followed in a rush, flowed along the rings after the two, until they swarmed under the canvas top like gigantic bees, in their efforts to get at the hated Medusa. And as they screeched and fought and tore at each other, the giant with its human toy gained the very highest pendant. Almost immediately the others closed in upon it. One, a half-grown animal, sprang, as though catapulted, to the rope that held this highest ring, paused there, gibbering, for a moment, and then swung its bulk down to one of the gorilla's legs. Two hoary, bead-eyed males fought for possession of the place vacated, and an inquisitive mother monkey with a baby clinging to its side tried to leap from rope to rope above the heads of the others and, falling to the ground, started all over again.

"Shotguns!" Charlot cried out, over and over. But the wall of clamor from the crowds below was impassable. Yet, even as he shouted, he discerned men with guns. They seemed to be trying to find opportunity to aim without risk of injury to the human bit in the center of that hanging swarm.

The other beasts were piling so rapidly upon Medusa, clinging so thickly to one another, and her and Spangles, that the latter two were soon completely lost to sight. And then, ominously, the whole fighting, screeching mass of them suddenly rotated with the peculiar jerk that told Charlot a strand of the rope had given way.

That it was a matter of moments when the whole legion would crash earthward with Spangles in its midst, he knew well.

It had all happened in the flash of a minute. There was no time to speculate. To jump was certain death. To return to the ground by the ceiling and wall struts and up the rings of the opposite arena would be fatal delay. The arenas themselves were so far apart that no one had ever, in the history of the circus, leaped the space between them. Yet Charlot felt that there might be at least one chance in fifty that he could make it. He pumped savagely; worked up the fullest swing possible; then, when the swinging had reached a maximum, lowered his body until he hung from the bar by his hands. Then on a vast final forward swoop, with his supremest effort of strength and direction, he let himself go, and went flying through the air.

He landed. It was upon the second rope, above the backs of the apes which could find no room on the highest ring but still loitered on the highest ring but one. Charlot had not aimed for the highest. He knew his added weight would have broken the remaining strands of the rope that held it.

Down this adjacent rope he slid—down to where the leftover apes clung. And then, suddenly, a most inexplicable thing happened. They stopped their gibbering long enough to turn wild, round eyes, snarling, leathery muzzles, and bared teeth upon him. There seemed to be a moment of paralysis among them, and then, starting to screech, they began to pounce earthward, one after another, until there was not one orangoutang left on the ring beneath Charlot.

He immediately slid down into it and pumped up a swing until he was able to reach the outer fringes of the creatures that clung, on the very highest ring, around the gorilla. And again, one by one, as he bunted against them, trying to seize first one and then another by the throat, they turned to gaze toward him with bronze eyes of horror, only to set up a more deafening clamor and to fall away to the ground. Finally the weight was so lessened on this highest rope that Charlot sprang to it. The remaining apes dropped away beneath him until there was none but Medusa left—and Spangles, hanging limply from her powerful arm, head and arms rolling. Creeping down the rope cautiously, Charlot with a sudden movement wedged his arm between Spangles and the powerful, stocky side of the beast. This one, too, turned a frantic gaze upon Charlot, and with a faint shriek that seemed to die in her throat, surrendered her prey before Charlot had time to land a blow between her eyes. She dropped away in terror to the ground beneath, and followed the others coweringly into the cage-car.

For, like them, she had seen her master, Cheng!

The crowds cheered deafeningly as Charlot carried Spangles from ring to ring until he reached the lowest. Here a little group waited for him: a strange man wearing a monocle and standing on a stepladder, close under the ring in which Charlot sat—and MacWhorter who, in the silk hat and frock coat he wore for his ring-master act, steadied the ladder for the stranger with one hand, while holding up a megaphone with the other, to plead with the audience to "kindly remain seated in the name of humanity." Karl the Klown, too, stood by, waiting, incongruous in motley, paint and steel-rimmed spectacles, holding a blanket and a glass of pink liquid.

Lastly, on the fringe of the group, there stood a woman. She had a patrician face, even-toned gray hair and the kindliest gray eyes Charlot had ever seen. She waited quietly, yet anxiously, and watched closely as the monocled man on the ladder reached up toward Charlot, received Spangles into his arms, and, holding her lightly as a baby, receded carefully down the steps, to the ground beneath.

"Oh, my darling!" breathed the strange woman as she fairly fell upon the girl, enfolding the bright head in her arms, putting back the soft hair and pressing her face lightly upon Spangles' forehead.

Dr. Karl threw the blanket about his little patient, then seized her hands, inquiringly.

"Why—she's moist!" he exclaimed. "Why—if her temperature isn't down to 99, I miss my guess!" He laughed delightedly, and took a couple of gleeful little dancing steps. "I believe it must have been the exertion," he added with completely unprofessional candor.

The boy could hear no more. The little party which had been moving away down the sawdust lane, with MacWhorter in the lead shouting away the curious through his megaphone, disappeared through the performers' exit. Charlot remained crooked in the ring, and the band struck up "The Starry Flag Forever."

* * * *

Three hours later, after the gigantic finale act was over—after nearly all the lights had been turned out, and the great show tent had been closed, and the last of the spectators had sauntered away—Charlot set out across the dark lot, aimlessly. His prayer had been answered. Spangles was to be well again. He had had ten years of the sweetness of her companionship and no one could ask for more. The two strangers were the Mainwarings of England, of course—Spangles' real father and mother—and now they had taken Spangles away—and she would soon be at the other end of the world, both geographically and socially. As for himself, Charlot realized, he would throw his little water-color box away. There could be no dreams without Spangles to dream them with.

How like Spangles the man from England had been, in spite of his monocle! He had a fine face; the features were almost as fine as Spangles' own. And the woman had Spangles' large, gentle, gray eyes.

* * * *

Charlot got back to his tent only after a long and aimless stroll. He heard voices inside. When he lifted the entrance flap, he was startled to see that the English couple had not yet left: they seemed to be waiting for Charlot—they and MacWhorter.

"This, Charlot," announced the latter, feet astride, "is Mr. Mainwaring—and lady—from Ashton-under-Tyne, England: Spangles' father and mother."

Charlot took the strangers' extended hands, one after the other.

"I say!" Mainwaring exclaimed. "That was splendid work, sir, if I may say so. My wife and I saw it almost from the beginning. We arrived here just after our daughter had—"

"Yes," MacWhorter interrupted him, "Dr. Karl dozed off out in front of Spangles' trailer, when you were there, Charlot: he figured you'd wake him up by coming out again, but he slept right through. And Spangles must have gotten out of the trailer to look for you after you'd been gone a while; she must have gone into the show tent stage entrance, and thought Medusa was you in your monkey outfit. Fever delirium, of course! The girl knows where the cage key is kept."

Mainwaring, gazing in astonishment at the interruption of the circus owner, waited courteously until the latter had finished, and then turned and addressed Charlot, again.

"Those are very original and, if I might say so, very arresting stage settings you design—"

"You see, Charlot," MacWhorter interrupted the Britisher again, "I told these folks all about you, how you and Spangles consider yourselves engaged and everything—and about those stage sets you paint. You see, he saw all those little papers hanging in Spangles' trailer and he asked me about them—and then I showed him those sets you made for the side shows."

When Mainwaring was able, he took his astonished eyes from the American circus owner a second time.

"Yes," the Englishman acknowledged to Charlot, "Mr. MacWhorter has told us more than one pleasant thing about you. And now,"—he adjusted his monocle and glanced apprehensively toward MacWhorter, in fear of still another interruption—"I've a proposition to make to you that would bring you along to England with our daughter and us if you cared to consider it—"

Charlot's eardrums turned somersaults in his head and he heard the rest as if he were in a dream:

"You see," Mainwaring added, "I was a producer when the actress Bella kidnaped our daughter. I still am a producer—somewhat more of a producer, if I may say so!—and your ideas interest me. Now I'm planning to put on another modern-art musical production at Drury Lane, the great new Drury Lane, you know, that supplants the one Bloody Hitler destroyed. It is my belief that your ideas are unusual. I believe that, with the opportunity to experiment on a larger scale, discarding and substituting to get your effects without fear of expense, you could contrive scenes for our show that might turn out to be the sensation of the year in London: the freshness of the youthful point of view and all that, you know? I should like to have you consider the matter of creating trial sets for the entire production."

"And also, dear," Mrs. Mainwaring hastened to add, "of continuing whatever personal understanding may exist between you and our daughter."

"You mean—y'all want me to go to England too? With Spangles?"

The Englishwoman's kindly gray eyes seemed to throw a mantle of tenderness over Charlot. She put an arm about his shoulders.

"That's right," she answered, simply.

"But—but Mis' Spangles," said Charlot, "going to have right many friends now—and she won't want to be studyin' about me no more. And you all don't know anything about me."

The strangers looked at each other with a twinkle in their eyes.

"We know two things about you, sir," said the Englishman. "You risked death on a very slender chance of saving her, really—which means you must love her, don't you know—"

"And then, too," added the woman who was Spangle's mother, "we saw the fall-blooming wood violets you hunted and picked for her—we understand they're extremely rare—and the little note attached: and that told us the other important thing about you, dear—that—" She turned to Spangles' father. "—that here at last, by Jove," concluded Mainwaring, "was one young man whose normal sentimental instincts had not gone modern!"

CHAPTER IX

THE LONELY MAN

Jim Craney, driving along Foleysburg Road in the darkness, had a rueful look on face when he realized the never-ending kidding he was due to get on the morrow. When certain full details appertaining to his rejoining the show would become performers' public property. Due to that full report which, Jim knew, he must make to Angus MacWhorter. And which report Jim had no intention whatsoever of not making; since it was his fidelity to facts, as he knew, that made MacWhorter put so much confidence in him.

Yes, Jim Craney would hear a-plenty, Jim Craney knew, how the Gr-r-reat Craney, expert driver—who had both talked himself past—and even practically bought himself past by a library book—a country Sheriff, guarding a shortcut passage to Foleysburg, should have gotten stuck in a bog off the Foleysburg Road.

Until, moreover, a pair of fool mules and a log chain, plus a block and tackle, had pulled him out!

Which was exactly whar had happened to Jim Craney.

And even had he been of a mind to say nothing about this sad, sad fact, the wagon-cage he was driving told the full story. For its wheels were encrusted with mud from axle to rims; the now dry mud ran up to the very floor of the cab. It had been a miracle, indeed, that the dry floor of Princess' cage had escaped.

It was, in fact, 1 o'clock in the morning!

Though this wasn't in the least worrying Jim.

Not now!

Not since, pulling away from Klum's store at 4 o'clock the day just closed, he had seen what he had seen—plastered on the off-side of that store! A 2-sheet which said—

But now he was drawing near the show itself. Which had *not* left Foleysburg! The great rent, small however at the distance, gleamed phosphorescently, luminously, because of the several lights that were always left in it all night so that if its 2 custodians shouted fire—fire could be fought—if fire there was. Though there was something hectic about that phosphorescence tonight—it was brighter—as though extra lights were burning—that seemed to say unusual things had happened tonight; that more people than usual in the show were awake—

But now, as he calculated he was a quarter mile off yet, the lights of his car-cage lighted up a figure on the road ahead which, at the very moment, shouted, "Hi, Jim!—draw up—it's me!"

The "me" was MacWhorter, taking one of his frequent after-show walks along a country road, lonely and brooding. Though he carried the loaded blackthorn cane that, for protection, he always carried on such occasions, he wore now, absentmindedly, the very silk hat which he wore in his late ring-master act; the long frock coat which he always forgot to doff. His great face, blinking at Jim in the headlights, was a sad and brooding face, and old-fashioned due to his sideburns.

Jim Craney brought his cage-wagon to a stop.

"Evening, Chief. Taking the—the old evening walk?"

MacWhorter drew up to the cab of the cage-wagon.

"Well, well, Jim—I see you made it all right, with Princess! What kind of a time did you have over that damned hills road?"

"Gosh," said Jim, "I didn't have to come by that hills road. Believe it or not, Chief, that Sheriff let me through by the Straightaway."

"The devil you say? But here—Good Lord, Jim—how—"

"Yeah, I know," said Jim ruefully. "But you've heard of the damfool frog in the bottom of the well who fell two feet back for every foot he jumped out? At least I got out! At—must be 'bout 1 in the mornin', ain't it?"

"About, I guess," said MacWhorter impatiently, "But good heavens, Jim, whatever happ—but wait—how did you ever grease that Sheriff? He wouldn't let us—listen—have to pass him anything?"

"Passed him one library book," said Jim laconically. "That he thought he'd want to read. Though *I* know he won't. But skip *that!* For—but say listen, don't you give a damn to know that you're the proud papa of 5 little lions?"

"Five!" ejaculated MacWhorter. "The devil you say, Jim?" He almost purred himself. "So she had 5, eh? Any trouble?"

"Just a bit slow, that's 'bout all. I didn't get started from Pricetown till this morning late. Partly 'count of her slowness—yes—but partly, too, 'count of another delay I had there; but which, in view of later things, ain't even worth the relatin' now. Anyway, Princess is just fine—and every kitten is finer yet."

"Bless her heart," said MacWhorter. "Give her—give her—by God, Jim, when you bring her in, give her the steak that Maggie's holding right now to cook for me when I get back. But see here—about this Sheriff now? Do you really mean," MacWhorter pleaded amazedly, "that you didn't have to pass him any money? Did—did he hint at wanting to be grease—"

"Say, Chief," asked Jim, "if you were lookin' for a gang of bankrobbers that had robbed a bank east of you, would you be botherin' to gibe a guy for a 10-spot?"

"A bank? What you mean, Ji—"

"Just that a bank was robbed—that's all I know—and that the robbers was on the same highway with me!"

"The—the hell you say? Did—but how do you know?"

"Passed 'em," said Jim, the laconicist.

"The hell you say! Well, did this Sheriff get 'em?"

Jim threw up his hands. "Search me, Chief. Hope so, anyway. For he was one swell duck. And the real reason he let me through was because he was fond o' cats. About all I'm in position t' tell you tonight—if you want facts—is what it feels like to sit on the hard land alongside a quicksand, under a big warnin' oil lamp swung by a pulley rope acrost by two trees, an' watch your cage-wagon sink a little bit every half hour."

"Jim, Jim, Jim!" groaned MacWhorter. "You don't mean to tell me you got bollixed up on that double by-pass tangle at Mill Creek?"

"What do you think, Chief?" asked Jim. "That this yellow stuff on these wheels is cake?" He laughed sheepishly. "Chief, I'm the prize boob, I guess. Not because I lost all the time I gained—that don't matter *now.*" And he waved a hand toward that distant tent which had *not* come down tonight! "But because I took the wrong pass—and damn near sunk to China."

"Well, you were safe," MacWhorter comforted him, "about going to China. There is hard bottom to that pseudo-quicksand, I heard authoritatively. But how'd you get out?"

"Through a kid. Rather, the kid's old man. The kid who appears to have the tendin' of that damned lamp. Which, after I took that road, I found, b'gosh, was a *warning* lamp!—instead of a guide lamp!—anyway, it seems the fool kid, who gets a dollar a month for tending two lamps, neglected his stuff and forgot to light the p'ticlar lamp that lights the sign describing which by-pass road *not* to take. He come along, shortly after I got bogged, to pull in the lamp that was strung acrost the bog, and trim it—and seeing I was up Mike's Alley he told me his old man, who had a place back in the woods a few rods, had two mules in a log barn—a locked log barn, incidentally, Chief—and a log chain—and a set of 6-pulleyed block-and-tackle—and could get me out like nobody's business. But the rub was that the old man went every night to some cross-roads tavern north o' there—and never got back till around 11 bells. And—

"However," Jim continued wearily, "to cut a long story short, he showed up fin'lly—a bit likkored, but hitting on all fours mentally—at least when it come to cussin' mules out!—and he had them critters out in th' twinklin' of an eye—a log chain—the block and tackle outfit what we hooked to a couple of trees with the lines back of the cage—and, with the kid and me pulling on the fall line—and the mules pulling—and the old man cussin'—God, he was beaut'ful—an artist!—why, hell, we came up out of the muck 10 minutes after the old man struck there. Suckin' the guts right out o' the very earth; taking half the bog with us—there 'tis on the wheels! I *did* have to slip him $5, however—but I got his receipt."

Jim Craney fumbled in his breast pocket and withdrew that penciled slip of paper which that demon mule-curser back at Mill Creek had given him. Which he handed down to MacWhorter.

MacWhorter seized it, lowered it carefully into the glare of one headlight, and read it over with a Scotch eye, nodding with satisfaction that seemed to say that bringing Princess and her five little lionesses, worth $150 apiece, through for $5 only was a real triumph; then he stowed the receipt away in a curious big leather wallet which, to open, he had to first unlock a small silver padlock holding it fast by two stamped rings. This intricate procedure accomplished, he resumed the conversation, one hand on lamp, one on stick. "Yes," he announced, "that must have been the fellow I was told, way ahead of there, had mules and tackle—in case of any trouble. Well, Jim, you did mighty well to bring the girl through for a five-spot."

"Thanks. But now I'll ask one, Chief. Here 'tis: What—in the name o' the 7 bells o' hell—induced you, after we were all booked and all, to play 2 nights at Foleysburg—instead of 1? Today *and* tomorrow?"

"Well, I'll tell you. I—but where'd you' first learn it?"

"Why—right back there at that country store that lay just ahead of Perkins Junction. As I pulled away from there at 4 sharp—in accordance with some arrangements I'd made with that Sheriff beyond the mountain—and after eating me some canned stuff, fixing a tire, and catching a spit o' sleep—well, as I pulled away from there, glad *as* hell that I had a through ticket through that smooth Straightaway, and could beat the pullaway at Foleysburg seven ways across the board, I took a last gander back—and whooie!—there, plastered against the offside of that store, was our regular 2-sheet, with, over its regular play label of '1-night-only'—a big green sticker stuck atop it sort of squeegee, screaming out 'Two Nights.' Boy, you coulda goosed me with a sody-straw! Of course I knew something had happened, all right. And—but was I glad, Chief—oh, I won't say why!—because I was scared as hell I might not catch up with you here."

"Why should you be scared, Jim? You had $50, didn't you? And besides—however, to answer your question, I made a long-distance call, early this morning—or I should say yesterday morning, now!—from that store—to Hootens Falls—to Pete Glassbey. To see what, if anything, there might be new on the advance work. And I caught him at the Mansion House there—and caught a double piece of news, Jim! A double piece of news that made our playing Foleysburg two nights a 'natural'—100 percent in the bag. For shortly before I rang him, fire had just finished consuming practically our whole next stop—Spottsville!—and—"

"The hell you say? Little Spottsville—wiped out? Ow!"

"Yes—but wait—that isn't all—Pete slipped up, somehow, on his nose when he booked us at Foleysburg—drunk probably, damn him—and muffed completely that there is to be a 4-county old settlers' reunion in town on the night *after* the booking he got us—my God, Jim—can you beat it?—muffing *that!*—why, it will mean, that reunion, at least another tentful—for tomorrow night. So right then and there—at that country store—I made my plans to play here two days. What else could I do? And so, as we pulled off, I had Slappy plaster a green '2-day' on the 2-sheet he'd just stuck up.

"But why, Chief? You couldn't get any business out of that faraway road and count——"

"Now stop ribbing me! I—I—I did it to ease *you* up, in fact. I knew you'd see it, in passing, and know you no longer had to burn your cylinders up catching up. In fact, God help me, I left a whole trail of those 2-sheets—but all revised, of course, to show a 2-days' playing—along Old Twistibus, just to—"

"Not to ease *me,* though," laughed Jim. "And you know it! 'Twas to leave the name o' MacWhorter for kids to gape at in godforsaken spots, wishing like hell that they—"

"Now wait!" pleaded MacWhorter, gazing up wryly at Jim's grinning face. And as a man grasping at a straw he added: "I—I—hrmph—I like to think that there are boys gazing at my name all over the country—and evolving ambitions in their hearts to make something of themselves—and to—oh, let's drop that argument, Jim. I've—I've had far too much trouble, and excitement, today and tonight, to be able to argue on things like that."

"Trouble?" echoed Jim. "Excitement? What—what all happened today *and* tonight?"

"What happened—today and tonight!" MacWhorter threw up his hands, including the one with the blackthorn stick. "What didn't happen? In all my days, Jim, I never saw 12 hours like the last 12—with hell-popping at a dozen pain——"

"My God, spring it, Chief, for God's sake! What happened?"

"Well, for one thing, that crackpot hell-popping reformer of Southwest City—the Reverend Zebulon Q. Holowynge, who has been making so much successful trouble for the liquor interests there that it bids fair to involve the liquor interests all over the U.S.A.—I tell you this, Jim, because, confound it, you never read newspapers en route—well, this same Reverend Zebulon Q. Holowynge, believe it or not, tried to close the show."

"Close the show!"

"Yes—but failed. Thanks to your not having caught up with us before he had to tail it out of town."

"Thanks to me," echoed Jim helplessly. "Failing to catch—I pass!—but—but what else happ—"

"Well, for another thing, the big monks got loose, and—"

"The—hell—you say! Anybody hurt? Any—"

"Well, Spangles—"

"Spangles? Good God!—she isn't—"

"Now, now, now," pleaded MacWhorter desperately, "will you let me tell this story in my own way? Spangles, she—now listen, Jim—now listen!—I'm an old man—my last doctor—that fellow in Croutville who gave me a complete going over for 25 cents and a pass to the show—said I would have to conserve my resources—and so, if I have to tell you about the Big Excitement tonight, I'll only be wasting my energies and my time—for it'll be told you tomorrow by 99 other people—and for all the rest of your days you're with this show. And, probably in 99 different versions. So—"

"But damn it to hell, Chief, I *do* have a bump of curiosity. You know I have. So—"

"O-kay," replied MacWhorter, very grimly. "But I intend to conserve my strength. Now I'll tell you one thing—or the other—the Big Excitement that happened tonight—or how this reformer hell-popper who succeeded in making powerful big-city liquor interests wriggle like eels, fell flat on his beezer when he tried to put the blocks to MacWhorter's Shows. So take your choice. One or the other. Take your choice."

"Hell—fire!" retorted Jim emphatically. "I'll naturally want to hear about a goshdarned reformer making a bust. Rather, how my fool accidents during the whole day, and all that, prevented this particular one from reaching first base. Specially if, anyway, I got to listen to this other story 99 ways around tomorrow."

"Let it be so then," returned MacWhorter with a sigh of relief. He was silent a moment, free hand on the nearest headlight.

"Well," he began, "this reformer—this Zebulon Q. Holowynge—just happened to be in town today, looking up in the Foleysburg probate records some old detail of some local penny-ante estate that was bequeathed to some reform institution he's one of the directors of. As I told you, he's made things so disagreeable for the liquor interests up there in Southwest City, by his—his supreme legal cunning—that he—"

"But here, Chief, we don't peddle liquor. So—"

"No, but we have a lioness, don't we? That is, when she don't stay behind to have kittens—and doesn't have to be brought up by a lazy good-for-nothing lion-driver who gets himself stuck in a bog." MacWhorter grinned malevolently.

"Your trump, Chief," agreed Jim contritely. "But what connection—well, wait—if this fellow—Zeb—Zebulon?—Q?—Hol—Holowynge!—tried to put the blocks on us once, he may again; so I'd—I'd like to know more about him. Exactly what kind o' hell—is he raisin' there in Southwest City?"

"Well, like all other cities of America which have tasted the return of liquor—*and* its evils!—Southwest City is today a mixup of wet and dry districts, no bigger, some of them, than 2 blocks long. And this old boy, from rummaging around law books and Supreme Court rulings, and finding that liquor can't be advertised in a dry district, is successfully preventing the beer and whisky delivery wagons from going down so-called 'public thoroughfares'—in short, the streets—of—"

"How?"

"Why, on the basis, Jim, that the very names of the companies are, in most cases, an out-and-out ad for the companies' products—like, for instance, the Southwest Distilleries Company—or—or the Foamy Beer Corporation. Get it? And so this old boy has them actually going down alleys—in the dry districts—alleys not being, you see, 'public thoroughfares'—going down alleys, like cockroaches—cutting from wet district to wet district—and one company, the Hi-Bubble Champagne Company, has even had to change its corporate name to the Happy-Water Corporation and handle mineral water, too, to make the name legal!—but the point I'm trying to get at is that this Zebulon Holowynge has started a prairie fire that bids fair to be taken up in hundreds of other cities. Now, I guess, you know who the man is who tried to shut us up bag and baggage tonight, and get us fined $500 to boot!"

"Well, I guess I do all right. But what on earth leverage did he think he had—or—or have—on our show?"

MacWhorter appeared to be actually enjoying the recountal of this episode, since it had manifestly terminated triumphantly for him.

"Well, it seems, Jim, that having been in the reforming business so many years, he knows a lot of crazy statutes concerning everything everywhere, and back to Adam. And somehow he knew—or found out while he was here—of an ancient statute of Foleysburg County, from way back in the '60's—and never repealed—which provided that anybody holding a lion or lioness or big-type feline in captivity in the county, could be fined $500—and any traveling exhibition so holding one could be closed and likewise fined. And so, seeing a circus playing here—seeing our showbills—and that one of Princess, doubtlessly—he—he just had to put his hand in. Indeed, what did he do but swear out a warrant against us on *that* old statute, grab the Mayor and Chief of Police under his two arms, and descend on us just a couple of hours before show opening. Boy, oh, boy, was I praying, at that moment, that *you* were asleep on the way—drunk—'most anything." MacWhorter paused. "Well, we told him that our lioness was back in Pricetown having kittens—and was to rejoin us only at Hootens Falls—we took him all over the lot—through the Big Top—let him assure himself, to 100 percent, that we had no big cat. So he just had to give it up. For it seems he was due to testify in court tomorrow in Southwest City, and had to make some jerkwater line 8 miles west of here by 5 P.M.—to get back there. The minute he pulled out, the Mayor and the Chief of Police sheepishly tore up the fool warrants he'd sworn out—but confessed that if he'd put the heat on 'em, they'd have had to serve 'em, and go to bat on them—the Reverend being so all-powerful in this part of the United States. And that," finished MacWhorter satisfiedly, "is why I haven't roasted you for getting stuck in a bog!"

"Thanks, Chief," was all Jim said. "It gives me plenty sat'sfaction—believe you me!—that my fool shortcoming's helped to hamstring a guy who has liquor wagons slithering up big-town alleys like cockroaches! But now comes a real question. With us scheduled to stay here 2 days, what if this fellow—"

"—returns—or sends a deputy back? Well, Jim, after he vamoosed out, the Mayor showed me where and how the show abuts right on a county line—a county where that old statute doesn't exist. That is, Jim, the show is in Foleysburg County, see! And this other county, hugging it, so to speak—in fact, you're in and on it right now!—Foley County, it's called, though it's tied up, like the other, by Old Tom Foley's crazy land grants, so far as use of electricity and electric wires and all that goes—well, that county—this county—is without that old statute. A fact! The Mayor showed me. So we've arranged with a fellow who owns a spit of land adjoining the lot—but in this—Foley County!—to let us extend the sideshow tent *just* far enough so's Princess' cage-wagon can sit on his land—in Foley County—and *not* Foleysburg Connty—and Screwface is even back there sitting on the road-side now with a lamp, to highball you to a stop and pilot you off into proper position when you do arrive. And so Princess won't ever be in Foleysburg County at all—on top of which, when we pull out tomorrow night, with you taking a special detour, she won't even have entered that particular county! Pete Glassbey should have known about that statute. He—but everything's hotsy totsy now, Jim. Certainly so far as any naughty ideas back in the head of the Reverend Zebulon Q. Holowynge go! Everything was hotsy-totsy after he blew out of town, except that—" And he sighed wearily. "—except that, after he did blow out—and we opened, on the dot, as usual—then the Big Excitement happened—my God, Jim, it's a wonder tonight that I'm not a wreck. For I—but see here—I'm tiring myself—I want to finish my walk in the cool fresh air—all's well that ends well; so drive on to where Screw-face is marking the county line, and put up where he shows you, and I'll take a look at the kittens before I turn in, and will see you tomorrow."

"Okay, Chief. You do look sort o' weary. Nerve-weary, I mean! Well, I'll pull on now. Say—uh—say—Florette—I 'spose of course she's still here?"

"Is she—still here? Good God in heaven, Jim, why wouldn't she be?"

"We-ell—"

"Oh, you mean—she might have jumped the show tonight?—because we're about to leave railroad territory? Well, even if she had any such idea in her head, she wouldn't have jumped it tonight—when we don't leave till tomorrow night! But good heavens—be yourself, Jim, won't you?—why would she jump our show?—any night at all?—Florette?—jump the sh— well, by the gods, Jim!—speak of the devil and he appears; but speak of a pretty girl—and she floats right out of the night!"

For MacWhorter had been looking casually back along the road as he had been speaking—and Jim's own eyes had been where his Chief's face was—and now, as both gazed down the road, a girl could be seen coming along it, just entering into full view in the lights. She was dressed in a gypsy costume with widely flaring skirt of many colors from which peeped a crimson petticoat; she wore a silken orange blouse, and a black silken headdress, and had a string of great brass beads around her throat, false brassy but ornate earrings in her ears; her curious heart-shaped face, with its dark eyes, was solemnly, unsmilingly grave.

"I'm off," said MacWhorter suddenly. "Somehow I don't believe I belong here. Yes, I'm off. For a half hour with God."

And off he trudged into the darkness into which he had originally been headed, a lonely and always pathetic man.

The girl was now in the full flare of one of the headlights. A vivid picture indeed, in all her rainbow colors. She gazed up at Jim wordlessly. Almost questioningly. Though there was no sign of her stopping. And he spoke, rapidly, desperately.

"Florette," he said, "wait!" She stopped. "I'm—I'm awful sorry that I spoke to you the way I did that night. I was drunk—yes!—but that shouldn't have had anything to do with—with what I said. I was a dirty dog, Florette—not worthy even o' drivin' the high-grade car I'm drivin' now. I love you, Florette—so much so that I'd hate to lose you—but whether I have, or haven't, I'll never speak to you again the way I did—what's more—if I *have* lost you—for Mondaine has got more than just that $1000—he's got—oh, he's got ever'-thing—but if I *have* lost you to him, I sure never will speak to any other girl—if any other girl there ever is in my future—the way I did to you. I learned more—since I pulled away from Pricetown this morning— than I learned in all Australia and South Africky, plus the whole o' my life. That's 'bout all I can think of right now to say—'cept that I hope—I sure do hope!—that you don't jump the show tomorrow night—when it leaves Foleysburg—but if you do—if you must—"

She had come closer to his cab platform. And now put a slender hand up on his knee.

"I'm not going to jump the show, Jim. Tomorrow night or any night. I wanted you, Jim—but I wanted a Jim that could swallow his pride. I've even been kinda hard myself, I guess, Jim. Too hard, I guess. In fact, Jim, I—I couldn't even turn in tonight—after the show—so upset I was; I couldn't even take the trappings off. And when I finally went out to the road—to try to catch a breath of night air without gasoline fumes in it—and saw, way up it; the two lights that must be you—then the glint of red and gold back of your cab—I—I just decided then and there—to stroll on up—and—and get it over with. To find for good and all—whether you were willing to let you and me—be wrecked for good. But I've been too hard, Jim. Yes, I have! But I'm so glad—so awfully glad—that you—but anyway, Jim, everything's all right now—between us—you haven't the $1000 that Cecil has—no!—but it wasn't Cecil's $1000 I wanted—I wanted only his consider—but everything's right now, Jim—it's you I wanted—and have got. The Jim that's the tender and right Jim; and I never was so happy in my—"

He reached down a muscular hand to her.

"Up! Come up here—and while you're comin'—I want to jest say that you keep your faith in me, and I'll get that $1000—for that chicken farm. I will, Florette—I will! I will—somehow. I swear I will. And with it in our mitts we'll jump this godawful life together, and start raisin' chicks. Maybe Mr. Mac'll even give us a young lioness, as a weddin' present, to eat all our chicks up! Up now!—for I want you to be the first of the outfit to see the Royal Fam'ly!"

She was in the seat by him now. Her head on his shoulder. His arm around her. And, driven by one hand—one arm—the cage-wagon, bearing Jim Craney, rolling stone—Gypsy Queen Rozequia, who was no gypsy— Princess, who was no princess—and five kittens that were nor even true kittens!—moved majestically down the road toward Big-Top Town!

CHAPTER X

THE PORCH-SITTING SHATTUCKS

Sheriff Bucyrus Duckhouse was engaged this early morning—the morning following the set-to between Cedarville County and Willis Creek County, so to speak—in a most peculiar pursuit. For he had in his hand a great flaring lighted flambeau made of a pine-knot torch, wound and wound with oilsoaked rags—and in his eye was the proverbial blood thar comes at least once in a lifetime to every human eye!

For, due to possession of a bare trace of Indian blood—$\frac{1}{64}$th, he reckoned—Cherokee, he b'lieved!—he was proceeding through that tunnel—slowly—and on foot—exactly like an Indian would—to find out whether that damned gangster mob's truck had even reached the tunnel mouth before it had, for some reason, turned back. And, if it hadn't, it was the Sheriff's intention to find at *what* point back of the tunnel it *had* turned back!

Illumination none had he obtained by the long-distance call he had made, late last night, to the motor-vehicle registration department night clerk of Southwest City, and the ascertainment that state license 888,001 had belonged to a woman invalid, Mrs. Hepzibah Green, 80 years of age, dead for 7 days, and the license plate itself reported stolen 13 days ago; and that other law agencies had already that evening made the same identical inquiries. Nor even more illuminated had the Sheriff been, so far as that went, by the other similarly distanced call he had made to the night once of the Southwest City branch of the Transcontinental Trucking Company, and his ascertainment of the fact that a special "beam-braced"—whatever in Sam Hill that 'uz!—truck of their small local fleet of such was stolen fully 3 weeks ago in the suburb of Upper Southwest City Heights, and never recovered. And which identical information also had been obtained, that very evening, by many law agencies.

So all night long the Sheriff' had tossed and tossed, going slowly crazy because of the problem of a truck that had somehow succeeded in getting off a high embankment many feet above ground; and because such a fool problem had no answer, he had concluded grimly that the entire crookedness laid to him last evening had been on that other end; that it was Jech of Cedarville that had let them back—Jeth, who had somehow temporarily gotten rid of his helpers—and that town banker, damn him, must have been in on it—must have been himself in trouble—why—

Though all that didn't make sense, either!

The light from his torch showed the great rocky arch above his head, carved in material impregnable except to the stoutest compressed-air-driven chisels—the ever gradually bending granite walls the curve of which had been designed to slow down the traffic—to correct a slight offset in the two Carthage Roads—and to avoid the geological fault outside of itself which, if cut into, might make the tunnel unsafe.

And now, about $3/8$ths through the tunnel eastward he came upon one sign of one vehicle: a bit of crimson and gilt which he recognized as having come from Jim Craney's circus wagon where its side, in turning, had just grazed the rocky tunnel wall too closely.

From side to side, top to bottom, he examined that tunnel. Not a rookery for even a misanthropic bat was to be found: wall to wall—arched ceiling to macadam—his eyes darted; he was, indeed, in no less than an actual stone tube!

Now he came out in the light of morning. And had found no evidence yet that the gangster truck had gotten this far. From now on, he realized, it would be a matter of inquiries from those few scattered souls who lived in the lowlands, and who might have been anywhere in and about the Gullies yesterday; in particular, indeed, from two sets of lone people living in those lowlands almost under the east tunnel mouth, and off from the Straight-away, who might, by the grace of God, have seen something—heard some-thing; though unfortunately for Bucyrus Duckhouse's wobbly hypothesis of crookedness at the barrier, those who saw nothing and heard nothing would be able to prove nothing concerning it!

The first habitation he saw, naturally, as he came out, gazing rightward, and downward, was the log cabin of Gran'ther Fiddlecroft, standing upon low log stilts, some 150 feet from the Straightaway pillars; and, gazing left-ward of himself, he saw, down in the gully, the rambling unpainted house of the Porch-Sitting Shattucks—known thus because they practically never did do anything but sit thus *and* eat!—and whose famed porch faced the very Straightaway.

Stamping out his flambeau, and tossing it to one side, he went over to the low concrete railwall which had by no means even obscured his vision, and, feeling along its outer face, found the top rung of the series of curved steel ladder rungs which had been sunk into the concrete at intervals, where certain pillars stood, to give entrance down into the lowlands.

So over the low wall he went, and down the wall and pillar beneath it he went, hand by hand. And reaching the bottom, a once-mud that had dried here for so many decades that it had the most amazing crack patterns in it, he tramped over it southward to Gran'ther Fiddlecroft's sprawling stilt-supported log house.

Gran'ther Fiddlecroft, who had once been a miner in the long ago, and who lived on a tiny life insurance annuity today, was engaged this early morning, just as he had been engaged for years, in the creation of that bomb-proof cellar of his which almost rivaled a chamber on the Maginot Line; so at least, thought the Sheriff, who had last viewed it but a week ago, but who had never seen the Maginot Line; what he had seen, up years before, had been only a trench. Gran'ther, by pure chance, stuck his head and shoulders out of his narrow entrance shaft, to one side of the house, even as the Sheriff came up. Gran'ther was, of course, standing on the ladder that led into the bowels of the earth, and remained thus standing, for he rose no further than the upper part of his red flannel undershirt.

He looked his age of 76, though his cheeks were ruddy; his gold spectacles hugged his face tightly; his locks were long and white. The arms that reached over the shaft edge were still powerful.

"Hi, Gran'ther," the Sheriff greeted him. "How's she go?"

"Got her a'most all shored up now 'ith them timbers I tu'k down one by one; w'y—I'm danged near ready to po're the concrete. Wisht I coulda had her that fur w'en them fellers was a-po'rin' th' Straightaway yonder. Moughta ketched a lettle po'rin' cheap."

"You still think," said the Sheriff helplessly, "that the Germans will someday get in this far?"

"Hell-fa'r, Duckhouse, them devils' bombers 'll kivver this hull kentry. Cept'n they won't jar me none! Who knows but mebbe I'll hatter re-pop'late this danged kentry 'ith Americans—ef they leave one likely gal." Gran'ther's face was so unsmiling that it was plain he believed that sheer patriorism could call forth supreme accomplishment.

He leaned his back now against his entrance slit—for slit was all it was: a veritable slit with plank-encased walls, and a hinged trapdoorlike cover that could be brought down right over it. Gran'ther was even now toying with the key that would lock that trapdoor from the inside—and himself—against a fleet of Heinkels.

"Well, Gran'ther," said the Sheriff dourly, "I don't reckon I stand much chance to git any he'p from you, 'ith you practically livin' down in the guts o' the yarth—still—you mought a-b'en up on terry firmy yistiddy around—but to cut sho't arg'ment, was you upstairs hyar yistiddy any time or times 'round five-thutty—mo' or less?"

"Well," returned Gran'ther unperturbedly, "I wuz—an' I wuzn't."

"Yo' wuz—an' yo' wuzn't? What in the devil you mean by that, Gran'ther?"

"I mean I stuck m' head out'n this hyar shaft o' mine oncet 'bout—oh—hell-fa'r—I don't know the 'zack time becaze that's why I stuck m' head out—to calc'late it from the sun an' th' sky—but jedgin' by the light gildin' that Smoky Ridge crest—and the sky—it must a-b'en five-thutty mo' or less, 10 minutes one way or t'other. Atter w'ich I went back on down and did me some work, fur them Germans, when they declar' war ag'in us, they won't—"

"Well, what I really want to know," put in the Sheriff forlornly, "is not whether you did this or that, but whether you seed an'thin' on the Straightaway w'en you wuz sky-scoutin' fur the hour?"

"Whyn't you ast me that fu'st?" complained Gran'ther with some asperity. "I seed so'thin' up thar I hain't seed sence I 'uz a kid, bowlin' up to the tunnel mouth like—"

"What, Gran'ther?"

"A sarcus wagon, dog my hide ef I didn't! A sarcus wagon 'ith a lion inside—I know it—fer when she bounced like hell on a chip o' loose concrete, that durn lion he roared like he didn't like roughridin' nohow!—an' dang it, I know lions, fer hain't I b'en to the zoo in Southwest City at feedin' time? But 'bout then th' sarcus wagon, whut 'uz slowin' down fast, it rolled on into the tunnel—and I went on down into my shelter wonderin' how th' wagon evah got on th' Straight'way. I knowed they wuz a sarcus som'eres 'bout, day befo' yistidday, but how come one of its wagons to git on *our* Straight'way, I cain't fig—"

"I—I gave it permission," said the Sheriff. "Besides, th' driver 'uz fetchin' me so'thin' very special from Elum's. W'ich he passed to me tother side th' mount'in." He was regretfully silent. "Well, thanks fur th' info, but it—but see hyar, Gran'ther—how long, mebbe, didya remain down thar? Hour?—half hour?—two hou——"

"We-ell," responded Gran'ther, a bit embarrassedly, "I—I fell asleep down thar." Now he colored beet red. "Fack is, Duckhouse, w'en I still had that bigger shaft what drapped down from onder my house, I—I moved th' pieces o' m' extra bed down it, an' I've sence set her up—in case them goddanged Germ—"

"Yes," put in the Sheriff hastily. "Well, you shore hain't much of a witness, Gran'ther, fur tellin' me 'bout traffic on the Straightaway last evenin'—but thanks anyway." He was regretfully silent. For Gran'ther Fiddlecroft's erratic existence had virtually destroyed one person who might have testified that the gangster's truck never even got this far—and thus helped to "check the bet" to the Jeth crowd—and—

"Good luck," the Sheriff said.

"An' keep yo're own eye peeled," warned Gran'ther, "fer fellers 'ith squar' heads." And lowering himself rapidly out of sight, he reached out and drew down the hinged trapcover over his departing head. And the Sheriff, left alone and deserted in Frog Gully, turned and went in the direction from which he had just come. Surely—surely the Porch-Sitting Shattucks would be able to do for him what Gran'ther was unable to do.

Very shortly he was passing under the elevated highway again, between two massive pillars, coming out from under between another two, and traversing another stretch of cracked ground toward that rambling unpainted house lying, with porch facing him, 150 feet off from the raised highway. The Porch-Sitting Shattucks were already now doing their stuff, for Grammaw Shattuck, in a grey wrapper, was in a rocker shelling peas—and smoking a corncob pipe as she did; Paw Shattuck, in brown overalls and jumper, was fiddling "Turkey in the Straw" from a most comfortable-looking overstuffed chair leaking stuffing at all points; Maw, in a jade-green wrapper that, though she knew it not, had been contributed to charity by the madam of Southwest City's most notorious sporting house, sat in a wooden spring rocker rocking comfortably and apparently enjoying to the full her blaze of color. Susie, the 12-year-old, in a dress made of flour sacks, was on the top step with a rag doll, and Benzy, the small boy, about 7, in sun-faded overalls and sun-faded hickory shirt, was at the step next below puttering with a kite.

"Hi, Folks," the Sheriff said anxiously as he came up. "How's the po'ch-settin' this mawnin'?"

"It's putty fair," announced Paw imperturbably, coming to the very end of his rendition. "Long's it don't rain. This hyar po'ch, y' see, faces the south rains. Guess it'll hold we-uns up long 'nough 'twell we won't have to 'pend on relief money no more."

This was a puzzler to the Sheriff. For the Shattucks had been eating on relief money for as far back as he could remember.

"Well, Folks," he said, putting one booted foot atop the lower step, "I'm down hyar to ask yo'-all to tell me—but wait!—when do you folks eat yo're evenin' meal?"

"We eat ev'y day," declared Paw, "at 3 'clock. An' have us a snack at bedtime."

"Good!" said the Sheriff. "Then, Folks, yo're my meat—so t' speak. For I'm askin of yo'-all to tell me evahthing yo' seed on that el'vated road back o' me yistidday 'bout five-thutty o'clock in the afternoon—ruther, from 'bout a half-hour back o' that to, say, a half-hour beyant—whilst you doubtless was settin'?"

"Well," replied Paw, obviously official spokesman for "yo'-all," "we can't tell you much 'bout th' half hour befo' that time, 'caze the whole pack an' passel of us 'uz down in th' cellar layin' out our mushroom farm."

"Mushroom farm?" echoed the Sheriff glumly.

"Yes. We're goin' into business—so t' speak—with a feller whut advertised in th' *Rural Companion* fur—fur mushroom growers. We-all got our cellar factory all laid out, with strings. Susie and Benzy they air goin' to have sections close to ourn, an' grow th' leetle white 'uns needed fur that heathen dish, chop suey. Grammaw she's s'lected her section, an' is goin' to grow th' med'cal Maltese mushroom what keeps people from pukin'. Soon's we git a-holt the $100 whut we need fur spores, we're all set. This hyar fambly don't aim to be on relief much longer."

"Then—then," said the Sheriff disgruntledly, "you didn't none of you see nothin' on the Straightaway?"

"Cain't say that," pronounced Paw, "becaze, when we all did come up and tu'k our cheers hyar, whut we sot in 'twell dark—'bout 8 'clock—we *did* see var'ous things."

"What?" demanded the Sheriff, pricking up his ears.

"Wa-all, fo' one thing, we fu'st seed a big grey motor truck go billy-hell into th' mounting."

"Truck whut b'longed," put in Maw, who had been to school and could read big words, "to th' Transcontynental Truckin' Company. One o' their fast freight trucks, 'caze it said all that in yaller letters on th' side."

"Ah!" breathed the Sheriff. "So it got there after all?" He rubbed his hands. Now he had the Jeth crowd! And asked: "And how soon'd it back out, turn 'round, an' go back?"

"Didn't come out," said Paw.

"Didn't come out?" echoed the Sheriff. "But it musta."

"Then we mus' be all blind," said Maw. "'Caze we all sot hyar 'twell dark an' the skeets driv' us in."

"You did?" said the Sheriff helplessly. "Wa-all—wa-all—wa-all, you see a posse come 'long the road any time?"

"That's whut I said 'twas!" spoke up Grammaw triumphantly, to her relatives, and blowing a huge cloud of smoke out of her mouth as she talked. "That thar big green car whut come 'long befo' dusk, an' riz up an' down evahtime its front tires went over taped bumps—an' with a man ridin' on each runnin' board and th' whole pack an' passel holdin' shotguns. They—they sot the car 'g'in the Fiddlecroft side, an' all got out and lit up 'lectric to'ches an' things—one feller lit a kind of a oil torch—and then, beatin' on pans and what, they all went into the tunnel."

"Went in?" repeated the Sheriff. "Did you recognize any—"

"Grammaw don't know folks 'round here," put in Maw, "but *we* do. I rec'nized th' leader as bein' Sher'ff Bill Jeth o' Cedarville—fur didn't I visit my sister thar a month ag—"

"And Stoeffhaas the banker," offered Paw, but wrinkling up his own forehead. "At least his squar' beard and his belly!"

The Sheriff's blood was running peculiarly cold now.

But Paw was continuing.

"Sher'ff Jeth 'uz wearin' a pillow or so'thin' tied to his foot—'caze he clumb up atop the pa'pet, befo' they went in, to peer in th' tunnel better."

The Sheriff's blood was colder yet. He essayed to speak.

"Wa-all—wa-all, what next—"

"Why, we jest sot an' sot," said Paw, amiably, "'cept'n Benzy hyar—who run 'crost the gully an' clumb up—"

"—clumb up," piped up Susie, breathlessly, "the rungs this side, nearly t' th' top, an'—an so'te a hid onder an' back o' th' par'pet!"

"And?" said the Sheriff faintly—but to Paw.

"Wall," said Paw helplessly, "they all come our 'bout 15 minutes atter they went in, still ca'yin' they guns, and Jeth limpin' on his cushion. And they all got into they car—Benzy he says they wuz sayin'—whut wuz they sayin', Benzy?"

Benzy piped up eagerly. "They says, 'We'll indict th'—th' damn crook—when the grand jury sets!'"

"An' off they went back," finished Paw, "from whar they come from."

"My God!" moaned the Sheriff, putting his hands to his head. "Wu'ss—wu'ss—an' still wu'ss! A gold truck dis'pears not on'y on a raised highway—but right inside a tonnel with solid hard walls. I—I'm goin' plumb crazy right this minute!"

CHAPTER XI

THE SHERIFF TRIES TO CONCENTRATE

Sheriff Bucyrus Duckhouse lay atop his bed, with its red and black and green patchwork quilt, occupying the one bare whitewashed room off the kitchen-office of his shack, trying vainly, despently, to read. The wall clock visible through the crack of the open door showed the time to be 11 o'clock in the morning—but the leaf calendar on the bedroom wall showed that it was the day after the one on which he had met up with stark mystery in a tunnel.

His two cats, Sebastian and Tobias, roosted on each side of him, paws curled under their breasts, affectionately contemplating him as the world's most wonderful individual.

The book he was trying to read, while the cynosure of two pairs of cat eyes, was a book of Chinese wisdom—no less, indeed, than the one that had been brought to him by the circus wagon which had transported one, Craney. It consisted of hundreds of curious and quaint aphorisms, based on Celestial ideas of thousands of years ago—like dragons, and prayer papers, and goldfish, and Cathayan silks, and temples, and slave priests—grouped together into alleged "systems" by which they might perhaps be applied to this or that modern dilemma or problem, but none of which systems applied even remotely to the Sheriff's problem.

Which was that of a man who apparently had had a sudden moment of aberration—some sort of epileptic fit—or—or cataleptic fit—while a truck-ful of gangsters rode past him—and had then come out of his fit with complete amnesia concerning the moment. Except that, by Godfrey, and Jupiter Priest, he could reconstruct in his mind a complete continuity of thought over that period while he lay waiting, waiting, for them fellers to bowl out. And consequently—

And so he read, and read—read aphorisms in straight sequence—and not at all for illumination, but to get his tortured mind off his situation. And, reading, paused after each one, and tried faithfully, persistently, to digest it completely before going on to the next—since that appeared to be the only mental gymnastics that did halfway help to make him forget himself—though half the time, he realized, he wasn't even concentrating to that degree.

Because his mind simply wasn't on the job of reading Chinese wisdom!

For he had seen himself indicted that morning in County Court. Indicted for letting through a truckful of bankrobbers when he had been pre-warned they were headed his way—and he had them inescapably blocked. And under the state ruling providing that indicted county officers of the law could not function until cleared of their indictment, or cleared at their subsequent trial, he had even seen his star, which, in the very courtroom, he had had to turn over to County Commissioner Hosea Jones, put—for the time being, at least—on the breast of Under-Sheriff Job Binks. Between Jeth and two of the latter's crowd as witnesses, Lucy the local telephone operator, and Paw Shattuck and Benzy Shattuck, Bucyrus Duckhouse's indictment had been a dizzy affair for him indeed. They had even sprung old Charley Sit-on-his-Own-Face, the old Indian who lived near the Indian trail, who had gravely and unblinkingly sworn in court: "Big buzz box on wheels—like big grey moth—with yellow marks on wings—pass Injun's place—going west—ask how quick out from deadwoods—give Injun firewater." Old Charley, the Sheriff realized, being of the tribe Cheyenne—and stock Algonkian!—could well have been protecting somebody who had traded him a bottle of hooch, by rendering spurious facts which the superannuated—but always imperturbable—red man had shrewdly picked up from his excited questioners. Unless, perhaps, old Charley really *had* met up with—

For, alas, a few tire tracks had been found on the trail, near its out-point on Southwest Road which itself led quickly into Southwest City Road, of identical pattern with those in a brief stretch of that Cedarville Road whose owner had damped it down with a watering can just before the grey truck had roared over. No significance in really proving anything, the Sheriff told himself angrily, in view of the many cars—including countless truck drivers and their sweeties—who drove, with their sweeties, into that sparse thicket up south of Southwest City—then on, on, on, for various distances, down the ensuing trail—cars and trucks with identical tire patterns to any of thousands of others. Just a piece of mosaic that added itself beautifully to the tale of Old Charley, the story of Paw Shattuck and Benzy Shattuck, the two Jeth witnesses, Lucy Hig—

And the Sheriff groaned.

He himself was prepared to put everybody in Willis Creek on the stand, when his trial should come up, to prove that the grey truck hadn't passed thataway; also, a half a dozen big city truck drivers—if such would have the decency to come forward—to prove that they and their countless brothers often drove their sweeties into the thicket which provided a secret ingress into the dead woods; and to try to tear Old Charley to pieces on the witness stand. But in the face of the mere existence alone of that amazing and almost secret detour—it was like trying to spoon up the Mississippi River with a teaspoon. And, being purely negative proof, wouldn't restore his own good name. Specially with that confounded rumor of the existence of that forged check wafting here and there—not quite in the open because nobody had the check.

"Goddang it to hell!" he said to himself, staring moodily at the book in his hands, as he turned another of its pages, "I hain't never had any amnesy in my life. So how could—" He came out of his own thoughts, and put them for a change, on the aphorism he was trying to read—he even read it till it registered—he digested it—then his mind, as though it was on a rubber band, flew straight back again to the thing that was driving him crazy. "How the hell kin a man have amnesy when he kin 'member ever'thin' he 'uz thinkin' at the time he had the amn—aw shucks!—it cain't—but now le's see—what's this 'un about?—dragons!—pshaw—who ever heered of a drag—by Jesus Christopher, them gangsters was *in* the tunnel when Jeth and his whole posse went through—they was a pay-off in there—'at's why Jeth an' them slicker townsmen o' his'n put on sich a fine indig'ant act with me—the gangsters, they lay in there 'twell dark, an—ah, shucks!—that set-up'd fall to pieces with that many townspeople in it—fur it—what's this un about?—a mulberry leaf—one o' them leaves that silkworms make silk from—Jup'ter Priest, but them old Chinkees 'd shore be surprised ef'n they knowed we spun our silk t'day out'n coal, an' called it nylon!—but would they?—sence they prob'ly wouldn' know what coal was, nor—say, I wonder ef I could be crazy, an' the folks around here don't know it yit?—that would make sence outa nonsense—which things air now—or air they?—well, I say they air!—big heavy truck—with heavy wheels an' engyne—carryin' a heavy box o' gold weighin' a eighth ton—an' 5 gangsters, countin' that old local confe'date we now know they picked up outside Cedarville—and it—it dis'pears right inside that thar stone tunnel—that tube—that—goddang it!—"

With a furious effort he broke himself loose from his hopelessly squirrel-cage ratiocinations. And succeeded in actually reading is aphorisms—and digesting them. Turned the page. And because of that single break in the continuity of what he was doing, recommenced his mental turmoil right where he had left off!

"—heavy truck and 5 gangsters—went in—but never come out—walls solid as hell—Christ, didn't I see 'em chiseled?—an'—an' I 'zamined 'em yistiddy mo'nin' goin' back through—'zamined 'em at every foot—at every danged inch!—they ain't a hole what you could even poke a crowbar into—say, I wonder, by God, if I could have had a sunstroke that aft'noon, an' passed out?—but good God in heaven—who ever heered of a man gittin' stroked by the sun when 'twas so clost to th' horizon!—prat'cally on the horizon!—an' me, old sun-dog, of all pussons!—besides—then that means th' truck dis'peared—fur it went in—an' it never come out—an' it never backed out, nuther, so—God, but I'm tired—I 'uz tired that day—I wonder—"

And as a last desperate experiment, he closed his eyes. To see *if* a man could drop off without knowing it. For he was desperately tired from last night's tossing. But he didn't even sway from the precipice of wakefulness. He could almost count the quarter-seconds his eyes were closed.

He opened them up again disgustedly. And went on reading where he had left off.

That is, trying to read and think at the same time.

"'A shaven priest'—now," he switched off mentally, "the whole danged Shattuck fambly'll be su'poenyed to 'pear at that trial—an' will!—as well as half a dozen o' the act'al hold-up witnesses—and the whole danged posse this time, bar none—but it'll be the Shattucks' story'll be the toughest fur me—fur they put them gangsters lit'rally in my lap—and they all hang together, and confi'm each other—say—I wonder ef the Shattucks could secretly hate me, and be in a conspi'cy to send me over the ro—but good Gawd, how could they?—wasn't I alluz kind to Paw?—I got him a job in this hyar town out'n his own caounty—but mebbe *that's* why he hates me!—but I give Susie that rag doll last b'uthday of her'n—an' I brung Grammaw some smokin' tobaccy last Christm—goddang it, I'm losin' my mind—I—"

He went on to another aphorism.

"I'm losin' my mind," he said, "that's what. I—I got half a notion—no, a whole notion!—to have one o' them ali'nist fellers 'zamine me all over—and then plead mental ab—ab—whatever t'ell it is—but now wait!—math'matics cain't lie—math'matics proves an'thing—now the sum o' the exits an' the entryances 'd have to be a even number o' times either one—fur—but Jumpin' Jup'ter, do I have to prove first that the World is round?—a'right—the sum o' the exits an' the entryances 'd have to be a even times either one—but wouldn't hatter be divided equally atween the two tunnel ends—or would they?—or—but no, they wouldn't—take the case of a car goin' in and backin' right out—thank God, there's one statement o' mine that stands firm on all its laigs—a'right—well, the sum o' the entryances an' exits has to be a even number o' times either group—an' ef they was one excess 'un o' either on the Jeth side, that'd prove th' Jeth crowd are crooks—and ef they was one excess 'un on my side, that'd prove I was a—a—a—well, why th' hell worry now 'bout what it'd prove, 'twell I see what we *do* prove?—a'right—well, Gran'ther Fiddlecroft seed Jim Craney go in—that's one entryance—an' I seed him come out—that's two—but hell-f'ar, it'd still be two even if Gran'ther wasn't in the pikter—now how the hell kin that be?—I 'spose 'caze o' th' simple fact that sence Craney come out, he had to have first went in—so—aw, skip it!—now Gran'ther may be a mite cuckoo on German invasions, but he shore told ever'thing straight 'thout ary promptin'—includin' 'bout that big cat's roar—so a'right—two is two—two makes two—two is alluz one plus one—now the Shattucks see them gangsters bowl in—that makes three—but goddang it—that's all it does make—three ain't four—three ain't—but atter all, who in hell says the exits an' entryances hatter be a even times either?—only me!—a goddanged screwy addlepated old coot who's beyond doubt in a 'arly state o' paresis, an'—"

He stopped, As his eyes, resting so long on one aphorism, caused his brain to take over and made him read it. And then, by sheer habit, to reread it. And then to digest it. At which, his eyes opened wide.

And he started up in bed, gasping.

"Whoops!" he yelled—so loud, that Tobias and Sebastien were but two cat-colored streaks flying through the air toward the crack of that door—"— the old Chinkees have solved it. Hoo-ray!"

CHAPTER XII

BLACKED MAN IN A CORNER

Sheriff Duckhouse, seated in the cheap hotel room of that city far, far from Willis Creek, his small alligator traveling bag by his side, a switch engine dolefully switching cars, in the inky night, outside the very window, sternly eyed the blacked-up man with gargantuan pink-striped wing-flare collar, and large banjo slung over shoulder, who faced him ruefully from a stiff chair some feet from his own. The room—such as it was!—was carpeted with cheap matting; its walls were papered with arsenical green roses; a tarnished rickety brass bed occupied one corner, and coiled under its one windowsill—and one end fastened stoutly thereto—was a coil of musty-looking rope, placarded by the inevitable flyspecked red sign reading *"Use in Case of Fire."* Downstairs, under the floor on which the two men were closeted, the raucous clatter of a tinny piano indicated a cheap tavern of sorts; but while it was noticeable that several instruments could be discerned accompanying the piano, not one of them was a stringed instrument—let alone a banjo. At least not just now!

"Aha!" the Sheriff was even saying at this very moment—a moment arriving after a conversation—mostly accusatory on the part of the Sheriff—which had been going on now for 15 full minutes, "I jest thought that th' *mode* o' th' payoff—w'ich I knowed I'd fo'ce outa you easy!—'d give me th' leetle clue I needed to yo're gang—yes, yo're gang, I said, even ef you air he'pin' on'y from—from th' outside—but, instid, I git m' clue in 'nuther way—however, it don't matter—fur as I've a'ready said, I knew, from a suttin' leetle so'thin' I read in a suttin' book o' Chinee wisdom which I've referred to more'n oncet t'night—*how* yo're gangster friends dis'peared co'pletely inside that tunnel—an' which knowledge driv' me shore an' straight to'd a suttin' man—brother, in a manner o' speakin', to th' leader o' that gang—a man now ca'yin' a banjo on his shoulder, nigger paint on his face, and a nigger collar whut never have I see on land nor sea, sence Hector was a pu—but skip it. So come clean now, Mr. Banjoist—*what* is that one clue to them fellers' hideout what yo' jest acc'dentally let loose you p'ssess?"

"I—I don't know," replied the blacked-up man stubbornly, compressing his red-paint thickened Negro-like lips.

The Sheriff's own lips closed together tightly. He was a changed Sheriff, from what he usually was around Willis Creek, for he was dressed tonight in his best black go-to-meetin' suit, with his boottops now under the cuffs of the top'short black pants, and he wore his Sunday Sheriff's bread-brimmed black hat. He grunted belligerently, got up, took off his coat, tossed it on the tarnished brass bed in the room, exposing in thus doing bright red galluses which were matched, in screaming effect, only by the enormous arsenic-green roses on the greasy wallpaper of the cheap room.

"Now yes you do," he averred. "I knowed—when I knowed ever'thin'—that th' one outsider who worked in with that gang would be the key to where they air. An' you can't come none o' yo're denials on—"

"We-ell," said the owner of the shiny black face, the chin of which was moist with sweat, "can—can I ask a question?"

"Shore—shore. Axe away?"

"Well, it's—it's this," stated the other. "Did Jim Craney, when you came up to him—at that show openin' hour of his—in and at the town where his show was playin'—did Jim Craney, when you told him that this book he fetched you from that country store had turned out to be the complete an-swer to that Cedarville County bank robbery—well, did Jim Craney ask you for a cut out of any reward?"

"Why should he?" demanded the Sheriff acerbically. "Fur fetchin' 'long a book to me? Didn't I pay him fur the book in a'vance? By givin' him p'mission to transpo'te his cat through my county? Why should I even give him a 5-p'cent cut fur *that?* A fair exchange is no robb'ry! However," he broke off, "to talk with Jim Craney on his own p'serves—a circus show—is much diff'ent from talkin' to him out in the wild deestrict where I live, and talked with him erig'nally—it 'uz able to show he's a white man, fo'ty ways 'round the board, and—however, let's git back to brass tacks, Mr. Banjoist. Now, ol' boy, yo're playin' in fur a thousand lousy dollars—looks like a million to you, yes—but is on'y a thousand—yo're playin' in fur an' with a dirty rascal who ain't even yo're real blood-brother—ain't even, by God, yo're leg'lly adopted brother—Al Mulhearn—a robber and, beyant all doubt, a ruthless killer—an' who'll have *you* bumped off either before the pay-off or after—but shore. So now you switch yo're play to me, and in with me, and I'll pass you th' same amount out'n my cut—"

"Meaning—"

"Meaning they 'uz a $2000 reward offered fur capturin' 'em—and I aim t' do jest that."

"You, you mean, and a half a dozen of the toughest G-men you can get—since G-men can't cut into rewards!—yes, I get it all right—but the point is: if you and those G-men fail to take just one of—of Al's bunch—just one!—that one'll eventually gun me sure, for my one protection—"

"—the dope you left in the saf'ty box ag'in just that—yes?—"

"—yes—my one protection—the clue to that hideout—won't even any longer be anything, once the hideout is found and raided. Jesus Chri—"

"And you think," parried the Sheriff, "that you ain't going to wind up in a shroud under th' present conditions? Why, you damned fool with a banjo, yo're livin' on borried time this minute. On'y thing that's savin' you is the fact o' them fellers layin' low—veree low!—in their hideout. Now see here—get wise!—you tell the Law—that bein' me, I regret to say—you tell the Law that hideout now—ruther, the clue you got to it—instid of when it's all too late—and the Law—me, again—'ll cut you in 50-50 on my take. An' you'll ride clear—as the man who he'ped d'liver th' gang to jestice. And—now wait!—ef'n you don't play ball with me," emphasized the Sheriff harshly, "I'll simply have to have you 'rrested right t'night. By the Chief o' Police of this city. And yo'll be sent 'ventually to Cedarville County, where a jury o' 12 farmers an' townsmen'll convict you as accessory to the crime, an' give you 10 years in—anyway, think hard. Think mighty hard."

"What d'ya think," said the other, equally harshly, licking red-grease-painted lips with a tongue, "I been doin' all this time?"

"Well, think fast then, instead o' hard," the Sheriff advised coldly.

There was a tense silence. A silence in which the blackface banjo-holder wiped off a chin dripping with perspiration. It blackened the ungloved white hand that wiped it. He seemed not even to see it.

"We-e-ell," was his unhappy reply, "I—I have thought. There's just one—one thing, how'ver. Will you put that prop'sition in writing?"

"Cert'ny—cert'ny." The Sheriff reached down for his alligator bag, took it up on his knee, opened it, withdrew from it a coarse ruled tablet, and on the top sheet thereof wrote, with a green-inked fountain pen he had, the tablet lying atop the flat handle of the chair he occupied. The while the switch engine chugged and snorted outside and below the very window, at times a blast of sulphurous smoke trailing in the open window. The Sheriff read what he had written, then handed it to the other. "Here 'tis."

The black-lidded eyes read it, squintingly.

"That's—that's 100 p'cent conclusive, I guess. So—so it's a deal. Except that I know somebody in that gun battle, that's sure to be, will get killed—and if it's you—this paper won't—"

"—won't be worth the woodpulp it was ground out of, heh? So that's yo're big worry, is it—my gittin' killed?"

"Well, under these circ'mstances, it—it is. But a deal's a deal. And a guy backed into a corner is able to see a fair deal—even if he does double-cross a boy what grew up with him for—"

"Come, come!" said the Sheriff. "Growed up with you—for no more'n a year—bulldozed you—wasn't square even with yo're father who tu'k him in—stole so'thin', I think you said, when he run away—turned into a gangster, bankrobber—a—a killer—why, goldang it, man, he double-crossed you—and yo're father—by turnin' into sich a kind of a man. Cain't you see how—"

"Yes," said the other hastily, "I—I know. I know. But it kind of goes against my grain to—but you're right." The white hand was stowing the precious paper, now folded, away in an inside pocket inside the short musician's coat.

"Well," its new owner began, undecidedly, "Al had an uncle when Dad took him in—an uncle who apparently didn't want to be bothered with Al, but who didn't have nobody but Al in the world to leave what he had to when he died. I don't know his name, though. Any more than I do the exact place where he lived. For I was only 7 at the time we had Al—my own father died when I was 9—and I got sent packin' myself to far rel'tives in the East who'd take me in. This uncle of Al's owned a cur'ous place in the country, what he use to live in in the summertime only—a place layin' south of Southwest City. That's quite all I can tell you where 'twas. We ourselves lived north o' Southwest City. North by several hundred miles. And when Al—a big boy to *me!*—persuaded me to take a bummin' trip with him to this uncle of his, I only know that we bummed on th' local freight south to Southwest City—trudged clear through the city on foot—and then went south by another line. Oh, Al knew the ropes; knew the way; knew ever'thing. I was just a brat.

"Anyway," the black-painted man went on, "this uncle was a reg'lar re-cluse. He lived that way in the city—though what city, I don't know—as Al told me; and he sure was livin' that way—when we found him in the country. For he was livin' in a big square one-room house—all made of wood—stout wood—but of one thickness of board only—the boards were well joined with wood-lathe stripping at the junctions—and tar-papered to boot—okay for summer—n.g. for winter! 'Twas situated where he wouldn't ever be bothered—by God, *couldn't* be!—by anybody knockin' at his door for directions, or asking for water, or any other damned thing. Including even hunters passing over his place. For the place was cut off from the narrow dark rutty road it lay on, by an eighth-mile deep strip of the dankest, rankest woods you ever see; it was in fact, cut off by woods a'most everywhere; the house, in fact, was on a fair-sized clearin' right inside a woods that occ'pied the whole tract, and which woods was contin'us with more like woods each side of it, a—a downright forest, no less!—the whole region—and, outside of Al's uncle's partic'lar tract, the forest land was being held in trust by some estate for some kid, yet unborn, but to be born—if, as, and when!—to some kid who even then was virt'ally in diapers, and then and then only—at the heir's major's, I mean—be turned over with a crop of trees that would contain a fortune if sold to a furniture factory or—or a pulp-paper mill. And because o' that—the restrictions, I mean, on the trees—and the fact o' pract'cally two matur'ties of 21 years each bein' involved—the whole tract of forest land would still prob'ly be there today, thicker and ranker even yet. Anyway—" The black-faced speaker wrinkled up his brows in recollection. "Anyway, at the time I viewed it, people wanderin' those woods were just hamstrung from even moseying over into Al's uncle's section of it, by the fact of the existence of a deep ditch, full o' water, coming into the roadway, and cutting off one entire side, and emptying into a creek, also full o' water, running along the rear of the holding at—at its—well, I think it was its north edge—though I'm not clear, see? Not clear at all t'day. Passage onto the holding by trespassers from the right was prevented by a narrow swampy stretch, the water in which couldn't touch this here high tract.

"But," went on the black-painted man, "there was a cunning path through them trees in front. A path cleared so's to be wide enough for a wagon or car. Lookin' straight at it, you couldn't even tell it was a way through. But if you followed it, ever—always takin' the *one* direction where no trees blocked you!—you could sashay right through it! But once 'way, 'way inside, and through, there was this pretty neat place. It—"

"What the devil did this uncle do with himself in there?" asked the Sheriff helplessly.

"Worked," said the other quickly, "on his wall. For alongside this living shack, when we got there—off from it by 25 feet or so—was a beaut'ful 30-foot-long wall, 6 feet or so high, with half a dozen diferent kinds of masonry work in it—sections of stones—sections of bricks—different kinds of coping even. That—that was this old boy's hobby. Like some people do fancy work, he ev'dently did wall work! I s'pose today that wall is in rack an' ruin—but doubtless still standing. On the other side of this house— about 30 feet off—was a good quality barn. Prob'ly built by the first man who cleared the place.

"And that's the place Al's uncle had. And which, when Al inherited it— for he sure musta have—bein' this old bird's only relation, he cert'nly would have—Al, prob'ly then well on th' crook, could use as a hideout far, far better than he could ever use the few lousy dollars the tract'd have brought. Of course, bein' on the crook, he'd have long since transferred his holdin' to a bunch of phony names and aliases—and so there'd be no clue t'day from any holdin' in *that* name, that's sure! But my b'lief is that he and his gang are there right now. He don't know I'm able to be tellin' anything of all this, for the simple reason that he don't remember anything at all about that trip. Reason I know is that when I see him last—before this last time, I mean—10 years ago—when I ran into him in the East—we had a couple o' beers and gassed over the old days. And he was wishin'—actually wishin'

—that him and me might have taken one bummin' trip in our kid days. He don't remember anything. He—"

"An'thing happen," asked the Sheriff shrewdly, "atter that trip that 'uz painful to him?"

"Did they? His uncle whipped him good—before he took us back; and then my father whipped him again—for risking my young legs under freight trains. And so—"

"Well, that's all explained by a feller named Frood," imparted the Sheriff. "Things what is painful goes co'pletely out'n the mind. 'Specially with long time, like is involved here. Two whoppin's—at each end!—hell f'r—he's got a complete amnesy 'bout this incident layin' decades back."

"That's right—whatever the explanation. But *I* didn't get whipped—and I remember everything. Everything, that is, but the location of this place—and I can't help you on that any more than I could show you where a needle was, in a haystack. I—"

"Hell-f'r," snorted the Sheriff. "With all yo're dee-scription o' the place, yo've as good as put it in my lap. It kin be found—easy. An' quick. Fur one thing, I kin git air service from this city what'll put me into Southwest City in time fur—hell, I kin even get a goddanged good sleep in prep'ration fur tomorrow's work. And which'll be to sift the farm plats, at the State Re-corder's, o' some of them counties lyin' south o' Southwest City—and pay attention only to ditch and creek int'rsections—and standa'd descriptions showin' woodsy or swampy land alongside or near. Hell—it's in the bag. Part of a big woods—prat'cally a forest—ditch 'long one side—creek 'long rear—marsh to tother side—and, to check ary place tallyin' with this, a wide trail through it from roadway back, if you follow the tree gaps keerect with your eyes—it's a problem a 14-year-ol' boy could solve, so—" The Sheriff had risen abruptly. Was putting on his coat. Took up his small bag. And turned to the black-faced man watching him unhappily.

"So," the Sheriff continued firmly, "keep yo're mouth shut from now on—if it's the last thing in the entire world you do. Fur it'll mean a grand to you—ef the button on yo're lip don't—uh—unbutton! It'll mean a grand, that is," the Sheriff qualified, "if me, an' the men I'll get, get them bank-robbers, and what they stole. And goddang it—quit re-proachin' yo'rese'f fur bein' a guts-spillin' louse. Yo're black face is—is a mile long. Why, this Chinee wisdom book, I tell you, laid you right acrost my legal knee—oh, yes it did—fur it told me *how* they dis'peared, truck 'n all, in that tunnel!—which driv' me straight as hell to—to a nigger wirh a banjo!—who was bound to be the key to whar they wuz today—if not becaze he'd know the hideout, then becaze he was to be subjec' of a pay-off—so of co'se you had to sing—or go to prison yo'rese'f. Ever'thing was finee, I tell you, an' in the bag, I tell you also, when I turned a suttin' page of a suttin' book."

"Well," said the other morosely, rising, "I don't know what you saw nor read—and don't care much, neither—but everything isn't finis, that's the trouble, 'bout this case—for you and your gang of G-men haven't taken those boys yet."

"Oh, well," sighed the Sheriff, "is an'thing ever sure in life?"

"Not by a damn sight," sighed the other lugubriously. "I—well, when—when d' you think you'll take 'em—that is—try to take 'em?"

"When? Well, I'll work down to 'em tomorrow mornin', by those plats. And the raid'll be done at sich time o' day or night as'll seem best fur—but see hyar now—don't, whatever you do, try to double-cross me atter I go away from here—'caze yo've on'y killed yo'rese'f dead ef you do. Fur if that gang finds out—from so'thin' comin' straight from *you*—that yo've sent—or had tried to send—a party o' th' Law ag'in 'em, they'll clear out—fur an'whar 'll be less hot than *that* place—but they'll make you to be a dead man fur what you did. Jest keep in mind that w'en you 'prised me of the dope by which myse'f an' the G kin get 'em yo' hamstrung yo'rese'f from double-crossin' us. Yo're not atween the devil and the deep sea, Mr. Banjoist—yo're atween a grand of sweet money—and gangsters' bullets a-trailin' you fur the rest of yo're days. Keep *that* in mind. And stop yo're fool innard quallums as to when, how and with whom they'll be took. Leave that to the G *and* yo'res truly—a man whose got guts 'nough not to be afraid of dirty rats whut lives by their guns; and brains 'nough to—hrmph—brains—yes!—to set by a tunnel mouth waitin' fur a truck what had vanished into thin black air t' come out. Brains—yes! Brai—but don't worry 'bout me, now. I'm worried on'y—so he'p me—fur a grease-painted banjoist who a'ready needs a whole ovahsized bed sheet fur a diaper becaze o' what he thinks he's went an' did. Now buck up, man—an' ef you get too nervous, cut yo'rese'f some blank paper strips, and count 'em like as ef they was 100 $10 bills!—bills which, *you* lucky black-faced devil, this here Jim Craney, who you ast me 'bout a minute back, could use like nobody's bus'ness—in the face of a love affair he's up ag'inst, an'—but skip it—good night, now—an' git back to yo're work!"

CHAPTER XIII

QUIET EVENING AT BILL TARG'S

Bill Targ, Chicago bookseller, sat in his cozy little shop at 335 South Dearborn Street, wondering this late evening just before closing time, whether bookselling had any of the compensations it was alleged to have! For this had been one of those strange and irritating days in commerce literary which proclaimed that at last double-feature movie bills and 24-hour-around radio programs had written finis to bookselling—in reality, of course, one of those strange and unexplainable days when people not only evinced no desire whatsoever to own a book, but actually perked up their noses when they went by a window full of such. And Bill Targ, familiar only with phenomena taking place at and in front of 335 South Dearborn Street, Chicago, did not know that every other bookseller in Chicago was wondering, this evening, the identical thing he was now doing. He knew only, indeed, what was going through the mind of a certain slender kindly looking young-appearing man, with blueblack hair brushed straight back from a high forehead, distinct green-brown eyes, and tweed suit, who sat at his desk in the tiny alcove-like appendage to his small bookshop, filling his pipe occasionally, looking out into the shop over the tables covered by books—and which man was Bill Targ!

The Targ shop, Chicago's one and only resort for so-called "literati," was curiously devoid, at this hour of 10:10 in the evening, of those rare souls who never—quite and absolutely never!—bought a book: *i.e.* the writers who wrote them—and the browsers who browsed them; but whose presence, at least, served to make bookselling, in moments when it was not profitable, an interesting and merry occupation. Most, if not all of the latter individuals were, at this moment, beyond doubt, listening to Fanny Butcher's weekly radio review of all the latest books, thus cutting down by a few hours, at least, their daily work of leaning against booktables, and by a few hundreds of pages, their daily leafing over thousands of such; and most, if not all of the former souls—the writers—were, at this same moment, most likely, foregoing the colorful spiritual and literary fare that could always be found in Bill Targ's colorful little place—for Bill made his place to be like that!—and were satisfying their grosser inner writing selves with sour red wine, spaghetti, and breadsticks at Joe's. That is to say, the Joe on Lincoln Avenue—or the Joe on Belmont Avenue—or the Joe on 63rd Street—or the Joe on Clybourn—or any of the 138 absolutely identical restaurants in Chicago called "Joe's."

But now an interruption to bookselling—rather, to non-bookselling!—took place, as an ugly-looking man in a brown derby hat, carrying an obviously secondhand book in his hand, entered the shop. He had thin crafty lips, close-set black eyes, and Bill immediately knew the newcomer was not interested in books whatsoever. Bill even wondered amusedly if Bill Targ's was now going to be held up—then decided that all hold-up men who would hold up a bookstore were probably already in the Lincoln, Illinois, Institute for the Feeble-Minded.

The stranger brushed across the shop, knocking off a couple of books from the corner of a table as he did.

"Hey—hey!" he shouted, looking angrily around. "Hows-about some service around this goddamn joint? I—"

But Bill Targ had arisen. And had become visible above that little occluding desk.

"I am the proprietor," he said. "We—ah—usually—in the book business—don't bother customers till they find what they wish. Anything I—can do for you?"

"Maybe—maybe not," said the thin-lipped man cryptically. He looked about the shop, particularly its walls, shifted his secondhand book to his other red hand, then gazed at Bill Targ again.

"I'm a c'llector," he said, "o' calenders—lit'ographed calendars. Got at least t'ree t'ousand of 'em. And a guy what was in some Chicago bookstore one night, tryin' to buy a copy o' *Lady Chitterling's Sweetie,* wit all the dirty words in it, said that one shop he was in had a queer calendar somewhere's on one of its walls—on'y, this guy by this time was 7 sheets in the wind, and didn't know where th' shop was—fact is, he not on'y don't know t'day whether 'twas a secondhand bookstore, or a firsthand one, but, by Jesus, he ain't even sure t'day whether 'twas a straight bookstore or—or jest a place where books, as well as other junk, was sold—anyway, this here calendar shows some rubes chewin' the fat on a rur'l tel'phone wire, an'—"

"Rubes?—chewing the fa—?—oh," admitted Bill Targ, "he must have meant this one. For if—if he were 3 sheets under the wind, I probably took him back in the office there to find out exactly what he wanted—but come in here—yes."

He motioned the stranger inside his little office-nook, cut off from the main shop only by the tall bookcase containing the mystery novels. And nodded toward its end wall where hung a calendar which, over the course of 10 long years, had hung on one or another of the walls of the various bookshops Bill Targ had possessed.

It showed a picture—rural, indeed!—rustic, to say the least!—across whose top, in snappy black-outlined crimson letters, was an advertiser's name—and his advertising message—and all of which ran:

CASEY'S BEER TUNNEL

Under the Sidewalk at State and Van Buren Streets,
Chicago. Visit it—and see Casey's Trick Clock!

The pictorial representation which the calendar held undoubtedly showed an incident which was taking place simultaneously in 4 different sections of space; for it was divided into three close-lying panels, two vertical, and one horizontal one underlying both; an individual in each panel was shown holding a telephone receiver to his or her ear, and from each panel to every other one a realistic representation of telephone wires, sailing across, indicated that the same moment in time was being portrayed. The individual shown in the right-hand vertical panel was an indubitable farmer, sun-browned and windbrowned, clad in faded blue cotton shirt with equally faded wire-mended black galluses, and wearing a battered grey felt hat flopping grotesquely up at one side; with troubledly squinting eyes, he was talking at a wall phone in what obviously was a country cross-roads store, for red gasoline cans, illuminated by rays of bright afternoon sun, were in sight, open cracker barrels, shelves of canned goods, and a few signs announcing chewing tobaccos. The individual to whom he plainly was talking—and who was shown in the left vertical panel—was an equally rural, but older, man, evidently a doctor of veterinary medicine, for he wore a short grey near-professional beard, had gold spectacles on his nose, and some kind of a huge cow-injecting syringe in his free hand, which instrument was silhouetted against the end of a stall—and a cow's very tail! The oddest thing about this professional-looking elderly man was not that he was coatless, or that he had his sleeves rolled up as though ready for some sort of medical operation, but chat the shirt he wore was a checkered hickory shirt—showing him to bc a true horse and cow doctor of the soil!

Underneath the two earnest conversers—the right one of which appeared to be asking information—the left to be rendering it—in the third and underlying horizontal panel, sat an old woman—except that she wasn't an old woman—she was an indubitable man with a woman's grey wig on him, neck and torso swathed carefully in a knitted shawl, and wearing silver spectacles of which one lens was cracked—a man with a large nose, and a visible gold tooth, trying to represent an old lady—listening hard to a telephone receiver, and evidently taking notes, for the model's talons held a piece of paper on which was writing of some kind.

And underneath the entire picture, in black type, was its title, which read with, underneath it, in turn—and running the entire width of the picture—the explanation which Bill Targ knew by heart, and which read:

> The picture shows a typical Southwest farmer who has called his veterinary, in a typical crossroads store, to ask what to do for his ailing sow, receiving exact instructions what to do; the veterinary is a man of the soil exactly like himself. As in all telephone conversations in the country, an old lady, with nothing to do all day but listen in, is taking in the whole conversation and making notes. She will be telling the whole countryside in a few minutes that Abe Jones's sow is ailing. This is a typical American scene.

The man in the derby hat was reading the caption puzzledly.

"There are words also," explained Bill Targ, "written on the paper held in the—uh—old woman's hand. Sort of—ah—microscopic—but purposely so, of course, so as to titillate anybody and everybody to read them!—for they're not so small that they can't be read."

"Well, *I* can't read 'em *that* small," said the derby-hatted man disgruntledly. "because I ain't my reading glasses with me. What do they say?"

"Well, they read," said Bill, who knew them by heart, "'Whoever enters The Tunnel between 5:26½ and 5:39½ in the afternoon does not emerge.'" He smiled.

"The—Tunnel?" ruminatively echoed the derby-hatted man. "Meanin', of course, this Casey's Beer Tunnel?—for short?" Bill Targ was nodding amusedly. "But why wouldn't such a guy e-merge?"

"Because," pronounced Bill Targ, though speaking in the tense of Casey's Beer Tunnel only, "he theoretically wouldn't want to! At least I didn't—one time when I made it on the magic dot of the witching hour."

"What the hell is it all about?" almost moaned the derby-hatted man.

"Well," said Bill Targ resignedly, "since you're interested in calendars, I suppose it's up to me to tell you about this one." He paused. "It was something gotten up by Mike Casey who owned the famous Beer Tunnel under the sidewalk at State and Van Buren near here; today the place is called the Cold Snack Cellar. Mike had an idea, when he got this calendar up, for a stunt—of sorts. Incidentally, when his brother snapped these types somewhere in the West, or Southwest, for the scene prospected, not an old lady in the entire countryside would pose as a listener—they were downright indignant!—and so, ultimately, Mike himself, with a wig on, had to be the old lady listener. And," went on Bill Targ, patiently, "Mike had a big trick wall clock which was fixed up by some clever clock mechanic to go at all kinds of different speeds, mostly fast, frequently reversing itself at unexpected moments and going backward for a while! And every day it was started off by the bartender at a different hour. And—as you heard in the matter of that fine writing!—anybody who came in there between the hours of—but wait—"

And Bill Targ turned down a two-inch bottom margin of the calendar which had been tucked up underneath at a time when, had it not been, it would have had to curl out over the top of a built-in book-cabinet containing rarer works and first editions, but which cabinet today was on the opposite wall-end closest to Bill Targ's own desk. The let-down margin of the calendar contained a lightly pink-tinted panel on one end of which was a blank area evidently once occupied by the tiniest of calendar leaf pads, and over whose whole extent, to the right, was printed or lithographed bright black type reading:

> A Crown Worth $10!—And Free Drinks and Free Eats!—from then to real and actual Midnight—to the Lucky Person or Persons Who Succeed in Entering Casey's Tunnel during the Minutes (on Casey's Trick Clock only!) corresponding with the Minutes shown on this Calendar. (See Writing on Scrap of Paper Held by Casey himself in his great Old Lady Act!) Try Your Luck! If you Enter the Tunnel while the Clock, on Today's Run, is within the range of minutes designated, a Crown consisting of a $10 Cashier's check—plus all you can Drink and Eat till midnight—is Yours. You're King of the Joint—and We Promise you YOU WON'T GO HOME!

"But—but w'at was the idear?" asked the stranger, after he had read this easily read announcement.

"Why," said Bill Targ politely, "people popped into Casey's Tunnel at all hours of the day and night to buy a drink, or a sandwich, figuring that if the clock, at the moment of their entrance, was at any minute between 5:26½ and 5:39½ they'd win. It brought Mike all sorts of business. And not many losses! For he had the clock geared to go like the very devil between those hours. People would go in—drink or eat—try to figure out that clock—go out—come back again—in the meantime, however, the clock would have slowed or sped up—or even reversed itself!—it was a case of 'guess' to the nth degree. Once *I* made it—on the nose! And, of all things, had only gone in to have a few words with a man who hung out there. Another time, three men barged in at the magic moment—and Mike had to pay off triple. But it brought business."

Bill Targ paused regretfully, for Mike Casey had been a great bookbuyer back when Bill, across the street from The Tunnel, had been managing the book department of Goldblatt's Department Store. "And that," he finished, "is the story of this curious calendar—since it interests you—and which I've always kept as an example in colored lithography. I had two originally—but an Englishman who was in here once—a chap out of London—fancied one—so I gave it to him—and I suppose it's hanging somewhere in London today as a perfect detailed example of the Scene American!"

Which, indeed, it was—though Bill Targ knew it not, for it was hanging, at this very moment, in the bedroom of a fake trance medium of Mile End Road, who now languished in Bow Sueet Gaol, not only for utilizing its vivid and extremely detailed picture as the source of a too objectively presented "trance," but for accepting 6 shillings for the same!

The derby-hatted man, looking back at Bill, was frowning.

"So you had two of'em?" he commented. "Might I ast what you charged this Englishman—is this'un in good condition?" He set down his secondhand book on the corner of Bill's desk, and went forward, and felt the calendar—the paper—looked at it back and front. "This is in party good condition," he said. "For a c'llection. W'at would you ast for it?"

"Well," said Bill modestly, "I'm not in the calendar business—I'm in the book business—but I *do* believe in building up collections of anything—however, I can hardly name a price for a thing that hasn't an intrinsic value of even 25 can—but maybe we can make a swap—what have you here?"

He tapped the other's secondhand book questioningly, for it lay upside down, and with its backbone off from Bill's gaze.

"It's a secondhand book," declared the derby-hatted man, "what cost me 10 cents, but what'll give this baby 5 bucks' worth o' sheer unadult'rated enjoyment w'en I c'n get around to readin' it, since—" And, with great triumph he added: "It's a book by John L. Lewis—"

"Sinclair Lewis, of course you mean," corrected Bill with a difficultly suppressed grin. "John L. never wrote any books bound this way."

"Okay—okay," retorted the other a bit testily. "What t' hell does it matter w'ich Lewis? The book's the on'y thing that matters. And this one's about that writin' feller, Jack London—rather, about his famous boat wit' which he made such a goddamned ass of himself that he—"

"The Snark?" echoed BiU. *"The Cruise of the Snark,* eh?"

The derby-hatted man was nodding gleefully. He evidently liked to see literary people being made fools of.

"Jack London did have a terrible time," Bill Targ admitted, always glad himself to discuss literary history, "with his *Snark.* There have been countless articles, monographs, books, and what nor, about that fiasco. Though none, I'm sorry to say, be Sinclair Lewis—so yours must be by still another member of the Tribe Lewis—however, as you said, what does it matter anyway, eh?" He smiled placatingly. "According to the very latest and most accurate dope on the *Snark* affair—" He shook his head disparagingly, however, at the other's battered book. "—dope that's later and more accurate than this could possibly be—London spent $30,000 building the fool boat—when he had aimed at only $7,000—and then everything went wrong after he embarked on it—"

"Big cockroaches," took up the derby-hatted man with gusto, "drove him an' his wife up to the deck—and kept 'em there—so's he couldn't even write his thousand silly words a day—oh, I heard a guy on the raddio tell a little about that *Snark* cruise—it's a scream, when you know it—but you seem to know all the facts on it yourself, buddy?"

"On Jack London?" echoed Bill Targ aghast. "Well, how could I fail when I have—" He plucked from a shelf on the wall 2 practically brand-new books. "Now here are the 2 most accurate and detailed accounts of that famous *Snark* voyage ever penned—for the one, a biography of London, is by his wife, Charmian London, and the oth—"

"Wiff? She wrote one too, eh? She had the low-down, eh?"

"Don't wives generally?" queried Bill gravely. "But here's *the* very, very, very last work on that *Snark* debacle. By one Irving Stone. A biography. Houghton, Mifflin and Company, 1938. *Sailor on Horseback* is the name of it." He opened it to page 225, and handed it over, thus, to the other.

Who proceeded to read voraciously, at the opened spot. He was, beyond all doubt now, a man who enjoyed seeing a literary man at the bottom of the latter's own pedestal. "Je-sus!" he exclaimed exuberantly, as he leafed his way greedily, hungrily, ahead, "it says here, in this passage, how the *Snark*—" He stopped, lost in glee.

Bill Targ was now leafing idly over the other's book, which indeed was a *Snark* book too, pausing here, and pausing there. But speaking. "Such account as you might hope to get from this work," he said quite frankly, "on Jack London's great debacle, would hardly be 1-2-3, if that, to what you could get from Charmian London's biography there—or Irving Stone's—since she was his wife, and Stone had access to material nobody else had—however, I see you looking at the calendar—and hugging that Irving Stone biography—which is worth $3.00, coin of the realm—wait—when new—as it now is, write your own figure!—so suppose, for your *Snark* book, which, though a bit moth-eaten, so to speak, and—and fusty, might be of academic interest to—ah—professional Snarkians!—I give you *my* ultramodern *Snark* book, containing the best and fullest history of Jack London's debacle—*and* the calendar—"

Bill stopped and grinned quizzically.

"It's a deal," said the derby-hatted man hastily. And who right now, as Bill could see by the fact of a page with torn-off corner being turned over by the other, was chucklingly reading about how the *Snark's* sails were all rotted when it was time to raise them. "Except," the derby-hatted man added, looking up, and with the cunning of the ignorant and illiterate, "that soon's I say 'Okay,' you'll raise the ante on me—making me add a buck or two?"

"Oh, no I won't," protested Bill. "For there are always—ah—Snarkians—wanting more and more details—and older details, at that—about Snarks!"

"Okay," reiterated the other promptly, closing the Irving Stone biography of Jack London. "It's a sale. Rather, a trade. But no crawfishin' now, fella! I bought that *Snark* hist'ry that you've been leafin' over, for 10 cents—an' on'y an hour ago—off'n an open stand in front of a store on West Madison Street—partly, yeah, to catch a good belly laugh outa, th' doin's o' that writin' fool, Jack London—bur partly also so's I could barge inside and lamp the inside of that store which I thought might have this calendar—except that it turned out that the store sold mostly crock'ry and secondhand household junk. So—well, is it still a deal?—or ain't it still a deal?"

"I told you," averred Bill with dignity, "that it's a deal. I'm thinking of collections, not of—"

"Sold!" The derby-hatted man hastily and emphatically waved, toward Bill, the *Snark* book which Bill had tossed back upon the corner of his desk. And tore the calendar loose from the two thumbtacks which held it up.

"I'll be goin'," was all he said. And with a sort of facetious, Hitlerlike salute to Bill, wound his way politely past the younger man, who stood politely aside for the other, out of the office-nook, and to the door of the shop.

Where, however, the derby-hatted man turned and stood, the Jack London biography hugged tightly under his elbow, and looking at Bill sardonically.

"Well, Buddy," he said, "le' me give you a hunk o' 24-carat advice. Next time a guy comes smellin' around f'r a queer piece o' junk—like a calendar—'r any other goddamn thing—and sayin' he's a c'llector, don't pay so goddamned much attention to his fakealoo. Put on your mental specs!—and boost the ante on him. Now this calendar you was so kind as to explain to me, was engraved by me. That is, the stone work was did by me. That's my trade—yowsah! And so I know a-a-all about this pikter. This very print even onct hung in my own boodoir—that is, a certain one of a hell of a lot o' boodoirs that I got kicked out of, f'r nonpayment of rent!—as a sample o' my work. And my old buddy and roommate in that partic'ler boodoir where this hung—an' who, I'm sorry to say, was a pickpocket—told me, when he croaked in the County Hospital, that, whilst him and me had lived together in that room, from w'ich he got shot into th' County, an' I had to hit a flop-joint for a while, that he'd stashed a C-note—that's a $100 banknote in *your* language, Buddy—ag'in the back o' our calendar, covered by a oblong of cloth." Bill Targ started. "An' Christ—by th' time I learn that, the people in that house is left Chi—their goods is sold all over hell-an'-gone—the house itself is torn down. And—well, *I* been huntin' this goddam calendar all over Chi—ever'where they was a few books outside or inside a store— ever since l heard, a couple o' weeks ago, from a screwball booze-soppin' friend o' mine, that he seen one such hangin' back inside such a store some goddamn where." The derby-hatted man was, even as he talked, peeling off the oblong of cloth that Bill had always thought was a mere mending oblong.

But which was proving to have been pasted about its margins only, and by, obviously, rubber cement. The derby-hatted man was even, indeed, right this very second, extracting from back of that cloth oblong a bright crisp green bill on which in one corner, as Bill could easily see, was the figure "$100." "Let it be a lesson t' ya, Buddy," the derby-hatted man went on, caustically, "t' keep your glims open. Goo-oo-ood—night!"

And out he went, and straight into a yellow taxicab that had just discharged a man at the curb—and disappeared into the night. Leaving Bill holding that battered 10-cent copy of a book dealing with the Snark!

With a sigh, Bill dropped to his telephone. And dialed a number on it. A man answered. A man whose cultured, well-modulated voice Bill immediately recognized, for Bill spoke.

"Mr. van Gelder, I've got a Lewis Carroll book here in the shop—somebody with a decided grudge against the name 'Carroll,' however, has scraped the 'Carroll' off both the front and the backbone, and—but now for the thing that will interest *you!*—it's *the* Lewis Carroll book you wanted so badly—yes—*The Hunting of the Snark*—oh, yes—yes—the edition which carries an acrostic poem, printed in fine script, to that little girl who enjoyed his *Alice in Wonderland* so much—yes, Adelaide Paine—but wait!—the acrostic poem in *this* copy is signed by him, and—forgery?—well hardly!—since this is one of the two copies he's known to have signed—in fact, this is the *other* copy—right!—the first edition—the London edition, yes—the first imprintation thereof—yes—with the missing folio number on Page 5—the reversed lines on Page 75—the errors of spelling in the text on Page 148—the upsidedown woodcut showing the mythical Snark animal—you bet!—the only such defective copy that escaped the publishers, and which never could be retrieved after that—that's right!—oh, the price?—well, you'll recall, I'm sure, that the other autographed frontispiece poem copy of this very same edition sold at the Irving Fletcher sale for $875—and this one would be even more valuable, since—but, to you, we'll say this one is $500 even—okay?—no, I really mean it—it's bargain day today at the Targ Bookshop!—yes, indeed, I'll stay open till you come—oh, no, no, no, don't bother even thinking to take care of that toni—all right then, *if* you insist—surely—cash *or* check—either is okay."

He hung up.

"Sometimes," he said, taking up his pipe and tamping into it, from an open tobacco jar on his desk, some of the dark weed, "I think that the bookselling business *does* have its compensations!"

CHAPTER XIV

THE HUMBLE CALLER

Al Mulhearn, his coat collar turned up about his throat because of the chill of early, early morning, but gazing triumphantly at the king-high bob-tail straight-flush in diamonds which he held in his hands, shoved to the center of the small green baize-covered card table in front of him $20 of the paper currency lifted from the Cedarville Bank exactly 84 hours ago. And 84 hours almost to the minute, moreover, for a leaf calendar on a wall now facing Al Mulhearn showed the date to be the 4th day after that of the robbery—while a tinny alarm clock ticking away on a shelf of the same wall showed the time to be exactly 4 A.M. of that day—in short, the hour of pre-dawn.

"I open her, Slim," Al Mulhearn announced to the man across the table from him, "f'r this double sawbuck."

"I'm in," declared Slim, his own coat collar up around his own throat, and shoving over $20 of his share of the same money. But, exactly as he had done a hundred times during the night just gone, he arose, peeled off his coat, tossed it lightly across the back of his chair, and sat down—coatless and lucky. As, at least, he appeared to believe, anyway!

The large 1-room habitation where the game was going on was thick—at least at its ceiling—with blue smoke. The smoke from countless cigars and cigarettes which had failed to completely ooze forth through the partly blocked-up chimney. The black shades of the windows, one each side of the big room, were drawn tight, snugly tight, to the very sills. Light was being furnished by a huge brass oil lamp, hanging by four brass chains from the ceiling, and adjustable as to height by a counterweight inside the four chains. The poker game itself was going on on a collapsible green baize table, set up about the middle of the uncarpeted but wood-floored room, with four piles of paper money around its edges and one in the middle!—several sticky whisky glasses—one bottle, a quarter full, of the same—and 4 folding wooden campchairs drawn up to the table. And all, moreover, occupied, for at Al Mulhearn's right was no less than Snipes Spurlock, coat collar around his neck—and at Al's left hand no less than Scarface Scalisi, the same. Around the edges of the room—except where the two oppositely placed windows were—and, in that other wall, the single door—were narrow canvas cots, with none-too-clean cheap blankets on them—6, all in all. In one corner of the room was a waterless, pipe-less sink, full just now to overflowing with crumpled dirty paper dishes, and with, above it, a huge water tank capable of holding many gallons of drinking water; near that, a 2-hole gasoline stove; and, near that, a tall wire wastebasket containing scores of empty cans—mostly baked beans and chili con carne—rearing themselves out its very open top. Around the stove and the sink, both, lay various cracker boxes, empty and half-filled, and dirty sticky can-openers in profusion. Bottles of whisky could be seen in all directions, some with sticky glasses near them, some without, some with upended corks near them—others with corks stuck loosely back in.

And reason enough—for the cans, the dirty dishes, and the half-consumed whisky bottles, for the gang had now been "dodging the heat" for close on to 3½ double revolutions of the clock!

And reason enough for that, too!—for even now, as Slim Yarnai shoved in his $20, a tiny battery radio, in one corner, which had been playing very lightly, commenced speaking:

"And now, folks, as we close this program which comes forth nightly, over Station SWLN, for night workers—victims of insomnia!—the late retirers of the amusement world—and other such, we give you the last-minute police news—such, that is, as is available as all morning papers start to go on press. First: nothing new on the bold bankrobbery perpetrated in the country far, far south—west *and* south—of Southwest City here. Nobody yet apprehended but the county Sheriff who let them through to safety, and who is indicted but free on his own recognizance. Every possible haunt of every possible man thought to be possibly involved in that robbery—plus the haunts of all other known crooks—are being watched continuously by the police of Southwest City and all cities hundreds of miles in all directions of Southwest City, but, of course, all the habitues of such haunts are, just now, 100 percent *non est—non est* meaning, 'not there'!—so as not to have to go up before the 'green-lights' for grueling questions which most probably can't even answer. All three crooks suspected of having possibly been the leader of that hold-up crew—Big Muscle Hop-fear—Al Mulhearn—and Long-Arm Dirks—are not in the least to be found; the three scar-faced men, 'Scar' Humpberry, Scarface Scalisi, and 'Slit-Puss' Mayfeedl—are lying low. Of course, folks, when all these specially looked-for folks finally *do* appear, it will be the old, old story: each will have a perfect watertight alibi for the day and hour of the crime—and each, as each will put it, cleared out to avoid hard questioning and police-wielded rubber hoses. So much, then, for the 'heat' now on Crookdom. Now, moving on to the case of the Murder of Millionaire Aubreyton, of 48th Avenue, it seems that—"

"Turn 'at goddam thing off," grunted Al Mulhearn. "Le's have a little peace n' quiet out here."

A tremulous hand of a considerably wrinkled, white-haired elderly man, lying fully dressed on a cot near the radio, but with warming blanket drawn partly up over him, reached out and snapped the radio off.

Now a man lying on a cot across the room from the other—and some 12 feet or so from the poker game—spoke. He was a hard-faced man, bronzed of face, wearing a warm sweatervest under his coat, and consequently without turned-up coat collar, and with the leather boots of an oil prospector.

"Jesus Christ!" he ejaculated, "but the Big Town sure stays hot, don't it, Al? I don't see though, myself, why you don't let me amble up there and pick up some inside info."

Al Mulhearn paused in the act of drawing one card only.

"Be yourself, Driller! Why, damn it, you ain't free from suspicion by a goddam sight—on at least two things *I* know of. An' wit' nothin' to do wit' their rubber hoses an' fists and greenlights, th' cops 'd put you on the carpet just on a gen'ral chanct—and hell, maybe wind up gettin' you positively identified as the guy who was hangin' 'round Cedarville, the prob'le advance caser—sure, that ain't conviction ev'dence—no!—but it'd be enough fer 'em to give you all they got. And before you got it all, you son-of-a-bitch, you'd yap somethin'—oh, yes, you would. You can't take pressure, Driller." He re-examined his retained cards carefully. "No," he continued, "th' place fer all us boys is this hideout—*till* the heat has cooled—then a bust in all directions. This is the A. No. 1 hole in all creation—last owned, as 'twas, in the name of a 'Mrs. Fanny Brewer-Stodges o' Liverpool, England'—" He chuckled grimly, thinking of the half-dozen cunning transfers of this wooded area in the years he had held it. "—an' now held in the name of th' 'Western City At'letic an' Huntin' Club'—an' wit' all taxes paid on it—wit' nuttin' but the primyevil forest all around it—in front of it—in back of—well, in back of it as far's that one holdin', acrost th' rear creek, wit' nuttin' back o' the trees on it but one deef par'lyzed bach'lor in a wheelchair who can't hear even nuttin' wit'out his ear trumpet. Ever'thing is jake. How many you drawin', Slim?"

Snipes, evidently out of this pot, was dealing.

"Two," said Slim, carefully regarding his hand. "After playing which, I'm checking out—and going to sleep. Driller, who's slept all night, can sit in in my place."

"With what?" asked Driller ruefully. "I've lost the last of *my* cut of the folding money."

"I'll advance you a grand," said Slim, looking at the comfortable pile of bills in front of him, "against your 1/6th cut in the gold."

"It's a deal!" came back Driller, sitting promptly up. "It's—"

But at this juncture there was a knock at the door of the shack. A gentle, kindly, courteous knock, however. A timorous knock, even—if one had had time to analyze it. And decidedly no knock, even Al Mulhearn knew, such as officers of the law—G-men, or any of that ilk—ever deigned to render. Now it was repeated, almost apologetically, and branded itself immutably as the knock of somebody who was lost in these woods.

The game had stopped dead. Quintetes of cards were being held rigidly in mid-air. Four free hands, however, had shot straight to back pockets. The free hand of Driller, on the cot, slithered underneath a blanket pad that was serving as his pillow. Now 5 automatics were in evidence. Al Mulhearn, gripping his own, was the first to speak.

"What th' hell—who th' hell—what th'—"

Snipes had two guns out now. One evidently from where it had been strapped on an ankle. He was edging off his chair—was crouching low behind it and the table side that was farthest from the door, guns angled above the table's edge.

"Easy there, boy," cautioned Al. "That's—that's some damn fool who's lost his way."

"Lost his way—at dawn?" snarled Snipes. "Christ, it's a posse—"

"Posse my behind," snapped Al Mulhearn. "A posse don't op'rate that wa—" He stopped. He was 100 percent convinced of his own words, but troubled in some vague way.

Again came the gentle knocking. So gentle this time that it branded itself as the knocking of a girl.

"Don't answer, Al—whatever you do!" This from Driller, raspingly. "It's a decoy—to get us to open up."

"Decoy my behind!" retorted Al Mulhearn. "If 'twas th' Law, they'd toss a rock ag'in the door—an' skip to hiding. It's some goddamn fool who's—well," he broke off helplessly, "if it *is* a decoy, that means th' joint's been found—but that's all we want in here, in that case; jest one lousy son-of-a-bitch on whose life we c'n bargain our way t' the dear an'—

"Here," he broke off, in sudden resolution born of the necessity of ending suspense, "fan them rods out o' sight—stick 'em behind you—all o' you—ready to use 'em if we have to—but don't show 'em in case it's somebody we got to explain that—that we're fishermen or somethin'—you know? Fan 'em, now."

Instantly, in synchronism with Al Mulhearn himself, 5 guns moved in back of 4 bodies—Driller's gun slithered in under that pillow-like pad of his blanket—Beebles, the gun-less one, was shaking like a leaf.

Al Mulhearn, his own hand gripping his gun behind him, strode to the door.

"Who's there?" he demanded.

"He-e-elp!" said what sounded immutably like a woman's voice.

"Crazee Annie!" offered Scarface, relaxing a bit.

"Maybe—yes, that's jest who it is," nodded Al Mulhearn, tlunking of that woebegone half-witted creature who was to be seen in and out on the roads at times. "Well, here go—"

"Don't open, I tell ya, Al," cried Driller. "It's a phony."

"Well, goddamn it," retorted Al, *"if* it's a phony, then 'at's all th' more reason wc got to yank her—or him!—inside here—our on'y ticket to an 'out' in case—hold ever'thing now—play inn'cent—but wit' your gats ready—easy on them trigger fingers!—I'll do *this!"*

He snapped a key in the door; shot a bolt; threw up a wooden bar. Flung the door open. With himself just inside the door edge. And gripping his gun behind him.

But there, outside the door, stood not the character, Crazy Annie—but a man's figure.

A figure whose arms were raised well above his head.

A most peculiar figure, indeed—and one which made Al Mulhearn's face, peeping from around the edge of the doorway, break into a hopeless gaze.

For the figure was that of a man of about 44 or 45, in bedraggled dirty once-white shirt, coatless and hatless, and with black trousers tucked clumsily into shin-high boots. Across his left shoulder was swung a cluster of pairs of indubitable handcuffs and indubitable ankle locks—so many of them that their very weight caused him to lean a trifle to that side. Half over his right ear, in a sort of half-cocked manner, was a biscuitlike telephone receiver, held to his hatless head by a steel springband, also sitting partly awry, and a small biscuitlike transmitter hung, by a couple of flexible wires, just to his unweighted shoulder. A flexible insulated wire was trailing down from the headband and back of him—into the slate-grey dusklike dawn of nowhere.

In the twinkling of an eye, practically, Al Mulhearn's gun was in the newcomer's belly, the gun-wielder himself still shielded—all but the arm that held the gun—and the one cold eye that peeped forth.

"Who's wit' you?" he snarled. "Speak fast or—"

"Nobody," said the newcomer. "I'm all alone. An' unarmed."

"What t' hell—t' hell—you want?"

Driller, in back in the room, was first of the men therein to speak.

"It's the Sheriff—the hick Sheriff—of that Willis Creek burg."

"'At's right, boys," admitted the latter imperturbably. "I've come to save all yo're lives fur ye."

"Come—to save—" Al's gun drilled a quarter inch deeper in the stomach. The upraised hands outside the door inched farther upward. "What t' hell—save our—I'm gonna blow you t' hell an'—"

"Now—Al!" The Sheriff's words were downright reproachful. "An' you boys back in thar, too. Didn't you hyar me tell you 'at I come hyar to save all yo're lives? I'm a man who don't b'lieve in massacrees—even c'mmitted by the Law. I—"

"Massac—" Something was stirring in Al Mulhearn's brain. This man—this man—had something on the ball.

"Goddamn you—come in here. March!"

The Sheriff, as one who knew exactly what would happen, stepped forward. "When you close the door ahind me, Al," he said gently, "let this hyar wire back o' me trail onder it. 'Caze ef that c'nnection breaks, boys, yo're all as dead as—as do'nails. That co'd is yo're lifeline!"

The cord was dropping by itself. Al Mulhearn was staring. "Keep'em up!" he warned. Then—"No, reach out with yer right hand only, an' toss that door back o' you shut." The newcomer did just that. Briskly and conclusively—so much so that the door closed tightly to. Though it did pass easily over the trailing cord, which now led out over the threshold. Al Mulhearn snapped the key in the lock. Stared at the wire scowlingly. Then shot the bolt. And dropped the wooden bar.

"Frisk him first!" he ordered his two nearest henchmen.

The "frisking" was done expertly, by Slim and Scarface, hands clamping the Sheriff's legs from boots up. Hands patting pockets and torso. Both men turned to their chief.

"He's not gatted up," said Slim. But his words were glum, as his eyes rested on that trailing wire.

"W'ere does that there wire lead to?" demanded Al Mulhearn, coming around in view of the Sheriff.

"T' th' chief o' th' posse," declared the Sheriff, almost reproachfully. "Th'—"

"Posse?" ejaculated Al Mulhearn.

"W'y, yes—th' posse what's surrounded this hyar house to—"

"Surrounded—this—"

"'At's right," nodded the Sheriff, again utterly reproachfully. "Yo're surrounded, boys—all o' yo'—so bad that they hain't a chanct in a million o' one o' yo' gittin out alive. As a matter o' fact—" His voice fell low. "D'ya object—if I kiver this transmitter a second—'ith the palm o' my hand?"

"Okay. Talk fast!"

The Sheriff reached up back of his unencumbered shoulder, and clasped that biscuitlike transmitter so that his palm covered it completely. "As a matter o' fact, boys," he said, still speaking low, "they don't aim—out thar—t' let one o' you git out alive."

"Don't—don't aim—"

"Take a look fu'st," pleaded the Sheriff, directly to Al Mulhearn. "So we all know what we're a-talkin' 'bout."

"Keep—keep this son-of-a-bitch covered," Al Mulhearn ordered.

His face—though he didn't know it—had gone grey.

He stepped to the one north-facing window. But before he did anything at all, he received a caution. It came from the Sheriff.

"Don't pull the shade 'way out, Al," the latter said quizzically. "Fur that's one o' my signals fur 'em to let loose."

"Let loose—wit' what?"

"With 4 machine guns able to shoot th'ough 5 inches o' plankin'—3 b'ar rifles able to do the same—one el'phant gun—an' a asso'tment o' eight .38's to .45's, able to bore th'ough one plank wall. Take it awful easy, man, will ya?"

Al Mulhearn pulled the tight-fitting black shade gently—very gently!—out from the window casing. And doing so, gasped. Turned olive green, in fact. For along the ridge of the low narrow barn facing the shack from but 25 feet away he could see, against the now definitely light grey sky, the tips of guns—he even recognized one, protruding very far up, definitely as a water-cooled machine gun—he saw the tips of conelike hats—made out the round semicircle of the front of a straw hat tilted up on its wearer's head—the wearers of all those hats were, he knew, lying on the short back slope of the barn, toes doubtlessly propped against rain gutter. He let loose of the shade as though it were white hot.

And turned.

"On'y way," he gurgled, though to nobody in particular, "is out that winder facin' th' ol' wall—an' into th' woods. On foot. A'right, boys—"

"Now wait!" pleaded the Sheriff, upraised arms so far sunken down now that his elbows were propped against his ribs, "yo'-all don't give Uncle Sam much credit fur brains, do you? Won't you take a keerful look, fu'st—out'n that south window? But keerful—very keerful—'caze one of my three signals is—" He said no more.

Al Mulhearn had crossed the room. Was drawing forth gingerly, micro-metrically, the black shade. Peered out the vertical aperture created. Turned sicker yet.

For he saw several more gun barrels pointed above the top of the old crumbling wall, facing the shack from but 25 feet or so of space; again, one machine-gun nozzle; a couple of hat-tips, at least.

He let go the shade speedily. And turned.

"Looks—looks like—" he half choked. "A'right, boys. We'll shoot it out, goddamn 'em. We'll—"

"Now, now, Al," said the Sheriff plaintively. "Have you lost the brill'ancy by which you made yo're truck an' yo're men dis'ppear inside that stone tube?" Al Mulhearn fixed but a savage gaze on the speaker. "That's what them fellers—" Again he cupped the transmitter. "—that's what them fellers aimed t' git you boys to do from the beginnin'. To try to shoot yo're way out. So's they kin onleash their artill'ry—both sides! Why, boys, ef you try to make it out th' door, yo'll pile up right in the do'way; an' the minute you busts th' fu'st pane o' glass, they'll c'mmence drillin' you—from both sides—through these hyer one-plank-thick tar-papered walls. You all will be as dead as—"

"Let's—let's surrender," groaned Old Beebles. "They—"

"Quiet, you yellow-bellied dog," bellowed Al Mulhearn. "I'll take it on th' lam. You'll all take it on the—"

"Let—let me take a look," begged the still shirt-sleeved Slim Yarnai, a bit of green as green as the stripes in his sleeves fusing with his bronzed complexion.

There was silence—but acquiescent silence. The while he peered, extremely carefully, through a slender gap in the curtain behind him. Then turned away, a bit white now. Crossed the room. Did the same with the barn-facing window. Turned away. Completely white now.

His face had told a complete story to all eyes riveted on it.

The Sheriff, however, was the one to speak.

"Boys," he said abruptly, "I got to make m' report now. Fur I've b'en in hyar at least 2 minutes—and ef I ain't heered from by 3 minutes atter I went in—they're gonna onleash. Is it—is it a'right?"

"To do what?" rasped Al Mulhearn.

"To jest talk—converse—in this transmitter—to th' Chief."

"Not, by Chirst, by a goddamn si—"

"Lat heem talk, Boss," begged Scarface. "Eef he speel wan theeng he no shood—we geeve him plantee slogs een guts—"

"Now, now, feller 'ith the scar," said the Sheriff, downright disgustedly, "don't be a—a—a Latin damn fool. An' that goes fur all o' you. You boys air co'rageous robbers—downright talented men. The way you snaked that box o' gold out'n that bank tu'k guts. Mo'n I've got. And the way yo'-all dis'ppeared inside that stone tube, tu'k brains—somebody's brains an'way. Now don't become 6-ya'r-olds now. Yo've lost yo're trick an' air on a new negotiatin' basis now. Wich same I pr'pose to 'stablish. An' ef my talkin' is int'rrupted, mo'over, they're to onleash. Now, fur God's sake, dumheads, kin I talk?"

"Talk!" commanded Al Mulhearn. "But—"

"Now wait," pleaded the Sheriff. "Kin I lay the hearin' dewdad atop this table hyar—it yells so loud when it speaks it likes to split a man's card—"

"Lay it, goddamn it," snapped Al Mulhearn, almost breaking under the suspense.

"Okay! Then kin I dump this tonnage o' metal what's on my lef' shoulder thar, coo—'ithout gettin' shot?"

"Dump it, for Jesus Christ sa—"

The sound of the mess of handcuffs and ankle irons clattering to the very table stopped further remarks of Al Mulhearn.

Now the Sheriff, businesslike, laid his headband on the table. The transmitter had enough wire thar, by leaning a bit over it, he could talk. Six men watched him grimly. Six guns held by 5 of them were being grasped. The Sheriff was, however, speaking!

"Who's on th' wire?" he queried.

Plainly and clearly the answer squeaked into the room, perhaps reflected a bit by the table top under the speaking device.

"Inspector Gridway, Duckhouse. How—"

"Good! Well, Inspector, I've wasted 'most all m' time in fool p'lim'naries—hain't even got yit t' th' thing I come in fur—so how 'bout addin' 2 more minutes now?"

"Go ahead, Duckhouse. You're wasting your time, though. I know that ilk. And my last words to you are that you are a mighty brave man to let yourself be riddled with machinegun bullets just to erase 6 rats."

Six faces at this moment turned sickly green, but continued to gaze at the Sheriff perplexedly.

The latter turned, hand over transmitter. "Y' see, boys, the least I could do as a law off'cer was to give one life fur 6. Oncet, back when I was young, an' that life was wu'th so'thin', I resked it—jest to snake a couple dozen Heinies. Now, t'day, I'm a older man by 25 years or so—and wu'th nothin' 'tall. An'—"

"Goddamn it to hell!" screamed Al Mulhearn. "Get—get—get to your point. What th' hell d'ya want? What's the prop'sition? What—"

"Wall, it's jest this," said the Sheriff. "Them fellers out yander want to exterminate you boys, while I want to save yo're lives. I got on'y one man out thar who's with me in this matter o' savin' yo're lives. The rest of 'em has give' me th' priv'lege o' tryin' to do it, sence 'twas me as unkivvered yo're hideout fur Uncle Sam."

"You?" This from Snipes. "Well, you straw-chewing son-of-a-bitch, that's all this baby wants to kn—"

"Easy, Snipes—pipe down." This from the leader. "We can kill him later. And shoot it ou—" But Al Mulhearn stopped. As he recollected the true significance of that picture he had glimpsed—of guns and hat tips—both sides of this lonely house. "Go on with your story, you rube bull," he snarled.

"Wall—" The Sheriff shrugged his shoulders helplessly. "I take it you boys know so'thin' 'bout County Jedge Pettridge?—o' Cedarville?"

"So what?" snarled Al Mulhearn. "Meaning—"

"Meaning," explained the Sheriff patiently, "that he's a man o' implic't honor?"

Driller spoke up. Graspingly, as a tired swimmer who saw a straw coming to him over the next trio of waves!

"They—they say, Al, in Willis Creek—that Pettridge is a man of his word."

"All right," snapped Al Mulhearn. "He's a man of his word—so—what?"

"And so," the Sheriff drove on, "I want to make a dicker fur you boys and him, fur he ain't fur this killin'—this—this massacree. He says ef yo'll give up and come out peaceable-like, he'll agree, at the trial, to give you all 10 years—which with good-behavior time off, 'll on'y be 7½."

"How the hell can he—"

"He's out thar," illuminated the Sheriff. "Ahind the barn—with the boys—but not armed. I sent fur him yest'day atternoon—as soon as this raid was schedooled fur dawn. He lit out fur Pricetown—and flew to Southwest City—an'—but what the billy heck does it matter how he got hyar? He's here fur the pu'pose I brung him. W'ich 'uz to do dickerin'. And—"

"Goddamn me!" snarled Snipes, "but I'd sure like to kill one judge—"

"Quiet, you young fool." This from Snipes' Chief. "The judge—uh—a judge—is the only answer you got f'r a short sentence—not that—"

"Kin I have him put on?" the Sheriff was inquiring patiently.

"Put him on," snapped Al Mulhearn, wiping off a very damp forehead with a coat sleeve.

The Sheriff spoke into his transmitter again. "Inspector?"

"Still on," came the same voice that had spoken first.

"Le' me speak to Jedge, will ya?"

There was a brief silence.

Now the voice that came forth, in rolling drawling intonations, from the transmitter, was a different voice.

"Judge Pett'dge speakin', Bucyrus."

"Say, Jedge," the Sheriff plunged in immediately, "the boys her don't seem to onderstand that you an' me—as off'cers o' th' Law—like to write our own kind o' finee on cases—'cept'n that we're two ag'in the pack, Jedge, an'—but I reckon they *do* want t' know I'm givin' them the c'r-rect low-down 'bout you bein' willin' to—"

"To give them 10 years each? Yes, I—but let me speak to the Mulhearn man."

The Sheriff thrust the transmitter toward Al Mulhearn, who took it, a bit unsteady of hand. And said into it a single grim:

"Hello?"

"Ah, Mulhearn. Mulhearn, I'll give you boys 10 years apiece fo' this job you pulled if you'll save Bucyrus an' me from bein' party to a massacre. That's min'mum sentence. An' the best I c'n do without bein' impeached."

Al Mulhearn said nothing. His eyes half closed. He was thinking deeply.

The voice resumed speaking in the receiver.

"The G-man chief here, Mulhearn—Inspector Gridway—wants to let fly ag'in you men—but says he'll give you all 3 minutes to come out th' way Duckhouse says it'll have to be done."

Al Mulhearn turned to the others. Unconsciously cupped the transmitter as the Sheriff had done.

"It's—it's up to you boys," he said, swallowingly. "'Twas a good job—but we flopped. There's a flop for every so many jo—but what now?—shoot it out?—if we do, they'll drill us through the walls and—"

"And kill this bastard," exulted Snipes.

"That bastard," Al Mulhearn almost wailed, "loves glory more than he does life. He—he ain't had any newspaper public'ty for 25 years, and is aching to—aw, forget him—now if we do shoot it out it's curtains f'r some of us—without none of us probably gettin' a single one o' them out there—against 7½ years apiece as things now stand. 7½ years, that is, if—if you boys can behave yourself. So which—which 'll it be?"

There was loud talking. Words flew across, and back across, the room like swallows darting for an opening. The most that could be gotten out of the medley of words was that all were agreed. For all faces were white. Except that of Snipes, which was a suffused red, showing that he was apparently motivated by the fact that, after the 7½ years was over, he could exterminate every single person who had—

"Well," said Al Mulhearn, almost too quickly, "speakin' for us boys, Duckhouse, we'll—we'll play ball. But how—how—"

"Well, fu'st," pointed out the Sheriff, "yo'll hatter put yo're guns—all o' yo'—on this hyar table, An' line up—all o' yo'—ag'inst that wall facin' the most o' them machine guns—yes, the barn-facin' wall. Where, ef you make a fu'ther wrong move, they kin drill yo' all dead. Yo'll hatter stick yo're hands around ahind yo'—while I have one o' you—say, the old gent yander—yes!—have him lock yo're hands together with these here cufflets—and yo're ankles by these anklets which have at least got 9 inches o' chain each. Then, when yo're all set, yo'll hatter walk out back'ard an' in single file—under them guns out thar—which I promise you won't be fired."

"A'right, boys," said Al Mulhearn, wearily, "Let's get it over wi—but wait—fix that up, Sheriff—fix—"

"Right!" The Sheriff had slipped the headband over his head so that the receiver covered half his car anyway. He was talking into the transmitter. "Who's on—oh, Sher'ff Gaylord? Well, tell the men out there, Sher'ff—an' Inspector—that th' boys hyar air ready now to line up. Facin' you folks who air on the barn. But don't shoot! Pass the word down the line now not to get 'cited. Easy now!"

From his repeated nodding, he was getting a completely affirmative answer.

Guns were already being tossed disgustedly on the table by hard men who knew that the end had been reached.

Al Mulhearn himself was first to give objective exhibit to what must be done. By stepping to the wall that faced the barn, and facing it himself, just left of the single forward-placed window, wrists crossed in back of him.

Driller, who had climbed out of his cot, and approached the table to get rid of his gun, took quick place next Mulhearn—to the latter's left.

Snipes, muttering throaty things, came next.

Then Scarface, biting a lip.

Then the shirt-sleeved Slim Yarnai.

Then Old Man Beebles, who had crawled off of his cot and stood erect, but shaking all over.

"A'right, Beebles," said the Sheriff, kindly, "go 'long them wrists—an' snap these handcuffs—one pair on each—just snap 'em, 'at's all—they're a'ready opened—then do the same 'ith these leg irons—and ef you do the job right, the Jedge'll give you probation. He said so to me."

"Probate—probate me?" quavered Beebles. "God, that's goo—" His trembling stopped completely. He was a new man—a new old man, that is! He worked like a man being exhilarated by an electric spark. Snapped handcuffs on crossed wrists. And completing that job, commenced snapping leg irons on ankles. It was almost evident that at some penal institution, back in his life, he had once worked doing this same thing to prisoners being transferred.

He stood up, nervously wiping his hands. Three pairs of handcuffs—4 pairs of anklets—lay on the table top yet!

"And—and I?" Beebles asked.

"Nothin'—fur the present," said the Sheriff. "'Cept'n to hold yo're guts up with yo're hands!"

Beebles, like a man trying to be 100 percent acquiescent, actually took hold of the sides of his abdomen. Which operation Slim Yarnai was disgustedly watching, by a head revolved around on his shoulders. Quickly, however, the latter, catching the Sheriff's menacing gaze, brought his head back to face the wall.

But the Sheriff, could anyone have seen him, was scratching his chin.

"You—feller who was jest lookin' 'round—turn yo're head around ag'in. I—I want to so'te o' an'lyze yo're face a bit."

The man addressed did as he was bid. His face was now gloomily dark. "For why?" he demanded.

"Wall," said the Sheriff troubledly, "I b'en goin' over some trash what was found in the stove of a house what was—skip it!—I b'en goin' over some trash that was burned by a city woman who lived fur a brief while in Willis Creek, an' in it they was a phot'graph of a feller—tu'k artistic-like—with lamplight, jest like this, shinin' so'te o' down'ard—feller with a black mustache an' a sho't beard—half of such, an'way—but that half what's left cert'ny, ef you ast me, tallies kind o' close with—"

"Oh, nuts," said the man who was being addressed. "I never knew nobody in your town in all my days."

"Wa-all—" said the Sheriff helplessly, stroking his chin, "my mistake then, I guess. My mistake."

He clapped his hands.

"A'right, boys. All o' you turn left now—qua'ter turn—so's yo're back'ards 'ith respeck t' th' door. Squad—left!"

All did.

The Sheriff regarded the 5 left legs fronting him sideways, the 5 pairs of contraptions on the table. Then nodded curtly to the old man still holding up his abdomen.

"A'right, Mister Beebles. Hook one o' these from each ankle iron to the ankle iron o' the feller next in line. I don't want you boys to git panicky—an' one o' you to make a fool break—and get all o' you shot."

Beebles, with alacrity, was carrying through this new simple hookup of human beings. It took him no more than 15 seconds, old as he was, to accomplish it. At each incisive click, the Sheriff nodded.

"And now—" asked Beebles, rising up "—what about me?"

"Shackle yo're own ankles," the Sheriff ordered.

Beebles did so, easily!

"Mr. Beebles," the Sheriff half laughed, "I never seed a man so used to shackle work. I—I b'lieve you could snap yo're own handcuff's ahind yourself. Try it! Go 'haid. Le's watch yo' do it?"

Beebles could—and did!

"Very good," complimented the Sheriff. "Yo've 'arnt probation. Git in front o' the goodlookin' slender gent'man—'at's right," as Beebles placed himself as rigidly in line as though he were shackled to it.

The Sheriff clapped his hands again.

"'Tention—squad! Back'ard march—single file—'long th' wall—to'des the door—'twell—"

The line stirred troubledly, but unmovingly.

Al Mulhearn, it seemed, was the obstacle.

"Listen here, copper," he rasped, "are you sure—when we start comin' out—the men out there won't start unlimberin' on us?—how 'bout callin' up on your wire—there again—tellin' 'em exactly how it's to be done—and when—so's—"

"But," expostulated the Sheriff. "I mought, by acc'dent, git th' man who pretended to be Jedge Petr—"

"Pretended—to be?" snarled Al Mulhearn. "Why, you lying hick copper, you—"

"Now—now," said the Sheriff unhappily. "Easy on them acc'sations, Al. Nobody has did you wrong. I am happy to say that I brung 'ith me the pussen'l promise of Jedge Pettridge, give' me on the long-distance phone last night, that ef I ever contacted you boys, and yo'-all ever gave up to me quiet-like, he'd give you 10 years. Evahthing's gonna be a-a-all right now, an'—"

"This is a hell of a note," rasped Mulhearn. "To have dickered with a G-man, pretendin' to be Hizzoner—all on the lyin' word of a hick cop—"

"—on the word," raged Snipes, jerking his hands violently, "of a hick copper. By Jesus—"

"Aw, cut it," snapped Al Mulhearn, whose nerves were frayed. "A'right, copper—the trick is pulled now—an' maybe you are on the level at that—call 'em up out there now, and tell 'em how we'll be com—"

"Call up?" said the Sheriff sardonically. "Hell-f'ar, I think I b'en botherin' that pore par'lyzed neighbor o' yo'rn what lives crost an' back o' that rear creek—back, even, of the trees what's back o' that creek!—e'nough this mo'nin'. Even ef he *has* played G-men in his day so much that he—he hates the guts o' fellers like you. An'—"

"Paralyzed man—" Al Mulhearn was tugging at his wrists. Which remained completely back of him. He was also kicking viciously sidewise—frontwise—backward—trying to only, that is!—for the left ankle that essayed to do this thing came to an abrupt stop in every direction it attempted a kick. He stopped that as quickly as he had tried it. But was bellowing forth with untrammeled lungs: "What th' goddamn he—"

"Shore," said the Sheriff easily. "That par'lyzed gent'man may be deef—yes!—but he ain't deef on no telyphone. And he's no more, that gent'man, a p'lice inspector or a jedge than is—is them broomsticks an' ca'dbo'de cutouts, what, 'ith th' he'p of a old ladder I unkivvered round hyar t'night, I plastered 'ith gobs of putty 'longside that barn ridge tonight in the half moonlight—and 'long the wall th' same—no more than is them cutout weapons—or hats or—or a posse. For—"

"You—you mean," Al Mulhearn almost groaned aloud, "that—you—you took us—without guns? Nor men? Nor—"

"'At's what I mean," nodded the Sheriff. "Took a bunch o' mangy rats 'ithout a bullet. Fur when *I* need $1000—*my* cut on this leetle job—to retire a piece o' my fool n'goti'ble paper!—I need it all—'ithout dividin' it 50 ways acrost th' board atween a whole passel o' county off'cers an' G-men." From the guns on the table he had been abstracting, as he talked, two, and now, with a sudden quick overturning of the table with his foot, sent it scuttling, guns sliding to the opposite wall. He strode to the door, twisted the key in the lock, shot the bolt, flung up the bar—and tossed the door open. The bright grey of early, early morning was here, the sky bright and vivid with color. "A'right," he continued, "git goin'—all o' you—back'ard." He stood off well from the door. "Single file. Back'ard. And don't meander a single inch as you pass—or they *will* be shootin'. From inside—not outside! Left!—left!—left!—'at's right—you hatter do them lefts together—keerful —an' quit yo're shiverin', you who's on'y in yo're shirtsleeves; the dawn *is* a bit cold; but it'll be warmer'n tarnation-hell in 60 minutes—even less— an'—a'right!—git started, all. Bend barn'ard—as yo' come out. Fur we're a-goin' fu'st to git yo're battleship-grey bodied truck out'n yander barn— an' the heavy box what's still in it—*ef* it ain't, it better be!—and then, atter you boys has clumb up into it by a gangway made from that ladder—an' I've locked you to a few eyebolts, or what-have-you, in it, by th' balance o' these handcuff gadgets, we're all goin'—but 'ith me drivin'—as fur as Willis Creek together. A-a-a-alll right! To the do'way—all! March!"

CHAPTER XV

INTERVIEW!

Uneasily, downright embarrassedly, Bucyrus Duckhouse faced the 4 men who represented practically all of the newspapers in the United States of America! The 4 men in question faced him eagerly, in the big high-ceilinged courtroom directly above the Willis Creek lockup—a simple courtroom of whitewashed walls and whitewashed ceiling beams, their pencils in their hands waiting for notes, their high-speed cameras at their feet. For, having arrived in a special small plane capable of carrying but 4 men only, no news-photographers were present at this peculiar meeting!

The Sheriff, almost defensively, had placed the chair in which he sat against the front high empty judge's bench, and which now loomed above his very head. The four men, in flat-handled chairs that had been used, often and again, by lawyers—and one, indeed, by witnesses—crowded against him eagerly, almost feet to feet. On each flat-handle was a trio or so of crumpled, but blank, sheets of news-copy paper, and the incumbents of the 4 chairs were waiting—on the humble words of Bucyrus Duckhouse!

Outside, visible through one of the side windows nearest the front of the courtroom, on the empty desolate land that lay that side of the low building, could be seen the bright red airplane that had circled about, but 10 minutes ago—and but 10 minutes, indeed, after the Sheriff's own arrival in Willis Creek!—for a landing, and had finally come down gracefully on the sundried land, setting free four intrepid adventurers after news for America. A throng of natives circled around the plane even now, the pilot keeping firm guard with folded arms.

The Sheriff was speaking.

"Gosh all hemlock, gent'men, yo' shore—shore par'lyze me—when you say th' story o' me corrallin' them rats is right now—this ve'y plumb nunute!—burnin' up th' Press wires to evv'y paper in th' U-nited States. And 'll be runnin' in evv'y city—as 'arly as th' noonday editions. I'm sure glad, though, 'at *I* got in hyar, as I did, with my cur'ous load, befo' the long-distance wires start hummin' to *this* town—'caze oth'wise, I'd a-had ten thousand fool questions to answer on the way. Shore wu'kked out nice fur me. But now you boys, who've started that story a-burnin' up them wires—

but, shucks, corrallin' them rats wan't no feat nohow—but hyar, will you tell me ag'in how the news o' my fool doin's traveled straight t' you a hour or so back, so's you could write out yo're stories fur dispatchin', and then, on top o' that, a'most beat me home to m' own home town?"

He swept his eyes uneasily across the four men who had descended on him like hawks, no more than 30 seconds after he had clattered upstairs from a certain stout basement lockup after having turned the key on a snarling, shuffling, cursing, ankle-locked line of human beings he had piloted therein. And having, immediately on top of that, tossed in, after the one of the line who was clad in vest only, the latter's coat so that he could use it as a cape. Snarling and cursing, that line of men, perhaps it should be said, with the exception of its leader, who, over the course of a certain bumpy ride, of several hours, had metamorphosed into a state of complete docility—into an attitude that was uncommunicative—into a mien that was 100 percent philosophical!

An odd ride, moreover, that bumpy ride. For throughout its component that lay within Willis Creek proper, the Sheriff, driving, had airily fairly told all inquirers who had shouted up at him amazed queries, that he was jest a-fetchin' in, for the Transcontinental Trucking Company, one (1) truck to be used as Exhibit No. 1 in the indictment tomorrow, at Cedarville, of Messrs. Roe, Doe, Moe, et cetera, bankrobbers—and the singular fact was, of course, that even as the Sheriff unblushingly handed out this misinformation, Messrs. Roe, Doe, Moe and et cetera, bankrobbers, were concealed from his view within the very thing he was driving!

And as for the actual locking up of that closely linked line of human beings comprising Messrs. Roe, Doe and others, that was an incident which had been unattended quite by any curious crowd, or witnesses, for the simple reason that the line's disembarkation from the battleship-grey bodied vehicle, down a ladderlike gangplank, had taken place within a certain closed high-fenced corral adjoining the rear wall of this very courtroom, and leading, by a short flight of steps up into the courtroom itself by a door just back and off from the judge's bench—or, by a stoutly barred door at the side of the steps, to the lockup below. Through which door—and down further steps—this shuffling line had been neatly conducted. And thanks to the further fact that Mr. Job Binks, Esquire—Acting Sher—rather, should it be said, reluctantly Acting Sheriff!—had been sighted lounging about the front of the building just before Bucyrus Duckhouse, temporarily deposed Sheriff, had unlocked that high corral gate with his keys, driven in, and locked the corral again—and that the said chinless Job Binks, upon a lustily roared command from deposed-Sheriff Duckhouse—and a promise of four bits in silver to come!—had meekly and acquiescently allowed himself to be posted on the inside of the courthouse-jail front door to keep all curiosity-seekers out, Sheriff Duckhouse was now alone within those sacred precincts over which, up to sometime ago, he had been virtually boss. Alone, except for these 4 eager-looking men who had successfully talked themselves past Job—and gotten in!

Thus the capture, by the Press, of the man who had captured 6 other men. Four men who represented no less than the News of the World.

To the Sheriff's right, in the small semicircle, and on whom his eyes were now resting, was Sidney Uher, who, in his almost too big black derby hat, and with his jowls, his gold spectacles, and his black-gloved hands, now wielding a pencil daintily with backs of gloves turned exactly so-so down, looked a thousand times more like a prosperous broker than the Southwest City representative of the world-famous Associated News Journals.

Next in the semicircle, as the Sheriff's eyes traveled, was Paul Dragoo, whose red hair, under his tilted-hack newspaperman's soft grey felt hat, and his laughing blue eyes, if not his grey flannel sports-like shirt, belied his being chief feature and news writer, at least in Southwest City, of United Print Features.

From here, the Sheriff's eyes roved helplessly to Jack ReQua, young, curly headed, hatless entirely, with unlighted cigarette drooping from corner of mouth, representing National Press Features.

And then to Kalvelage Lantree, impeccably dressed, with purple velour hat leaning against side of chair, with thin mustache, with brown eyes, looking far more like a screen-hero actor from Hollywood than the Southwest City representative of East-West Newspapers.

The red-headed Paul Dragoo was answering the Sheriff.

"No mystery about *that,* Sheriff Duckhouse. This paralyzed bachelor who helped you out on that portable phone circ—"

"Fine feller," said the Sheriff, emphatically. "Wouldn't consent—in a'vance nor atterward—to cut in on a blamed penny o' th' reward!"

"Why should he?" was the comment, here, of the handsome movie hero. "He's very rich. He's Aubrey DuCastle—in case he didn't tell you—once-famous stage actor—and even actor-produc—but I see you know that? Well, the point of the matter, Duckhouse—and I'm answering for you, Paul!—is that after you drove off from his front gate early this morning, with that battleship-grey bodied truck—and those fellows locked inside it to, I thinly DuCastle told us you later told him, a couple of eyebolts you found there?—" The Sheriff was nodding confirmation about the eye-bolts which indeed he had found. "—after," went on Lantree, "you had cut around the roads northward to come past again by DuCastle's place—to hop off and tell him everything came out okay—he got to thinking of all the publicity the newspapers had given him in his famous days—and so—"

"—and so," put in the black-gloved Sidney Uher, disgruntledly, "he finally—oh, several hours after you'd pulled away—he finally called up the Southwest City offices of each of the 4 syndicates which we gentlemen have the honor to represent, and gave each of us the story as you gave it to him briefly in his open window before you pulled out—told each of us all the facts—replete even to the plank you laid across that creek, from the rear of his place to the rear of that hideout place—the cardboard cut-outs you made up in his house—the putty he had brought out from town for you—also the portable phone and 500 feet of wire—and the whole showdown inside the shack, of which he heard every word—and our respective stories were getting written and put into telegraphese, and each of us, in turn, getting ready to beat you here, while you were still perhaps 50 to 75 miles out from here. We met at the airfield, we four!—each with his cameraman—like comets on our way to—to Mars; the one available plane with wing-slots and so forth that would chance a landing here—for its pilot has been down this way before—was that 4-seater—so we all grabbed our cameras away from our cameramen, hopped in—and here we are, locked with you in an empty courtroom, above a lockup with 6 gangsters, demanding the story."

"Wa-a-all," said the Sheriff helplessly, "thar hain't no story, that's the trouble."

"No story?" echoed Jack ReQua, shifting his unlighted cigarette, with his tongue, dexterously to his other mouth corner. "Hell, man—when a man takes 6 armed gangsters with not a weapon but a phone and his guts, and a flock of handcuff's and ankle locks from a trunkful of props used in *The Lights O' London,* DuCastle's last actor-manager production!—it's a 6-11-66 yarn—well, I pity *you* if you subscribe for nation-wide clippings on it at 2 cents per column inch!"

"Aw th' devil!" expostulated the Sheriff. "Hardest thing 'bout takin' them fellers was th' job o' standin' th' goddanged smell in th' hideout whilst I done so—'at's what I said!—them fellers hadn't bathed nor nothin', fur a consid'able number of days, an' bein' onder a hell of a lot of emotion'l disturbance, they shore give all they had—to their sweatin'! Fo'tunately fur them havin' to stick thar like a lot o' hawgs in a hawgpen, they had gen'rated their own stink; so they wasn't able to smell themsevves at all, at all—but fur me!—comin' in from the clean outside—whooie!" He wrinkled up his nose at the very memory of it.

"Well, sweet-smelling gangsters or sour-smelling gangsters," repeated Jack ReQua, "taking 6 of 'em armed, with not a weapon but—"

"Aw," expostulated the Sheriff again. "'Twas the on'y way to take them polecats. Hell, they thunk they knowed how t' play poker—they hain't never seen *real* poker in their li—"

"Well, they did this morning at dawn, all right," chuckled Kalvelage Lantree, the movie-like press correspondent. He paused a second, then pressed on. "However, Sheriff; we're here, y' know—to find out from you whether any of 'em has squawked to you yet—as to how the hell they ever pulled that vanishing stum in that tunnel; for surely, a man like you—who took 'em cold—with $2000 on the table—"

"Two thousand seven hundred fifty-four," said the Sheriff, tapping his breast pocket. "The bank's."

"Well, a man like you—who took 'em cold—with that much money in sight—wouldn't have passed 'em through, that day on the ro—"

"'Nough!" sighed the Sheriff. "And still folks don't b'lieve me." He paused glumly. "Well, the leader, Mulhearn, has obleegingly tolt me a few highlights o' that vanishment, what I 'uz intrusted 'bout, jest afore I come upstairs, but o' co'se I didn't need nobody to squawk nothin', sence it was my knowin'—from a book o' Chinee wisdom—proverbs an' sich—*how* th' gang did their vanishin' act, what put it in th' bag fur me to track 'em down to their—their lair. So I reckon now yo'all'll not on'y want to know how they did it—but what the old Chinkees could know 'bout it, heh?"

"Want to know!" said 3 of the journalists, all in unison.

And then, from a fourth, obviously speaking for all: "If the finis to this crime case was written in an old book of Chinese wisdom, this is the news story to end *all* news stories! For Lord's sake man, speak fast—and where's the closest phone with long-distance service?"

CHAPTER XVI

ELUCIDATION

"Any phone in town 'tall," the Sheriff replied promptly to that last direct question, "'ll give you long-distance. An' 'caze you kin git Pricetown an' Brocktown, t' th' east an' northeast, sim'ltaneously—an' Janestown an' Billburg, t' the west, th' same—th' whole y o' you'll be able to talk to your chiefs at Southwest City at one an' the same time!"

Now he became thoughtfully silent, as a man marshaling certain threads in his mind.

"They's so many strange threads to this case," he began troubledly, "that I—I ha'dly know whar to begin." He did essay to do so, nevertheless. "However, th' day that truck an' its murd'ous crew vanished into thin air inside that tunnel—"

"'How Gang of 5,'" quizzically repeated Kalvelage Lantree of East-West Newspapers, obviously forecasting an intriguing headline of sorts, "'Out-Einsteined Einst—'"

"Better make it a gang o' 6," put in the Sheriff grimly, "ef you figger to include *all* its members that 'uz then down in this neck o' th' woods—and 7, ef you include also a suttin' feller Driller who was in the hideout, *his* work did."

"Gang—of 7?" repeated the black-gloved Sidney Uher. "One in the hideout?—6 in this neck of—"

"The gang," explained the Sheriff super-patiently, "on th' day most of its members 'vaporated—in a manner o' speakin'—into cool dank tunnel air, had one member who wasn't in on the actual heist; oh, you kin take my word fur this, 'caze I've talked to him, a banjo on his shoulder, and black paint on his fa—"

"Musician, eh?—when he's not gangstering?" This from Sidney Uher. "Well, what's his na—"

"Better le' me tell this, boys," pleaded the Sheriff, "'thout int'ruptions. And then you kin ast all ye' wa—a'right!—well, this gang member who wan't in on the actual stickup, he was—"

"—was inside the tunnel?—waiting?" nodded Jack ReQua.

"No, no, no," complained the Sheriff, emphatically. "He 'uz travelin', in a vehicle containin', amongst other things, suttin' glass raddio bulbs an' sich-like gadgets in it, as could—well, glass bulbs, 's fur's that goes, e'zackly like some what was inside the battleship-grey truck—an'way, he 'uz travelin' 'long Old Twistibus—"

"You don't mean," put in Sidney Uher suddenly, pencil aloft in gloved hand, "that the bankrobbing contingent had a confederate with radio-sending apparatus to—to time 'em on something?—or—"

"Wall, so fur's timin' things goes, I'll hatter axe you fellers w'ether you even know 'bout this turr'ble road what par'llels Ca'thage Road West an' the Straighta—"

"Who doesn't know about Old Twistibus?" laughed the movie-hero-like Kalvelage Lantree. "With Uncle Sam tossing away millions of simoleons to detour it out of existence, and—but see here, Duckhouse, this confederate traveling along Old Twistibus—with radio-sending apparatus—what was he supposed to time—"

"Sa-a-a-ay!" broke in Paul Dragoo. "I've got it! That is—listen, Duckhouse—is there any truth at all in the story that when the sun gleams on the west face of Smoky Ridge Mountain straight horizontally, some section of the mountain actually moves—but oh, hell, my question sounds craz—"

"Does it?" said the Sheriff. "I cain't see as it's any mo' mirac'lous fur the sun to move a mount'in than 'tis fur th' sun to raise up a million billion tons o' wheat out'n the ground—why!—but hyar—I'm delayin' the story o' how them fellers 'vaporated!—so 'spose I follow this confed'rate an' git him over with, an'way? A'right. Wall, it's 'nough to mention that he 'uz travelin' Old Twistibus whilst they 'uz goin' into the tunnel—"

"Watching the sun on Smoky Ridge," nodded Paul Dragoo, "and signaling them—"

"He 'uz havin' oncommon good luck, too," went on the Sheriff imperturbably, "on gittin' through an' out ag'in—whar contact 'uz poss'ble with th' gang—sich luck, b' God, as I'd probably never have in a month o' Sundays. F'rinstance, he found a bridge down at a place called B'ar Creek—yet found, 100 feet 'r so down that creek, two newly felled trees acrost it, an' a whole stock o' new lumber piled up fur somebody's house-to-be. What does he do but lay planks acrost them trees, an' go acrost like— like—nobody's bus—but the p'int is," he finished, "that this confed'rate we're discussin' fin'lly come out o' Old Twistibus, an' 'bout 4 hours atter he went in. Cl'ar, ain't it?"

"Clear as mud," admitted Kalvelage Lantree.

"Oh, it'll cl'ar up as I go 'long," the Sheriff promised. "And now—" But he did pass a hand helplessly over his brows. "I 'spose now I should go back in time some years. To whar two threads fu'st come t'gether—one bein' that of Al Mulhearn, locked up downstairs, this gang's leader—and t'other bein' this—this musician you speak of—an' both wuz little boys. Livin' t'gether fur a year on'y under the latter feller's father, Al Mulhearn bein' a tooken boy—you know—not adopted?" Notes were being made, but puzzled notes.

The notes, however, engendered one question. An almost insolent question from Jack ReQua.

"Well," he said, caustically, "since you have only 6 men downstairs, and they may protect you on this tale—oh, yes, Duckhouse—*I'm* being frank—protect *you* for some protection you can give *them*—well, is there anybody at all who can confirm your—er—narrative—of a 'confederate' traveling, in a vehicle with radio tubes, along Old Twistibus that day?"

"Yes, they is," nodded the Sheriff satisfiedly. "They is. 'Caze both roads, y' know, sprout from a common jonction. Yes, they is sich a feller. He driv' up to this jonction not long atter the bankrobbin' crew did—and he seed some surprisin' things. He—well this feller—his name is Craney—Jim Craney—"

Notes were being made.

"And he's a circus-wagon driver fur the MacWhorter Shows. A feller who I'd give' p'mission, that afternoon, to come th'ough th' Straight'way. Sense he assured me he 'uz th' last wagon—and 'uz transpo'tin' a lioness and some newly bo'ned kittens. He—"

"Well, what'd he see?" This inquiry, which emanated from Sidney Uher, was caustically skeptical.

"Well," retorted the Sheriff, "as he bowled lickety-hell over a gentle rise in th' road ah'id of him—and down plumb into th' cup o' land constitutin' th' jonction—Perkins Jonction—he found hisse'f clappin' on his brakes danged fast—fur blockin' his very path 'uz a battleship-grey bodied truck—with two men in stripet trucker's clothin' standin' near it—Jim says he glimpsed a man standin', gun in hand, close t' the rise in each o' th' right and lefthand roads goin' out o' this jonction—in his ears, even, was the sound of a 'splosion—comin' from beyant a rise what lay on the direction he had been goin'—he seed a man comin' over that rise shoutin', 'I've blowed the barr'er!—so come on, boys!'—and, as he clumb meekly down out'n his cab—fur one o' the stripet-clad fellers was on the runnin' board, with a gun on Jim—as he clumb down an' out, an' the other stripet-clad man turned, gun in hand—an' stuck it even in Jim's stomach, Jim saw—"

"Al Mulhearn, of course?" nodded Kalvelage Lantree.

"Yes, and no," said the Sheriff'. "He seed Jerome Craney—as his paw had leg'lly named young Al y'ars ago—his own foster-brother who—"

"Then," said three of the journalists all together, "Jim Craney—was the confederate—on Old Twistibus—who made that robbery a success?"

"Right," admitted the Sheriff sadly.

CHAPTER XVII

VANISHMENT!

"Yes," the Sheriff pressed on, after a second's pause, "Jim Craney 'uz mo'n that that day—he 'uz th' fly in th' ointment—th' monkey wrench in a bee-oot-ful piece o' machinery—th'—an' by the way, he really was transpo'tin' a gadget with raddio tubes in it—but onder his seat—'twas a po'table raddio he'd picked up sho'tly back fur a gal he loved in th' circus—but couldn't give it to her account a quarrel they'd had. And I want you fellers to be kind, in yo're news stories, 'ith Jim Craney. Treat him right, will ya? He's a really fine feller—cur'ous duck in some ways—likes t' sometimes refer to himse'f as 'Jim Craney' as ef he wan't himse'f—though, alas, he cain't do that no more now, sence he's 'cided that from now on—y' see, I talked with him 'arly this mawnin', by long-distance, from some crossroads store, whilst my grey truck an' my hawgtied gangsters in it wuz parked outside—I talked with him an' th' gal he's in love of—a gal named Florette Smith—she's stickin' to him, in this—an' they have both 'cided that from now on—'count the news stories that'll be writ—they'll be abandonin' th' name Craney fur a new one—one what they kin use when they marry, an' own their chicken farm what they'll be buyin' outa the cut from the $2000 possible reward money I'll be givin' him—*I—hope!*" The Sheriff's face gloomed up. He shook it off fiercely. Though not before Paul Dragoo put in a salient question.

"Two grand reward, heh? Well yourself?—what do *you* figure to do with your end of any reward money—if there ever is any?"

"Oh," said the Sheriff morosely, "retire suttin' negot'ble paper I have issued. Or—or b'en said to have." He was drearily lost, shook his mood oh—went on. "An'way, gittin' back to this Jim Craney, I int'viewed him, 'ith blood in m' eye, at Hootens Falls, whar the circus was playin' fur 2 nights, up to night afore last. A busy town—not on no railroads e'zackly, no!—but on water—sence there is a railroad what c'nnects it d'rect t'— 'at's right—'at's right. Wall, I cotched him 'doublin' in grease'—as it seems the circus fellers put it!—jest goin' on in the big ensemble to increase th' number o' funmakers—he 'uz blacked up—totin' a phony banjo—and so I didn't stop the show, no—sir! No, I int'viewed him in his room in the hotel, 'longside th' lot an' railroad, atter he come out the tent. The p'formers, lots of 'em, was qua'tered there that night 'caze MacWhorter 'uz havin' th' trailers overhauled. Well, I so'te o' trapped pore Jim—heaven he'p me!—fur I introduced myse'f as a friend o' Sherif Duckhouse's!—an' Jim tolt me all 'bout meetin' Sher'ff Duckhouse—on th' Sher'ff's side o' th' mountain—that day—an' givin' him a book, an' all—an' then I up and tolt him I 'uz Sher'ff Duckhouse myse'f—and that I knew he'd went th'ough by Old Twistibus that day—that I knew *all* 'bout it, and—how!—even outside the A. No.1 proof I now had that he hadn't even ever seed the Straight'way.

"I tolt him plain, boys, that sence he went that godawful way—and onder the sarc'mstances he did!—he'd b'en paid or promised so'thin' sweet to do it—oh, I had him, boys!—had him 7 ways acrost th' board as access'ry atter th' fact ef not afore th' fact—he hadda admit all, includin' the pay-off he was to get—an' though I got no clue t' them gangsters' location from th' method of th' pay-off, I *did* cotch a clue Jim had—out of days when he was a boy with Jerome Craney, his foster-bro—"

"One minute!" This from the derby-hatted Sidney Uher. "Was this Al Mulhearn legally adopted by Craney's father?"

"No. He 'uz on'y t'uk. Old Man Craney *did* take him into County Court, however, and had his name changed to Jerome Craney."

"Ah!" Uher turned to the other men. "There's an interesting factor, boys. For that man Mulhearn is one of the few individuals in the world who actually *possesses* two names—both legal! A fact! See Supreme Court in the case of Milliman *versus* Adineau—where a child below age—and not adopted—has been nevertheless given a legal change of name by a foster parent. The child retains both—owns both—may deed property under each—is, in fact, *both individuals!* In your stories, boys, you can now refer to Mr. Mulhearn—logically—legally—and wordily!—as A. Mulhearn—or as J. Craney! Shoot, Sheriff?"

"Wall," the Sheriff went on, "this was what happened that day in th' lonely cup o' land representin' Perkins Jonction. Jim's sho't-lived foster brother Al—*I'll* call him Al now—drillin' a gun in Jim's belly, snarled: 'What the goddam' hell, Jim, are you doin' here—nosin' into our jug-heist—with a MacWhorter's Show wagon and—'

"Well, Jim talked damn fast—he knew well that a 'jug-heist' was a bankrobb'ry—an' he talked damn fast—'ith them guns nuzzlin' him; he tolt Al how he'd talked 'ith me on the phone—plumb desprit then becaze of a girl in th' show he was losin'—losin', ef fur no other reason, 'coze he couldn't even get $1000 t' take her outa the circus!—tolt Al how he'd tolt me def'nitely an' abs'lutely he 'uz th' last wagon—how I 'uz lettin' him th'ough th' Straight'way count of a lioness an' some newborn kittens—

"Al, he sez, almost screamed aloud. Fur Jim, boys, with his lion wagon an' his lions, had killed the heist! A fact! Fur would yo' b'lieve it, of all them gangsters there, on'y one could drive?—drive sat'sfact'ily 'nough fur the kind o' des-prit travelin' they had t' do—an' they babbled 'nough right then an' thar fur Jim to pick up the info that them fellers had a lion cage on wheels, with a sick par'lyzed lion in one co'ner of it, cunnin'ly cached some'eres up the line, an—"

"Where?" asked Jack ReQua promptly.

"Yes, where?" repeated Kalvelage Lantree. "The highway being on stilts."

"Rather," qualified Paul Dragoo, "how'd they run their wagon and sick incumbent thereof in—to wherever they had it?"

The Sheriff leaned back in his chair and hooked his thumbs triumphantly in his red galluses. "I'd say, boys," he announced triumphantly, "that you'd never guess—in a thousand y'ars—none o' you—'zackly *whar* they had their cage-wagon and lion hid. Fur it—but to the story! As Jim 'uz able to pick things up from the 'cited talkin', th' gangsters 'uz goin' t' transfer theirsevves an' their swag from the truck to it, at the proper p'int—ditch th' truck—fur th' time bein'—an'—"

"And now I'll ask one!" bit our Sidney Uher savagely. "Where were they going to hide it?"

The Sheriff again raised a hand patiently.

"Whar they had had the other 'un hid, o' co'se, Mister Uher. Yes, I know, th' highway 'z on stilts—shore!—but le' me tell the story—an' you boys write it? Okay! Well, th' gangsters quite plainly, as Jim 'uz able to pick up, 'uz gonna come th'ough the mountain as a 'last wagon' what had barged th'ough a blowed barr'er gate—tellin' a vivid story 'bout a battleship-grey truck and some bad-lookin' men back thar ahind 'em—they knowed, y' see, I'd stay on my side o' th' mount'in on'y, 'count of a suttin' big standin' local reward fur pepperin' a bankrobber—an'way, a suttin' handsome feller amongst 'em called Slim 'pears t' be a regular nat'ral actor—he had onbuttoned his stripet trucker's jacket whilst Jim 'z bein' nuzzled with guns, an' his reg'lar coat jacket, onderneath that, 'uz onbuttoned also—an' so Jim 'uz able to see that this Slim had on a complete MacWhorter's driver's show coschume under his 2-piece truckin' outfit—under his inner coat and outfit, I should say—even, b' God, a sho't bull whip!—as it happened, th' feller Slim even had, in a compa'tment under the seat, a grey felt hat 'ith its edge tacked up 'ith a stitch so's to give it that—that Austral'an roll!—in sho't, boys," finished the Sheriff wearily, glancing at a silver turnip he withdrew from his pants pocket, "they had timed th' date o' their heist 'ith the playin' of the MacWhorter Shows at Pricetown!—plus the show's havin' to come through west'ard to Foleysburg—very beeootiful a'right—oh, the coschume?—made by one o' the gang molls, I l'arned a leetle while ago—made e'zackly atter one o' the many lith'graphs papered 'round the kentry!—an'way, this Slim, nat'ral actor as he was, was to talk 'em through, an' b' God, 'ventually did—followin', however, in this case, Jim Craney's style an' manner o' talk—an'—

"Why—the big feller Al tolt me, on'y a leetle while ago as I was lockin' 'em in downstairs, that he 'uz inside the gangsters' closed circus wagon, leanin' plumb ag'in its front end, even as it drawed to a stop, two-thirds th' way out'n the tunnel on my side. They knowed me fur t' be me, immed'ate—'count Jim havin' tolt 'em how I'd tolt him I 'uz wearin' my check'bo'd shirt that day! He—this Al—yes—watched Slim's an' my whole chinfest, both of 'em bein' plenty flabbergasted at findin' me posted thar—of *all* places. He says he 'uz even wipin' off his fo'head 'ith a bandanner, inside th' wagon, whilst I 'uz doin' the same ident'cal thing outside. He says th' puzzled look on his face, when I refused Slim's offer—which it seems Slim knew I would!—to stay an' he'p gun fur the gangsters, was'nough in itse'f to have bored right th'ough to me! And this Al says he said, with a puzzled gesture, as they driv off later, 'Not my fun'ral'—which, indeed, it hadn't b'en that day—thanks to *my* wooden head. And thus," finished the Sheriff, "it was that J. Craney come th'ough the mountain that *day*. But not *my* J. Craney.

"Fur my J. Craney was the monkey wrench that t'uk his-se'f out'n th' machin'ry fur $1000—*to* come!—plus a lot o' fool soft soap 'bout brother love. Bah! Fur ef they had killed him—or kidnaped him—they was nobody could drive his damn cage-wagon and lioness out'n the way—there 'twould be, standin' 'crost the jonction—with the result that a pursuin' posse—or the natives back a ways—would be phonin' ahead 'bout it and the p'sumed 'last wagon' comin' through then'd be stopped—questioned—'zamined—"

"And a male lion, with a mane, found—instead of a female?" pointed out the curly-haired Jack ReQua.

The Sheriff grinned amiably.

"That pore devil—Jim Craney," he continued, "lost his fool head, it seems. Only chanct he ever had to 'arn $1000, it seems. An' easy way, too. He no longer had t' worry 'bout a suttin' turr'ble problem o' catchin' up with his show, an' fixin' up a suttin' quarrel with his gal afore she jumped it—fur as he'd driv off from the last kentry store, called Elum's, he'd found a lith'graph announcin' his show'd be in Foleysburg 2 days 'stid o' 1. And his gal had und'lined, in a suttin' letter to him, that she'd remain 'twell 11 bells o' the night the show pulled away from Foleysburg. As fur the newborn kittens he'd b'en tryin' to protect 'ginst too much travelin', it come to him—so he says—like a flash that them kittens had b'en travelin' an' joltin' fur weeks an' weeks—inside their own mammy—ever sence they was—was kitten seeds! They could, he realized, take th' turns an' dips of Old Twistibus as easy outside her as they would a-had to do inside her. So—so he turned over to the gangsters a red book he had 'ith him—a book he 'z bringin' me from that store fur to read—yes, the Chinee wisdom book, no less!—tolt 'em the on'y p'int o' dee-scription he had 'bout me: my checkerbo'de shirt!—give his promise he'd keep his trap shut—took theirs on th' matter of th' thousand—an' dived into the Hills. And the hillbillies thar don't know yit but that he 'uz jest a wagon trailin' a show what *did* go through thar 'bout 11 hours before. Jim got through fine—got stuck in a bog off Foleysburg Road late at night—got out no mo'n 14 minutes atter he went in, thanks to a man an' some mules livin' alongside!—an' the mud all over his wheels accounted fur his 'purrent slowness comin' th'ough by th' Straight'way.

"He even met up with his boss on Foleysburg Road—an' surmisin' that them gangsters *had* met up a'right with the Sher'ff he himse'f had been talkin' to on the wire, he made up a story 'bout *himse'f* havin' met the Sheriff!—even 'bout bringin' me through that book!

"And that ends the story, boys," the Sheriff finished simply. "The gangsters, atter they rolled leis'ly through my town—fur I'd even sent out th' word, God he'p me, that th' last circus wagon would be a-comin' th'ough!—they turned no'th at Southwest City Road Crossin'—and was soon lost. While Jim Craney, when he come out into Foleysburg Road at lonely Simpson's Jonction, he tu'ned south—and was also soon lost—to this story. Now, of co'se, havin' got his thousand by a honest way—I— hope!—an' my assu'ance, which I got by phone last night from Jedge Pettridge O' Cedarville—Jim Craney's ready to test'fy 'gains' this brother who never was a brother at all, but an unjustifi'ble bully and a dirty little crook—against all these fellers, in fack, who'd have but bumped Jim Craney off, oth'wise. An' that's the story of how a battleship-grey truck dis'ppeared in a mountain!"

"All but," pointed out Sidney Uher, grumpily, "where they had hid the lion cage and sick lion that they presumably brought up into the mountain—and where and how they hid the truck that they left after them—and how they regained it afterward. Could you ride us to the point—and show us the whole *modus operandi?*"

"Ride you an'whar," said the Sheriff amiably, "yo' like to go. So foller me, please, all, to the on'y veh'cle they is now that I kin take you any place in—the truck, yes!—follow me th'ough yander door—" He was pointing at a door off and back of the raised judge's platform. "That door leads to what we call the stockade—outside the co'teroom—from days 'way back when th' tethered hosses o' witnesses an' all had to be pertected from Injuns." He had arisen, and was leading the way, around the judge's bench, along the platform, to the door; all the newspapermen had arisen likewise, were following him, were clustering about him even as he turned the knob of that door. As he flung it open, it revealed, down a short flight of 5 or 6 wooden steps, a dirt-floored stockade about 30 feet square, built of tall 14-foot-high logs, pointed sharply at their tops, and the contact spaces between them cemented solidly with mud so that neither through that wall—nor over it!—could human eye peer. Part of the impenetrable wall could be seen, on closer inspection, to be a tight-fitting 8-foot-wide gate, just now barred, however, by a drop-beam across its entire width, but showing how the Sheriff had driven in here today.

But there, inside the stockade, facing the very doorway—though facing it rearwise—stood a most peculiar vehicle!

A vehicle, the strange reason for whose original construction—prior, that is, to the bizarre use to which it had really been put!—could probably never be guessed by anyone; but which reason the Sheriff well knew; and which was—

For the vehicle consisted of a more or less standard truck chassis on which had been bolted an aluminum floor, and from the corners of which floor, moreover, had been erected simple, but most peculiar construction work. Construction work—as was evident from viewing its inner and unpainted portions—entirely of light aluminum. And resembling, at first quick glance, nothing so much as some curious gargantuan metal box kite, gone crazy—or standing in readiness, on half-posed wings, for drunken, careening flight! A thing constructed, as was to be brought our later, by a master aluminum-welder and micro-machinist, yet not nearly so difficult to create as to guess *why* it originally had been created!

For, lighted up inside as well as out, by the bright morning sunlight falling within and on it, it could be seen to be, basically, but a rectangular skeleton work of aluminum—obviously strong, obviously rigid as well—made by welding, to each corner of the aluminum floor, a tall vertical column consisting of a 2-inch-thick, square cross-sectioned aluminum bar; and then in turn welding, to the tops of these bars—and to each other—four horizontal beams of the same bar material. Within each rectangular "frame" thus created, excepting the one which lay just back of the driving cab, had been installed, on midwise-placed horizontal pivots, a great panel of light aluminum designed to revolve exactly like a cheval mirror, and to comprise, when in proper position, the truck's side, or rear end, or top, as the case might be. Cunning snap-lugs riveted to the inner surfaces of the skeleton work showed how these revolving panels could be locked firmly into either one of two positions: paint, on all the outer surfaces of that rectangular skeleton work was of grey—grey which could fuse with more grey of similar shade!—or, as grey can do, blend artistically with areas of gilt and crimson! And which function of that grey was conclusively brought out by the manner in which, just at this moment—though for reasons perhaps known best to the Sheriff!—all the delicately pivoted, revolving panels swung at various angles from their correct positions. And thereby revealed—

Indeed, the rearmost square panel was at this moment so far revolved on *its* horizontal pivots that only its comparatively thin edge, and the projecting hancock of what appeared to be a small swinging trapdoor within itself, and a couple of apparent handgrips screwed into its now uppermost face, were visible to the men crowding in the doorway and looking down at the strange vehicle. The position of this panel had, as a result, allowed the pivoted "roof"—also for some reason unlocked, and swinging free—but obviously not in balance!—to automatically take up a position of about one-quarter tilt, and the uppermost area of that roof was battleship grey. The right oblong panel, revolved just now about one-quarter way off the vertical, on its horizontal axis, showed, on its inner surface, some black outlined yellow letters painted against a battleship-grey background, and reading, though upside down, TRANSCONTINENTAL TRUCKING COMPANY," plus some additional words; while the other oblong side panel, swinging at this moment almost horizontally, showed on *its* uppermost face gilt-tinted crimson-stained papier-mache work whose relief-molded convolutions held strange crude figures suggestive of carnival and circus the world over.

And the square front end piece of this curious oblong skeleton— unturnable itself, on pivots, because of the standard black cab which hugged its position—stood, just now, entirely removed, against a rear wheel; cunning machined drop-lugs on its edges would have revealed, at least to a mechanic, appendages which could be dropped into receiving apertures in the front vertical columns; the particular face of this panel visible to the men in the doorway was encrusted with more of the gilt-tinged red papier-mache work seen on one side panel: the side not visible was, obviously, a battleship-grey!

"For—the love—of—" the curly-headed Jack ReQua, back of the Sheriff's left shoulder, was saying. But was interrupted by the Sheriff, whose person was more or less neatly blocking the path down to this curious device at which 4 faces were dumfoundedly peering.

"I'm airin' it out well," apologized the latter. "Sence it'll be State's Exhibit Number 1 at the trial. Them 6 pieces o' ripe cheese what rode hyar this mo'nin' inside that—that skelington work, didn't make the trapped air inside smell any too good! An'way, that's w'y ever'thing, just now, is swingin' looselike. Sorry y' cain't see, from whar we stand, the green state license plate—stolen, o' co'se!—what's riveted on the upper face o' that end piece that's showin' on'y edgewise to'ds us—or th' gold an' black Fed'ral int'state license plate—also stolen, as I now know—what's riveted on the onder face o' th' same end piece."

But Paul Dragoo of the red hair was speaking. Over the Sheriff's right shoulder. And excitedly.

"By the gods!—a trick affair!—with sides, and top, and rear end, that can be swung 180 full degrees around—and a front end piece that can be lifted out, turned about, and slid back on—and the whole become, at will, a circus wagon or a truc—"

"But will you all take a look inside!" the derby-hatted Sidney Uher, craning over the red-headed man's shoulder, was actually now shouting. And the black-gloved hand that now reached over the Sheriff's own shoulder was pointing downward and within the framework, toward the farther end of the platform nearest the cab. Not, however—as it appeared—at a heavy-looking wooden box, with seals and stenciling and what not all over it—including the black-stenciled letters "ESTATE OF JASON WHIT-WORTH"—no!—but at a curious little mechanical-electrical device, off to one side of the box, consisting evidently of a phonograph record atop a phonograph turntable, standing atop a more or less open cabinet with lead storage batteries in the bottom section of the cabinet, and various tubes and electrical appurtenances in the upper section.

"Oh, yes," nodded the Sheriff. "A phonygraft record o' all the wild any-mal cries o' Afriky. But all shaved off 'cept'n th' stretch representin' the roar of a lion—an' marked keer-ful' with white crosses at each end. Them gadgets *inside* th' open cabynet, howev'r, is sound amplifyin' stuff. When them fellers'd run the phonygraft record over th' white cross-marked stretch of itse'f, a lion'd roar—inside! And—what's that—the skelington work stuff itse'f? Shore I know how an' whar it come into bein'. Now, an'way. So hold yo're hosses—yo've all got all day to inspect and photygraft the thing—an' this 's the on'y time, so he'p me Hannah, that I'm a-goin' to tell these curi-ous facts afore the trial." The Sheriff cleared his throat; blocked the doorway a little better; felt fountain pens scratching behind his shoulders. "'Twas designed, that thing yander—an' secritly built—an' all inside his own big private garage, w'ich happened also t' be a private machine shop, too!—by a so'te o' lone wolf o' Southwest City—bachylor an' all that, y' know?—named Hupe Furr, who 'uz an expert A. No. 1 mechanic, in both alum'num an' th' micro-machinin' thar'of, whatever th' hell that is—though it must be so'thin' to do 'ith the amazin' way them panels fits the oblongs they swing in—hardly a ray o' light or—or a 'skeeter's eyelash kin pass atween, an'—however, this feller Farr 'spected 'ventually to patent the contraption, an' offer it to the likker intrusts o' Southwest City—t' th' likker intrusts all over th' kentry, in fact—so's they could—"

"Liquor interests?" This from the handsome face of the journalist Lantree, edging in over the Sherif's shoulder.

"Yes. As a sound truck fur adv'tisin' likker in cities what are grabbin' up the scheme o' this reformer, the Rever'nd Zebulon Q. Holowynge, o' Southwest City, who, as you fellers ought to know, has sewed things up so bad there that not even a wagon with a liquor dealer's name kin skin through a dry deestrict! The idee was to send the truck out, with its crew pervided with a map o' the city showin' wet deestricts—an' its phonygraft-amplifier a-playin' nice loud ma'tial music, an' the truck itse'f displayin' ord'nary ads or an'thing on th' sides—and on the roof, too, fur people livin' in sec-ond stories and up'ards—and then, on crossin' into a wet deestrict, spin the danged sides an' roof an' hind end over—turn the front end, too, ef 'twas a big deestrict—and there, on all the new faces exposed, 'd be ads advertisin' bourbons, Scotches, beer taverns, or what-have-you—atter w'ich the crew'd turn the truck faces an' top an' ends all 'bout again on rollin' out. No more back alley slitherin' an' all that fool stuff; no more—

"But," continued the Sheriff, "Hupe Farr up an' died—all these facts, yo' understand, I got from Al Mulhearn whilst lockin' him up downstairs— Farr up and died, b'Godfrey, on th' very day he'd machined th' last layer o' moly-cules off'n th' last panel o' his contraption—an' fitted that last panel keerful into place! The on'y feller to whom he'd confided his strange inven- tion 'uz his cousin, a suttin' man named Driller—also locked up downstairs jest now. An' Driller, in turn, had tolt Al Mulhearn 'bout this cur'ous de- vice. An' at the time of Farr's death Al Mulhearn was study-in' our a suttin' proposed heist. An', bein' a so'te o' magician, was seein' how he could use that contraption bee-ootifully. 'Specially sence he'd b'en 'prenticed, as a kid, fur 3 long years, in the ornymental stucco work business, and is still, so he claims, so durned good at th' trade t'day that he kin—but, to make a long story sho't, fur you boys air champin' at the bits to take 'bout a million pickters o' that thing—Farr conveni'ntly got struck by an auto an' died, in th' hospital, at th'—th' phys'log'cal moment; Driller, who 'uz at his bed- side w'en he died, immedi'tely phoned Al—and so, late that night afore Farr's premyses could be inspected, Driller run th' machine out—an' to the Mulhearn gang hideout. An' 'twas Al himse'f who not on'y painted the out- side battleship grey an' letterin' fur one side o' them panels, but did all the encrustation tint work on the other sides. Cur'ous thing 'bout the danged de-vice," went on the Sheriff, disgruntledly, "'uz that sho'tly atter th' gang rid out onto the Elyvated Highway with it as a truck, they flopped one side over!—an' from that time on it 'uz viewed—by people on diff'ent sides of it—both as a battleship-grey truck *and* a circus wagon—fu'st by folks livin' 'bout 10 miles out—and, later, th' same ident'cal thing, by folks clost t' th' very mountain. The—the results—o' sich double viewin' like—like to have driv' *me* insane."

But it was doubtful whether the Sheriff's last words were even being heard. For, while he had been talking, four individuals, more or less held in leash back of him, had finally slithered past him, two each side—were down the steps—four cameras, in fact, were busily snapping the strange wheeled device from every angle. So busy were all, indeed, that it was doubtful whether certain newly rising sounds betokening the arrival of automobiles, on the road outside and off from the stockade, and men's voices, were no- ticed.

So the Sheriff, being no longer of utility as a doorway bar—since there was nothing to bar—came majestically down the steps, too. And, thumbs hooked in galluses, joined the others. Just in time, in fact, to catch a ques- tion—hurled point-blank at his head.

For the red-haired Paul Dragoo, camera in hand, had turned.

"But hey—hey, Sheriff!" the latter demanded. "What the hell was the Chinese aphorism that gave you the lowdown on *this* piece of quick-change machinery?"

"Well, 'twas jest," the Sheriff explained, with supreme patience, "a sayin' of a ol' philos'pher who—acco'din' to a footnote printed onder it, an' writ by the compiler o' the book it was in—had b'en the fav'rite disciple o' an even more famous old feller—even tended th' latter in th' latter's last days—l'arned all he knowed from his master—the latter bein' Confooc'us who—"

"Why then," put in Jack ReQua, "the philosopher you're referring to would have been one, Tze Kung?"

"That's it!" nodded the Sheriff emphatically. "Tze—Kung—right!"

"Well, what—what did Tze Kung say?" demanded Lancree.

"Well, he merely said," struggled the Sheriff, "that ef'n a gang o' bank-robbers, figurin' to flee a bankrobb'ry in a battleship-grey truck, could so'te o'—o' fix things so's they could revolve th' sides an' ends o' that thar truck to be so'thin' else—say—a circus-wagon—or what-have-you—they could jest pass outa th' pikter as bankrobbers—an' ride th'ough to safety as so'thin' else. That's—that's all Mist' Kung said."

"Oh, come now, Sheriff," retorted Jack ReQua. "The old Chinese could never say *that*. For in 400 B.C., when Confucius and Tze Kung both lived, the Chinese had no *banks*—hence no bankrobbers!—no battleship-grey trucks—or any other kinds of trucks!—nor circus wagons, either—let alone, God in heaven, trucks with cunning pivoted aluminum sides built into riveted aluminum skeletons. So, come on now—what did that aphorism say?"

"Wa'all," the Sheriff sighed, pulling from a hip pocket that quite crumpled and folded page whose top item had given him the complete answer to *this* mystery, "Mister Dragoo kin read it aloud." And he passed it to Paul Dragoo, who was closest to him.

The latter unfolded it eagerly, the while 3 fountain pens poised aloft. Aloud, Dragoo read slowly:

> "'If nobody will sing your praises, put your jacket on inside out—and sing them yourself!'"

A loud laugh rose simultaneously from 4 Gentlemen of the Press. But it came to a sudden stop as a sheriff-like figure appeared in the doorway looking down on the stockade. At the newcomer's shoulder was a round Teutonic-looking face with a square black beard. Other faces could be seen hovering in back of those two.

"Hi, Duckhouse?" called the sheriff-like figure in the front. Bucyrus Duckhouse had turned quickly at the sound of the call. Thinking that it just might have come from a certain opaquely glassed door, with heavy iron bars, that lay to one side of the steps. But saw, immediately, where it *had* emanated from.

"Why, h'llo, Jeth," he called out. "H'llo?"

"Well, we're here, Duckhouse," said the newcomer.

"Thanks to that phone call you give us, an hour an' a half back, from Ribbey's Crossroads. We're here—Banker Stoeffhaas included—an' with 3 cars and a dozen temp'rary deputies—to fetch those fellers—an' that sweet box they lifted, an' which I see yonder!—an' that—thar State's Exhibit Number 1 you told me about—on to Cedarville. And now—" He was holding our, somewhat undecidedly, two long pink-tinted oblongs of paper. "These checks here—"

The blackbeard, back of Jeth's shoulder, was talking.

"I haf made them out, Mis—uh—Sheriff Duckhouse, as you said you wished dern—when you rung us. But haf I efferything right? One, for $1000—to James L. Craney? One, for the same—to Bucyrus H. Duckhouse?"

"'At's right, Mist' Stoeffhaas," Bucyrus Duckhouse nodded. "'At's right. An' thanks!"

Bill Jeth held out, however, only one of the pink-tinted oblongs. Which Sheriff Duckhouse, being close to the foot of the steps, reached up and took from the other's fingers.

Jeth was speaking. Somewhat embarrassedly.

"Well, there's the Craney one in your hand there, but see here, Duck—Bucyrus, this business of our holdin' your check for a few months—and advertising in all the local an' big city papers that anybody holding *any* checks or instruments ag'inst you—forged—n.s.f.—or—or what-have-you —be presented to us for taking up—well ain't you—uh—ah—afraid, Du—Bucyrus—uh—ah—well, you know, that—that rumor?—well, ain't you afraid that that check—re-referred to in that rumor—will come—"

Sheriff Bucyrus Duckhouse raised a hand.

And smiled sadly.

Smiled, because of certain remembrance, fresh in his mind from this very early morning, of how a certain coat, owned by a man called Slim, but unrestorable to the latter for wearing because of the sad fact that he had been handcuffed to certain other men behind him and in front of him!—and said coat therefore being transported prisonward by the Sheriff, driving a battleship-grey motor vehicle—being even sat upon, as a sort of seat cushion, *by* the same Sheriff!—had proved to contain some goddanged hell-f'ared so'thin' which, at every lurch of the vehicle, had pricked the Sheriff's underanatomy so agonizingly that, at the 10th such lurch—when it had caused the Sheriff to rise up off his seat with a scream of agony—he had furiously examined the coat—had seen curious golden prickles protruding from it!—had felt something crackle in its lining—had ripped open the lining a bit—

had found a sealed envelope inside, with godawful prickles sticking out of *it,* and which envelope, when held against the now-bright sun well above the horizon, had showed within itself an apparent cactus leaf silhouetted against an oblong of paper unmistakably bearing a figure reading $1000 and Bucyrus Duckhouse's own signature; and he smiled a bit more broadly as he recollected the expeditious manner in which that envelope had been ruthlessly torn open, its cactus leaf—a gold cactus leaf—tranferred immediately to the inside of the Sheriff's shirt—where it was right now!—and envelope and oblong of paper both tossed atop a smoldering deserted tramp's fire at the first railroad crossing, where, before the Sheriff's eyes, they had turned into fine black ash. And the Sheriff spoke—and quite confidently.

"That thar check, Jeth," he said, "'ll never show up. 'Caze—'caze it don't e'zist. But in squelchin' naughty rumors, one has t' squelch 'em in a—a—rad'cal way, don't you know? So you folks please adv'tize the e'zack way I *ast* yo' to—all bout the kentry hyar—an' in the Big Town—and then, w'en the alleeged check don't never show up—an' yo're all 100 p'cent confident they never was sich a thing!—I'll be a-gittin' m' reward check jest in time to be usin' it fur to marry M'liss—hrmph—you newspaper boys want to see them gangsters afore they start east?—a'right—ever'body down to th' lockup!"

www.ingramcontent.com/pod-product-compliance
Lightning Source LLC
Chambersburg PA
CBHW031408250626
47155CB00004B/1457